The Golden Star
of Shanghai

California and its rise
from the Gold Rush

Book 1 of the
Charles Townsend Reed Saga

Clifford Louis Gans

**Rip Roaring
Press**

FIRST EDITION

The Golden Star of Shanghai
California and its rise from the Gold Rush
Book 1 of the Charles Townsend Reed Saga
Historical Fiction
ISBN 978-0-999071106 print edition

Author Website: cliffgans.com

For Val,
one more step in a journey together.

"Let history crown the heroes and villains. For me, I just wanted to leave the world in a better place than I found it."

Charles Townsend Reed,
near the end

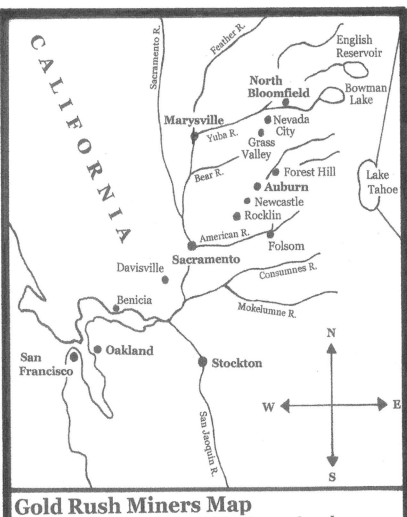

Gold Rush Miners Map
1 inch is 20 miles or the width of your thumb
*copied from old Del's map

California, September 2013

"Tom, are you sure you know where you're going?"

"It's not far," I lied to Jen, my wife, who sat beside me in the passenger seat of our Honda SUV. "I saw it on a brochure in the motel lobby. It's an old historic mining town from the Gold Rush. The desk clerk said it was good, worth a stop. It's some kind of ghost town now."

"Okay, but you know where you're going?"

"The desk clerk said to take Highway 49 to Rock Creek Road," my voice trailed off, studying the one-way road, wide enough for only one vehicle, hoping for no oncoming traffic as we wound up the twisting, beat-up mountain road, climbing up out of a river canyon at barely 20 mph. "I trust his directions. I mean, he gave us a cash discount of 10% when we checked in. Who needs hotels.com," I crowed unconvincingly, "and all those other sites, 'book early and get the best deals,' you just need to bargain is all."

Jen didn't answer, but I detected a slight "yes, dear" nod, preferring, wisely, to quietly concentrate on the road, helping me peek around blind turns, our view obscured by tall pines, trying to avoid a head on collision and impending death. I spun the steering wheel on yet another switchback, the tires grinding with the turn, no guardrail and a steep embankment, a long way back down to the river. My confidence began to shake, wondering if this really was a good idea. I quickly put the defeatist thought behind me, thinking back to the beginning, a mostly unplanned vacation, a road trip the length of California, where something new pops up at any minute. I remembered those giant statues of Paul Bunyan and Babe the Blue Ox from just a few days ago, how a roadside attraction grabs your eye and says, "You Must Stop." And you do stop, despite whatever your teenage daughter says from the backseat, "Daad! Not again."

Looking back, that stop up north was worth it, if for no other reason than to add a "Bigfoot Country" magnet from the Trees of Mystery souvenir flub dub shop to the refrigerator door, a refrigerator cluttered top to bottom, side-to-side, with a lifetime of magnetic bric-a-brac of every place Jen and I had found time to visit over the course of nearly 20 years together. The black stain-resistant, frost-free, ice-dispensing monolith was a true piece of modern art, a monument to places to go and things to do.

We crested out of the canyon, the road widening to our relief but turning from cracked pavement to gravel. I kept the speed down, the wheels crunching loose stones that pinged in and out of the wheel wells.

2

"You're *sure* this is the right way?"

"Uh, yeah, the guy said the road goes to gravel for about 6 miles before we reach North Bloomfield."

I looked into the rear view mirror, seeing our daughter, Kendra, fixated on her phone. "Kendra, quit texting your friends. We need some help here. Look up Malakoff Diggins State Park."

She raised her head, eyes meeting mine in the mirror, hearing the request. She wrapped up a rata-tat text, a burst of 40 characters, which was probably some Amber Alert message to a friend, "trapped on vacation with parents." I was amazed by her dexterity with the tiny keyboard, accurately tapping away on this bumpy road. If it were me, it'd read like a randomized stream of alphabetical gibberish. Plainly, this was a modern skill I would never own.

Kendra's voice rose above the road noise, "You're going the right way," expanding the map on her phone with a flick of her thumb and index finger. "It's just up ahead a few more miles."

"Good," Jen said, thankfully, "I can't take much more of this road."

"Interesting," Kendra read, "Tripadvisor, four-and-a-half out of 5 stars, 60 reviews. North Bloomfield is the number one thing to do in Nevada City and Malakoff Diggins is 'the least visited state park in California, located on the western slope of the Sierra Nevada Mountains, 75 miles northeast of Sacramento, elevation almost 3,300 feet.'"

"Could have something to do with the road," Jen reiterated.

"It's home to what was once the world's largest hydraulic mine, operated by the North Bloomfield Gravel & Mining

Company," Kendra explained.

"Tell me more," I said, encouraging a synthesis between the virtual world and the real world. It was a point of pride for Jen and me, seeing how Kendra used her phone. The limits placed on devices years ago paid off in a kid who knows how to use technology in the proper context, to highlight and enhance engagement with the physical world around you, to meet people and see the scenery first, especially on vacation. I could think of few things worse as a parent than to have a self-absorbed kid, mindlessly addicted to games or social media, their entire adolescence consumed by gigs and mega gigs of constantly streaming data. Whatever happened to play? I used to ride my bike when I got home from school, played catch or touch football in the street. Of course, back then, there were only five TV channels and no microwave oven. You want something to eat, it took a while. Aw, forget it. I'll wait till dinner and ride my bike instead. I shouldn't be so harsh. A soda slurping geek will probably grow up to rule the world, transforming some start-up into a tech giant, though he will always be a social misfit, desperate for a date with my daughter. This was all hard won wisdom, I figured, the graying Generation X perspective of knowing what the world was like before the IT revolution, before the Internet changed everything.

"Not much else to say. There's a small museum, hiking trails, a small lake."

"Good thing Kendra is so adept looking things up," Jen said. "I don't dare turn my phone on."

"Either of us turns our phone on and we'll spend the next 3 hours answering work emails. We're on vacation, let's enjoy vacation," I pledged, swearing an oath to dismiss the 21st century curse of 24/7 employment, work that seeks you out and finds you anywhere anytime.

"Just read my Out of Office message," Jen said slowly, to no one in particular, "reach out to the contacts listed."

I agreed, but as managers with different companies, we always worry about things going wrong, a process not followed, a deliverable not met, schedules and budgets, and even if a colleague ably stepped in, at minimum, you'd be copied on every email anyway. I gazed into the future, the dreaded first day back from vacation, logging in and seeing an inbox runneth over.

"Our companies can live without us for a couple of weeks," I offered in a hopeful tone but surrendering to the inevitable, "but, at some point, we'll need to use our phones…"

"Love my phone, hate the constant tether to work," Jen grumbled, picking up on my thoughts.

"It's a modern day scourge, but where'd we be without Yelp? It's put us on to every 4 star local restaurant and diner throughout this trip."

We both thought back on our favorite meal so far, so many choices, a culinary tour de force of authentic farm to fork ingredients, local ambience, establishing a real sense of place that no franchise or chain restaurant could ever do.

"We've eaten at some good places. I've been writing them down in the journal, in case we ever get back to any of these towns."

"I hope you've got all the craft breweries. We've stopped at so many."

"That last IPA was so good," Jen recounted, "but think of

the calories…we need to hike more."

"We need several *long* hikes," I said with a grin, but who knew beer could be this good? Incredible varieties that we loved, especially the big bitter India Pale Ale bombs, created by mad scientist brewers, using Citra, Simcoe, or some esoteric Mosaic hops, which has reinvented the beverage. May God smite me with stone or strike me down with lightning if I ever touch a Bud again.

"GPS is a godsend too," Jen reminded, "no more wrong turns down some rabbit hole. Just think how much better it'll be once they link your destination with close, available parking."

"Self-driving cars next," I said, amazed at the rapidity of change, wondering at the implications, especially when AI kicks in, a worldwide game changer for everyone and everything.

"When that happens, will people still take road trips?" Jen asked.

"I suppose so. It'll be just like flying on a plane. We'll passively stare out windows or into our palms, at some screen, except we'll have more legroom."

Jen speculated, "We'll be able to program any destination and it will constantly offer a stream of suggested activities – other stops, sights to see, food choices, anything, based on our personal profiles, likes and dislikes."

"All that and more," I said ruefully, thinking back to when I was a kid. My Mom and Dad would pile my brothers and sister into the back of the car and we'd take a family vacation. Dad would rent a trailer and hitch it up to his big V-8 Buick and we'd drive to Yosemite, fighting all the crowds and noise. I remembered a national park experience that seemed more like Woodstock than any transcendent John Muir moment. I pulled on the thread of memory, walking it back to my 10-year-old mind, our campsite neighbor's boom box blasting Led Zeppelin well past "quiet time," Robert Plant's banshee voice ripping through the valley. I asked, from my sleeping bag, in the darkness of the trailer, "Who's that?" and my old man answering, a man whose musical tastes ranged from Hank Williams to Johnny Cash, saying glumly, "You don't need to be listening to that shit."

"Tom, what are you laughing at?"

"Nothing, just thinking back to an earlier road trip when I was a kid."

I could feel Jen's eyes on me, her psychic stare.

"The one in Yosemite, when you became a fan of Led Zeppelin?"

"Man, we've been married too long. I know of old couples that finish each other's sentences, but now you're finishing my thoughts. And we're not even old yet, well not so old. Here, I'll try you again. Guess what I want for dinner?"

Jen feigned exasperation and then theatrically placed a glistening fingernail to each side of her head, slowly rubbing her temples. She closed her eyes and concentrated in a mock Vulcan mind meld sort of way, her lips voicing a short, incoherent mantra. When satisfied, she gazed up from her trance, saying solemnly, "You want Chinese, but will settle for a burger and sweet potato fries."

"You left out the beer," I quibbled and we both smiled.

I dodged more rough patches in the road and watched the dust boil away from beneath our wheels, roiling particulates obscuring the rear mirror view, framed by still more ponderosa pines. I was about to ask Kendra how much further when North Bloomfield came into view. "Hey, everyone, we're here."

I pulled the Honda onto a small strip of dirt used as a parking lot, just off the road that bisected the rustic old town. We parked beside a magnificent silver Class B motorhome, sparkling in the sun, the dream toy that Jen and I so longed for. It was the perfect ride, small but luxurious, with all the modern amenities. It also got an amazing 22 miles to the gallon.

We got out of the Honda just as the two Class B occupants emerged. We smiled and said "hello," the pleasantries returned with a distinct European accent. I asked, "Deutsch?"

"Ja, bist du Deutscher? Ich heisse Helmut. Das ist Gregor. Wie heist du?"

Jen and Kendra stared at me. I said, "They're German. This is Helmut and he's Gregor." They smiled and nodded again, men in their early thirties, lean and lithe, probably from riding their bikes to and from work each day at some tech company in Stuttgart or Munich. Both looked ready to tackle a 500 mile stretch of the Pacific Crest Trail, scaling the heights and doing a handstand on each peak. I introduced myself, then Jen and Kendra, explaining that we were Americans and that I speak a little German, "Ich spreche nur ein bisschen Deutsch. Do you speak English?"

"Ja, yes," Helmut answered with the cool detachment of a German speaking a second language as an afterthought. "We are like many Germans who come and enjoy holiday in your country."

"We've met so many Germans and other Europeans over

the years," Jen shared. "I think there are more Europeans in the parks and on the trails now than at any other time. The fall is the best time to visit. The weather is good and kids are back in school, smaller crowds."

"Es ist our first time here, in this part of California," Gregor explained. "We wanted to see a real Gold Rush town."

"That's why we're here too," Kendra chimed in. "We started from Grass Valley. Did you drive the motorhome on this crummy road to get here?"

"We were in Nevada City. There ist a better road to get here," Gregor pointed in the opposite direction out of town, "longer but we did not want to take a chance getting stuck because es ist a rental."

"Can't help but admire your wheels," I said, gently knocking my knuckles on the Roadtrek Adventurous with the Mercedes-Benz sprinter chassis.

"Here, take a look," Gregor said, holding the door open so we could peer inside.

Jen beat me to a compliment, gushing an elongated "beautiful."

One glance and it was easy to see why this was the favorite motorhome for German tourists, the streamlined organization of space and efficiency. We'd seen many over the years, on the road and in campgrounds throughout the western half of the U.S., all the way up into Canada, with each model year looking better than the last. "You don't want to know how much we want one of these."

Gregor said, "Ja, es ist an amazing machine, very comfortable, though very expensive. We have been travelling for almost a month."

"A month? That's a long time to be on the road," Jen said.

"In Germany and all European Union countries, every worker receives 4 weeks of vacation by law," Gregor answered, "but we are lucky, we have 8 weeks for our travels."

"Must be fun," I said enviously. "We've been doing a mix of hotels, campgrounds, and we've become big fans of yurts. Do you mind if I ask what it costs to rent a rig like this?"

Helmut interjected with even more proficient English, and from the tone, he was more a discontented than a happy camper when it came to considering the amount. "Very expensive, $1,700 per week, but it is the mileage that adds up. The first 100 miles is included but every mile up to 300 miles is 50 cents per mile and once you go above that, it is 80 cents per mile," he said, detailing the pocketbook pain. "Our plan should have been to buy a used motorhome and then sell it a month from now when we leave."

I gave a sympathetic, "ouch," and wondered "that probably doesn't include a security deposit?"

Helmut's forehead wrinkled with more angst before Gregor interrupted, "We are on holiday and nothing ist ever inexpensive when travelling, but this ist a very beautiful country. Such wide open spaces are unimaginable in Europe. To drive and see all of this ist a wonder. There ist ein German term, *Wandervogel*. It means wandering bird, to seek out the freedom of nature without society's restrictions."

"We're on our own *Wandervogel*, seeing the parks, hiking, finding good food and drink," Jen replied. "Have you been to Yosemite?"

Gregor, enthusiastically, "Ja, hiking in Yosemite. We climbed Half Dome, up the back with the cables last week, very memorable with most spectacular views. I don't know what was harder, the climb or obtaining a permit for the hike, but the German Alpine Club has been very helpful in planning our trip."

Jen said, "Yeah, the crowds of hikers are huge on Half Dome. Everyone wants to do that as a bucket list hike. Tom took me in October, when everyone was back in school, just before the permit system started a few years ago to control the crowds. I was so tired afterwards. Funny, the cables, I mean, the heights, didn't bother me."

Helmut said, "As long as you hold on, and keep your feet firmly planted, moving between each board, you will be fine, though, I must say, the general fitness of many Americans makes me think few can make such a climb, especially if one starts on the valley floor."

The distended stomachs of Americans, spilling over waist-lines, it's the first thing every outsider notices. I commented, "It must be getting pretty bad in the U.S. when a great sausage and beer drinking culture like Germany is so impressed, too much television, fast food and computer games."

Helmut clarified to avoid offense, "I only say this since it is apparent you guys are not like others in your country, since you enjoy the outdoors and you each appear fit."

Like a gunshot, a voice erupted, snapping us and the small group of people milling about town to attention. "Did all of you pay your visitor fees?!"

We froze and stared at a squat, stern looking, gray-haired volunteer ranger, perched on a wooden plank porch to the North Bloomfield Museum. The woman continued to bellow in both directions down the street.

"You have to pay your fees inside!"

Jen broke the silence, "So much for 'welcome, thanks for coming.' Ms. Ranger could sure use some tips on customer service, rather than making us feel like deadbeats who climbed in over a fence."

"It's not what you say but how you say it," I agreed. "I'm sure she thinks she's doing a great job...scaring everyone." I kick-started the conversation with our new German friends back to life, "Let's go pay up. Helmut, Gregor, maybe we'll see you guys inside the museum."

We left the German duo to close up the motorhome, and we walked toward the small clapboard building that served as a museum. As we neared the entrance, the woman barked again, "Town tour starts at 1:30. You'll see inside these historic buildings and learn what life was like in a Gold Rush mining town!"

As we passed, she gave us a stink-eyed look, "Have you paid? It's $8."

"We're going inside to do that now," I answered softly, hoping she would drop her voice a few notches.

Jen couldn't let it go. "You know, it would be nicer if you were less accusatory. I mean, instead of demanding payment, try saying something like 'Hello, welcome and everyone *please* remember to pay your park fee...'"

Jen stopped and the two stared silently at each other, the older woman's face pinching up into an uncomprehending, "What? Are you trying to tell me how to do my job?"

Jen shook her head, giving up, saying, "Nevermind," and fell in behind us, walking through the museum's open doorway.

Kendra whispered, "That didn't go well."

"Let's look through the museum and then the town tour will start. Maybe she'll mellow by then."

"You mean Mom or grizzly ranger?"

I raised an uncertain eyebrow and paid our fee with the ranger behind the counter, who was slightly more engaging. I asked, "She always like that?" having to explain no further since this ranger had heard it all before.

"Ruth is Ruth," she said in a flat officious voice. "We're pretty remote so we don't get many volunteers. We take who we get. Here's your change, tape this on your driver's side window, not your dash. Next."

I thought, "least visited park," yeah, for a reason.

It was Jen's turn this time, providing a consultant's evaluation, "no people skills so let's put them in a customer facing role." She shook her head, "who hires and manages these people?"

I tried to make light of the apathy, smiling, "Just wait until the town tour starts. They have badges, you know, the *official* license to drive us through the streets like mules. Yah, mules. Yah, mules!"

We walked back outside just in time to see Helmut and Gregor getting the freeloading, deadbeat treatment. Jen and Kendra stayed in the porch shade while I ran the receipt back to car, taping it in the window.

"Have you two paid your visitor fees?"

"Nein," Helmut said.

"I didn't say $9. I said $8."

I locked our car, chuckling at the misunderstanding, thinking some Abbott and Costello Who's on First? hilarity would ensue but that would be wishful thinking.

Helmut removed and held out his debit card.

"What do you think I am, an ATM? You don't pay me. You pay inside," she snapped.

I walked back up behind, defusing the encounter, "Follow me, guys. I'll show you where."

We passed Jen and Kendra on the porch, I said, "Still think it's a training issue?"

Kendra answered this time, "It's a politeness issue."

1883

C harles Townsend Reed opened The Golden Star of Shanghai with Wei Lu a little over a year ago in the gold mining town of Auburn, California. They formed an unlikely partnership. Reed, an Anglo white professional gambler and Wei Lu, also known as John John, was the proprietor of a thriving Chinese laundry, washing the duds of almost every miner in the Sierra Foothills east of Sacramento. Their venture, established in the old part of town, on the plaza, was formerly a hotel – the American Hotel – whose run ended when fire gutted its interior, a brick edifice the only thing left standing. Refurbished and renamed, The Golden Star of Shanghai straddled the unofficial border between Auburn's white community and its neighboring Chinatown, one foot in each camp.

The plan was to lure both races into the saloon, with Reed offering liquor and games of chance, while John John minded the kitchen and laundry out back. The endeavor proved successful, especially after Reed brought in a slew of dance hall girls. More and more miners came out of the hills, lining up for a turn around the dance floor with their favorite painted lady, purchasing a $1 ticket with half the amount going to the lady herself. It was no surprise to Reed and John John that the popular girls earned more money than the miners, especially after Reed offered a commission on every whiskey guzzled. The ladies enthusiastically embraced the idea, and began finishing each dance with a flourish, twirling the prospector's back up against the bar, ending with a suggestive bumping of hips. The whole dance-drink combination became something of a tradition, where one begat the other, becoming downright un-American to not end a dance without a bump and a libation. Of course the ladies of the line worked in cahoots with the barkeep, who surreptitiously dispensed cold tea or sugar water into their glass instead of whiskey. When the smiles and conversation ended and a new miner lined up, the final bill was tendered to the hapless dirt digger, showing all drinks being whiskey, the heavily marked-up kind.

It was wholesome fun and the miners didn't really feel much like victims. They were glad to be had, willing conspirators in a weekly ritual – a wink and a smile, womanly attention – packaged in ruffled skirts and petticoats, net stockings and garters. They were defenseless to these charms, the low cut bodices and exposed bosoms, women rubbing their seductive shapes provocatively against the miner and his pocketbook. The loneliness of a miner, the lack of female companionship, everyone knew time with a lady came with a price.

The Golden Star of Shanghai was a respectable house and

not one of ill repute. One could drink and play cards, faro or roulette, eat in the kitchen, but prostitution was to be found elsewhere. Everyone felt a little guilty about this, lathering up the clientele without a particular means of expression. John John solved this by ushering the aroused out the back door and down the alleyway. Brothels were to be had in any direction, with each bawdy house paying a fee for patrons led their way. A short walk was all it took to reach these sporting women, doves who had fallen farther than their dance hall counterparts, women who serviced the desires of men.

The miner's sabbatical, a one day reward for the week, was a respite from the miserable, backbreaking grind of everyday life. Clean yourself up and get into town, take a break from the 12 hour days toiling in filthy conditions, eating one poor meal after another – fried or boiled meats, usually salt pork or fatty beef, with a helping of potatoes or hard tack. The unappetizing grub, along with putrid water, guaranteed a passel of bellyaches and other digestive maladies. Diarrhea and dysentery was commonplace and everyone seemed afflicted with a chronic case of the backdoor trots. Some thrived in the shared misery, others grew despondent, withdrawn. A dedicated few still remained who hoped to strike it rich on their own, independently. With the Gold Rush more than 30 years old, most miners had abandoned or sold their claims. It took machines and large investment to dig deeper, to reach the riches. The easy to find placer gold was long gone, prompting many to leave the hills behind to take up a new vocation. Most became farmers in the valley, the rest stayed and hired on for a wage. It wasn't much, but it was what they knew, counting on one of the big mining outfits, like the North Bloomfield Gravel

& Mining Company, to take care of them.

Behind the bar stood Willis Connelly, a friend of Reed's, who, when he wasn't master at arms for the establishment, also drove stagecoach and freight to and from the nearby towns and mining camps. On Saturday nights, Willis could be seen coolly surveying the hall, making sure everyone was enjoying themselves without the devil getting loose on their person, compelling them to do something dumb, like punch a dance hall girl or interrupt the piano player. Reed, John John, and Willis were of equal minds that one could have a lively time at The Golden Star of Shanghai, just so long as people held their liquor and civility reigned. Ruffians and scoundrels were not welcome, but one stopped by anyway.

Why he was here was anyone's guess, and both Reed and Willis watched Russell McGirt with interest, seated at Hai Lon's faro table, consistently losing gold piece after gold piece.

Reed moved up beside Willis at the end of the bar. Willis was the first to speak. "Why's he here, and not playin' at The Skidmore?"

"Not sure. Probably has something to do with our new Chinese dealer. I've been thinking he would make a run at us. Thinks all Chinese are stupid, can't possibly beat him at cards, but with Hai Lon pulling in the winnings, I'm thinking he's reconsidering that notion."

"What do you want me to do?"

"Just keep an eye on him and get your scatter gun ready down below, in case he wants to grab the pot. He probably thinks the law won't do anything to a white man, even if he tries to steal the money back. Have you seen the Dutchman?"

Willis, looking over Reed's shoulder, answered, "He just came through the doors, walkin' this way."

Mr. Chang, master of the kitchen and temporary barkeep, approached Wim Van der Hoof, saying in his limited English, "What you drink?"

The Dutchman snorted, "I will drink anything, but not from you, yellow dog. You, white man, fetch me a beer."

Reed looked to Willis, "Is he talking to you or me?"

Willis volunteers, "I'll handle it," stepping in and placing his hand on the shotgun that rested on a shelf beneath the bar. As he walked toward the Dutchman, he slid the shortened twin barrels down the shelf, aiming it directly at the Dutchman's middle.

"You're name's Wim, isn't it?" What'll you have and what's wrong with Mr. Chang here gettin' you a drink?"

The Dutchman faced Willis. His ruddy complexion under red moppy hair reminded Willis of a spotted tail end to an appaloosa he once owned.

"Yes, my name is Wim and if you truly knew me, not just my name, you would know I don't take my liquor from any slant-eyed Chinese," he sneered in a Dutch lowland accent.

Reed stepped in. "Then this isn't your kind of place, Wim. We already know enough about you and aren't interested in the rest. Take it out on the street and don't come back."

The Dutchman set his jaw, wiggling and twisting his neck in the manner a snake does when swallowing a rodent. Once choked down, he spewed it back up, racist invective through clinched teeth, "All these heathen Chinese can go back to where they came from. We don't need a single one of them, taking our gold, establishing themselves in our town, our state, our country. The Transcontinental Railroad is built. We don't need their hammers, picks and shovels anymore. Move on and leave this country to the white man."

Reed answered, "You don't sound like you're from these parts yourself. I'm not so sure we need another Dutchman either."

Willis broke in, "Especially this one."

The Dutchman looked up at Willis, a tight smile on his lips.

"Give him a beer, Willis, and then get out, Wim. You're not welcome here."

The glares ended when Mr. Chang plunked a beer down in front of Wim, a short pour in a tall glass.

The Dutchman grabbed the beer and swallowed it in a single quaff, banging the glass on top of the bar. He smiled at Reed and Willis, "Sure. Leave all of this," he said, his eyes rolling up and around, expansively, "leave all of this to the Chinese and, yes, the bean eaters too."

Reed returned the grave smile, "Why stop there, Wim. I say we give it back to the Indians, too. There's a few Maidu remaining. Seems like the Christian thing to do."

Wim, laughed, saying, "Do-gooders, just like all those farmers in the valley, building farms, roads, schools. I will leave once my friend is through with his game," another snake-like shake of the head gesture toward McGirt.

Six eyes turned to McGirt and Hai Lon. It was easy to see that McGirt had moved rapidly from agitation, to frustration, to impending eruption, the penultimate climax to a game of cards decidedly not going his way.

Reed moved to the faro table, standing behind Hai Lon as he called the turn, when a final bet was placed on the order of the last three cards played. Of course, McGirt, feeling a surge of gambler's confidence, placed a bold wager that busted him out and ended his night of erratic play.

"You lose," Hai Lon said in a detached, nonchalant voice.

"I '*lose*.' Is that right, Chinaman? I know how to play the game," McGirt's voice rising. "I know what losin' cards look like, you cheatin' son of a bitch."

Hai Lon said nothing as he cleared the table. He just slowly turned his head, stopping for an instant to stare at the space where McGirt had once stacked his chips and gold coins. It looked like empty prairie land. Others in The Golden Star of Shanghai noticed the ruckus and began to find their way to places out of danger, through side doors and into the street or standing closer to some piece of furniture that could provide protection.

"You slant-eyed coolie. You cheated me. I want my money back. And…what're you lookin' at, Mr.?"

"I'm Charles Reed. I run this place. What makes you think you were cheated?"

"No white man *ever* loses to a Chink Chinaman," McGirt said plainly.

The statement was pure racist hate, a malignancy formed over a lifetime, pounded into his thick skull the same way a blacksmith beats on a red-hot horseshoe.

Reed challenged, "You see that sign on the wall over there? It says, 'This is a Square House. Please report any unfairness to the proprietor.' I'm the proprietor. I trained Hai Lon myself. You got a square game. Now clear out and take the Dutchman with you."

McGirt, defiant, stoked his fire, "I don't give a shit about you, Reed, the Chinaman, or your bit house saloon. You're all a bunch of shit eaters so gimme my goddamn money back or I'll take it back myself."

Reed had always known where this was headed once the two walked in. One didn't make a living as a professional gambler without confrontation being an unwanted part of the life of cards and wagering. Reed noticed McGirt's slight lean forward in his chair, his hand slipping down to his hip. In an instant, Reed had his Remington out, cocked, and pressed up against the fleshy spot between McGirt's eyes. "Sit very still and put your hands on the table," he said in a firm, even voice.

McGirt, bewildered at the speed of Reed's draw, simply complied, resting his hands on the green felt.

Up against the bar, the Dutchman reacted, reaching into his coat but getting no further.

Willis had the shotgun out and pressed into the Dutchman's back. "Move, Dutchman, and I'll blow your pink skin in half."

The Dutchman's gun remained in his coat, an empty hand back at his side.

Willis acknowledged the decision, "You done good Dutchman. Now I won't have to scrub your bloody mess up from our nice clean walnut floor. Would've needed Mr. Chang to help me toss your carcass in the pig trough out back."

"Hai Lon, take his gun, will you?" Reed said, pressing the Remington's barrel more forcefully against McGirt's forehead, the pressure creating a round indentation in the skin.

Hai Lon removed the long-barreled Colt from McGirt's person, while Mr. Chang moved in to disarm the Dutchman.

Reed looked at Willis and received an all clear look in return.

"You're not robbing from him, you're robbing from me," Reed said, pausing to let the statement sink in. "You're supposed to check these guns with Sheriff Huntley when you cross into town. You see, cards, liquor, women and guns don't mix very well so the town removes one. Guess which one?"

McGirt argued, "I see you got one?"

"You're in my place of business, my property and it's lawful for me to have it to protect my goods, my people. Everyone walking these streets checks their firearms on entry, especially the unwanted types like you and him."

The Dutchman croaked, "More civilization."

Reed answered, "Yes, that's right. Hard to build a town, attract money, open businesses, when bullets whiz up and down the streets and bullies try to have their way. City leaders don't like it and neither do I. Now get out."

McGirt stood and joined the Dutchman. Crossing the room, they stopped in the doorway. McGirt turned and issued a threat, "I'm going to remember you two. You're going to regret doing what you just done. We'll meet up again," he spat before the two stomped out of the saloon.

The commotion over, people began to reappear, from behind columns and out from under tables. Reed looked to Elsa at the piano and she launched into a lively tune, everything back to normal.

Willis said to Reed, "He's right about that. Them two ain't forgettin' tonight. If not today, tomorrow, they'll look to bushwhack us."

"I suppose so," Reed agreed, "but, Willis, do me a favor? When they come for us, it won't be with these guns. Take them to the kitchen. Have Mr. Chang heat the barrels and bend them in the vice out back, straight up into the air, so the only thing they'll be able to shoot is the clouds in the sky."

Reed reached behind the counter and poured two glasses of bourbon. He slid a shot glass to Willis and took a sip from his own. "I'll check them with Sheriff Huntley and let him know what happened here tonight. We can't afford to be known as some bucket of blood saloon."

"Good idea, though, I have to say, Reed, you're one fast hombre on the draw. I never get tired seein' that move. McGirt was nowhere close to clearing leather. He only had time for his eyes to widen, big like saucers."

"Practice and a card player's dexterity," Reed explained. "Also helps to choose the right gun. In close like this, a lighter short barrel, like my Remington, will be out on the dance floor faster than that big hog leg Colt. Take him forever to wrassle that hunk of metal from his hip."

"Yep, and you know exactly when to draw. You never let the other fella get the drop on you. You're always first."

Reed nodded, taking another sip of bourbon. "First and fast and you can take control of any situation. I've rarely ever shot my piece. It just comes down to fast, disarm, send them on their way."

"Tell me again about your time playin' cards with Wyatt Earp and Doc Holliday in Tombstone. You cleaned them out on their own turf. They didn't cheat you or nothin'?"

"Willis, the straightest game a professional gambler ever gets is with another professional. Earp's a pro, steady, teetotaler, drinks nothing but coffee, very clearheaded. I liked him. Doc Holliday, on the other hand, sickly and mean, fueled by whiskey and more whiskey, but very loyal to the Earps.

Never seen any one man drink so much and be able to stand, let alone play faro. But, when it comes to cards, if Doc wins he wins and if he loses he loses. He's just like Wyatt in that regard. A man makes a wager and the cards do all the talking, but the game better be an honest one or things will get ugly and not even Big Nose Kate will be able to settle the dentist down."

"What does the good Doctor see in her, other than her big pickle nose?" Willis asked, slugging down the glass of Kentucky's finest, the warm liquid splashing down in his belly.

"Many a man, not just the Doc, admires her handsome curves and looks the other way when it comes to the big nose part. Honestly, it's not about the nose. The two just like to drink, and drink…"

Young Charlie Yue approached Reed and Connelly, a letter in his hand. In English he said, "This came for you earlier today, Mr. Reed." He handed over the letter and returned to the kitchen.

Reed opened and read the letter. He looked up at Willis, "It's from Lester L. Robinson, president of the North Bloom-field Gravel & Mining Company. He wants me to pay a call on his office at the mine. Says he knows me by reputation as an honest gambler and is interested in a private game."

"That big, muddy hole in the ground above Nevada City?"

"Yeah, I've heard enough talk about it, but not many people other than those who work at the mine ever get to see it. It's a secretive place for all the activity that goes on there. I suppose that's reason enough to not pass up the opportunity."

Reed paused, thinking to himself, hydraulic mining, entire

hillsides blasted away by water monitors in search of gold, becoming more intrigued at the prospect of a visit. He looked up from the letter, smiling, "Besides, who am I to deny a man a chance at placing a few lucrative wagers? There're few names bigger in California than L.L. Robinson. He's a man worth meeting."

"Well, Charlie, you best be on guard. McGirt and the Dutchman oversee all them miners workin' at that North Bloomfield Mine. Don't want any of them $2 a day workmen endin' their shifts with loose nuggets in their pockets. Woe unto those who try to sneak a little gold out for personal use. Much blood spilt and bones broken for those who try."

"I won't have to worry. I'm just going to play cards with their boss. I figure I'll be under his protection," Reed surmised.

"Just to be safe, I'll go with you. Hank Monk is drivin' the stage to Nevada City and on to North Bloomfield. He'll use me as his second alongside him so I can be nearby."

"Suit yourself, Willis. I figure by the time we get up there, enough time will have passed so that everyone's head will have cooled off."

Willis laughed at the impossibility of that.

Charles Reed entered the kitchen to The Golden Star of Shanghai, bustling with activity as many cooks prepared dishes in flaming woks for the nearby dining room. Since partnering with John John, the restaurant had thrived. Most people could at least mask any anti-Chinese sentiments, so long as the food was good. Reed himself had taken to the

Asian diet and noticed, as most everyone does, that the bad belly problems that plagued everyone but the Chinese, went away. The rice and vegetable laden fare from John John's larder, in place of the usual meat and potatoes, calmed one's shit chute considerably. Since switching to the diet, Reed, and Willis, too, had not used any opium to quell runny bowels or a plug of blue mass to open them up. Reed was even beginning to like the hot green tea with, what was it, he thought, lemongrass?

John John sat sipping tea, alone, at a table adjoining the kitchen. He closed the small book he was reading and looked up at Reed as he approached. "You should have killed him."

"It may very well come to that, but, in the meantime, we have to abide some semblance of law and order," Reed explained.

"Easy for a white man to say. The law protects you. My people are forgotten or, as the murderer McGirt knows, a resource to be exploited, like the yellow metal buried in the hills. Even the black man, once a slave, is freer than my people," John John asserted.

"You know yourself, J.J., you'll get no argument from me at the injustice of it all, but as partners, I do provide a great deal of cover so our enterprises can thrive."

"And I am grateful, my friend," John John acknowledged with a slight bow of the head, with Reed questioning the sincerity of the gesture.

"McGirt and the Dutchman are gone now. I don't think they'll be back, at least not so boldly as to use the front door," Reed predicted.

"The great Chinese dealer experiment, is it now over?"

"Hai Lon's table has less action, but we shouldn't give up so easily. We're doing well enough to try this a spell longer. Besides, nothing's going to change unless whites and Chinese mix and understand each other better. The dining hall is certainly working out."

John John sat silently, sipping his tea.

Reed changed the subject, "so how's our laundry business doing?"

John John rose from his chair and the two walked through the kitchen, exiting a back door and into a dark narrow alleyway, the vices of white Auburn to the right, the opium dens and prostitution of Chinatown to the left. Reed and John John chose neither, stepping into the laundry, another brick building that sat directly behind the saloon. It too was built to better withstand the many fires that periodically claimed the town, the last just three years ago when most of Sacramento Street went up in flames.

The air was hot and steamy, with piles of laundered clothing folded on one side and piles of filthy work clothes on the other. In between, clotheslines were strung about as garments hung to dry. Heated metal vats boiled with hot water and soap, Chinese laundrymen, sweating heavily, used wooden bats and washboards to agitate and stir the dirt and stains out. John John's trusted lieutenants lined each wall, overseeing the work.

John John unlocked a small windowless office and he and Reed entered. On the table was an oil lamp, a scale, an array of small gold nuggets, and two pouches of gold dust. John John said, "This is just from the last week."

Reed pushed the brim of his hat back off his forehead,

whistling, "Un-beee-lievable. It's no wonder why our laundry prices are so low for miners. I hope we're still running the wagon out to the mines to pick these duds up?"

John John nodded and smiled, "and they think us idiots for doing it. If the fools only knew how much gold was in their pockets, cuffs, shirttails, they would give up mining and start a laundry."

"The laundry produces more gold than most claims. All washed into the bottom of the vats," Reed continued to shake his head in amazement.

John John observed, "It is unsurprising to find gold dust in folds and creases. What is surprising is the many pouches and nuggets left behind in pockets. I believe this is because most miners are so drunk that they simply do not remember where they have placed their purse."

Reed agreed, "Yep, everyone is too roostered up for their own good. They can't find their hat let alone their gold. We must have fifty hats up front. People grab whichever one they want when they leave."

"The white man's consumption of alcohol is truly extra-ordinary."

"A lot like those Chinese corpses with hollowed-out cheeks sucking the bamboo pipe in the opium dens around the corner," Reed countered.

John John did his slight bow again. This time it was sincere. Touché.

They placed the gold in a strong box and returned to the alleyway. John John asked, "You are off to visit your whore?"

Reed answered "Yes," turning to John John, "but this is none of your concern."

John John protested, "A prostitute for Dai Lao is a concern. There are many others you can choose from. You are also well aware that our tongs are rivals."

"You mean Pig Face," Reed said derisively.

"Yes, Pig Face. Respectfully, you must be careful. He is especially cruel to his prostitutes and even his miners, poisoning them with the opium he controls."

"I don't work for him," Reed declared flatly.

"That is true, but your increasing visits have not gone unnoticed. If you have feelings for her, she could be used against you, me."

"I'll make sure that doesn't happen," Reed snapped, done with the conversation. He walked a path away from John John, toward Chinatown, and into the night.

Reed heard the whispers of *gwai lo* as he moved along the brick walled alleyway and into the heart of Chinatown's red light district. Everyone moved in a manner suspicious of one another. Chinese in long changshan shirts and skull caps, their pigtails dangling down their backside, knocked on doors and crossed into their own forbidden world – sex, opium, gambling. As a door opened, Reed could hear the lively play of fan-tan from inside, a version of roulette popular with Chinese – somebody winning, somebody losing.

Reed stopped and leaned on a brick wall. Opposite he could see Chan in her second floor window, a bright light illuminating her fine white skin. She sat, as she always sat, pensively, waiting for the workings of the world to impose its will upon her. Reed just watched, studying her movements –

minimal, sublime. He wondered how much she thought of him, thinking back to the beginning, when both were a cipher to each other. He knew mystery was an attraction, exotic, that little things revealed themselves in time. Everything was unrushed with Chan, and, in time, he learned her story and she his. Now, he felt in his heart, they were creating a new story together.

She had told him of her past, recounting her kidnapping in Hong Kong and the years after the Taiping Rebellion, millions dead, famine, subsistence living. With life so hard, many families willingly let their daughters go to America as one less mouth to feed. They could find work and send money back to the family. Others were lured by promises made by importer agents who spoke of high paying jobs or marriage to a success-ful Chinese merchant in San Francisco. All lies. Young women were bound to contracts that amounted to indentured slavery, as the cost of ship passage, food, board, and continually com-pounding interest imprisoned them in a world of prostitution with little chance of parole or escape. For Chan, it was different. When the false promises no longer held any allure, the agents simply began to kidnap women, trolling the urban centers or the rural landscape for any face, pretty or otherwise.

Torn from her mother and father, forced onto a ship from Hong Kong to Guangdong province, Chan joined several other captive women. They were placed on another ship bound for San Francisco, manned by a sadistic crew, prisoners of the Hip Yee Tong, the notorious gang that spooked John John. He said their reach was far, with agents in China and bounty hunters in America, hatchet men, criminals, who protected and extended its illicit trade. The Hip Yee Tong relied on an elaborate system of informants, rewards, and bribery to maintain control of their prostitution empire, tracking down and punishing any woman who dared escape.

Once off ship, the appropriate customs and immigration officials bribed, Chan was housed in a *barracoon*, a filthy holding area of one hundred women facing sale or distribution to brothel owners, some of whom having already paid a negotiated price. Chan was held till the end, auctioned off like a fish in the market to the highest bidder, for $2,000 in gold. Though Chan would not consider it luck, she was lucky to have been purchased by a wealthy Chinese man. Other women were less fortunate, sold off on a sliding scale of degradation, the prettiest destined to Chinese brothels serving high-end clientele, others relegated to lowly cowyards and cribs, 25 cent screws by the lowest paid laborers of any race – laundrymen, teenage boys, sailors, drunkards.

After a few years, almost used up, addicted to opium, afflicted with disease, these women would be freighted from the city and out to the mining camps. Here the harshest treatment and the final humiliation was inflicted, moved about in a cat wagon, the last bit of profit wrung from their bodies before death. Within this world, no matter where a woman stood, she was merely chattel, her life stolen for profit. Chan's banishment came when she fled her wealthy suitor, an abductor posing as a husband. With no one to help, and white police either bribed or uncaring, she was quickly hunted down and returned like a piece of property. Beaten and stripped of her clothing and adornments, she was sold and shipped like a package, hands bound, on a journey downward, to Dai Lao, Pig Face, away from San Francisco, a step closer to the

THE GOLDEN STAR OF SHANGHAI

dreaded mining camps, to Auburn.

Reed pounded a fist on one of the black double doors, which were nicked and splintered by years of use, hanging on heavy iron hinges. How the doors survived the last town fire was anyone's guess. Half of an ancient Chinese woman's face appeared in the gap between the two doors, an intricate web of thin wrinkles etched into her skin. A wedge of reddish light spilled from inside, cutting a slash into the dark alleyway. Reed said nothing, one look satisfied the old woman, who opened the door to the *yin chong*, the man who wants sex.

Reed entered the space. He was well acquainted with its layout. Other Chinese men sat about silently, waiting for their time to go upstairs and into the crib of their own sing-song girl. They stared at Reed blankly, with no emotion, through black slits. The large thug in the corner, the Baotu, as Chan called him, sat on his small wooden stool, arms crossed over his expansive belly, contempt rising up out of him. His only movement, a slight curl of the lip, a sneer that lifted half of his mustache, which looked like two mule tails pinned on each side of his mouth, a large, empty, fleshy patch under his twisted nose.

Reed moved past the ancient woman and up the stairs to Chan. He no longer cared what these Chinese thought of him, the white man who appeared to do as he pleased, going straight up to *cao* a beautiful Chinese woman, a woman often alone – alone because no Chinese man would touch her. They would never press their flesh against her, run their hands down her length, place their lips to hers. Chan was a *jianmin*, a sexual pariah, a woman who had prostituted herself to a white man. Reed was hated for having soiled her, taking her away from their own lustful urges. The insult was particularly galling now, a year after enactment of the Chinese Exclusion Act, a federal law that prohibited all Chinese immigration into the United States. With Chinese men far outnumbering Chinese women in California, to lose one so beautiful to a white man fueled their rage, especially now with the imbalance a permanent reality codified into law.

Reed knocked on Chan's door before opening it. She stood facing him, her hair up, in a white laced bodice and bell shaped red skirt, its folds covering many colorful petticoats below. Being dressed as a white woman, untraditionally, was part of the shame she bore, Pig Face's way of marking her as an outsider in his Chinese bordello. Reed did not care if Pig Face was playing mental games. He preferred Chan's saloon girl appearance. Clothing would be beside the point, anyway, for the both of them, once they retreated to the bed, enjoining themselves in one another. For Chan, any stigma attached to attire meant nothing once Charles arrived.

In his eyes, she was radiant, tall for a Chinese woman, lithe and proportioned, with skin so pure and unblemished as to be ivory. Touching her was like stroking the feathers of a dove. Reed placed his hat on a brass wall hook and took off his coat. From its pocket, he removed a small package tied with string. "This is for you."

"Charles, always with a gift," she said, a smile on her face. She opened the package, inside a pearl necklace. "It is beautiful, Charles. Where did you get it?"

"Nothing like it in Auburn, that's for sure."

"San Francisco? But you have not been there recently. Where?"

"Something new. I had the necklace sent to me from Chicago. A fellow named Montgomery Ward has invented a mail order catalog that everyone calls the Wish Book. It's 250 pages long and Ward claims to have 10,000 items available for sale, all through the mail."

Chan, amazed, "Really?"

"Only took a month for the necklace to get here. Of course, all the merchants in town are frothing mad, now that there's somewhere else to buy from. Going to kill business on Main Street America they say."

Reed closed the gold clasp around Chan's neck. He reached for a mirror and held it to her face. She gazed at her reflection, studying the pearls, saying again, slowly, "Beautiful." The layered nacre crystals produced a bright luster and a glow deep from within the pearls. A similar glow rose up inside Chan and Charles, a welling of hearts, seeing both together, he standing behind her, casting a gaze over her shoulder, their eyes met and held on the mirror's reflected surface. Her hand went up, placing it over his hand that rested upon her shoulder. Chan turned and kissed Reed long and passionately, wrapping her arms around his neck, pulling him tight. He returned the passion, absently tossing the mirror onto a pillow and placing a hand on each side of her waist, resting atop her hips. The kiss continued pressing and turning forcefully, tongue on tongue, probing, both startled by their open-mouthed teeth clicking against one another, but still not breaking the seal. Their lungs strained at the physicality of the act, the ferocity of their love.

Reed's right hand slid into the small of her back, using his strength to pull her body even more tightly into his, her breasts squeezed decisively against his chest, their hips no longer merely touching, now locked together. His hand moved from her back and over the curve of her behind, cupping a cheek in the palm of his hand. The skirt and petticoats rustled in protest and the dense fabric was far too much for Reed to stand. Their lips parted with a gasp and an inhalation, sucking on the long cut off air. They stared again deeply into each other's eyes, a ravenous lust driving their desire. Each shared the same thought – that these clothes simply must go.

Chan, smiling, pulled Reed's tie loose, sliding it out from its collar and onto the floor, the buttons of his shirt next, stripping him to the waist. Reed did likewise, unlacing the front of her bodice, separating its halves, revealing her perfect breasts, nipples distinct and blooming in the candlelight. Soon they were lying side by side, naked except for Chan's pearl necklace. More kisses, hot and physical, Chan's lips raw due to the short unshaven bristles on Reed's upper lip and chin, a sting that Chan did not mind in the least, the best kind of pain, causing her lips, mouth and tongue to flare and swell, accelerating her passion. He moved on top of her, hard and stiff in the saddle, a coo of delight as he made his entrance. He arched his back and Chan moved a hand up, stroking the hair on his chest, biting her swollen lower lip, her white upper teeth pinching down on the lipstick covered surface – puffy, round, and glistening a fiery crimson that spurred his desire. He looked again into her eyes, nothing said, just the same invisible thought they had shared numerous times before, rising up out from her – do it to me again, Charles, and again. He happily obliged, moving with a powerful intensity, stirring her pot, finding a cadence and alternating rhythms, pulsating, sweating, nurturing, and coaxing their zeal for one another to a crescendo.

Reed said, "Do you want me to do it to you?" repeating the phrase again between breathes. He continued with the refrain, teasing her, "Do you, do you, my pretty little, dirty little Chinese girl? You like this too much, my China Doll. Let me hear your voice, sing-song girl, sing your song to me."

Reed kept at it, his desire growing with each quickening thrust.

Chan demanded, "Speak to me, Charles, speak to me," digging her nails sharply into his back.

He indulged her fantasy, "You need your white man hard atop you, don't you? You love being a white man's slut, my naughty concubine."

She smiled, "more, go on, go on."

"You're so bad so very bad for what you do to me. And what I do to you…you hate yourself so much for enjoying it so. What's your answer, Chan? What do you want? What do you need? Do you want it now? Do you?" he said with a greater push for emphasis.

Chan's teeth clenching, eyes squeezed shut, a nerve quivered reflexively in her right eye lid, her lashes snapping to its beat, fluttering like the wing of a bird. Her breathing grew quick and shallow, her being about to burst, moans of pleasure replaced by wide hungry eyes open and demanding, locked on his. She answered a definitive, primal, "Yes, yes…"

Reed fulfilled the request, though, at this moment, he had little say in the matter, succumbing to his own passion. He moaned his own tune of delight, which was returned simultaneously by Chan's own release, her mouth opening, a slow exhalation through her mouth and nose, an elongated purr of ecstasy escaping deep from within, lovemaking by a man clearly in love with her and she with him.

When the pleasure had run its course, their heartbeats slowing, Chan said, "You bastard, Charles. I should slap you for making me feel the way you do. You are so inside my mind, my thoughts. You know what I am thinking secretly. What I desire. How is it you know so much, that you can reach so far into my *ch'i* – my heart, my body, my soul?"

Reed thought about it a moment, "Just attentive, I guess. I know what you like, who you are. I learn a little more each time. I like trying out ideas, things that will arouse you even more, better for the both of us. Let me know if there's something special you want said so I can add it to our repertoire."

Chan laughed, "Charles, you are doing fine as is, but I do hate you for knowing me so well in this way. It is a little unnerving," she smiled at him, "but I'm glad you do know, know how to pleasure me and that the joy is good for you too. It is very uncommon that a man and a woman know each other so well. I suspect that we could do most everything in life together, without uttering a single word."

"We clearly have a way with one another, that's for sure," Reed agreed.

They sat quietly in bed for a while, pondering the depth of their love.

Reed broke their trance. "Tell me again about your parents? How it is you speak English so well."

"My father is a merchant. In the years after the Opium Wars, our family traded tea and silk with the British. My mother was a keen advisor to my father and knew our businesses as well as father. Sitting quietly and observing, she could discern one's character quickly, knowing who was trustworthy." Chan paused, recollecting her past, a life forgotten if not for Charles's interest, which she deeply appreciated. It allowed her to see her parent's faces in her mind, to hear their voices, laughter – tapping into memories, a mental visitation that provided comfort.

"Our success came from learning to speak English and knowing its customs. We knew many government authorities, ship captains and traders. This all happened as the influence of Great Britain grew in Hong Kong and at the mainland treaty ports – Shanghai, Canton, Ningpo, Fuchow, and Amoy – where Great Britain maintained favored nation status. Eventually, we served as mediators and interpreters for the British in their communications with Chinese officials."

"We? You and your parents?"

"No, I have a brother. He too is in America, somewhere. I had hoped to find him when I fled, but it was not so." Tears welling in Chan's eyes, "Charles, what is to become of us? Is everything so hopeless? Will I ever see my mother and father again?"

Reed shook his head not knowing the answer, so much of the world beyond anyone's control. "I give the old lady downstairs plenty of money to keep you away from other white men. I don't know how long the agreement will last now that Chinese women can no longer set foot in America. Scarcity may make Chinese men forget their aversion to you, degrading yourself to me, a white man. I suspect the payment is bound to go up."

"Dai Lao has said nothing to your offer?"

"Nothing yet. He can't seem to come up with a price for your freedom. Probably wants to bleed payments out of me for as long as he can before coming up with a purchase price." Reed shook his head in disgust, "It's as if the Civil War is still being fought, people buying and selling others."

Chan said, her voice cracking, "Dai Lao cannot wait too long. You may tire of me and walk away. He may end up with nothing. I'll then end up in the mining camps."

"I'm not leaving you. Women may be scarce now but I figure Dai Lao and the Hip Yee Tong will find a way to get around the Exclusion Act, smuggling women in sooner if not later. I can still make a deal with him. Don't give up, you hear me?"

Chan nodded, "yes."

Reed poured two glasses of wine, a bottle of red from Amador that he had left behind on his last visit.

They clinked the glass rims together, "We deserve a better world, Chan. Few of our problems are our own making. We just have to find a solution, somewhere to get off this bad buggy ride."

Chan quietly said, "Despite our predicament, if I had not been abducted, I would never have met you, Charles. We would have remained an ocean apart, unknowing of each other's existence, strangers." She looked up at him, "If we passed by each other on the street, would we even notice each other?"

Reed thought about it, saying, "Funny how the world is, but I can assure you, I would most certainly smile and tip my hat to a lady so beautiful."

"Charles, you always say such nice things."

"As a filthy white man, I have to do something to improve Chinese relations."

"Then we must degrade each other some more, my dear."

Charles Reed walked to the Telegraph Stage Line office the next morning. It was cold but the sun was out as the streets of Auburn came to life, storefronts opening, wooden planks broomed of dust. Reed's first stop at the Auburn Jail was pleasant enough as he recounted it in his mind. Sheriff Asa Huntley was at his desk when Reed handed over McGirt and the Dutchman's guns, telling the tale of last night. They shared a cup of coffee and laughed at the outcome, with Asa hanging both guns by their trigger guards on the jailhouse wall, both barrels bent at a ridiculous angle. Asa said, "will make for a good conversation piece."

"Yeah, it'll take everyone's mind off how bad this coffee is. You sure you used coffee beans? Tastes like you made it with dirty gravel. I almost chipped a tooth drinking it."

Asa smirked, "Budget's tight. City don't allocate much for the finer things in life, like that suit of clothin' you're sittin' in."

Reed rolled his eyes, reckoning it was so. He reached into his suit coat pocket, removing his billfold, "which reminds me," he said, handing $50 to Asa, "for this month, might help with the coffee supply."

Asa said, "Obliged," accepting the municipal fine for operating a saloon and gaming establishment. Asa collected the fine from all such places in town, including brothels, as part of his duties. Even though there was a law against gaming and prostitution, a monthly fine was preferable to jailing people, especially since it was money going to the town, lowering the tax burden on other lawful businesses. Reed had learned early, that if one's operation was a two-bit dive and caused offense to the city's residents, it would be shut down, so he strived to be as discreet and upstanding as possible. Asa placed the $50 inside a stitched leather foldover pouch, "Property of the City of Auburn" burned onto its pebbled-grain calfskin side. He locked the pouch in his desktop drawer.

Asa said, "you mentioned you're heading out to the North Bloomfield Mine and Mr. Lester L. Robinson. That's some fancy company, one big bug, but you best be watchful with them other two workin' at the mine. I doubt these are the only two guns those desperados own. Willis goin' with you?"

Reed nodded, "Willis is looking to ride along with Hank Monk."

"That's good, more for Hank than you."

"Why's that?"

"Hank's not lookin' good. Got a wicked cough. Not gettin' any better, either. He could use a hand with Willis beside him. The man should be restin' in bed and not riskin' a last stop in the bone orchard."

Reed noted the observation, saying he was "sorry to hear that."

Hank Monk is a stagecoach legend, the Knight of the Lash, barreling a coach at breakneck speeds around the windiest Sierra mountain roads. He is probably the most famous person in this part of the state, carrying every person here or there at one time or another. Reed and Asa recollected the story of Hank delivering Horace Greeley of the New York Daily

Tribune to Placerville on time so he could make a lecture. Hank told Horace, in no uncertain terms, to keep his ass plunked down on the seat and to put something else in his mouth other than his complaining words, because "ole Hank'll getcha there." Of course, the stage made it in time, with Horace ricocheting around the interior like a popped kernel of corn, the leather thoroughbraces banging and bouncing throughout the mad dash. When Hank drew the stagecoach to an abrupt halt, he flung the door open, spilling the bruised and battered journalist onto the muddy streets of Hangtown. Greeley wobbled to his feet and promptly threw up his afternoon lunch in full view of his paying audience, right there, in front of the theatre. Hank laughed heartily, admonishing, "Don't tell me or anyone that I didn't get you here in time." It caused everyone in the street to burst out laughing. The story made the newspapers, naturally, every mining camp, and even Mark Twain himself used the tale when he opened his lecture at the Nevada Theatre, saying that "whenever Hank Monk takes me anywhere, audiences are instructed to wait. People don't need to be picking me up out of the street like a sack of taters, dazed like a duck hit on the head by an oar."

Reed got up from his chair and moved toward the door. "So long, Asa. I'll see you in a few days."

"You take care, Charles. When you get back, you might pay a visit to J.C. Boggs. He's got his saloon up and running and could use some advice. I don't think his heart's in it. Once a lawman, always a lawman."

"I'll do so," Reed reminded himself of all of this as he approached the Telegraph Stage Line ticket window and purchased his passage to North Bloomfield about 45 miles from Auburn. Reed noticed Willis Connelly readying the stage. The two men spoke.

"I hear Hank's got a bad case of the croup."

Willis just shook his head, "Pale as can be, and I can't get him to stay put in bed. I can make this milk run without him, but he's insistent."

As Willis finished saying this, Hank Monk appeared in his low-crowned, wide-brimmed felt hat, linen duster and long gauntlet gloves pressed between his left arm and ribs, a soiled kerchief in his hand. He was unloading a nose full into it as he came to a stop, croaking, "Mornin', fellas."

Reed dabbed at his own unshaven lip, gesturing to Hank to take another swipe at his mustache and lip where the ghost of the last blow still lay, a silvery web glistening in the sun.

Hank excused himself, "Oh, sorry," and wiped again. "Can't seem to kick this here cold. Down in my lungs and hardening. Figure the bumpy road will loosen it," he rasped. "Allow me to hock it out." He paused, gathering breath, "just need Willis here to yell at the team of horses."

"Hank, you need to be in bed restin' before this becomes pneumonia," Willis objected, "if it isn't already. You're going to kill yourself."

"Willis," Hank coughed, "I appreciate your concern, but what I need is fresh air to open my nose up. Hell, you can take the reins. I'm just goin' to sit on top of this box and do my restin' there, wrapped in a blanket, and let the wind do its job. You just help me get on up and everything will be fine. No place I'd rather be." Hank turned and then took a seat on a bench for passengers, landing hard, leaning to one side, waiting for the hostlers to finish harnessing the horses and the passengers to load.

Reed looked at Willis, sharing a thought that it was not "fine." "Can't stop a man from doing what he thinks is best," Reed said, surrendering to Hank's stubbornness.

Willis shook his head, taking Reed's gambler's kit by its handle and loading it with the rest of the freight atop the stagecoach, behind the driver's bench.

Reed opened the stagecoach door and helped the widow Louise Cornet onto the stage along with her young daughter, Abigail. Abigail was followed by an older couple he recognized as Jasper and Mildred Fanch, devout Christians and leaders of the local Temperance Movement. Reed extended his hand to help Mildred aboard. Their hands almost touched before she shuddered and pulled back, stepping up of her own accord. Her husband followed directly behind her, saying, "Move along, Mildred. Take a seat."

Reed wondered what the refusal of his hand meant, but figured he would learn all about it, just as soon as he took his own seat. Once inside the passenger compartment, Reed stared at the couple. Jasper gave off a hard gaze while Mildred looked away absently, fearing to make eye contact with the Lucifer in her midst.

"Is there a problem, sir?"

Jasper Fanch leaned forward quickly, a sermon at hand. "You're that heathen gambler Charles Reed," pointing a finger. "What is the Devil himself doing holding the door open for my wife?"

"Common courtesy, sir. I do it because it's the right thing to do, not because I need another poker chip to get into heaven."

Louise Cornet rustled slightly, beside him.

Jasper Fanch reddened, "Such insolence was never spoken. You're the Devil, Mr. Reed. No amount of good deeds can undo the temptations offered by that house of sin of yours." Jasper rose up a few inches from his seat, his spine stiffening as the carriage swayed on its leather straps, he practically spat, "gambling, demon liquor, women, all tools of the Devil, the Devil I say!"

Reed shook his head, thinking he had left this kind of righteous fervor behind in the east, escaping west, where people didn't tell other people how to live their own lives and where judgment is left to the Lord himself, and not to His self-appointed earthly minions.

Jasper preached on. "You wear your fancy silk duds, but I see who you really are. You best get to church and make amends with the Lord Almighty before it is too late and you burn a fiery everlasting death in hell."

Reed glanced to his side, asking a question to Louise Cornet, "Is my pointy tail and pitchfork showing?"

Louise Cornet tried to suppress a laugh, but couldn't.

"Let's get along, Mildred," Jasper exclaimed. "We have the Lord's work to do and won't be sharing any stage with his likes." The two exited the stagecoach quickly, too quickly, as Jasper shoved Mildred out the door. She stumbled going down the stairs, her short legs reaching for ground and coming up empty, the cold roadbed of Auburn in her face. Willis was there to lend her a hand up. The Fanches ignored Willis, as they continued to squawk at one another, blaming the fall on Reed as more work of the Devil, rather than on mere clumsiness.

Reed, Louise, and Abigail watched the spectacle from the

stagecoach window, while Willis just shrugged and continued his work.

"Quite a bit of feather dustering for so early in the morning," Louise Cornet said.

"A horse can't help but to shoo flies with its tail and a missionary's work is never done. Best they stay and buzz the town, rather than this stage. It would've made for a long journey," Reed observed.

"I'm grateful they're gone," Louise confessed. "Since the Fanches arrived in town, church has not been the same, with all their fire and brimstone talk. Everyone is a sinner and damnation this and damnation that. It's all I can take." Louise looked directly into Reed's eyes, "They made me feel like I killed Josh myself, like I did something wrong, some sin, God's punishment for his passing."

"I'm sorry about Josh. He was a good man and deserved a better end." Reed had heard how it had happened, a minor cut to a hand sharpening an axe, leading to infection. He lost the arm but not the blood poisoning, more infection, fever, delirium, a hard way for the timberman to go. "Don't listen to the Fanches. It was nothing you did, Louise. If God wanted to speak to you through someone, He wouldn't be using the Fanches. It would be a messenger sent with comfort and compassion, rather than shame in mind."

The stagecoach pulled away from the station, moving briskly past the train depot, and beyond the town limits. Periodically, Reed could hear Hank's heavy, deep cough, among the clomping of horse hooves. The cough was followed by a powerful spit, a wad of phlegm pin-wheeling into the wind. It sounded like an entire lung was coming out.

At Grass Valley, Louise and Abigail Cornet departed from the stage. Louise would leave Abigail in the care of her sister, Henrietta. With Josh gone and his wages, Louise was searching for work herself, thinking there might be a position available at the Holbrooke Hotel.

Reed wished her well and offered his sympathies again, saying "if the Holbrooke doesn't work out and if you don't mind working in a house of sin, you'd be a welcome addition in the kitchen of The Golden Star of Shanghai." He appended his offer with a smile and the requirement, "you'd have to be willing to work alongside a wicked heathen like myself and the Chinese."

Louise returned the smile, appreciating the offer, responding, "Poss-ib-ly," elongating the word.

Willis handed down a small suitcase from the top of the stagecoach that Reed grabbed, relaying it to Louise. She said, "Thank you," smiled again, and walked away, Abigail's hand in her own.

Reed asked Willis how Hank was holding up, as hands began swapping out the horses for a fresh team to carry them along the next leg of the route. Willis gestured to a nearby bench where Hank was curled up, asleep, mouth agape, his rolled up duster under his head. "Didn't talk much, but he did say the bumpy ride helped, loosening the gunk. I'm sure you saw how much of it he spat overboard." Willis gave a second look to Hank, adding, "Downed a bottle of patent medicine too, said it was a phlegm-cutter."

"What kind of patent medicine?"

Willis pulled the empty bottle from his pocket, reading the label, "Hostetler's Cure-All Bitters, $3." He handed the bottle to Reed who pulled the stopper and sniffed the lid.

Reed pulled back, "Whoa, mostly hooch, probably some kind of dope opium too." Reed read more of the label, "'Soothing tonic that cures coughing, dropsy, biliousness, stomach ailments, high blood pressure, low blood pressure, women's troubles, baldness.'" Reed shook his head in disbelief, "yeah, right, all of that. This tongue oil is probably what's killing him. You sure you don't want to just get him a bottle of his favorite bourbon? If John John were here, he'd be pumping Hank full of that hot green tea of his."

Willis suggested, "Let's let Hank rest on that bench for a bit. You're the only passenger movin' on. I need to deliver this satchel of mail to the post office. I can then run into the drug store and get him another bottle. He says he'll need it to make North Bloomfield. We can get along then."

Reed nodded okay, saying, "That'll give me time to visit The Mercantile. I have an idea for a piece of jewelry."

"For your lady friend?"

"No, myself, something Jasper Fanch said."

"I wouldn't make a habit of taking on any ideas from old Fanch. Every time I see him, his pinched face reminds me of someone sucking on a sour pickle."

"He called me the Devil," Reed explained. "I want to live the part. I'll see you back here in a few."

By the time the two regathered, Reed had Hank up, leaning on him, wrapped in a blanket, ready to mount back up. Willis said, "They didn't have any Hostetler's but the druggist said this tonsil varnish works just as well. Hinkley's Liniment cures everything but the women's troubles."

"You hear that, Hank?" Reed teased, "you're on your own when it comes to those cramps."

Both Reed and Willis laughed, hoisting Hank back to his perch.

"Blast you cussed fools. Just get my darn ass on top and gimme the bottle so I can have a swig. I'll let you know if I need help birthin' any babies," Hank muttered.

Reed and Willis continued laughing as the stagecoach pulled out of Grass Valley toward the Anthony House on the Virginia Turnpike. The three picked up a bite to eat, ham and biscuits, paying the $4 toll to cross the turnpike's 11 miles to French Corral, which included the covered bridge at Bridgeport, spanning the South Fork of the Yuba River.

As the stage climbed out of the South Fork drainage, Reed was amazed at the denuded Sierra Nevada countryside. Most all of the sugar pine trees had been cut from the landscape to serve the mines, used to build miles of flumes to direct water to the diggins or to timber mine shafts. It was a depressing sight just seeing the foothills themselves touching the sky without a crown of trees.

The stage pulled into North Bloomfield late in the day, stopping at the Ostrom Livery Stable. Reed and Willis helped Hank to Miss Ellie's boarding house of comfort, or ill repute, depending upon one's point of view, so they could bed down for the night. Hank managed a few words, "feelin' a little better," but still looking horrible, the Hinkley's Liniment numbing his symptoms and dulling his mind. Miss Ellie and the sporting girls of Mill Street would look after him in a different manner than they had during his numerous past visits, but no less comforting, tending to his feverous misery.

Willis cautioned, "If Hank's not any better tomorrow, we'll need to fetch the doctor."

Miss Ellie bent over Hank, concern in her eyes. A light knit shawl fell from her shoulders to reveal her bare white shoulders, black choker necklace, and ample bosom in a corseted blue velvet dress. Two large jewels were sewn into the dress where Ellie's cleavage met the edge of the brocaded fabric, her tied up red hair and golden hairpin glittered in the room's candlelight. "Doctor here ain't much good," she said. "He's probably puttin' on a drunk right now at King's Saloon, already crawlin' into a second bottle."

"The Hinkley's Liniment is almost gone," Reed said as he shook the bottle for all to see. "He'll need more bug juice in the morning."

Ellie disagreed, "He don't need any more of that. I'll fit him out with a mustard plaster to pull the poison out of his lungs. He just needs rest and something to eat that's easy on his stomach. I can make him up some soup that'll do the trick. And just what're *you* gawkin' at Mr. Willis Connelly?"

Busted.

"Pardon, ma'am," Willis stammered. "I was just admiring your, uh, jewels right there in the valley of those, uh, mountains." Willis looked to Reed for help. None was forthcoming.

Ellie scolded, "I should call you out to your schoolmarm sweetheart Miss Alice, Willis. How she feel if she knows you were ogling me in a carnal sort of way?"

Reed offered, "Willis just wanted to know if they're real…the jewels, he means…I mean."

Ellie laughed, "You blushin' boys wear more rouge than

me. Of course they're glass jewels, but these two babies," she crowed, cupping each side of her chest with red-nailed hands, "*are* for real, no padding required." Ellie lifted and bounced her comely figure for effect.

Hank, playing possum in bed, came to life, "What a time for me to be sick when a go-round is to be had, Ellie. That's the cure I need."

They all broke up laughing at a resurrection worthy of the Holy Spirit.

"You just get well Hank Monk. We'll be knockin' boots again soon enough," Ellie consoled, kissing him on the forehead.

Smiling, Willis and Reed left the room to Ellie and Hank. Willis chuckled, "Hank seems to have found some energy. Might need to get some of that Hinkley's Liniment myself if it helps that much in the saddle."

Reed jested, "I'll remember, next time Hinkley pulls his snake oil wagon into town, we can have Alice offer a testimonial to the townsfolk on how it worked or *didn't* work for you."

"Get on outta here, Reed."

In the morning, Reed and Willis breakfasted with three other boarders, drinking coffee between bites of eggs and sowbelly bacon. Reed had sent an advance message to Mr. Lester L. Robinson, saying he would arrive at the North Bloomfield Gravel & Mining Company office at noon. Willis departed directly after breakfast, walking to the mine warehouse located on the rim of the Malakoff Diggins, not far from town. Willis was acquainted with Mr. Hadley, who operated the warehouse, directing the heavy teamster wagons delivering iron pipe to the mine. He would hire on for the day with Hadley, who could always use another skilled teamster, like Willis, to handle the mule teams and their heavy burden. It provided a good reason to be about if McGirt and the Dutchman caused a ruckus. Willis carried the tool of his trade, a rawhide lash and popper that was as deadly as any knife or revolver.

When noon came, Reed had reached the mine and was escorted through its main gate. He didn't see McGirt or the Dutchman, but he did see a large number of riflemen patrolling the outskirts of the massive hole in the ground. There was a great deal of activity far below, giant streams of water shooting over a hundred feet from water monitors positioned about the mine. The action of the hydraulickers continually expanded the muddy pit, washing the gold-laden gravels to sluices for collection. Reed figured Willis was down in the muck, among the torrents of water and debris, working a 20 mule team on one of the many heavy wagons delivering pipe and hosing that crisscrossed this tear in the earth. Reed reached the mine office, perched near the edge, overseeing the entire endeavor.

A wooden platform and protective rail overlooked the rim. Reed could see even more of the massive expanse that was well over a mile long and almost as wide. The bottom looked to be at least 500 or 600 feet deep in places. It was hard to believe man could make a hole so big.

Reed said to the rifleman, "Quite a sight."

The rifleman eyed Reed suspiciously, all but saying, "who

said it was okay for you to look?"

He mumbled from some place low in his throat, "In there," using his rifle to gesture to the office front door.

Reed turned from the man and walked to the door, figuring he could take it from here, glad to be done with the escort.

A dour woman in pince-nez glasses, hair pulled back into a bun, looked up from a ledger book. She was annoyed at being disturbed in the midst of a calculation, adding up a long column of numbers. Her questioning, "Yes?" betrayed not the slightest hint of humor.

"Charles Reed, here to see Mr. Robinson."

At the mention of her boss's name, she forgot her annoyance, "Oh, yes, Mr. Reed, please come in. You're expected." She left her desk and ledger behind, approaching Reed with a smile. "Forgive my brusqueness, Mr. Reed. I'm Miss Potter. Our offices are quite nice when compared to the scene outside. Please come this way."

Reed was ushered into a small carpeted banquet room, lined with books, mining and engineering tomes for the most part. Reed could see through the doorways to the personal offices of the men he would meet. He agreed with Miss Potter, quite luxurious when compared with the mud hole outside.

A smiling man, dressed in a dark suit, vest, and tie approached, a cigar between his fingers, "Ah, Charles Reed, good to have you join us. I am Lester Robinson, though please call me by my initials L.L., most people do."

Reed stepped forward, shaking his hand. L.L. was an inch or two shorter than Reed, with close-set focused eyes. Reed could make out a row of tobacco stained lower teeth, encircled by a beard and a large handlebar mustache that drooped down to his jawline. He moved in a marked, decisive manner, the swagger of a man with a plan, willing to move the earth to get what he wanted. Reed just had to look at the pit in the ground outside to see that it was true.

"I'll do so, L.L. Please call me Charles. Glad to join you and to offer my services. It's not everyday that I receive a sporting invitation from the president of the largest mining outfit in California."

"Yes, California is the land of opportunity in more ways than one. Please let me introduce my associates, Mr. Hamilton Smith, superintendent and chief engineer of the mine and his first assistant, Mr. Henry Perkins."

Reed shook Smith's hand, a forceful grip, with no words of greeting, just a small smile and a slight nod of acknowledgement, not unfriendly, but no nonsense. Perkins, the junior of the two and shortest, was coatless, in white shirt, red tie, and suspenders, a prominent mustache as thick as a raccoon's tail hung under his nose. He struck Reed as the bookkeeper, which was true, a man keenly aware of the cost per ton.

"Hello, Mr. Reed," Perkins said.

"Again, please call me Charles."

Smiling, Perkins said, "I'm not sure that I can do that since our aim is to win money from you. We can't really do that if we're on a first name basis."

Reed countered, surveying the group, "All three of you ganging up on me so soon, before the first card is turned?"

L.L. interrupted, "Forgive Henry. He's a bit too eager telegraphing his intent. We propose a private game, Mr. Reed, um, Charles, friendly and by all means fair. The reason you're here is that you have an exemplary reputation for honesty and a square game."

"Thank you, L.L. That's what I offer. I can bank faro, poker, three card monte, many games of chance. It's obvious that such esteemed and accomplished men, like yourselves, leaders in your field, are looking to pit your skills up against a professional gambler." Reed said this, though he thought these men with their fine silk suits would find it far beneath them to rub elbows with the North Bloomfield riff-raff who worked the mine and the people who serviced the men in town. "You can play anyone. It's the matchup you're after. Am I right? I can see, looking at Henry, that here's a man with a *system*."

Smith spoke up, "And this is why Henry will never win, too impatient, overconfident. It shows all over his face and actions. Am I right, Charles? A man like yourself can see this all too plainly in the novice." Smith's gaze at his assistant spoke volumes about how much further sonny boy here had to go to walk out of his boss's shadow.

Reed eyed Smith, clearly a man to watch, a man of economy and detail, who could cut to the heart of the matter in an instant, and of the three, probably the most formidable player. Reed played along with the older man, "Yes, Henry, you need to listen to your boss, if *the system* is to ever win at cards, you must learn to control your bodily functions." Reed made a mocking nervous twitch gesture, flapping his hand quickly to and fro, an egregious tell to a big hand.

Smith and L.L. laughed heartily while Henry stewed, managing a stiff grin.

"My, my Charles already inside Henry's head. What a splendid start we are off to. Please take a seat." L.L. waved his arm, motioning everyone to a table.

L.L. suggested, "Shall we start with faro? Again, it's nice to have a visitor at our table. It has been a while since we received a guest."

"I believe the last person to occupy that chair, Charles, was the Baron de Rothschild himself, who visited the mine a few years ago," Hamilton Smith recollected.

Impressed, Reed replied, "That's some mighty deep pockets. I doubt my bank can hold up against his. I can back this game. I can't back Wellington and the British Army at Waterloo. What was a Baron doing in North Bloomfield?"

"Hamilton and I led young Edmond on an inspection of the mine," L.L. explained. "The Rothschilds are major investors in mining. Here, Colorado, around the world."

Hamilton Smith added, "Yes, the Rothschilds are interested in American expertise, equipment, and its application around the world, South America, even as far as Australia. You see, no one is finding gold or precious minerals just lying on the ground as they did here in 1849. All the placer gold you could kick with your foot is long gone. It takes major investment and engineering to operate a mine like the North Bloomfield, to dig down deep into the rich layers of gravel, like the blue layer, 130 feet deep, though we can, *and are*, digging shafts much, much deeper than this."

Reed asked, still turning cards and managing the action, "Shafts? I thought this was a water operation?"

Smith, the engineer, expanded, "Water is used to wash away the upper layers of gravel. We sink a shaft, sometimes 200 feet to the channel containing the gold. Miners then dig an adit, which is a horizontal tunnel, slightly downward, hundreds of feet long. We construct multiple sluices in the adit so one is continually flushing gravel while another sluice, with its water stopped, is cleaned of gold."

Reed amazed, said, "still a costly proposition."

Smith answered, "I testified to the California State Legislature in 1878 that between $35 and $50 million have been invested in hydraulic mining statewide, producing $18 million in gold annually." Smith shook his head, "The lonely prospector with a pick and shovel will soon be replaced. Men of capital, of industry, have now taken over."

"Like yourself, Mr. Smith?"

"It's what I do, Mr. Reed, construct and design mines to attain the highest profits for myself and other investors, like L.L. here and to a lesser extent, Henry." Smith never missed the chance to stick it to his subordinate.

"Sounds like you're making a bundle and made a good impression on the Baron, though…sorry, you lose," Reed said, smiling, as he turned a card from the dealing box and collected wagers.

"I admire your style, Charles. It's like today, with these games," L.L. imparted. "We lose a little in the short term, but will profit in the long run, if for no other reason than to introduce ourselves to the Baron."

"So you threw a few bets to one of the richest men in the world?"

"Eddie was happy winning, who isn't," Henry said, as he examined the case keep that Reed updated, an abacus like device that allowed the players to see previously played cards in order to speculate on the cards remaining in the dealing box. The case keep discouraged card counting and allowed everyone to plan their bets.

L.L scoffed, "a mere trifle, lost change in order to establish a friendship, part of business. Hamilton, wouldn't you agree?"

Smith, his eyebrows arching over spectacles, placed a new wager on the faro board as Reed pulled the banker's and player's cards from the dealing box. "Yes," Smith said with a measure of pride, "mining operations in America are the most advanced. He needs us to tell him how to use his money."

Reed wondered, "Still, you've got a big operation here. I can't see any of you leaving for Australia, Africa, or even Mexico."

Henry Perkins smiled, "The North Bloomfield Mine has seven large Craig monitors working 24 hours a day. As Mr. Smith said, investment comes from San Francisco, New York, London, Paris. The mine has expanded enormously in the last ten years, requiring a large amount of capital."

Reed observed, "With the water cannons, the monitors, it looks like you need fewer men. It's not like the Empire Mine in Grass Valley and all the Cornish working the hard rock veins."

Smith took over. "Quite so, 100,000 tons of gravel are processed each day from the mine. We flood the mine with not just water but light. We generate our own electricity with water power, allowing the mine to work non-stop, but, as I said a moment ago, every week or so we do stop most of the monitors and remove gold from the sluices."

Reed ventured, "How much gold?" not expecting an answer.

Henry absently volunteered, "about $5,000 on average."

L.L. and Hamilton frowned at the bookkeeper. It was one thing to speak in statewide, general terms, quite another to be specific to the business. Henry looked down quickly, knowing he had spoken too candidly.

L.L. deflected, "We are all quite proud of our endeavor, some more than others," leveling a gaze at Henry. "But the monitors are a labor saving device. Where it would take a man with a pan $15 in labor to process a cubic yard of gravel, we can now process that same amount for 15 cents and you're right, we are not going anywhere when such profits can be made in these diggins."

Smith remarked dryly, "That is if the farmers don't shut us down."

L.L. looked at Reed, "Do you know anything about the Anti-Debris Association?"

Reed knew all about the Anti-Debris Association, but saw no point in revealing all his knowledge, spitting it out like Henry. "I know all the slickens from the mine has to go somewhere and that it flows downhill, into the valley, piling up in farmland and orchards, the streets of Marysville and Sacramento."

"Poppycock," L.L. declared. "Mine tailings, slickens, as you say, are captured behind our series of dams and other holding reservoirs. Any releases of flood water that these farmers are complaining of are mere nuisances and nothing more." L.L. gathered breath, "It's outrageous that farmers make these wild claims and bring suit in court. Farmers have no legal bearing on the actions of mining. Why, it is within the rights of any prospective miner to enter *any* public lands settled by farmers or ranchers and claim the mineral rights below the surface, if they so choose."

"What about their crops and cattle?" Reed challenged.

"This is a mining state, Charles, started by prospectors. Much like our water rights of appropriation, 'first in time, first in rights,' a legal principle in long standing, to the first days of California, that placed mining at the pinnacle of its economy."

"So you can trespass onto anyone's land and own the rivers?"

Perkins spoke, "You speak like a member of the Anti-Debris Association, Charles."

"I'm a professional gambler, who plays at Devil's Advocate. I'm sure you gentlemen have already been wrasslin' with all these arguments anyway so you can plot your next play. I'm not saying anything you haven't already thought of. Besides, we all know the courts will decide everyone's fate."

L.L. agreed with the assessment, "Charles, I like you more and more. Gambling is a respected vocation, particularly in the west, though you would make a fine lawyer, railroad man, or dare I say it, hydraulicker."

Reed turned his head in consideration, "Lawyering, maybe. Railroading, I got my fill of following construction gangs, playing cards and earning my early stake in life, but hydrau-licking, not likely, especially if it means working beside the likes of Russell McGirt."

There was a pause, L.L. searched for an explanation, "a regrettable but necessary part of mining. Without Mr. McGirt's oversight, I'm certain a significant amount of gold would fall into the hands of thieving employees. Wages are $2 a day and $3 to our many overseers, who watch the entire process, partic-ularly when the sluices are emptied of the gold. Of course, I've heard the stories, the tales, a nugget here or there smuggled out in a hollow boot heel, but without firm oversight this mine could not operate and would suffer irreparable losses."

Smith added, "We put up with Mr. McGirt's odious persona, but it's what the job requires. Does the punishment always fit the crime, who is to say? But he certainly is effective."

Perkins, looking to redeem himself, upped the storytelling ante. "McGirt caught a fellow the other day shoving two small nuggets up his nose at the end of the shift. When confronted, he denied it, saying he had a head cold, but McGirt made him blow into a handkerchief."

L.L. looked perplexed. "McGirt owns a handkerchief? He must have borrowed it."

Perkins continued, "Well, he wasn't blowing with much enthusiasm so McGirt raised his horsehide flogger, ready to bash in his nose, but at that instant this fellow lets out a blast of air, shooting two nuggets onto the floor, like they came out both barrels of a shotgun."

Reed shared a look with L.L. and Smith.

Perkins, now getting excited, kept the story going. "McGirt picks up the nuggets and sees them covered in snot. He tells the man he needs to return these, but has to clean them off first. The man didn't know what to do so McGirt busts him in the mouth, saying, 'swish 'em around and give 'em back to me clean and if you swallow 'em, I'm going to cut 'em outta your belly.'"

Smith eyed Henry, "There's a point to all of this?"

Henry, needing to wrap it up, concluded, "This here fellow spits the two nuggets and a tooth into McGirt's hand, clean as a whistle. Of course, McGirt then flogged the man ruthlessly in front of the entire crew. The Dutchman then threw him out the front gate, knocked out cold and in a heap, arms bent like a scarecrow."

Reed quipped, "McGirt must be going soft on you. That sounds practically mild next to what he does to the Chinese."

"Few Chinese work in the diggins now," L.L. remarked. "Those we have are outside, maintaining the flumes and ditches."

"Chinese is how McGirt and the Dutchman make money when not in the mine," Reed explained, "particularly since no Chinese can bear witness against them in court. Fair game to cheat, steal, and murder any they meet, especially those working their own claims away from prying eyes. Shoot 'em, take their property, take their gold."

L.L., unsurprised, "Frankly, I get enough of Mr. McGirt when he is here at the mine. I don't need to know about any of his outside pursuits. It's plain that you are not an admirer, Charles."

"I've had a recent run-in and I'll be honest, though effective for your purposes, he's a man of low character and turpitude, someone to avoid. It may seem shocking for the times, but I don't believe yellow hordes are anything to fear. There wouldn't be a Transcontinental Railroad, mines, dams, flumes, or a Golden Star of Shanghai, for that matter, without my Chinese friends. Work wouldn't get done without the Chinese, but if I snapped my fingers and McGirt and the Dutchman vanished from the face of the earth, would anyone truly miss them?"

Perkins answered, "This mine would miss them for what they provide."

"The leaders of mine, perhaps," Reed corrected, looking at

L.L., "certainly not the miners themselves."

L.L. conceded, "Maybe cholera or typhoid fever will do the job and not require the snapping of any fingers, but I see your point, Charles, the two are an abomination and…"

The conversation ran out of steam. Silence fell over the table, a brief moment of reflection as the talking ended, the pace of faro accelerating, everyone concentrating on the game.

Though men of means, the wagers were small and the hours passed idly with glasses of brandy and copious cigar smoke filling the air. The conversation moved on to other, more pleasant subjects, like travel, places visited, people met, things seen. With only three cards from the dealing box remaining, Reed called the turn. Each player now had to predict the exact order of the last 3 cards. Both L.L. and Henry lost on the first card, while Smith dropped out on the second. It was near midnight when the game adjourned, none too badly damaged by the day's play, a good introduction to each other.

Tired, L.L rose from the table, "I want to thank you for coming, Charles. I know there is only a small house edge with faro, but perhaps tomorrow we can try some of the new types of poker being played, which I'm sure you are a well acquainted with." L.L. looked to the others who nodded agreement. "Please be our guest tonight. We have comfortable lodging here and it would be our pleasure to guide you through the mine tomorrow, like Baron de Rothschild, so you can see our investment – how the mine operates. Shall we say 10 a.m. for a tour?"

"I look forward to it and our game tomorrow. Gentleman, thank you."

The four tossed back the remaining brandy in their glasses,

snuffed out cigars, shook hands, and bid each other "good night."

Reed looked out a window, a glow of light emanating above the rim of the pit, the investment still hard at it.

North Bloomfield, California 2013

A t 1:30 the town tour was scheduled to begin. People gathered on the wooden plank porch at the entrance to the rustic North Bloomfield Museum. Early arrivals sat in the shade of the covered porch, fanning themselves with the state park brochure, the temperature a hot 95 degrees. About 25 people had joined the tour, most being Girl Scouts from the nearby Chute Hill Campground, the last few late arrivals running in flip flops the short distance from Blair Lake, just up the street, some still wet from swimming in the watering hole, brightly colored towels covering their shoulders. A Girl Scout parent counselor explained that Blair Lake was originally a hydraulic mine that proved unprofitable. Generations ago, it was dammed and became the local place to picnic and swim. Jen, Kendra, and I thanked her for the local knowledge, Jen saying, "I hope the town tour is as informative."

The Girl Scout counselor, Nancy, agreed, "We've been camped for just a few days with the girls, and I'm really looking forward to this. We live just an hour or so away and had no idea how rich the history is in the area. The woods and trails are all so beautiful."

The stern gray-haired volunteer ranger reappeared, surveying those gathered. She looked at her watch, 1:31. She turned to face Nancy in the crowd and said in an accusing tone, "I'm not waiting any longer. Anyone late is just going to have to catch up." The inference clear to everyone that Nancy did not know how to control all these girls.

Nancy quietly said to those of us standing nearby, "Oh, God, she's not giving the tour, is she?" She made a quick gesture, waving the back of her hand to the ranger, "go ahead, go ahead, don't wait, we're all here." Nancy looked back to us, "That woman is really a piece of work. She has been hounding us at the campground, 'don't do this, don't do that, who said you could pick up a rock or climb a tree?' I'm surprised she hasn't told the birds to stop tweeting. I can't take her much longer."

The ranger, now in docent mode, shouted from her wide lipless mouth, "I'm Ruth Leek and I will lead the North Bloomfield town tour. We'll go into some of the historic buildings you see about and you are to not touch anything and walk only where I say. Follow me." She turned and was off.

Everyone shrugged, so much for the ground rules.

Ruth marched a few yards to a water cannon displayed close by, everyone following in her footsteps. She stopped abruptly beside the rusted iron hulk that must have been 15 feet long, with a 10 inch wide nozzle, a posted wooden sign named it "The Hendy Giant, used by the hydraulic miner in his quest for gold."

"First thing, let me get this out of the way – don't ask me about mining."

We all looked at one another puzzled, each thinking, we're in a mining town, what else are we going to talk about?

"If you want to learn about mining, speak to the docent at the gold panning demonstration in China Garden," Ruth announced.

A girl scout raised her hand and said, "Didn't they hydraulic mine here? They didn't pan for gold."

Everyone knew the young scout was right. We could see the water cannon in our midst and had all at least glanced at the state park brochure, describing a brief history of the Malakoff Diggins.

Ruth returned to her theme, impatience in her voice, "What did I just say? I said do not ask me about mining."

The young Girl Scout wilted and withered, withdrawing to a safe place behind her fellow scouts. It was the last Ruth would hear from any of them.

Ruth returned to her script. Jen and I wondered how scant it would be with the major industry that built the town removed from the narrative. We just shook our heads silently, saying, let's go with it, but we were both thinking the same thing – if this is anything like the crummy Tower Bridge tour in London, from our early life together, with its lame animatronics, we cut our losses and move on. Only get to London or even North Bloomfield a few times in a lifetime, not going to waste precious vacation time here. I can still hear the incredulous Cockney docent now, as we bolted from the room, "Wot? You don't want to stay for the show?" Uh, no, definitely not. Let's go, Jen, got to be more interesting sights down the Thames at The Tower of London.

Kendra was tapping away on her phone.

"North Bloomfield was originally named Humbug City in 1851. Many towns in early California shared the same Humbug name, which was another way of saying there's no gold in these parts. It's all a hoax." Ruth paused for breath, letting the statement sink in. "In 1857, over 400 people lived in Humbug City, with some 70 buildings. The people of the town said it was time to build a post office, but the U.S. Postal Service said they needed to change the town name since there were already too many Humbugs in California."

A pudgy older man to my left, in plaid walking shorts, high white socks and Birkenstocks, dryly said, in a voice intended for those standing close by, "and we're staring at one now."

Those who heard it, shared looks and smiled, as the man's wife nudged him with the point of her elbow to cut it out.

Ruth glared out at the crowd, her look one of "are you getting what I'm saying?" as if we were all dense.

"There was a public meeting and the town came up with a new name – Bloomfield. Turns out, there was already a Bloomfield in Sonoma County, so they had to change the name again. This time they added 'North' to Bloomfield and the Postal Service was happy." A pause, "Isn't that something?"

We all returned the look, yeah, I guess so.

Ruth barked, "This way," one foot pounding in front of the other, striding briskly down the street.

Kendra spoke softly, reading from her phone, "'North

70

Bloomfield sits on the San Juan Ridge, between the Middle and South Fork of the Yuba River. It is known for the Malakoff Diggins one of the world's largest and most profitable hydraulic mines.'"

"Kendra's got something," I said. "Kendra go on."

"'Water cannons or water monitors were used to wash away tons of gravel, boulders, and dirt in search of mere ounces of gold. A single monitor could launch 1.1 million gallons of water per hour at a rate of 150 feet per second, with a force of 5,000 pounds per square inch, washing away hillsides and cliffs. The power of the stream could kill a man 200 feet away, with 50 pound boulders riding its crest, or disintegrate a 3 foot thick brick wall at a distance of 50 feet.'"

Gregor, walking beside said, "That ist very powerful. Tom, are the Malakoff Diggins close?"

"Just down the street, through the cemetery. We're going to walk there once the tour ends."

Nancy asked Kendra, "Can you please say that louder so the girls can hear?"

"Oh, sure." Kendra repeated and continued reading, "'The miner that operated the monitor was known as a piper. Pipers were paid more than other miners since their expertise was needed to prevent cave-ins that could injure or even kill miners working alongside the monitor.'"

Kendra paused briefly, skipping ahead, editing the document on her display screen, sifting for more nuggets of information. "'In 1876, lighting was added to the mine so that it could operate 24 hours a day, with wage earning miners working one of two 12 hour shifts, 6 days a week. Electricity for the lighting came from a nearby hydroelectric powerhouse station.'"

Jen said, "Six 12 hour days, yuck."

I said in my best one-percenter voice, "Quit complaining. Take your $2 a day or I'll move you to the night shift. Make you work with the Chinese who I'm paying half as much."

Gregor and Helmut chuckled, "Tom, the robber baron."

I laughed back, "Jen and I work in corporate America, but we feel it's not the government's job to make the rich richer than they already are, especially at the expense of everyone else, who work longer and harder for less."

Helmut said, "Ah, Tom and Jen, progressive German Social Democrats, let the revolution begin."

Jen called out, "Bring back *both* Roosevelts, power to the people. Overturn Citizens United."

Helmut and Gregor laughed again, reminding me that most Europeans and Canadians were more clued into American politics than the natives. If you polled Americans about the Middle East, half would say it's located somewhere near North Carolina and that the country of Jordan is named after a Chicago Bull.

Kendra brought us back into the moment, saying, "This is really getting interesting. Listen, 'One hundred million gallons of water were used each day by the North Bloomfield Gravel & Mining Company. The company's president estimated the mine would use *16 billion* gallons of water in 1876 alone.'"

"Wow," I said, "those are some ginormous numbers, especially when you think of the current drought in California." I now saw that over half the tour group was walking beside Kendra. The rest were up ahead on Ruth's heels.

Jen asked, "Kendra, where did all the water come from?

How'd it get here?"

"One second, Mom," Kendra paused, awaiting a new document to download. "'The North Bloomfield Mine constructed numerous dams, with hundreds of miles of ditches and wooden flumes to carry water from higher elevations down to the mine. The Magenta Flume alone was 1,800 feet long and 125 feet tall with a water channel 7 feet wide and 16 inches deep. The mine owned eleven Sierra Nevada mountain reservoirs, including the English Reservoir, which was then the largest in the state.'"

Ruth yelled, "What are you people doing back there? Come along. I haven't got all day."

A little more giddy-up in our steps took all of us up to Ruth, who stood in front of King's Saloon. She pulled a ring of keys that bulged from one of her front hip pockets. "I'm going to open the door and you girls, especially, go in an orderly manner. Watch where you walk – no running, shouting, or touching."

Everyone moved into the saloon successfully, without Ruth issuing a single detention slip.

It was the quietest saloon anyone had ever set foot in, cowed by Ruth's intimidating manner. She seemed satisfied, as we stood shoulder to shoulder, in a circle, staring at one another under the low, white-washed slat roof ceiling, trying unsuccessfully to brighten the dark interior.

Ruth, ever the minimalist, said, "This is a saloon. It's where people came to drink."

Silence.

A young woman in a yellow print sun dress, an array of bracelets on her wrists, sunglasses in her hair said, "*And..?*"

Ruth replied, "And, it's a saloon. Look around."

Kendra bumped her arm into my side, showing me another document from the Internet.

I said aloud, "Hey, Kendra, that looks interesting. Why don't you share it with everyone."

Kendra smiled and jumped at the chance, "'King's Saloon was built in 1860 and was remodeled as a saloon in 1873. It was owned by Jack King, a man noted for his large size and ability to deal with any loud or obnoxious drunks.'" Kendra looked up to see the group was with her. "'Beer was the most popular drink because it was so inexpensive – just 5 cents a glass. Mr. King stored the beer in kegs in a cellar beneath the floor, in an attempt to keep the beer cool when no refrigeration was available. He would disappear down a trap door every time a keg ran dry behind the bar.'"

Kendra said as a postscript, "'King's Saloon was one of perhaps nine saloons in North Bloomfield at the time.'"

Looks of satisfaction all around, as people looked down, searching for the trap door.

Ruth said nothing, two lasers staring at Kendra. She walked her squat body out into the sun. We followed, slowly.

Pupils flared and adjusted quickly as the tour group exited the saloon's dark interior for the sun-drenched brightness outside. I could see Ruth trudging up ahead in her bent gait, crossing the street, not quite as fast as before.

Kendra said to all, "And as you look down the middle of the street, the building at the end is now used by park personnel, but in the distant past it was once a house of ill repute, owned by a popular local madam named Miss Ellie."

Jen and I just smiled at one another. Go girl.

The group landed in front of Knotwell's Drug Store, another example of Miner Shack Modern, white clapboard with a pointed shingle roof. Everyone was trying to squeeze into the shadow cast by the small building's covered front porch, anything to escape the sizzling heat.

Ruth said, "Let me unlock the door and, once inside, don't touch anything. Just look."

Someone said, "We heard you the first time," the revolt fully on.

Ruth wiggled the key back and forth, straining on the stuck lock. From behind, it looked like she was choking a duck. Finally, the lock turned and the twin, glass paneled doors opened. Everyone quickly filed inside, away from the oppressive heat, shuffling onto the varnished wood flooring, past a red-faced Ruth, exhausted by her ordeal with the dead bolt. Polished wooden countertops ran down the side and back wall, lined with white shelving, displaying hundreds of colorful bottles – powders and elixirs, patent medicines to cure any ailment.

Ruth said, "This is a drug store and where you came if you got sick. On the walls are the types of medicine used."

Here we go again, lowered expectations.

A woman spoke up, "Ruth," trying for the gentlest tone possible. "Can you *please* tell us what kinds of medicines were available and what people used them for?"

Ruth shut this line of questioning down in a hurry, "I don't know. Look at the bottles. There's writing on them. Just don't touch."

The same old man in Birkenstock's from earlier said, "Yeah, I get it. They just give you the keys and we do the rest." This time his wife did not elbow him. "Hey, where's the kid with her phone? What have you got for us, princess?"

Kendra held up a finger, indicating just one second. "'Knotwell's Drug Store was owned by Mr. A.A. Smith. The 1880 Census shows John Knotwell was a boarder of Mr. Smith. In 1881, John Knotwell married Smith's daughter Nettie. When Mr. Smith left town, he turned the drug store over to Nettie and John. Nettie Smith-Knotwell went on to become the first woman pharmacist in California.'"

The crowd "oohed" and another said, "now we're learning something."

The woman who asked Ruth a question from a moment ago, made eye contact with Kendra, "Can you find out anything about the medicines?" silently mouthing a "thank you" at the end of her question.

Kendra nodded an affirmative, her fingers quickly moving and scrolling across her display surface.

Ruth, looking perturbed, exclaimed, "What's that you've got? What are you saying?"

Kendra ignored the grizzled ranger, saying aloud, "'One of the most popular patent medicines was Lydia Pinkham's Vegetable Compound, which was purported to be the only positive cure and legitimate remedy for the peculiar weaknesses and ailments of women. In 1875, a bottle of the tonic sold for $1 and she claimed that all the ingredients were pure vegetables from various roots. The tonic, in fact, contained 21% alcohol, while many other patent medicines went even further, adding a large portion of opium to the mix.'"

Jen said, "You've got to be kidding."

"I'm not, Mom. I'll read more, 'Pinkham's Vegetable

Compound was used to also treat pneumonia, kidney disease, constipation, appendicitis, tuberculosis, and even infertility. With Lydia's picture on the label, she soon became the most recognized woman in America. Her grandmotherly looks and kind, innocent smile appealed to consumers who believed in the compound's curative power. The use of shrewd imagery and advertising drove sales to over $30,000 a month in 1881. Many women, based on their trust of the product, wrote to Mrs. Pinkham, seeking personal advice. These women would receive a personal reply from company writers until the early 1900s, long after Lydia Pinkham had died in 1883.'"

"That's hard to believe," a woman said, approaching Kendra. "Feel blue, young ladies, have some booze and opium."

Kendra turned her phone to the woman, displaying a photo of the bottle's label – high collar and a gray-haired bun pulled back on the smiling old devil herself.

Kendra reasserted the theme, "'With no legal restrictions, the use of opium, morphine, and cocaine, along with alcohol, were common ingredients found in most medicines, patented or otherwise. Few pain relievers existed, so the use of opiates before regulation in the early 1900s was more widespread than people realize.'"

A man said, "cocaine in Coca Cola."

Kendra continued, "'In the United States, annual imports of opium rose from 24,000 pounds in 1840 to 500,000 pounds by the late 1880s, with most of this coming from Turkey. At that time, there was an estimated 200,000 addicts in the United States, with two-thirds to three-quarters of these being women.'"

Audible gasp, followed by a collection of different voices, "Is that true?" "Really?" "It's on Wikipedia, it must be true."

Another woman spoke, "What were they all taking it for?"

Kendra answered with more from her phone, "'For women, morphine derived from opium was dispensed by physicians and pharmacists to treat female problems associated with menstrual pain and, to a lesser extent, pain caused by the tiny Victorian waists fashionable at the time.'"

Someone said, "What?" another said, "It's just like that scene with Scarlett O'Hara in Gone with the Wind."

"'Pressure from laced corsets and undergarments on the lower abdomen caused many types of pelvic pain, including prolapse to the uterus.'" Kendra paused, "'Laudanum, morphine suspended in alcohol, was a popular remedy, with some women drinking a quart or more a week to relieve their pain.'"

Kendra had everyone riveted. "Here's a quote from a young woman addicted to drinking laudanum, 'It got me into such a state of indifference that I no longer took the least interest in anything, and did nothing all day but loll on the sofa reading novels, falling asleep every now and then, drinking tea. I always seemed to be in a half-dazed state…my memory dreadful. Does anyone who has gone up to three or four ounces a day, and is suddenly deprived of it, live to tell the tale?'"

Kendra looked up at the crowd of tourists, pausing for dramatic effect, "'Many women in the Temperance Move-ment, who advocated the prohibition of alcohol, and spoke widely condemning the dangers of demon whiskey and rum, were themselves addicted to laudanum and other opiate based patent medicines, many containing 80 proof alcohol or more.'"

More shocked reactions as we all learned more about the demythologized Old West.

A Girl Scout cried out, "Hey, come here. I found a bottle of Lydia Pinkham's Vegetable Compound."

Helmut had his own phone out, looking up more information, as others got into the act, "Fascinating," he said. "'Opium was also used as a cure-all for many types of pain – as a sedative, to help coughs, insomnia, but mostly to alleviate diarrhea or dysentery, where it was well-known to lock up ones runny bowels caused by poor diets, polluted drinking water and, generally, unsanitary conditions.'"

Helmut looked up from his phone and got a group nod to go on. "'During the Civil War, the Union Army used 2.8 million ounces of opium tincture and powder and over 500,000 opium pills, where it was called God's Own Medicine, with soldiers lining up each day for a dose.'"

Kendra said, "I've got more. 'Mercury laced blue mass pills were used commonly as a purgative, with physicians and pharmacists devising their own recipes. Many historians believe Abraham Lincoln took the medicine for constipation, but suspect he was really taking it to treat his depression. It was incorrectly believed at the time that mental disorders originated from poor digestion and improper secretion of bile from the liver. Lincoln was, in essence, poisoning himself, since daily use of 2 to 3 blue mass pills exceeds by 9,000 times what is currently considered safe.'"

Ruth's anger got the best of her, "Who do you people think you are!" she roared. "This is my tour, not yours!"

Gregor retorted, "Dumme frau, you should be taking notes.

We are learning far more from the young lady than from you. She should be giving the tour, not you. Leave us the keys to the buildings so that we can get into them ourselves and you, back into your hammock, so you can eat more potato chips and watch your stupid reality television shows."

The Girl Scouts shouted in unison, "Yeah!!"

With that, Ruth snarled, "They don't pay me enough to take this shit. In fact, they don't pay me anything. I'm a volunteer. You should be grateful I opened the doors for you."

We all stood quietly, thinking, get it out of your system, the full Mount Vesuvius. It'll be good for you, Ruth.

"You people are on your own." She turned and stalked off, tossing the key ring over her shoulder, a sharp bang when it hit the floor.

Most people stood silently for a moment, then a variety of voices were heard: "What a crank." "They don't pay her anything?" "Her tour was worthless." "The pretty girl explained more than she ever did." "I hope she retires that docent's vest for good." "They need to screen their volunteers more carefully." "Anyone know a good place nearby to eat?"

I bent down and picked up the key ring, saying to Jen, "I'll make sure these get back to park headquarters."

We both looked to Kendra. Nancy was taking a photo, the Girl Scouts draped all around her, everyone smiling. Others in the group then stepped forward, asking if Kendra would likewise pose for a photo with them. Kendra happily obliged, cameras and niceties exchanged back and forth, multiple selfies with arms outstretched – everyone drinking in the positive energy. I made sure to get a photo of the happy time myself, something for Jen and I to view in our dotage.

Malakoff Diggins, North Bloomfield, California 1883

Bright sunlight welcomed Reed, L.L. Robinson, Hamilton Smith, and Henry Perkins to the mine overlook. Reed's hat brim sheltered him from the glare out of the southeast, crisp blue sky with billowing cumulus clouds providing a canopy above the immense pit.

"I walk to this spot every morning and I never cease to be amazed," L.L. rhapsodized. "Isn't it spectacular? a monument to man's ingenuity."

Reed stared into the colossal abyss for a second time, the view opening as he stepped up to the overlook's wooden rail, eyes straining into the distance, trying to find the dimensions to this ever-growing hole in the ground. The vast panorama was truly a jaw-dropping sight that no one would forget. It got your attention.

"I agree," Reed said, "but what do you see? a big hole or a money-making machine?"

Smith spoke up, "As an engineer, I first see the problem and then a solution. I design and build that solution, a machine that can generate profits with, of course, gold being the output." He waved his arm from one end of the horizon to the other. "The mine is one vast machine – water, flumes, monitors, sluice boxes – all connected in a gigantic earth moving enterprise to achieve profits, gold."

"Not exactly the soul of an artist, but I hear you, Hamilton, pride in what you've built, and anyone can see it took a hell of a lot to do this," Reed offered.

"Follow me, Charles. Let me show you Hamilton's masterpiece."

The men walked a short distance along the rim, riflemen were walking about, protecting the mine's perimeter. The men reached a staircase, then ladder to a plank deck, where they entered a wooden framed elevator operated by a rope hoist. Perkins handled the standing rope control, lowering them to the bottom of the pit. At the bottom, Reed gazed up at the rich layers of gold bearing auriferous gravel, pancaked one on top of the other in the looming cliffsides. The men were so deep that the sun did not directly touch them. It was colder in the shadows and Reed felt considerably closer to the center of the earth.

L.L. shouted above the din of activity, rushing streams of water, the blast of the water monitors erupting into the earthen walls, emitting a mist of soil-laden red foam. "Take a look, Charles. Over 350 million cubic yards of ore-bearing gravel, all around us. Enough to keep us washing away for the next fifty years."

Smith said, pointing above, "The upper strata only pays off

a few cents per cubic yard, but the blue layer gravel, down near the bedrock, we see our best return. How much, Henry?"

"$5.40," Henry said, pausing, "and the blue layer deposits are 130 feet thick."

Reed looked all around. He said to no one in particular, "So how much gold is here?"

Perkins with his numbers again, "at least $70 million."

Silence, while the amount sank in.

L.L. sighed pleasantly, "And to think, we bought up numerous claims years ago, for next to nothing, once the surface placer gold was gone."

"If those prospectors only knew the riches that lay deeper beneath their feet," Perkins commented.

"They could not reach the gold," Smith protested. "It takes capital, engineering, and heavy machines to move this amount of earth. For the prospector of yore, this gold might just as well be sitting on the moon."

"The Comstock Lodes are playing out in Nevada," L.L. said, "hard-rock mining, like the Empire Mine in Grass Valley, is pure chance, scouring through granite in the hope of finding a rich vein. It's all so very labor intensive, all the Cornish miners, too expensive. Investors are looking elsewhere to place their capital with higher profits and a better rate of return."

L.L. pointed toward a water monitor, a hissing hundred mile per hour jet ripping into the cliff face, boulders and rocks raining down in a rich slurry. "The monitors lower our labor costs immensely and, as you can see, 100,000 tons are blasted away each day so the return on investment is high, especially since we know gold is in these layers of gravel." L.L. paused, "We just need to get our hands on it."

A large, heavy wagon carrying sections of cast iron pipe tied down and stacked ten feet high rolled by, its wheels compressing the soft soil with 6 inch ruts. Reed saw Willis and another man walking beside a team of 12 mules pulling the wagon, rawhide whip ready in his gloved hand. Both men shared a look of acknowledgement before going back to their business.

Reed said, "If I'm not mistaken, it seems the mine slopes toward this end, down where you have that small lake and short dam."

"A surveryor's eye," Smith said, "follow me and I will show you an engineering marvel for the age." The men began walking the length of the mine, staying on what appeared to be the only dry trail along the bottom, though it was still impossible to keep some of the muck off one's boots and trousers. Reed would turn them over to the laundry when he returned to Auburn, but doubted he would be lucky enough to find a gold nugget in one of the cuffs.

Smith explained, "In order to move gravel more quickly away from the cliffs, we have constructed a series of eight vertical mine shafts, each 1,000 feet apart."

L.L. interjected, "Before we built the tunnel, a swale appeared at the base of a cliff we were washing. We did not want the pipers wasting time and water pushing the mass of dirt uphill and into sluice boxes."

Smith took over, "Since the advent of the tunnel, the gravel is washed down to the western end of the mine to the small lake and holding dam. It is then funneled down the vertical shafts, all connected to the horizontal tunnel beneath our feet, located deep in the bedrock, where the gravel and debris is washed over a system of sluices for the first 1,900 feet. As you observed, Charles, the tunnel runs downward, with gravity moving the gravel currents."

"And that's where the gold is removed?"

Perkins answered, "Yes, each run lasts two to three weeks and then we shut the water off. The heavier gold is captured behind riffles in the sluices, like you see in a washboard or on wooden blocks. The sluices are coated with a quicksilver amalgam that attracts the gold but not the dirt and sand. We use about 15 flasks of quicksilver, over 1,100 pounds, for each run. This amalgam reduces the amount of lost gold flushed out into Humbug Creek, down at the far end of the tunnel, where more sluices and undercurrents are located to capture any remaining gold."

L.L. and Smith cringed, clearly uncomfortable with Perkins sensitive disclosure.

"But we won't be going there," L.L. said in an admonishing tone.

"So how long is this tunnel? It's a long ways to the creek."

"It starts at the western end of the pit," Smith replied, "extending over a mile-and-a-half long. We started construction over ten years ago, in April, 1872, 175 men drilling the eight shafts. I surveyed the line myself and at the bottom of each of these shafts, working in both directions, on 16 faces, we began digging and blasting with Giant Powder."

"Sounds dangerous."

Smith shrugged indifference, "The early forms of dynamite were hazardous, but it was the diamond bit drilling machines that accelerated the tunnel's progress. These drills are powered by water pressure. Amazing devices, we received the drills in

1873 and completed the tunnel in late 1874, when all eight shafts were finally connected. Henry, final numbers?"

Perkins, more numbers committed to memory, "Tunnel length, 7,874 feet. Over 400 men worked on the tunnel at a cost of $551,243."

L.L. appended, "And we could not have built this without the Chinese. Their experience with tunneling for the Central Pacific Railroad in the Sierra Nevada mountains was most helpful."

For Reed, the scale was almost impossible to grasp, "All that way...Hamilton, you must have felt quite a bit of pressure making sure all those shafts lined up. Not a place to make a mistake."

Smith smiled his man for the ages smile, the intrepid engineer, "What pressure?"

Reed responded with a grin, "Yeah, all in a day's work."

"But we didn't stop there, did we, Hamilton?" L.L. boasted.

"No, since completion of this tunnel, we have constructed five branch tunnels with more vertical shafts, with two or three terraced steps."

"What are they for?"

Perkins spoke, "As the monitors wash the debris down the shafts, they fall down each step. This helps to break up the large chunks before they reach the sluices. If the debris does not break up and clogs the tunnel, we'll send men down to drill and place more Giant Powder to blast away the obstruction."

"So how many tunnels do you have?"

"All total," Perkins thought, "almost 20,000 feet of tunnels."

"Come again?" Reed said, astonished.

L.L. this time, "That's right, Charles, *20,000 feet*."

After a shake of the head, Reed said, "But all this debris goes somewhere. It flows out the end of the tunnel, as you said, down into Humbug Creek. It's what's got the Anti-Debris Association farmers and all those folks down in Marysville and Sacramento so hopping mad."

L.L. shook his hand dismissively, "At the end of the tunnel, at the lake and dam you see here, we sift all the coarse debris as it flows over a descending series of undercurrents and is then dropped into Humbug Creek and down into the South Yuba River."

"Seeing what you're moving here, it must all be piling up?"

"Winter runoff moves the tailings down the South Yuba canyon," Smith asserted. "The large pieces are contained behind brush dams and never reach the farmers."

Reed was astounded that Smith would even try this response, "Hamilton, I've been to Marysville and back. The brush dams were destroyed by the first heavy rains, just a year after they were built. They didn't hold anything back. What's left of them are busted up and overwhelmed with slickens just running over the top." Reed stopped to look at each man before continuing with what he and most everyone accepted. "With all the tailings *still* running into the valley, it's no secret that the Anti-Debris Association has kept after you with all their court injunctions to stop mining these hillsides down on top of them."

L.L., exasperated, but acknowledging reality, said, "The Drainage Act was ruled unconstitutional, but only because southern Californians successfully argued that they should not be taxed to pay for a northern California problem."

Reed challenged, "The state assembly did spend $500,000 to build brush dams."

"Yes and, regrettably, the brush dams did not achieve their objectives," L.L. conceded, "but we miners stand pledged and willing to build a new dam in the South Yuba River narrows that will impound all coarse debris, just as Judge Temple ruled last year in the suit filed against the Gold Run Mining Company."

"But the Anti-Debris Association refuses to compromise and we will not build another debris dam until they cease their incessant litigation, one injunction after another," Smith added with disgust.

"So your mines are operating illegally, in defiance of these injunctions?"

"A matter of opinion, Charles," L.L. countered. "Our attorneys can play the injunction game too. We have one from our own sympathetic Nevada County Superior Court that prevents the local sheriff from trespassing onto mine property." L.L. paused, a hint of a smile on his lips, "therefore he can't serve or enforce any of the Anti-Debris Association injunctions that seek to shut us down."

Reed observed, "It all sounds like a crazy game, but I do read enough from the newspapers to know it's all changing with Judge Sawyer looking into the matter. It's now a federal case and not part of the state courts."

"Until Judge Sawyer rules, we're operating as we always do and we're even adding more monitors. We will see a return on our substantial investment. Judge Sawyer is an original forty-niner. He came to California as a prospector, like so many others. He knows mining is the past, present, and future for the state. A jurist with this experience will surely recognize mining's value when he decides the case," L.L. confidently predicted.

"You must like the cards in your hand, though adding monitors is a nice gambler's hedge. Get it while you can, because sometimes the cards don't always turn up aces," Reed remarked.

"Look around you, Charles. Do you really think anyone is going to stop this?" Smith argued. "We're witnessing a great industrial age, economic progress on a scale never before imagined. It is vitally important for this work to continue so we can extract the resource. California's livelihood, its very survival is at stake."

Smith made his own prediction, "You'll see, fifty years from now, we'll wash the last of these gravels bare, collecting all the gold. We'll then move on to other hills and ridges, building more shafts and tunnels."

Reed nodded in agreement, the congenial guest, but secretly doubted whether any of this was good for anyone other than the men standing in front of him and the rest of the mine investors in San Francisco, New York, London, and Paris. How could a few people pocket such wealth from afar, while everyone else suffers the consequences, caught up in an uncontainable river of debris, having to live with the resulting muck? What about their property and livelihood?

"Time we move on, gentlemen," L.L. said, leading the group forward. L.L. pointed to the cast iron piping, stretching out to each monitor. Offhandedly, he mentioned, "The water flows down from our mountain reservoirs, mostly from Bowman Lake, where we expanded the stone dam, along the

Bowman Ditch, but we have many other reservoirs and miles of ditches to manage the flow of water into the mine."

"The English, Crooked, Island, Middle, Round, Shotgun, and Sawmill Reservoirs, to name a few. Roughly, 2.2 billion cubic feet of water," Perkins added, his facts and figures always at the ready.

"What's that in gallons?" Reed asked.

Perkins again, "About 16.5 billion gallons."

Reed whistled, "Can't imagine what the farmers in the valley could do with all that water."

"More Devil's Advocate, Charles?" L.L. acidly remarked. "The fact is that if you're a hydraulic miner, then you're also in the water business. Our water rights are the most extensive in the state and we paid handsomely for them, over $4 million."

Smith added, "That expense includes building the world's first long distance telephone line to manage the flow of water from the reservoirs."

"Here?" Reed said, surprised, "I read about Mr. Graham Bell's invention in the newspaper, but thought the only telephones were back east?"

Perkins, again with the details, "The Ridge Telephone Company, it cost us $6,000 to string a 60 mile wire line from French Corral to Bowman Lake, using Mr. Thomas Edison's parts and instruments."

"More wonders of the age," Reed complimented. "When you boys get after it, you certainly get after it. Most impressive."

"I venture there's nothing man cannot accomplish when he puts his mind and capital behind it," Smith declared.

"I wouldn't expect you to say it any other way, Hamilton," Reed said smiling.

The men reached a second wood framed elevator and were hoisted back up to the top, out of the great pit, the sun striking their faces halfway up, taking the chill out of the air.

L.L. said, "Charles, let us show you one last sight, the most impressive of all."

The men walked past more guards and into a large, barn-like structure, the mine's foundry and refinery. Heat and the smell of burning metals greeted their noses upon entering. Men were moving about in protective clothing, stiff leather aprons and long-gloved hands stirring and working furnaces filled with molten metal. Tools were everywhere, a man hammering at a forge, molds ready to receive the molten brew. Amalgams to purify gold were arrayed in flasks on shelves and tables – mercury, potassium, cyanide – all used to process and shape the gold into bars of varying sizes. Stacks of wooden blocks from the sluices were piled about, gassed free of mercury in retorts, where the gold was then collected. Odorless arsenic mixed with other toxic fumes to contaminate the air everyone drew into their lungs. Reed would never know how fortunate he was to come and go so quickly from this place, avoiding the poison these men inhaled each day.

The group approached a heavy, locked door. L.L. simply nodded, and the gatekeeper withdrew his keys and opened two iron locks, sliding a big bolt out of the door frame. The men stepped into the room, closing the door behind them. L.L. threw a lever switch illuminating the room, "We have electricity here, too."

"My God," Reed exclaimed. His eyes focused on the

massive gold bar displayed prominently in the middle of the room, set upon its own altar, the overhead lighting glistening off its golden surface. Reed stared into an eternity of color – ambers, yellows, browns – alive, almost moving, metal that formed in the earth eons ago. He touched its surface, slowly running his hand along the top, his mouth agape. Smaller gold bars were stacked in racks around the thick metal slab. They formed a simple frame to the behemoth in the room.

Reed looked to Perkins, who smiled bright white teeth, the gold bar reflected in his spectacles. Reed didn't even have to ask.

"Five hundred and twelve pounds, one-quarter of a ton," Perkins said in awe, pausing to swallow a gulp of air, "One hundred and fourteen thousand dollars."

L.L. was smiling too, "It's something of a showpiece, used to impress our investors in San Francisco. After it makes the rounds to a few board rooms and brokerage houses, we'll then transport it on to the San Francisco Mint, taking gold coins in return. They'll be deposited into the mine's bank accounts and a portion will return to the mine as payroll and operating expenses."

"I probably don't have to tell you this, Charles, but it's the largest gold ingot in the world," Smith said, stating the obvious.

The men then just stood in a circle, silently staring at the glittering object, hypnotized by its power, intoxicated by its golden spell, Reed fully understanding the allure of gold fever and how it changed men.

* * *

Reed heard the disturbance in the air first, a faint rustle, nearly imperceptible, a vibration. It was almost intuition, but the fact was Reed had exceptional hearing, and knew when to act, like now, leaping backward as the two pound hammer thudded into the floor at his feet. L.L., Hamilton, and Henry were shocked backward, with L.L. uttering, "What the devil?!"

The men, in unison, looked upward, into the high rafters of the foundry. There, among the trusses and beams, in a hole in the roof, the face of Russell McGirt glared down, disappointment etched, having missed his mark.

L.L. shouted, "What is the meaning of this, McGirt? You get down here and face us with an explanation this minute!"

The men heard the tick-tocking of feet slowly walking along the roof to an edge, then a ladder to the ground.

McGirt entered the open double doors to the foundry, striding right up to Reed, meeting his gaze head on. He said, to no one's belief, "We're patching the roof. The hammer must've slipped."

L.L. blasted, "Did you not think to yell a warning?! Someone could have been killed."

McGirt slid a sidelong look at L.L., dismissively saying, "Yeah, but they weren't."

Reed said, "You need to work on your aim next time."

"There won't be a next time, smart guy," McGirt spit, "things just happen."

"From above, from behind, the way of a coward," Reed replied.

"A what?"

"You got shit in your ears? You heard me, McGirt. You're a goddamn coward."

McGirt could not contain his mad dog rage. He lunged at Reed, who like before, was ready, kicking out a leg and using the man's momentum to toss him over his hip. Reed reached for his pocket pistol, a double derringer that was in his palm before McGirt even hit the ground. He pulled the hammer back and again had a barrel up against Russell McGirt's forehead, a foot hard on his chest, the same dumb look on his face as before.

All work in the foundry ceased as the men gathered to see how far this would go.

"This is a real slow moving bullet. You can even see it in flight, but it doesn't have to travel far," Reed warned, punching the end of the barrel hard into the skin, a jab that tore open a half-round circle of flesh. "God knows it won't hit anything passing through your skull."

Reed then flipped the short gun over in his hand and used the point on the gun's sight to dig deeper into McGirt's forehead. He clawed with the gun, like a crude dull knife, slicing and twisting a jagged line, cutting it down to the bone. The action caused the first half-circle wound to bloom and expand, the skin ripping loose. McGirt let out a high-pitched squeal that pierced the air, blood gushing in a roaring stream down into his eyes. A pink patch of flesh fell to the ground as Reed pulled the derringer away. A rodent would make dinner of it later that night.

Reed took his weight off McGirt's chest, releasing the man. He said to L.L., "You don't need to be employing a man like this. He's more trouble than he's worth."

No one standing nearby came to McGirt's aid. They felt, to a man, the comeuppance was long overdue. One man spoke,

Wendell Akins, "'Bout time someone took McGirt down a notch. He threatens us workmen in the mine, in the foundry, all of us." Wendell looked about, seeing he had everyone's attention, including the Dutchman who now came running into view, carrying his shotgun. Wendell raised his voice, "McGirt and the Dutchman, they issue fines for bullshit infractions, confiscating our wages because we don't wear our hats right or our toes point the wrong way. Just horseshit they make up so they can steal from us, pocket our wages. If anyone complains, they break a finger, an arm, maim us, threaten to kill us."

McGirt sat up, fire in his eyes, teeth bared, anger radiating from his blood covered face. He drew his finger across his neck, gesturing directly at Akins, a dead man look.

L.L. spoke, "Is this true? I won't have you attacking any of my guests or any of the men employed by the mine."

McGirt, staunching the flow of blood with a beat up leather glove, muttered in disgust, slurring what Reed clearly heard, "You're one tough stud broad, eh, Mary?"

"What's that you're saying? Speak so I can hear you," L.L. demanded.

McGirt staggered onto his feet, still holding his head with the glove. "If I don't beat 'em into line, then you'd have nothin'," he said angrily. "It's all about fear. You get what you want with fear. It's a useful tool, just like a hammer that comes outta nowhere." McGirt's voice grew louder, "You want me outta here, you do so at your own risk." He shot a menacing look at L.L. "Without me and the Dutchman, I'd wager far less gold makes it into this foundry, into your soft girlie hands, your silk pockets. You need us."

McGirt's unhinged soliloquy briefly ended. He removed the

leather glove from the gouge in his head and stared at the red clot sticking to the make-shift bandage. New blood immediately erupted from his head, hemorrhaging into his eyes and down his nose, spilling onto the ground. It forced him to stuff the glove quickly back up against the wound. It still wasn't enough to shut him up, picking up on his delusional rant. "These boys 'round me," he sputtered, spinning in a drunken circle, "are nothin' but scum, every one of 'em a thief."

Wendell Akins, already a McGirt target, threw all in, speaking his piece, "You're a murdering liar, McGirt. We ain't goin' to take it like the Chinese any longer. You took everything they got and now you've moved on to us. We know who's doin' the stealin' and we're all lookin' at 'im. You're the biggest cutthroat thief in the hills. I'll say the truth to your face again and again, until the sun goes down, you lowdown two-footed sack of shit."

L.L. had heard enough. He shouted, "The shift is over! Everyone get out, go home!"

McGirt shuffled out the doors first, picking up the Dutchman, who turned and walked at his side, his filthy hand still applying pressure to the knot hole in his head. He would stagger to the infirmary, where the layman on duty, a carpenter, really, crudely sewed the rim of the crater together, creating a jagged line in the middle of McGirt's head that looked like the crack in an egg. The layman would agree, being McGirt, he wasn't inspired to do his best work, secretly enjoying each time he stuck the bastard with the needle.

Other men patted Wendell Akins on his back, shaking his hand, congratulating him for his brave talk. They formed a party at his side, walking him safely out the mine's front gate, down to King's Saloon for a well-earned drink.

Smith and Perkins stood silently against the foundry's back wall, both trying to look as much like barn siding as they could. L.L. spoke, "I suppose you're right, Charles. It's up to me to send those two on their way, to clear them out of here. They are an obscene disgrace to humanity."

"Too much murderous rage walking amongst the decent," Reed seconded. "The Lord put him on this earth and it'll be up to men to fix His mistake, send him to hell where he belongs."

"And you're prepared to do this, Charles?"

"I could have shot McGirt dead on this very spot and not one man standing here would ever step forward and say they witnessed me doing it. Only the Dutchman and his shotgun prevented me from performing a public service."

L.L. sighed, knowing it was true. No one would complain if Russell McGirt was cut down and plowed under, one less villain to menace society. He considered the predicament, "Kill McGirt and you'll have to kill the Dutch blackguard too."

Reed pressed his tongue against his back teeth, nodding, "That's right. With the trespass injunction against the Nevada County Sheriff, it's not like you're going to get any help from the law out here at the mine."

"I'll be leaving tomorrow for Auburn. Those two are still in your kitchen. Perhaps the three of you can put your heads together and engineer a solution, like you do everyday for this mine. But remember, fear is a bad advisor. Find your counsel elsewhere, from within, look in the hard parts of your heart," Reed said looking at Smith and Perkins who joined them.

Perkins, his hand shaking, agreed, "Whatever it is, it needs to be painful."

Road to Grass Valley, California 1883

The stage had filled with passengers by the time it pulled out of Nevada City. Reed had ridden inside the Concord stage when it departed North Bloomfield, but now elected to ride on top, in the open air, seated behind Willis, who was driving. Beside Willis sat Lemuel Taggart, in the conductor seat. He wasn't a conductor for the stage line, just a large, round man from Sacramento, a scruffy salesman for Captain Ruhstaller's beer. From the look and smell of him, in tattered black coat, moth-holes chewed through, exposing a once white shirt, he could stand to stop drinking so much of the product he was employed to sell. Lem tried to doze, but was roused by each bump in the road. Willis feared the man would fall right off in his stupor, slouching further down until the shock of a chuckhole jolted him awake and upright in his seat.

Reed clapped Lem on his back. "Lem, ole buddy, let's trade places. You're bound to fall off if you sink any lower. You can stretch out back here and sleep it off."

Lem slowly rolled the meaning of the words around in his head. He exhaustively considered the sounds and combination. Finally, he unlocked the code, a tell-tale flicker of recognition in his half-mast eyes. He said nothing, just an upright head bob of acknowledgement that could have been caused by another bump in the road. He moved his bulk toward Reed, rolling over the top of the bench seat, more like a tumble, a controlled fall, bouncing to a halt, his derby staying firmly planted on his head.

"Thatta way, Lem. You made it." Reed got up into a low crouch, placing his hands on top of the bench seat and nimbly pommeled over, landing next to Willis.

Reed glanced back and saw that Lem was already sound asleep, nodding off before he even sat down.

Willis said, "Good idea. What took you so long to think of it?"

"I know we both like a beer, but if I wanted to smell like a brewery, I'd get a job there. At least now the odor's behind us."

"Yeah," Willis replied, adding a giddy-up, "Hah! I'll make sure the horses keep us ahead of it."

"There's a business to get into, growing hops," Reed contemplated, "taking over more of the valley everyday. Lem should be happy. I ordered a few barrels of their steam beer from him before we pulled out of Nevada City. The Golden Star of Shanghai could use a little more selection. I didn't know he was going to walk into The Nash and drink their supply dry."

"You ever notice how good beer tastes with John John's Chinese fare?" Willis observed, "especially when it's iced cold and with those hot peppers and noodles of his. Damn that's good. Me and Alice can't get enough."

"Fire and ice, burns a hole right up your nose, in a good way," Reed agreed.

Coming back down the foothills, Willis was taking it nice and easy, gently gliding the stage into each turn, unlike Hank Monk who lived for speed. Reed inquired, "How's Hank doing? He getting any better?"

Willis grimaced, "He left Miss Ellie's before we did. Said he had to get back on the road. Heading back to drive the Placerville to Genoa run for The Pioneer Stage Company, then on to Carson City. Said to Ellie he was up for it. The mustard plaster must've done him some good."

"I bet it was the romp with Ellie that done him the most good."

"Amen, brother," Willis replied, thinking of Alice, while Reed thought of Chan.

Willis said, "I heard what happened at the foundry with McGirt. Hadley had me moving loads up and down from the rim all day. Wished I was there and sorry I wasn't, but from what I heard, you done handled it. Say, you believe the size of that mine?"

"It's a sight, that's for sure, all the riflemen guarding the place. You ever make it down to the end of that tunnel dumping into Humbug Creek?"

"I delivered a load of mercury flasks that way. They prime the sluices with it to get the gold to stick to all them wood blocks. Funny silvery stuff, heavy," Willis answered.

"You see much debris spilling out that end into the creek?"

Willis laughed, "Oh, you should see it, rocks, boulders, tree stumps, you name it. The whole ridge is being washed down to the South Fork of the Yuba, directly or through escape boxes in the flumes and sluices."

"I figured that was so," Reed said, lamenting the half-truth. "They told me they were catching all the coarse debris, but they didn't want to show it to me."

"Yeah," Willis agreed. "They have their golden reasons not to. If I lived below, I'd be madder than an old wet hen, too."

"Before they built that big drain tunnel, it took nine years to mine a little over $200,000 in gold, with barely any profit," Reed explained. "L.L. now says they'll end up with over

$500,000 for this year alone and even more in the years to come if Judge Sawyer sides with the miners."

"Them some big numbers to ponder. Say, how'd you make out anyway with them rich fellas?"

"Got into some poker last night. Let's just say they were a bit rattled by the tussle with McGirt, affected their play."

"So you're coming home flush?"

"$1,000 flush," Reed answered.

"Oooh-wee, son of a bitch, that's some serious dinero, Charlie boy. I need myself a raise with you so loaded down."

"Well, you'll earn it keeping things civil at The Golden Star of Shanghai. McGirt's madder than all hell now. We've lit into him twice and he's never going to forget it, especially when he wakes up each morning and sees himself in a mirror. That big ole notch in the middle of his head staring right back at him, it'll remind him of the score he needs to settle. He'll be in Auburn soon enough."

"Bullshit, that jackass just needs to pull his hat down and forget about it. Next time we won't even leave him with a head," Willis predicted. "Maybe them mine owners will do the deed for us? Sounds like they got some gumption back."

Reed shrugged, not knowing. "L.L. will telegram me if things change. He might be sending half of the Sierra Nevada mountains down into the valley, but he's learned. He hates McGirt and the Dutchman as much as we do."

Willis pulled the stage to a stop on West Main Street in Grass Valley. They would rest and perform a few other duties before pushing on to Auburn, about 25 miles away.

"I'll be back shortly. Need to pickup my order at The Mercantile."

"Fine. Hostlers need to change the horses, I need to hand off the mail, and some people are gettin' a bite to eat so take your time," Willis said before entering the Telegraph Stage Line office to report to the division agent.

Reed walked to The Mercantile. He found the same small bald man from before, with round spectacles. He came around the counter to shake Reed's hand.

"Ah, Mr. Reed, step this way," the clerk said, smiling. "Our goldsmith completed your piece this morning. I have it right here." The clerk raced back behind the counter, unlocking a drawer. He placed a small, black velvet cushion on the counter between them. "Let me rub it up first," he said, taking a polishing cloth from his pocket to the lapel pin. He placed it on the velvet, saying, "I must say it is very nice, indeed."

Reed was also impressed with the Devil's Trident, remarking, "Yes, nice engraving work, from the bottom of the handle up to the tines."

"I can weigh it for you if you like, but I can assure you it is solid gold," the clerk pledged.

"Not necessary, I can tell by the feel. It's got some heft for a lapel pin."

"Then allow me, Mr. Reed." The clerk clasped the pin through the left lapel, running the prong down through the button hole, noting, "I especially like how the prong is threaded. There, securely on, please, the mirror."

Reed studied his reflection, tugging his lapels down against his chest, liking what he saw – the gold emblem contrasting nicely with the black suit coat.

The clerk said, "Your farm must be doing quite well to afford such a luxury item."

"Farm? What farm?"

"The pitchfork…wheat, hay? I assumed you must be a successful farmer."

"Oh, no, it's a…Devil's Trident. You see…it's a long story. What do I owe you?"

"That will be $57, sir."

"Can you please throw in a few of those red silk pocket handkerchiefs?"

"Certainly, Mr. Reed. I'll add them to the invoice."

Reed took one and folded it roughly, stuffing it in his breast pocket near the pin, thinking the red silk might help sell the Devil part. He looked again in the mirror and shrugged at his success.

He completed the transaction and arrived back at the stage as the last passenger in line stepped aboard. He hopped up on top, returning to his seat next to Willis.

Willis looked over at Reed, "Why you got a pitchfork pinned to your coat? You turnin' into a farmer?"

"Remember? Jasper Fanch," Reed said with a smidge of irritation. "He called me the Devil."

Willis looked again, "Oh, yeah, right," he said, releasing the brake, the stage creeping forward. "Still makes you look like a farmer. Next time have them make you a tiny Devil, the whole critter, with the horns, pointy tail *and* pitchfork."

Reed sighed, "Yeah, I'll get right on that," pulling the brim of his hat down over his eyes, letting the conversation go.

Malakoff Diggins, North Bloomfield, California 1883

The riflemen outside the mine offices ran like mice the moment Russell McGirt appeared, scampering away as if someone had tossed cheese on the ground. Just one angry look from McGirt wisely sent them on their way, off to protect some other part of the mine.

Miss Potter stood in the doorway, hands on hips, "You're not treading that mud through here."

McGirt stopped and looked down at the reddish soil caking his boots.

"And what happened to you? You've got two shiners and a dent in your head. Did a mule kick you?" Miss Potter said all of this in a tone that conveyed a sense of invulnerability. It was a power she did not possess.

"Get outta my way," McGirt growled, shoving her aside. It was just another outrage in a lifetime of offenses directed at the fairer sex.

Miss Potter let out a short scream at being jostled so violently, hitting the wall and sliding down to the floor, her pince-nez glasses breaking on the floor, shock registering on her face.

McGirt marched into the banquet room where L.L. Robinson, Hamilton Smith, and Henry Perkins warily awaited.

McGirt glared at Smith and Perkins, ordering, "You two get outta here. I need to talk to the boss."

Both Smith and Perkins hesitated, looking to L.L.

"It's alright, gentlemen. I'll call for you if I need you."

"Let's smoke a cigar, Henry," Smith said, whispering softly to L.L. as he passed, "We'll be just outside."

Both men walked out of the banquet room, moving past a wide-eyed Miss Potter, seated back behind her desk. Smith quietly repeated the same message, pointing to an area in the sunlight.

Miss Potter shook her head vigorously up and down, body language that pleaded – don't go far.

The men walked a short distance to the mine overlook. Smith opened his coat jacket, not for a cigar, but to show the revolver holstered at his side.

Perkins nodded and opened his suit coat, too, revealing a Remington, the one Reed recommended, short and light, purchasing it first thing this morning. The two men stood waiting, keeping their eyes on the office building, trying to detect any movement in the windows or loud sounds from inside.

"Everyone thinks they're a tough hombre now," McGirt smirked. "No one knows their place anymore."

Incredulous, L.L. scoffed, "After yesterday, you find that surprising? Mr. McGirt, you are one sadly deranged individual. Get out of here this instant. You're fired. Did you hear me? You are no longer a part of this mine. Clear out. Begone and take that filthy Dutchman with you."

McGirt moved toward L.L., pushing him into a corner, up against the wall and bookcase.

"See here now, I will have none of this ruffian business," L.L. protested, giving ground.

"I ain't goin' to shoot you," McGirt sneered into L.L.'s face. "No, you'd be missed, not like the Chinamen or the mudslingers workin' this hole."

McGirt grabbed hold of L.L.'s tie and tugged on it like a

leash. L.L. saw McGirt's thick dirty fingers up close, black streaks of grime under each nail. But it was his smell that was most offensive. With all the water running through this mine, L.L. thought, you'd think the man would use some of it to bathe.

"Your partners, who you make all that money for, would raise a ruckus, get the law after me. Probably hire guns to hunt me down, too."

L.L. met the challenge of McGirt's glare. He managed, "Oh, yes, we would have a reward on your head – dead or alive, with instructions on the former not the latter."

McGirt looked away, feeling the world standing in his shadow.

"Seeing what happened yesterday, all your victims," L.L. said in a determined voice, "there would be little trouble in raising a posse to hunt you down. I now have met plenty of men who would gladly take turns skinning you alive."

McGirt smiled, "Yeah, done my job too good." He then released L.L., turning away, walking to the center of the banquet room. "I should kill you and would kill you, but I got other plans. See, I made a lot of money here, being paid a salary to take even more from everyone," he laughed. "Goin' to cost me a lot to leave this place and I'm not goin' away for nothin'. You need to pay me off. I figure it'll cost you $4,000, no, $5,000 to make me go."

"I'll do nothing of the sort, you lunatic. That head wound Charles Reed gave you must have turned your brain to mush. You've plundered your last here McGirt."

McGirt removed his battered hat, which had sat awkwardly on his head due to the large bandage tied around it. He rubbed the bandage, feeling the bump below. The pressure of his touch caused a blood-yellow pus stain to seep up through the dressing, making it look like someone had urinated on his head.

"That Chinese lover, he can blow all he wants about what he done to me. Makes no difference, I'll deal with him next, along with all them shitkickers in Auburn. They're all a bunch of Chinese lovers. Not like the folks in Roseville or Rocklin, when we ran them out in '77."

"Do I have to say it yet again? Remove yourself, you lout," L.L. demanded.

"No, get the $5,000. I want it and I want it right now. I've been to San Francisco. I know people too, people who know you. I learned all about your bachelor marriage to your fat old Frenchy partner. Yeah, the one that blew his own head off when the creditors came after him," McGirt insinuated.

"What are you talking about?"

"I gotta say more?" McGirt chided. "Francois Pioche, the two of you gone punk for each other," he said contemptuously.

McGirt then stood upright, at attention, hand solemnly across his chest, like he was speaking in front of schoolmaster. He then mockingly recited a short limerick that taxed his feeble memory.

> *"Young cowboys had a great fear*
> *That old studs once filled with beer*
> *Completely addle'*
> *They'd throw on a saddle*
> *And ride them on the rear"*

McGirt burst out laughing, barely completing the final

verse. His mood then suddenly veered to anger, "You're going to pay me that money or everyone in these parts will know – mine investors, and 'specially executors of your wife's estate." He nodded, "That's right, the ones that sued you in court for helpin' yourself to all his" he paused, mood flipping again, "*ass*ets." He bellowed even harder than before, delighted at his lame play with words.

L.L. stood quietly, disgusted, uncertain, considering the blackmail, thinking of Francois, now dead some ten years ago.

At that moment, Hamilton Smith and Henry Perkins returned, each with a revolver leveled at McGirt's chest. McGirt stared into both barrels, his spine stiffening his posture upright and defiant.

Smith spoke, saying evenly, "We heard a commotion."

L.L. ended the matter, like he did in the foundry, declaring decisively, "McGirt, our business is over. Go and be damned."

Frustrated again, McGirt put his lid back on his head. "You'll regret this decision," he threatened, his lip curling into a menacing glare. "All of you!" he shouted, adding Smith and Perkins to his book of revenge. He then strode out the door, banging it loudly behind him.

Miss Potter entered the banquet room and along with Smith and Perkins, looked to L.L., who seemed to be battling himself, a temblor of anger quaking from tightened fists up through his arms, coursing through his body. He shouted, "Threats, the man only knows how to threaten, lie, and steal!"

L.L. reached for a carved glass vase, gripping it tightly. He contemplated throwing it out the window, shattering it and the window into a million pieces, but he didn't. Instead he restrained himself, smiling slightly, thinking how Francois would have been appalled by such a reaction, destroying such a lovely vase.

L.L. found a better place to be, at home within himself, locating the peace and comfort that comes from pleasant memories. He reminisced, picturing Francois's smile, the twinkle in his eyes, his jocularity. Francois, so cultured, so refined, who collected art, furniture, books, a banker and land owning mogul, a capitalist who invested in everything. His accomplishments were endless. Much more than L.L. would ever do. Francois, the developer of entire blocks in San Francisco: Market Street and its railway, the San Francisco Gas Works, the Spring Valley Water Company, the city's source for drinking water, numerous mining endeavors, including the North Bloomfield Mine. There were the railroads, too, with L.L. himself president of the Sacramento Valley Railroad venture. Despite all of this, Francois continued to do more, lavishly celebrating life, sharing his fine tastes with friends and visitors alike. He single-handedly created San Francisco's culture, importing fine chefs, spirits and wine from France, supporting industrial fairs, education, every imaginable charitable and philanthropic cause. L.L. recalled all of this, his friendship, his love – a most remarkable man, one who deserved a better fate than a Navy Colt pistol pressed to his temple – too many projects, overextended, no new capital available to keep the creditors at bay. To hear the voice of McGirt standing in this office, *his* office, uttering the name, Francois Pioche, was an affront, an outrage. Francois deserved respect, recognition, a statue in the town square. Russell McGirt deserved nothing but an unmarked grave.

L.L. stirred from his reverie, back in charge. "Miss Potter, I need to send a telegram to Charles Reed this instant." He abruptly stopped, turning up his nose and sniffing the air. "Would someone please open the windows? We must get that foul odor out of the air." Hamilton and Perkins, readily agreed, each moving to a window. "Miss Potter, do be so kind as to have someone stop by to clean the mud from the carpet and," he added, slowly drawing a finger down the elegant curve etched into the glass, "please order some flowers for this vase. I want all trace of McGirt removed from this mine. May he never curse this place with his presence ever again."

The moment was right, his prey in sight. "You there, get outta the way. You're not doin' it right," McGirt yelled, shoving the piper from his perch beside the Little Giant water monitor and onto the muddy ground.

The piper quickly found his feet, shouting above the deafening blast of water, "What are you doing? You don't know how to operate this machine! You'll get somebody killed!"

McGirt shoved the man down again, punching the piper in the chest, the blow knocking the wind out of him. He then kicked the man hard in the side with the point of his boot, breaking two ribs. The piper, dazed and in pain, gallantly tried to rise, but could only manage to lean up before falling back.

McGirt was no expert at the intricacies of water monitors, but he had seen enough in his time in the mine to give it a go. He grabbed the lever that controlled the Hoskin's Deflector, a flexible semi-ball joint between the end of the discharge pipe and the 10 inch nozzle. Its invention was a major innovation in

1876, allowing pipers to accurately aim the stream of water through the subtle movement of a lever, a balancing act that demanded a great deal of skill and dexterity. In the practiced hands of an expert piper, familiar with its workings and the mine terrain, more gravel could be moved efficiently with less water. Most importantly, a skilled piper knew how to work alongside other men, keeping those who pushed the ancient riverbed gravels excavated from the face of a cliff safe, preventing cave-ins and errant blasts that could kill those nearby.

McGirt manhandled the lever, pivoting the water monitor wildly to his right, over-shooting his mark, raining a powerful jet on a second, smaller water monitor providing additional current to wash the pool of gravel down a channel running along the floor of the mine, toward the underground sluices. Men were knocked from their feet as the water lit into them, some slipping into the rushing channel. McGirt jerked on the lever again, returning the nozzle to his left and swinging it upward, pouring a blast into the upper reaches of an over-hanging ledge. Men scrambled for safety as debris rained down, rocks and boulders of every shape and size. One man in particular, Wendell Akins, working with his fellow miners in the shadow of the bluff, was struggling mightily in the river of debris, wading waist deep in the torrent and slogging hard for higher ground, out from under the looming ledge, rocks battering his legs. With each tiny step, Akins could hear the deep rumble of rocks pounding and grinding around him, deep heavy booms echoing through the water as they bounced past him. The thunderous sound and shuddering vibrations spurred him in his flight for life.

When McGirt sparked this cave-in, this avalanche, he was

intent on killing Akins, but now his bad aim was turning the episode into so much more, with the water monitor tearing into everything. He giggled at the destruction, rocks falling, men fleeing. He returned his attention to Akins, who continued to strain in the mud red flow, seeking sanctuary. He would be goddamned if he were to let the man who spoke out against him crawl away before the world fell in on him. McGirt worked the lever again, driving the monitor's nozzle back to the right, raking Akins with a powerful stream of water that violently snapped his neck, instantly knocking him unconscious. The force of the impact blew his hat yards away from his head, high into the air. Akins body went limp, slowly sinking face down in the churning river of mud and gravel. McGirt whooped with glee, pleased at halting Akins desperate march. "Who's a useless sack of shit now!" he crowed, spitting his invective at the top of his lungs.

McGirt flipped the monitor again, elevating the nozzle to its highest point, a celebratory spout of water geysering high into the air. It produced a fine mist spray that mixed with the blue sky, riding upward and then cascading back down to earth. The water soaked ledge suddenly broke loose, tons of earth tumbling down in a roar as a hurricane of muck buried the body of Wendell Akins. McGirt let out an unheard laugh amongst the cacophony, a gale of displaced air enveloping him, leaving behind a residue of small mud droplets that coated his face, his clothing. McGirt's body spastically jerked up and down with joy at all the destruction he had wrought. He stepped away from the Little Giant, saying to the piper still on the ground, "Those men need to watch where they work," smiling his grit covered teeth that jutted in every direction, "a man could get hurt out there."

Men hurried to aid their fellow miners, laboring to free anyone trapped, buried, or drowning, tending the injured. Some hours later, Wendell Akins body would be retrieved, washed down a shaft with tons of debris, his body splayed out in every which direction, resting at the bottom of a sluice, silver globules of mercury laced with gold adhering to every depression and crevice in his flesh, ringing an eerie circle around his remaining cold, dead eye. For those who recovered his remains, lifting him to the surface, it was as if they were carrying a sack of onions, every bone shattered. A stamp mill pummeling quartz could not have exacted a worse toll on a human body.

McGirt did not stand idly by, he moved quickly from the mine while the calamity continued to play out. He was soon outside the mine, reaching the Dutchman. Both mounted horses, pulling along a mule packed with their goods. McGirt said, "Time to skedaddle. I know where a Chinese mining camp is set up. We can pay them a visit on our way to Auburn."

"People will be looking for us if you done what you said you were going to do," the Dutchman said.

"They have to find us first. I know an old coot, lives in a beat-up miner shanty, outside of Auburn, around Foresthill. Rance somethin' or other, German name. We're goin' to stay with him. Let the dust settle down, before makin' a run at misters Reed and Connelly."

The two kicked their heels into their horses' underbellies and were off.

Malakoff Diggins, North Bloomfield, California 2013

"I thought this would be a brief pit stop, just a few hours," I said to Jen and Kendra, "but now I think we're going to be here all day. This place is really interesting. You guys up for it?"

Jen and Kendra both stuck one leg out, Jen pointing, "We have our hiking shoes on."

Kendra added, basking in the afterglow of newly anointed town tour director, "Dad, I'm having the best time. What a great day."

Jen on cue, "Tom, lead the way."

I grabbed my backpack, perfect for a day hike, loading it with bottled water and sunscreen, taking point, pathfinder to the "*I gotta see this*," Malakoff Diggins, once the largest hydraulic mine in the world. We were barely off, when we side-tracked to a stop at the small historic town cemetery. We quietly walked through rows of plots, reading headstones and dates belonging to people long since passed, people who once called North Bloomfield home. We were joined by many generations of a family escorting two elderly sisters, both well into their eighties, a relative on each arm, guiding them up the slight grade, bare packed earth sprinkled with dried pine needles. The group entered through a small iron gate, slowly gathering at two headstones, laying a bouquet of flowers at the base of each, phone cameras preserving the event.

A young man in a San Francisco Giants ball cap and a week old beard, walked nearby, examining other markers. I said, "family plot?"

He smiled and said, "Yes, I'm the grandson-in-law, married a granddaughter," he lifted his arm, gesturing to a plump young woman in sunglasses, pale blue top, and white shorts, her nose, arms, and legs red from too much sun. "The sisters grew up here. This was their home. They were among the last to leave. Nothing more than a ghost town until the State Parks took over the place in 1965." He looked down, kicking a small pinecone, "There's still no electrical power, only diesel gener-ators and a few solar panels. Hard to believe over 2,000 people once lived here."

"Must be strange for the sisters seeing the place after so much time?" Jen asked.

"Not at all, they've had a great time seeing all the old buildings they grew up in, amazed at how so little has changed." He paused, looking back at the sisters, "Tilly is in a bad way, healthwise, though she has more energy today than I can remember. She and her sister, Marjorie, wanted to see the place one last time, visit their parent's graves, walk the streets, dip their toes in Blair Lake."

I said, "Sounds like lives right out of a Mark Twain novel. It's great they had this homecoming. I'm sure it brought back many fond memories."

"It sure has. Like everyone, I had no idea about the history surrounding this place. Well, everyone knows about the *Gold Rush*, but you really don't know until you see a place like this." The young man noticed his wife calling for him. "Gotta go. Nice talking with you."

The young man returned, conferring with his wife. Jen said, "They want you."

I walked over and was happily enlisted into taking a family photo. While everyone was gathered up, Tilly and Marjorie stood behind their parent's headstones, smiling at one another, the bouquets of brightly colored flowers contrasting vividly with the granite stones, monuments to loving parents gone now over fifty years. I quickly snapped a picture of the two sisters and their parent's together. The image briefly displayed in the viewfinder, sunlight angling through the trees, pleased I captured a candid moment. Others then mustered into formation, moving and crowding in beside the matriarchs, three generations of children, spouses, and grandkids. I framed the group, taking three more photos. I then returned the camera, handing it back to the young man and his wife. Thanks all around as I departed from their lives and back to my own. From over my shoulder, I heard the young wife say, "Ooh, that's a good one of Tilly and Marjorie." Mission accomplished.

We re-joined the trail, walking through a shaded forest. The trees abruptly ended and we found ourselves at a mine overlook, one of many vantage points available to hikers walking the Rim Trail. We stepped to the edge of the precipice, a vast panorama opening up into the far distance, our eyes dazzled by the immense open space. We breathlessly took it all in, silently scanning the remains of a huge pit, now teeming with vegetation.

"Do you believe this place?" Jen said.

"People talk about it, then you see it. Sure is something, over a mile-and-a-half long and almost a mile wide."

Kendra gave her opinion, "It sort of reminds me of Bryce Canyon in Utah, the sedimentary layers, the same orangey red colors." She paused, examining the park brochure, "'iron in the soil turns red when exposed to air, iron oxide.' Hey, look over there. They even have hoodoos, like Bryce."

"Yeah, it's a massive eroding pit," I said, "a man-made canyon that formed in a fraction of time, just a few years, not over eons."

"Look at all the trees ringing the bottom," Jen noticed. "It's been years since anyone mined here."

Trees had definitely made a comeback, conifers of white fir, ponderosa and sugar pine grew inside the mine, climbing up the sides to the steep perimeter cliffs. Further down, in the center of the mine, a colorful carpet of manzanita, native shrubs and grasses grew in a low wide strip, running the length of the mine, where, presumably, water still flows. Above the rim, nearby mountain tops encircled the mine with dense stands of pine forests. These trees, in their solitude, stood silent watch over nature's incremental encroachment, taking back what it once owned, a process now well over a century in the making, returning life to a once dead hole.

"Let's find the trailhead leading down," Kendra urged.

"The map says it's off to our right. It'll take us to the Diggins Loop Trail, the best way to see the bottom of the mine."

We fell in behind Kendra, who found the trailhead to the almost three mile loop. We watched our steps as we switchbacked down the chalky white, parched soil, loose pebbles all around that acted like ball bearings under our feet. I asked, "Anyone know why it's called Malakoff Diggins? Malakoff, it's an unusual name."

"I've got this one, Dad. I downloaded a few files back at the cemetery. I don't think we'll find much phone reception once we hike down into the mine."

That's our daughter, always thinking ahead.

"A lot of French miners settled here in the late 1850s, early 1860s," she said. "They were veterans of the Crimean War and the area reminded them of their victory at Fort Malakoff in Russia."

I thought "no shit" but didn't say it because I need to set a proper example. I substituted, "I wouldn't have thought this place could ever look like Russia, but, then again, I've never been to Russia and I didn't fight in the Crimean War."

"It was a major victory, breaking the eleven month siege of Sevastopol, leading to the end of the war," Kendra added.

Impressive, "Major in business and get a minor in history."

Jen tapped me from behind, a subtle reminder of Kendra's first choice – music, years playing piano. I quickly corrected myself, "Major in music, minor in history." I shrugged, "Just do something you love and have a passion for." As I said this, I wondered whether any career advice mattered anymore? You study one thing and then end up doing a job you never even intended. It was the same for Jen and me – get a college degree and in with some company. Show you can work with people, build and manage effective teams, move further up the ladder by obtaining some Performance Management Process certification, wear your Six Sigma green belt proudly, have a bigger cubicle, welcome to the upper middle class. Pays the bills, but hardly feeds the soul.

The thought of work again, need to push it out of my mind. Jen and I run the rat-race for fifty weeks a year. These are our two weeks, get back to vacation, but it's hard to do when Jen and I feel it already, the vacation hourglass running out of sand too quickly and the omnipresent tug pulling us back to our computer screens. Stop it now, quit thinking of work.

We continued on the trail, winding down and around creases in the cliffside, a wavy roller coaster caused by uneven erosion. With the topside rim constantly worn by the elements, the perimeter of the mine was actually expanding, albeit slowly. Erosion from the cliffs had to go somewhere, with gravity depositing the earthen runoff down into the pit through a vast network of vertical cracks and gullies, trying to fill the mine back up. Come back in a billion years or so and you might find just a shallow depression.

We worked our way from the cliffside, reaching the bottom through a thin line of trees rooted at the base of the cliffs. We walked out into the open among patches of shrubs and manzanita, dry crusty soil, darkened in places by thin streams of water emanating from the cracks and gullies above. We continued our trek down the length of the mine, not sure if we would complete the entire loop. As we walked, we saw many segments of rusted iron pipe, ten to fifteen long and at least 16 inches in diameter.

"Boy, look at all the piping they left behind, just abandoned."

"They're called penstocks," Kendra explained. "They were more durable than the original canvas hoses that couldn't take the high water pressure. These were laid throughout the mine – on the ground, buried, or on trestles – all funneling water to the monitors."

"The water pressure came from just the elevation change, didn't it? From the higher mountain reservoirs," Jen said, answering her own question. "Well, that and just the height change from the rim down to here would be enough. How many monitors did they have?"

"You're right, Mom, about the pressure. From what I can tell at least seven large monitors were used here."

"That's a lot of water. What was it? One point one million gallons *an hour* for just one monitor," I said.

Jen tagged on, "Twenty-four hours a day. I still can't get over that amount while we can't even water the lawn during this drought." She cast her eyes around, shading her brow with her hand, "Explains how this mine got so big. Where did all of the dirt go?"

"We need to keep hiking this way, down to the lower end of the mine. There's another trail down there, Humbug Creek. All the tailings were washed downhill and into the creek, which feeds into the river," Kendra said, "and the river runs all the way down into the valley."

We meandered south, Jen saying, "It's really kind of pretty now, all the plant life coming back."

After a mile, we came across a wooden sign saying, "Hiller Tunnel." We looked around and decided it must be off the trail, down a short but steep incline beside the trail. We took a pass on exploring for the entrance and decided to reach the far end of the mine, walking on a narrow boardwalk bridge that intersected a pond, the mine's low point, where green vegetation floated on or pointed out of its surface as lilies and glades of cattails. Past the boardwalk we found the end, a large water monitor mounted as a display piece near the base of this final cliff, where the trail began to loop back around. Kendra and I jumped up beside the cannon, modelled on Civil War artillery that hurled cannonballs, rather than spouting water. We posed beside the wooden box counterweight at the inlet end, loaded with hundreds of pounds of rocks to contain the massive recoil.

Jen said, "It's so big that it's hard to get you guys and all of the monitor in the picture."

She clicked off a few shots and then a few close ups with just a portion of the orange red metal between Kendra and me.

We decided to forgo the rest of the Diggins Loop, backtracking the way we came in. As we returned to the Hiller Tunnel sign, I was pulled by its allure. We consulted the map. I said, "Look, there's a trail here that leads out of the mine toward the Humbug Creek Trail." I pointed to the side trail that worked its way up and out. "You guys take it and I'll meet you there by way of the Hiller Tunnel."

Jen and Kendra froze, both looking at one another. Jen said, "Bad idea, Tom. We shouldn't separate and besides, you don't know what's in that tunnel. There could be snakes, spiders, bats."

"Dad, something could cave-in. You'd be stuck. Are we supposed to go in and get you?"

I waved off the worries, "If it's unsafe, there would be a sign saying so. It's the middle of summer. There might have been tons of dirt washing through it years ago, but nobody is blasting water monitors anymore. I bet there is barely a trickle running through it this time of year."

Jen surrendered, familiar with my little boy moments, "We're not going to be able to talk you out of this?"

"If it's unsafe, I'll just come back out and get on the trail you're using. Here, see on the map. It's only 600 feet. I'll be walking right under you. It won't take long. I'll probably even beat you to Humbug Creek."

"Right, sure you will" was the consensus.

I turned and worked my way down the embankment, bushwhacking a few trees and sure enough, there was the Hiller Tunnel entrance, embedded into the hillside, an array of boulders sitting on its doorstep. "Hey, hey, here it is," I shouted, stepping in and around a small stream that dribbled into the black oval.

"What do you see?" Jen yelled from above.

"A lot of black, but I've got my headlamp," I yelled back, removing it from my backpack. "This will work. I'll be fine. I'll see you in a few minutes."

A final "You be careful," belted out of Jen, as I began hopscotching on rocks, staying as much out of the water as possible, stepping and climbing over small boulders and into the darkness. The tunnel was only about six to seven feet wide, the floor very hard, slick and uneven. The sides and ceiling the same, faceted by chips, picks, or blasts carved into the rock when it was constructed. I braced my hands on and off the walls for balance, alternating left and right with my hands and feet, bounding forward slowly, but safely, slightly hunched, straddling the stream between my legs that ran from a thin film to pockets and holes a foot or more deep. I soon gave up on my feet staying dry, an impossible dream, but a meager price to pay all in all. After frog walking some hundred feet or so, I turned and looked back at the entrance, the sunlit oval now just a small dot far away. I felt miniaturized, like I was walking through the tiny aperture of some long camera lens. Condensed water droplets released their handholds from the ceiling above, plunging the short distance down, cold liquid pin-pricking my scalp, the back of my neck with each splash, the jolts heightening my senses. The hot summer temperature, though only a few hundred feet away, plummeted at least thirty degrees as I navigated this damp dark pipe.

As I continued forward, the tunnel began to bend slightly, or so it seemed, always moving slightly downward. The oval entrance behind me was gone, its sunlight replaced by inky blackness. My headlamp provided a good forty feet of light and I was thankful that I had recently replaced the batteries. It was all so very black ahead, beyond my lamp's beam, like the vacuum of space, with no sign of a sun at the far end of this wormhole. When I stopped my progress, I heard only the sound of my breath in the confined space, heart beating, and the drip and movement of water, eerie reduced sounds that were few and easy to discern, primordial. The sounds receded with my movement, one foot in front of the other, sloshing forward through the underground plumbing. I found my pace, gaining confidence, despite the unpredictable footing, thinking that if I can move forward safely, I should do so. I didn't want to unduly worry Jen and Kendra by dawdling, but what a cool adventure. They would love this. You know what I should do? Where's my camera? I need to make a video of this. They need to see what this is like. Kendra will show me how to post it on YouTube so all my co-workers can see it too.

I found my camera in the large front pocket of my cargo shorts. Sure phone cameras are better now, but I was old school, trusting in a single device with high resolution and a powerful 30x Leica lens. Amazing how photography has changed, now all digital, with massive SD card storage. My college photography class days spent in dark rooms, using toxic chemicals to develop rolls of film, dodging and burning prints, a thing of the past. Something lost, perhaps, but a whole lot gained.

I clicked a few still photos, the flash a lightning bolt through the air. I then spun a dial, setting the camera to motion picture mode. I pushed a button, the motion picture icon blinking "action." Rather than dead air, I began to narrate the action, a spontaneous, unrehearsed script in my head. "I'm in the Hiller Tunnel under Malakoff Diggins State Park. This tunnel was dug in the 1850s by Gold Rush miners and served as a drain to the largest hydraulic mine in the world. It's almost 600 feet long and…WHAP!…Uhh-oh, son of a bitch."

It had happened suddenly, without warning. One moment I was standing and in the next my feet are above my head, slipping out from under me when I shifted my weight, losing traction on the green slime that coated the rocky surface. I slammed down into the stream, a flop onto my right side, lucky to have not struck my head, knocked cold, drowning in six inches of water. I laid still for a moment, taking inventory, bells ringing between my ears, trying to get my wind back. I needed a tube to snake down into my lungs so that I could pump them back up. I stuck my tongue out, exhaling air with a wheeze. I seemed to be in one piece but soaking wet and cold. Somehow, I had hung onto my camera, which I had the wherewithal to extend into the air without it banging on the rocks or plunging into a pool to short out its electronics. My backpack had absorbed some of the impact and, despite the aches, I was fortunate to not be more seriously damaged.

Footfalls behind me, splashing, I turned to look back, two headlamps bobbing up and down with each step.

"Ahoy," the German accented voice called out.

"Helmut, Gregor? That you?"

"We heard a splash and thought it could be a big animal, so we hesitated," Gregor said.

"No, just me body surfing."

Helmut made an assessment, "Tom, I think you need to wait for the tide to come up."

Gregor moved in beside me, saying, "Are you hurt? Let us help you up," whereby each man took ahold of an arm, pulling me back onto my feet.

Helmut said, "Wasser has run through this tunnel for over 150 years, scoring the bottom, algae, very slippery, easy to go down."

"I'm fine, thanks for the lift up. Knocked the wind out of me along with some pride," I admitted. "Too much Francis Coppola," I said, holding up my camera.

"You need a GoPro camera like this," Gregor said, pointing to the harness contraption around his shoulders and across his chest, the small camera mounted in the center staring out.

"You Germans think of everything."

I launched the playback on my camera, the three of us watching, a dim view of the tunnel, my narration, then wham-splash, "son of a bitch" bringing a collective chuckle to my Hindenburg moment.

"Yeah, yeah, it could have been you," I said, trying to alleviate my clumsy embarrassment.

We moved on together, grateful for the company, a sunlit oval exit now visible a few hundred feet ahead. As we got closer, a silhouette of Kendra appeared, shouting, "Dad, is that you?" her voice echoing down the pipe.

"It's me, along with Gregor and Helmut."

"We thought you were gone for good," Kendra exclaimed, "that we'd never see you again."

The three of us, intrepid explorers, emerged into the sunlight, our eyes trying to adjust, warm air starting to work on my wet clothes, the hairs on my arms prickling upright. I could see Jen sitting on a rock up on the embankment next to the trail, legs pulled up to her chest, arms wrapped around her knees. We crawled out of the drainage and up to the trail, joining Jen.

"What happened? You're soaking wet."

"Uh, yeah, a little mishap, hon, about halfway, no permanent damage."

Gregor and Helmut smiling, Gregor cracked, "He'll show you the movie later."

I looked at the Teutonic Two with a wry smile, "Thanks, I knew I should have deleted it before we got out. I'll never be able to go spelunking again."

Auburn, California 1883

C harles Reed read the telegram silently, folding it and slipping it into the inner pocket of his suit coat. He handed a dime to the young boy who had run the message to him, thanking the boy for his effort, which still left him out of breath. The boy politely removed his hat, the sun highlighting his freckled face and wayward curls. He made a slight bow, saying, "Thank you, sir." He then turned and ran back to the Western Union Telegraph office in search of more work, more telegrams to deliver.

Reed continued on his walk to the Parkinson's Building, repeating L.L.'s telegram in his head, not surprised by its contents.

"Our mutual problem headed your way. Lucrative reward to any who takes action. Best be on guard, L.L."

Reed reached the Parkinson's Building and entered John Craig Boggs' saloon. It was early afternoon and business was dead. Reed saw J.C. leaning back in a chair, his neck extending with the back of his head just reaching the wall. The position was precarious and Reed thought the chair was about to kick out from beneath the large man. J.C. was unaware of Reed's approach, his eyes fixated on the ceiling, knowing the slightest wrong move would topple him to the floor.

Reed said, "Best lawman in the state held prisoner by a chair. How'd you get in that position?"

Two pupils moved in the still, unmoving head, "How else...boredom."

Reed grinned and grabbed the chair, setting J.C. Boggs, the former Placer County Sheriff, solidly back down onto all four wooden legs.

"Thank you kindly for your help. You just stoppin' by for a visit or are you a payin' customer?"

"Yeah, you could use a few more of those," Reed observed.

J.C. walked behind the bar and helped himself to a bottle and two shot glasses. He poured bourbon for Reed and himself, doling out a friend's portion, taking a seat. "Try one of them bread rolls. They're good with the butter."

Reed took a bite, "Still warm, good."

J.C., like always, straight to the point, "What the hell am I doing runnin' a saloon, Reed. There's too many in this town already. You and John John got most of the business – good drink, food, a sportin' chance with cards and the ladies. Heck, I should be at your joint now havin' some fun. Feel like I'm sittin' in my own tomb."

Reed looked around at the dust and gloom, offering an assessment, "You might make it as an undertaker, but that would mean bringing in some flowers to brighten the place up."

"What? You don't like what I've done? Look at that grizzly bear over there, brings character to the place." J.C. tossed back some bourbon, "Every saloon should have one."

Reed gave a sidelong look to the old mottled bear, posed on its hind legs, one paw extended in a hapless swipe, glass eyes and bared teeth trying to look tough. Anyone could see the bruin's heart really wasn't into it. To Reed, it looked like a thick, mangy rug tossed over a coat rack. "Uh, huh, goes real well with the curtains."

"What are you talkin' about, Reed? We got no cur..." He stopped himself, reflecting on the ramshackle surroundings, "Yeah, I see what you mean," he said, taking another sip.

"Asa said I should stop by, give you some advice."

J.C. laughed, "Asa's a good man and makes a good sheriff. That is for an old merchant seaman. He ain't afraid of much, but he's right. I ain't striking it rich as a saloonkeeper." He took another sip of bourbon, "No one's striking it rich anymore. The mines are all owned by outside money. Everyone else is now a *wage earner,* pecking away like hens for a few kernels of corn. They make just enough to eat, drink and whore."

"For many, that's enough," Reed commented.

"They must be doin' it in your place, 'cause they sure ain't doin' it here," J.C. said, discouraged, casting his eyes around the dull dark room. A lone customer sat at the bar, his head slouched down on its surface, sound asleep.

A bartender stood idly by, greased hair slicked back, black bow tie, earning his keep by swatting flies. A sharp "WHAP!" on the bar sending another fly into oblivion. The abrupt crack

THE GOLDEN STAR OF SHANGHAI

caused the lone customer's face to rise up out of a thin pool of saliva, shocking him upright on his stool, a strand of spit coming and going with the movement, snapping apart halfway up. The bewildered man absently dabbed at the lower lip end of his spit trail, wiping it with the back of his sleeve, exposing a mostly toothless mouth that opened and closed like a fish, swallowing back the remaining slobber.

J.C. shook his head, disgusted, "Shit, my best customer over there, Rance Mueller, is one of my oldest enemies. Twenty-five years ago he used to ride with outlaws Tom Bell, Texas Jack, and even spent some time with Rattlesnake Dick. Rance was in on many of the holdups, but I never caught him in the act. Should be sittin' in that new Folsom Prison, bustin' rocks, rather than takin' up space in my saloon, you layabout buffoon."

J.C. yelled this loud enough for the man to hear. "Yeah, I'm talkin' to you, you odd old stick." J.C. then waded up a bread roll, launching the packed dough across the room. It struck Rance in the back with a thud that sounded like a fist punching a sack of flour. The impact left a glob of butter stuck to Rance's tattered red flannel shirt.

Rance slowly stirred from his stupor, looking over his shoulder, vacantly squinting out from alcohol addled eyes, not feeling the bread roll or hearing a word, awakening from a dream he needed to return to. He gazed dejectedly at his shot glass – empty. With nothing to imbibe, Rance lowered his face back down onto the bar.

"At least you're tappin' him for a little coin," Reed said dryly.

"Ain't enough stickin' it to tired old road agents like Rance.

Gettin' out of this business and into somethin' else."

"Before you tell me about it, I need you to keep a watch out for Russell McGirt and Wim, the Dutchman. They're headed back this way. Figure it'll be a bloodbath this time."

J.C. was all attention now. "That a fact? They're an evil pair, those two. I've got no use for 'em. I ever tell you, oh, back some seven years ago, we had a bad murder. Fellow by the name of Oder and his wife, robbed, shot and hacked to death, gruesome act. They were keeping house for another man named Sargent. Sargent was found a half mile away with five bullets in him." J.C. paused for more bourbon, remembering the event, "He died the next morning but before he did, he described three Chinese assailants, one being Ah Sam, who used to cook for families in Auburn. The murders came about because of a $120 mining claim Sargent sold to these vipers. They wanted the claim *and* they wanted to repossess their money." J.C. stopped, considering his words, "You think folks hate the Chinese now, you shoulda seen it then."

Reed said, "Bad?" spurring the tale on.

"The crime shocked the state. It became the excuse for McGirt and the Dutchman to lead a lynch parade through Placer County, every town – Rocklin, Roseville, Loomis, Penryn. They destroyed every hut, shop, joss house they could find in every one of them Chinatowns. If you was Chinese, you were driven out of the valley – innocent people guilty of nothin'. It made no difference, get out or be strung up. McGirt shot his mouth off the whole time, saying they were the Vigilance Committee, restoring law and order. They were just an angry mob seekin' vengeance, breakin' heads and lootin' Chinese property every step of the way."

J.C. ruminated some more, "You know, Reed, Chinese make the easiest targets, everyone blames 'em for low wages. The mines and railroads could pay everyone more with all their profits, but they don't. They're just in it for themselves. What is it the newspapers call 'em now – robber barons. Makes me boil thinkin' of old governor Stanford, Crocker, all those rich fellas. They stand up all high and mighty now sayin' 'there's too many Chinese' when they're the ones that got rich bringin' thousands of 'em here to do the dirty work, layin' their railroad tracks for half the white man's wages."

"Ugly times back then. Figures McGirt and the Dutchman would be leading the pack," Reed said.

"It took every inch of me and every deputy in the county to tamp down all the anti-Chinese fury. In fact, the mob was even going to run my own Chinese cook out of town, but I stopped 'em."

"How'd you do that?"

"I convinced them to let him be, because he could help me track down the wanted men, which he did by asking the Chinese leaders for help, collecting information, leading me to two of the three. I arrested Ah Fook in Folsom and soon learned Ah Sam took his gun and hatchet out to the Gold Strike Mine in Plumas County. I rode out that way, warning everyone I met. Ah Sam got himself cornered by some of the miners I spoke to. As the miners were coming to fetch me, Ah Sam pulled the trigger on himself, preferring a hole in the head 'stead of a trial and a hangin'. Well, a hangin' at least. No one was going to wait around for a trial. The mob would've stormed the jail to get Ah Sam, but he deserved it, had it comin' to him for killin' those folks the way he did. Wouldn't have caught 'em, though, without Chinese help." J.C. looked into his empty shot glass, "Most of the Chinese that fled back then, ended up in Newcastle or Auburn, much more tolerant communities."

"You made it through them tough times, rounding up all them highwayman. You should be proud you're still standing. Everyone in the state owes you a debt of gratitude," Reed said sincerely.

"Kind words, thank you, Reed. You're right. I've lived through some tough times and I like to think life is better than the early days of California. I'm speakin' about the *real* Gold Rush, '49, into the '50s, when things were just startin' out. Never have so many low-lifes gathered in one place at one time, all with gold fever, many willing to rob, shoot, and steal from their fellow man when they couldn't find gold for themselves. Don't get me wrong, there were good folks, but unless he was known to you, family or a partner, you trusted no one."

"McGirt and the Dutchman want to bring those days back and we can't let it happen. People are going to die, and it ain't going to be me."

"Those fast hands of yours, I don't believe you have anything to worry about. Good folk will stand up. They always do. It's the side of life to be on, especially when the likes of you and me are around to remind them of their innate goodness. Anyway, I'm done peddlin' beer and whiskey. I'm sellin' out. Reed, you need any of this stock?"

"I'll take however much of this bourbon you got left. Good stuff."

"Ah, a man with fine tastes, one who appreciates a worthy

sippin' libation," J.C. said with a grin, splashing more into their glasses. He nodded toward Rance, "Not like a bum who pours it down his gullet so fast that it never even touches his tongue." J.C. shook his head, "I wouldn't waste a drop of this liquid gold on that old sot. I got plenty of bottles of hair tonic and some other stuff that takes paint off wood for him to swill down."

J.C. held the amber liquid in his glass up into the light, admiring the barrel-aged goodness, "Had it shipped straight out of Kentucky. Nothin' better was ever placed in a bottle. I can sell you my remainin' cases, but I'll need to keep one or two, hide it away from Louisa now that I'm goin' to settle down."

"What are you aiming to do?"

"Well, I can't compete with a card shark like you, Reed. The fruit tree business is goin' along nicely. Me and Louisa have settled right in on that patch of land I purchased down yonder in Newcastle. The house is sturdy and we're goin' to spend more time sittin' on the porch and watchin' some trees grow, plant a few more orchards, too. Good money shipping dried prunes back east. Once the railroads get the train cars with ice up and runnin', I'm thinking plums, pears, maybe even peaches and oranges. Fresh California fruit is the new Gold Rush."

"That's a good plan. I wish you luck with it, J.C."

Both men stood, shaking hands, J.C. said with a level look into Reed's eyes, "I could always count on you and Willis whenever we posseed up and the law needed a hand. You take care of yourself, Reed. If the shootin' starts, you can count on me to be there with my Colt and Henry shotgun."

"Thank you, friend."

"Hey there, before you go, what'll you give me for the grizzly bear?"

"Can't help you there."

"You sure? Well, I suppose it might look good in the Newcastle house?" J.C. pondered.

"You better chat that up with Louisa first," Reed reminded.

"Yeah, you're right. I don't need to go there. I reckon it would clash with her curtains too." J.C. then turned toward the bar, shouting, "Rance! Clear out before I put my boot up your ass, you two-footed keg of whiskey. We're closin' up. Buy your hooch from somebody else!"

Reed walked out the door, standing off to its side. He checked his pocket watch time, looking up as the body of Rance Mueller came tumbling out onto the street.

John John, entered the Quong Hi Company store with Mr. Chang and Charlie Yue when the day was at its hottest. They were grateful to find the shade of the interior, even though the walk was but a short distance from The Golden Star of Shanghai. Mr. Chang and Charlie placed their empty wheel barrels outside, near the entrance. Mar Ying Toy and his wife Leo Gim Moy were among the most successful Chinese merchants and grocers in town. Their success was hard-earned, the business expanding with a new brick building on Chinatown Hill. The hard-working couple, along with John John, and another merchant, Kee Chin, formed the Boss Chinese of Auburn, community leaders who maintained the Joss House as a temple of worship. Years earlier, with the arrival of the first Chinese, the temple was established and strategically placed at the entrance to the red light district, where its impact met with mixed results. Dai Lao, representative of the Hip Yee Tong, was noticeably excluded from the council for obvious reasons.

Mar Ying Toy greeted the men happily, conversing in their native Cantonese. Initial pleasantries were exchanged before John John began selecting herbs and vegetables for The Golden Star of Shanghai's kitchen. John John's practiced nose inhaled the latest batch of five spice powder, containing cinnamon, fennel, star anise, cloves, and Sichuan pepper. John John liked what he smelled, bowing to Leo Gim Moy, who stood apart, but was nevertheless keenly interested in John John's assessment.

John John said, "Unusual, but excellent. Are you sure there are only five spices?" The power of the number five has long held healing and curative powers in Chinese culture. The depth and complexity of this blend caused John John to doubt its makeup and adherence to tradition.

Leo held up a hand with all of her digits extended, insisting five. "I changed the portion amounts for each spice. That is why the blend is a little different – lighter, cocoa color."

John John nodded his approval. "Leo please join me while Mar fills Mr. Chang and Charlie's wheel barrels with rice and vegetables."

The small woman moved to John John, adorned in a fine silk robe, bright eyes, two interlocking gold rings dangling from each pierced ear. John John had always been impressed by Leo, the mother of Mar's three small children. She was the power behind his throne. He knew both Mar and Leo were very much in love, her intelligence and his work ethic had made for a powerful union. John John thought Mar's best trait was his good sense to defer to his wise wife on any important decision. This was not because Mar was unintelligent. No, rather, it was due to his wife's ability to consider all possibilities before making a decision. It was a trait John John could appreciate, reminding him of his mother.

"Mar is quite lucky to have you as a wife, Leo," John John said. "Can I ask a favor? I would like to see your gardens. I have dined on its bounty for so long, but have never seen them."

Leo granted the request with a silent nod, leading John John through the back of the store, emerging onto a shaded porch with pails of water and gardening tools organized and ready for use. Numerous potting beds, some on the ground and others raised, stood about, overflowing with lemongrass, ginger root, and coriander. The sight was lush and green, an aromatic wave filling his nostrils with each step. Leo had strung white sheets to dull the intense sun rays. She adjusted one sheet to better protect her coriander plants, saying, "The sun is very harsh this time of day. The plants will burn with too much sunlight."

"None of our cuisine would be possible without these ingredients. We are truly indebted to this garden and your dedication to it. My partner, Charles Reed, will be most pleased with the coriander. What he calls Chinese parsley." John John broke off a stem, sniffing and then eating the leaves, chewing into the pleasant lemon lime flavor, "Delicious."

"The Spanish call it cilantro," Leo said. "I find I use the leafy herb more and more when I cook, not just the seeds. It is a robust and hearty plant that grows easily in this climate, like so much else." She grew silent, her intuition at work. Leo knew John John was smitten with her, but also knew he would never act on such an impulse. Their relationship was one of mutual admiration and respect. All the same, Leo knew that closer ties would benefit both. She spoke frankly, "My youngest sister is visiting next week. She is legal, making it into the country before the Exclusion Act took effect last year. I think it appropriate that you should meet her."

John John was somewhat taken aback by Leo's directness. He paused and considered the words carefully. This was not idle conversation. It was tantamount to an offer of her sister for marriage. He was silent for a long time, with Leo becoming anxious with each passing moment. "You have spoken to her of me?"

"Yes, I have written many letters describing you. She has known of you long before leaving Guangdong Province."

"Do you write with a flattering or scathing pen?"

Leo smiled, "I don't need to tell you the answer to your question."

"Tell me more about her."

"I admit prejudice, but she is the most beautiful of all my sisters, very inquisitive, graceful. She is a fine cook, working with Mar's uncle in San Francisco. He has a popular dim sum tea house in the city. We are planning a fine dinner to mark her arrival. Please tell me you will be our guest?"

"Of course, I would be honored to meet her."

Leo smiled, "You two will make a good match."

John John said nothing, looking into Leo's eyes, a solid unwavering gaze that conveyed all of her vaunted wisdom. He felt the effect of its weight, just like Mar. He returned the penetrating gaze with his own, a meeting of minds, pondering the prospect of a matrimonial arrangement.

The gaze continued unbroken, until both were mutually satisfied with the sincerity of the offer and its honest intentions. John John blinked an ending, signaling his interest. He initiated the next step by simply requesting, "Her name?"

"*Ah Cy.*"

John John raised an eyebrow, murmuring softly, "Lovely."

Though far from complete, John John sensed the import of this moment, saying, "I look forward to the introduction, Leo."

"I am certain you will be very pleased. Here, let me show you the vegetables."

The garden extended behind the shop well past herbs, with rows of plants rooted into the ground, leafy greens like white and green *bok choy*, *yow choy*, and the Chinese broccoli known as *gai lan*. They stopped at the garden edge, examining the Chinese spinach, *hin choy*, with its magenta and green leaves.

"My favorite green," John John said, "though the odor is not very attractive."

Leo laughed, "Horse dung vegetables. It is how they thrive. I learned this as a girl in China."

Beyond the garden a line of Chinese women in conical straw hats appeared, led by the Dai Lao's big man, the Baotu.

Leo said, "Another day laboring for Dai Lao, on their backs when his opium fiend miners return from prospecting to breaking their backs now with petty hard labor."

John John watched as twelve women began their exertions. He studied their actions, curious at the work being done. Were

139

they picking up rocks and moving them, clearing the land so a structure could be built? He gave up, looking to Leo, "What are they doing?"

"It is Pig Face's way of control," she said. "At first, I thought they were clearing rocks from the land to plant their own garden, but that would be too useful. It began weeks ago, when they started to gather rocks into a pile. The pile was moved from one side and then to the other, over and over."

Incredulous, "Why? For what purpose?"

Leo stoically explained, resigned to the thuggery, "to be mean, evil, to strip out all hope from the girls' hearts."

They watched silently as the women bent and lifted in the hot sun.

Leo broke the silence. "Even the big man was bored with the continual movement of stone. I see now he has them stacking rocks along the property line, building a small pathetic wall."

"It is appalling."

"With the Exclusion Act, the Hip Yee Tong's prostitution empire is threatened. It is very risky and expensive attempting to smuggle new girls into America, providing them with legal documents," Leo explained.

"You would think this shortage would make him act more kindly to those he enslaves."

Leo looked to John John, "This is Dai Lao. He is a brute, an unthinking animal. His mind is demented from sucking too long on his bamboo pipe. He knows no other way." Leo provided a new wrinkle, disclosing, "He is now extorting protection money from us."

It was a disturbing revelation that John John responded to

wordlessly, with only a look that signaled to Leo its significance and his support.

They watched as the Baotu shoved a woman to the ground. A few of his loud words carried on the breeze to them. They heard him accuse the woman of only moving small stones and should instead lift and stack larger ones. Two other women, engaged in this labor, unsympathetically joined in, hurling insults and epithets at the woman on the ground. The fat-bellied thug pointed the women to a bucket of water. As the one woman attempted to stand, he shoved her back down. It was plain from this distance that she was expected to continue working, no water for her.

"They all hate her." Leo paused and then said, "You do know she is your partner's whore."

John John turned to Leo, "I did not know."

"Your friend Reed treats her well and the others resent it. Strangely, if he were to beat her, the others would likely leave her alone."

"The Japanese proverb, *the nail that stands up is hammered down*," John John whispered.

"Poor Chan, what a terrible fate for someone so young and pretty," Leo said.

"What is her name?"

"Chan…"

John John left Leo's side, stridently marching across the adjoining field, and past the thirsty women. John John came up behind the Baotu, who was still menacing the fallen woman. He kicked the Baotu behind the left knee, collapsing it. It exposed the thug's right flank. John John dropped all of his weight down onto his left elbow, striking a heavy blow to the ribs. The Baotu went down on top of the woman. John John rolled the large man off. He lifted the woman up from behind by the waist, spinning her around to face him as she came to her feet. John John saw nothing but the straw conical hat that he immediately tore off, exposing the top of her head, black hair parted. He reached with his index finger for her lowered chin, gently lifting her head. Her eyes were closed, tears running down her cheeks. She expected a cuff to the cheek. When none came, she opened her eyes that widened into recognition. John John mouthed one soft word, "Sister."

They embraced, she saying his name "Wei, it is you" over and over again. The joy did not last as the Baotu seized John John by the back of his neck, pulling the two apart. The powerful man slid the crook of an arm beneath John John's chin, pulling him in close, lifting him from his feet, trying to crush his windpipe, suffocate him.

Chan kicked at the Baotu, screaming, "Release him!" When the kicking proved futile, she picked up a rock and tried to bring it down on his head. She missed her target, landing a glancing blow on his thick neck.

John John's world was growing solitary and dark, blackness creeping into the sides of his vision, unconsciousness soon, followed by death. He tried repeatedly to drive his heels onto the top of the Baotu's foot to break the grip, but was missing with each strike, only a small puff of dust to show for each effort.

Suddenly, the grip was broken. John John was on the ground, the world returning, air rushing into his lungs, color coming back to his face. He rubbed the sore spot on his neck, turning to see his rescuers. Leo had led Mr. Chang, Mar, and

142

Charlie to his side. Mr. Chang held a pitchfork, its tines directed at the Baotu's throat, a look of determination on the old man's face. Mr. Chang had used the blunt end of the handle to jab the Baotu in the head. Its force had released John John, but the giant had now scooped up Chan, who wiggled and fought his grip. The Baotu sneered at the group in contempt, a red welt shining out from the side of his head. He shouted to the whores to return to their den. They ran off obediently and he backed away slowly, clenching Chan tightly, retreating to Dai Lao's stronghold.

John John teetered onto his feet, faint, lightheaded. Mar and Charlie steadying him. His weak voice uttering, "take me back. I need to speak to Charles Reed."

Reed stood again in front of the black double doors. This time he didn't even have to knock. The ancient woman opened both doors, light spilling out from the crowded interior. The aged face, impassive, stood aside, granting passage. The sound of many voices raised in anger halted, these strange foreign words hushing in a final echo that evaporated into nothingness – all eyes silently on him now.

Reed was expected, the unwanted *gwai lo* customer seeking an answer to his whore's fate, willingly stepping into the rat hole, incense and the stench of opium filling the air. Gaslights burned their reddish hue as Reed walked a narrow path surrounded by sallow faced miners and laborers, each holding various weapons – knives, short swords, and hatchets. They began thumping them to their chests in angry displays, their voices rising, bitter Chinese words hissed out at Reed who ignored them, not caring to understand. His business was with their boss, the bastard at the back of the room.

John John had tried to stop him from going, but he could not be deterred. He needed to know that Chan was alive and he could only do that by walking this path, through this slit in an enraged crowd. He kept his head up, unrushed in his determination to reach the back of the den. He found fat Dai Lao reclining on a couch, his long bamboo pipe extended above an oil lamp, heating the sticky tar like substance that he pulled deep into his lungs. His skull cap was off, displaying a massive forehead, half shaven to the top of his head, no eyebrows, a long braided pony tail running down the length of his spine. He wore a black changshan shirt that resembled a smock, along with baggy black trousers that stopped halfway down his shins, exposing a few inches of hairless yellow skin, then white socks and black slippers. One fat leg was crossed over the other, the top foot bobbing up and down in endless repetition, oblivious to its own motion. Reed had seen others before, so opium afflicted that they would begin scratching imaginary itches, obsessively scraping a cheek until they had opened a hole in their face. Dai Lao wasn't there yet, but that time was not far off.

The Baotu loomed beside Dai Lao, standing, arms crossed in opposition, Chan curled up at his feet. Reed's eyes met hers, scared but still defiant.

Dai Lao chuckled at seeing Reed, saying in his broken English, "You know she is mine, not yours."

"You may own her, but her heart is with me."

"Should I cut it out and give it to you?" the fat face replied, rippling with laughter.

"You've seen my offer. I can buy her from you. It's been done before. We can agree to it now. Name your price."

"It amuses me to see the white man so weak, humbled and unable to have his way. We have done much for America, but now life is harder. Look at my people, miners, ditch diggers, railroad workers – how ungrateful – their labor builds this country."

"Not much of a life, working played out mines and abandoned claims, contract labor you hire out, pocketing the wages. No wonder they're all homesick, crawling deeper into the pipe. Does anyone ever pay off their debt, the ship passage, interest, and all the other expenses thrown in that keeps them bound to you?" Reed asked.

Dai Lao waved a dismissive hand. "Their fate is like Chan's – in my hands. They have no choice but to settle their debt. Their labor is mine, like you say, mining, ditch digging, or even prostitution – they do the work I say. It may be a meager peasant's life, working for these crumbs, but sitting here, on top of it all, I have no complaints," he chuckled again, dragging more toxic vapor into his lungs.

"I don't doubt life is good for you and those you reward," Reed said, staring at the Baotu. "Too bad few in this room speak English. They don't know a better life exists beyond your control. We fought a Civil War and now you're the new slaveholder." Reed looked around the toxic den, "But it will all come to an end. Look at you. You're more beholdin' to the pipe than they are, more so everyday. It will be your master soon enough."

Dai Lao scoffed at the suggestion. "How we live and what we do, our customs," he said, holding up the pipe, "is none of your concern. The powerful have their roles and the weak accept their position," he nudged Chan in her back, tapping her with his bouncy foot for emphasis. "Chinese people are used to this arrangement. It is the way of the Hip Yee Tong." He then said something in Chinese to the Baotu, who dragged Chan to her feet with a gasp, spinning her back to Reed. The Baotu seized her collar with both hands, tearing the garment in half to her waist, exposing her back.

Dai Lao laughed at the Chinese characters now tattooed onto Chan's back, black ink harshly contrasting with her fine skin. "Allow me to translate, Mr. Reed. The calligraphy is quite good. It says 'prostitute, whore' and that is what she is and all she will ever be. You see, the world is full of people but America is not so full of Chinese and may never be again, especially women. Even though she has been touched by the white devil, she now is a scarce commodity, valuable. With far more Chinese men to women, it will be just a matter of time before my countrymen forget Chan's sullied past with you. Perhaps, a week of no payment required will spur business for her flesh."

Anger boiled up in Reed, "Kidnap women off the streets, hold them against their will. It's what you would expect from a Pig Face."

The jovial sadism was replaced by anger. He violently slammed the long bamboo pipe onto a table, shattering glass, scattering other paraphernalia. "Do not insult me with that offensive name. In this part of Chinatown, I rule. Chan will learn humility and obedience to me. Go, Mr. Reed, our meeting is complete. Chan is not for sale to you and never will be. Her body is not her own. I will tell her how to use it. She is

146

no longer a white man's toy."

Reed had run out of options. Drawing his gun would do no good. Both he and Chan would be cut to pieces. He knew it was over for now, but hated the thought of leaving Chan in this place, hating himself for his inability to free her now from this bondage.

Dai Lao spoke, "Last time I say this, go while you can. We both know I cannot kill you. Despite the white man's loathing for the Chinese, he allows us to rule our own communities so long as we display sufficient compliance. Your death would draw unwanted attention from the authorities, but I can certainly have you thrown out in a most painful way."

Dai Lao spoke again, rapidly in Chinese. The Baotu moved toward Reed, while other lackeys crowded in, their voices rising. Reed cast a last look at Chan. Their eyes met briefly. In that moment, he tried to send a message of hope and courage – that this was far from over. Reed was then pulled away from Chan, pushed in between two picket lines of Dai Lao's minions. He was shoved and bounced from one side to the other, back toward the doors. He struggled to remain upright. Finding his balance, he began to carve his own pathway out. Dai Lao's scum jabbed him with the hilts of their knives and swords with each step. Reed then felt the point of a blade prick his ribs, another into his back, stinging nicks that caused him to wince. He saw more hatchets poised above his head, waving menacingly, threatening blows that would cleave his skull wide open. He endured it all, walking now in an unhurried step, reaching the ancient woman who flung open the black doors. He crossed its threshold, finding sanctuary in the street. The thick doors slammed shut, followed by the clang of a heavy iron bolt sliding into place. Reed moved into the darkness, back to The Golden Star of Shanghai, consumed by one thought, freeing Chan.

As he passed the corner of a brick building, a small gap in the tightly constructed street, John John emerged from the shadows. "I could hear the uproar out here."

Reed minced no words, "We need to take Chan by force and we need to do it soon. I've got a few ideas."

"A plan is already in motion. Mr. Chang is gathering men and arms. They are already drilling by the light of the laundry. Willis is retrieving Mr. Boggs."

"We're going to need everyone and we're going to have to find a way through those heavy doors."

John John nodded, "Mr. Chang has an idea how to gain entrance."

"Keep an eye on the building. We can't allow Pig Face to move her without us knowing."

"It is being done."

"I'm sorry it's come to this, J.J."

"Do not be sorry, Charles. My sister, Dai Lao, a tong war is inevitable. Nothing can stop it now."

Foresthill, California 1883

"You got anything else to eat," McGirt asked Rance Mueller, as he and the Dutchman finished off the remaining venison jerky.

"You done ate all I got," Rance protested, annoyed at how quickly the chewy meat had vanished. "Didn't you two pack any vittles on your ride? I can hardly fill my own belly, let alone your two big mouths."

Rance immediately knew he had put his hand too close to the fire. McGirt stood, his eyes cross, "You shut the hell up. You should be happy to have our company, livin' here like you do, some used up old prospector. Can't hardly believe you was once an outlaw, riding with them early toughs."

"Give me more of that whiskey in that jug," the Dutchman demanded.

Rance hesitated, picking up the jug. He wanted the liquor for himself, but the weight of the jug was such that there was barely a shot glass worth remaining. He relented, walking the jug to the Dutchman, who removed the cork, upending the contents down his throat. Rance could tell the Dutchman was upset with only one swallow and that more couldn't be pulled from the jug.

"You've got more? get it," he slurred.

"I ain't got more. Dadburnit, you eat all my jerky and drink all my whiskey and still want more. You need to go into town if you want more," Rance declared, taking another stand.

"We ain't goin' to town. You are," McGirt ordered, throwing a pouch of gold coins to Rance, who fumbled them onto the floor. His leg bones cracked like matchsticks when he bent over to pick up the pouch.

Rance ogled the coins, "That's more gold than I've seen in a while."

"You're goin' into town to get us horses," McGirt said. "We need good ones because when we leave, we'll need to make a fast getaway."

"This is for what you done in the North Bloomfield Mine?"

Rance ventured. "The Nevada County Sheriff is lookin' for you. They say you done killed a man named Akins and maimed others with a water monitor. People know it was no accident."

"Forget about them troubles, they're over. We're on to somethin' else. You're goin' to help us to rob the payroll to the North Bloomfield Mine. It's comin' through from the San Francisco Mint just like it always does." McGirt looked to the Dutchman, reminding him that "we used to meet and escort it half the way from Marysville to the front gate. Them guards don't know nothin' about any accident at the mine and even if they did, we can wear masks," he decided. "People look away when you point a gun at them. None of them guards will give us any trouble. They ain't goin' to stand up to our hard stares," he said, smiling at the ease of the plan.

"Do not forget the first problem we need to take care of," the Dutchman reminded.

"I ain't forgot," McGirt snapped.

"What else you plannin'?" Rance asked.

"There's a man in Auburn we aim to kill. We'll do it quickly and move on to the payroll. If every county sheriff in the state wants to saddle up after us, so be it. Murder, robbery, don't matter how much offendin' we do. They still have to catch us and they can only hang us once," McGirt said with malevolent laugh.

"You fixin' to kill that Reed fella for puttin' that mark on your head," Rance gushed, tapping his own forehead at having figured it out.

"Shut up, shithead. I don't need any more back talk from a billy goat like you. You do what we say and get used to it.

Fetch us them horses. We head out tomorrow. Any money left, use it to buy more food and liquor for tonight," McGirt ordered. He issued a final warning. "You get to town and you get back here. I don't want you sittin' in a saloon drinkin' the day away, spillin' to people what we just talked about. You get back here fast, understand?"

Rance understood, but his wily mind still planned on a good soaking atop a stool. These two desperados, holed up here, would never know if he stopped momentarily to take in his cure.

Rance said, "I'll get the horses, but while I'm away, you two need to earn your keep. I want you to dig a new outhouse pit. Between the three of us, the darn thing is filled up."

McGirt wrinkled his nose. "You're outta your mind, old fool. I bet you dug that pit when you got here thirty years ago. That's all you out there," he said, jerking a thumb over his shoulder toward the shithouse. "Ain't none of us is stayin' once we light on outta this shanty. That includes you, 'cause you're now a part of the gang."

"Well, if I'm part of the gang, you can at least do somethin' other than drinkin', eatin' and shittin' while I'm away," Rance groused, treading into a new area of annoyance. "You two need to quit usin' my Farmer's Almanac I got on a hook out there. You boys usin' it and throwin' it into the pit before I ever get a chance to read it."

The Dutchman had heard enough, "Maybe we upend you into the pit. Stick your face in it so you can read it now, eh? That's what we do to welcome new gang members."

Rance, backing up, "I'm just sayin' that's my readin' when I empty my bowels. Goin' to be down to just my catalog soon enough. You don't understand what it's like livin' by yerself for years. A person gets set in his ways."

McGirt said, "Forget your almanac and catalog, get some ears of corn. We can eat 'em and put the cobs in the privy. Use those instead. Besides, I told you we was leavin'.'"

"I'm through with corn cobs," Rance said, exasperated, mumbling in a low voice, "they don't agree with me."

"I'm done with you, old man. You need to get into that outhouse now and read ahead if you want to know what's on them pages," McGirt advised. "By the time we rob that payroll and get outta here, you'll be so rich that you can use greenbacks to wipe your ass," he said with a grin.

Auburn, California 1883

"Do not trespass into this lodge of sin," Jasper Fanch implored from atop a wooden box positioned in front of The Golden Star of Shanghai. "Demon whiskey, the firewater of the Devil himself, shall cast you into his bosom, poisoning the Lord's spirit that lives within you. Lucifer's embrace will steal your very soul, denying to you all that is wholesome and worthy in a life schooled in the truths of the Bible," he proclaimed, holding the holy tome aloft for emphasis. Less than a dozen followers waved their picket signs up and down in support. A few other onlookers stopped and then went back to their business, unmoved by the sermon, having heard it many times before. The signage "Help Me Keep Him Pure" and "Mother or the Saloon?" were slogans that had worn off long ago. With the last "amens" called out, the Fanch temperance stump speech reached station, boiler cooling, engine losing steam.

Mildred gushed to Jasper, "Wonderful, as always dear." She celebrated by reaching into her purse for her medicine, swallowing two mouthfuls of laudanum. She repeated the ritual daily, two mouthfuls in the morning, two when Jasper started a speech and two at the end. Several more swigs would follow, depending on how the day unfolded from church until sundown. Along with Jasper, it provided Mildred with the strength to soldier on in the Army of the Lord.

Two men in dark suits and wide-brimmed hats had watched the demonstration with indifference, seeing it wind down and break up. "That temperance talk is sure findin' its way into every town. I thought Marysville was the only place afflicted," one said to the other.

The two crossed the street and entered The Golden Star of Shanghai. Willis Connelly nodded from behind the bar, asking the gents, "What can I get you?"

Both men said "beer" and Willis obliged.

"Let me know what you think," Willis said. "It's a new steam beer from Sacramento."

They sipped and nodded approval. "Say, barkeep? I don't know your name?"

"Connelly, Willis Connelly."

"Mr. Connelly, you wouldn't happen to know the fellow that owns this establishment, Mr. Charles Reed? My name is George Cadwalader and this here is another George, George Ohleyer. We've come from Marysville and we're hoping to have a word with Mr. Reed. That is if it's convenient?"

"I heard of you fellas. You're from the Anti-Debris

Association. I've seen your names in the newspapers, tryin' to stop all them slickens from washin' out your farms."

"That we are," George Ohleyer said, taking another quaff.

George Cadwalader explained, "You see, we're planning to visit the North Bloomfield Mine, guests of the president, Mr. Lester Robinson. We heard Mr. Reed was recently a guest there, too. We were hoping to have a word with him. Ask him what he saw, those he met. If it's not too much trouble?"

"I was out there myself with Charlie. Helluva hole they got out there, mighty impressive. You'd think God himself had a hand makin' a mark that big in the earth."

"If you owned a farm or lived in the valley below, you'd think it more the work of the Devil," George Cadwalader rebutted.

Willis scrunched his face, "Everyone is talkin' too much about the Devil these days. We lay the problems of the world at his hoofed feet, invoking his name. You'd think he was causing all our woes, but I ain't ever seen him about. Figure he doesn't exist. The problem is with *people* who act like the Devil, mostly out of selfishness and greed."

Both Georges digested Willis's brand of western wisdom with a no argument nod and a shrug.

"So you've been able to see the mine yourself?" George Ohleyer asked, "past all the guards?"

"I did indeed. Why don't you fellas hold your britches. Let me see if I can get Reed, so we can all talk this out once. He's a busy man at the moment, but I reckon he's up for a bit of speakin, seein' as you come all the way up the hill from Marysville."

"That would be splendid, Mr. Connelly," George

Cadwalader said.

Willis walked through the back and into an office, where Reed and John John were deep in discussion, John John taking notes in Chinese, while Reed wrote his own in English.

Reed looked to Willis, "Fanch still out there pounding on his Bible?"

"They wandered off a while ago. The devoted is gettin' smaller each day, down to just them older lady folks."

"Mildred still drinking from her purse?" Reed said, shaking his head. "We've got nothing that strong behind the bar."

"All them ladies sure do like to imbibe in their *medicine*, though Mildred seems the most touched. I've seen the druggist make it for her. He's got to sweetin' it up with sherry wine or port to cut all the opium bitterness. Puts in some cloves and cinnamon too."

"What do you need?"

"Two fellas from Marysville like to speak with you. They're the two that lead the Anti-Debris Association. Say they got an invitation from your friend, Mr. Robinson, to pay a call on the North Bloomfield Mine. Curious to know what's out there, what to expect," Willis explained.

Reed looked to John John, "We good?"

John John nodded "yes" and moved from the room.

"Bring 'em back, Willis."

Reed stood and shook each man's hand as they were introduced. Along with Willis, the four took seats around the office table.

"The leaders of the Anti-Debris Association, a farmer and its lead attorney," Reed said as he looked to each man. "Willis says you're invited to the North Bloomfield Mine."

"That's correct, Mr. Reed," George Ohleyer began. "Litigation is moving through Judge Sawyer's federal court and, well, everyone in the state is awaiting the verdict that will decide the fate of California."

George Cadwalader spoke succinctly, "As you know, our case rests on the principle that no man in his pursuit of wealth has the right to destroy the property of another."

"Yes, more farmland than ever," Reed said. "Those fields and fruit trees make for a prettier sight than what you're going to find out at the diggins."

"That is exactly our point, Mr. Reed," Cadwalader exclaimed. "Will we have a lush garden for many Californians or will we degrade the land into a cesspool for the beneficence of a few, wealthy mine owners, tycoons, many of whom live outside the state? We've court orders and injunctions in place that should have stopped hydraulic mining years ago. The debris and brush dams aren't a solution. They're just a miner's ruse. It's plain to anyone with eyes that these structures are deficient, overwhelmed, collapsing, with nuisance debris leaking from and spilling over their tops. Any talk of compromise, of the miner's building a new debris dam in the Yuba narrows that will solve all of this is treasonous. We will not drop our litigation in favor of dams that simply do not work and will never protect the valley."

Ohleyer picked up where Cadwalader ended, "We're all well aware that the hydraulickers continue to mine unabated, openly defiant of the county and state court rulings that aren't being enforced. We believe the miners are overconfident with regards to the pending litigation before Judge Sawyer. An offer to tour the mine is another manifestation of their arrogance."

"They're proud of what they're doing out there. It's quite ingenious, but I agree with you, it's not like they're doing this for everyone's benefit," Reed conceded.

"Crystal clear water above the mines reduced to cloudy silt, a brew unfit for drinking or irrigation, even the salmon are dying out having to swim in it. Slickens and tailings filling the valley and riverbeds, making flooding ever more likely and more destructive. Did you know that the riverbed just east of Marysville is now fifteen feet higher than the surrounding farmland? It gets worse as you move further up the Yuba River and closer to the North Bloomfield Mine – twenty-six feet higher at Daguerre Point, an astounding *eighty-four* feet higher at Smartsville." Cadwalader shook his head appalled at the state of affairs. "Only the smallest boats can now make portage from San Francisco to Sacramento and on to Marysville. Steamboat Slough is filled up with debris, navigation impossible. Everything must move by wagon or by the greedy hands of the railroads. The boatmen no longer have the rivers to move crops or any other freight. Their livelihoods are affected too, just like the farmer."

Ohleyer added, "I came to California as a prospector and, like many others, I'm now a farmer. We did well early tilling the land, but once the big hydraulic mines started up, we've been inundated with more destructive floods every year. The floods of '75 were very bad, eight feet of water and mud in the streets of Marysville, a little boy drowned, livestock too. We've built levees to wall in the city and fields, building them higher each year and they're still not high enough. Where does it end, I ask you?"

"I hear you. No one minds a prospector digging out all the

gold he finds, but he sure as hell doesn't need to drop the whole hill down on everyone while he does it," Reed sympathized.

"I make plenty of stage and teamster runs," Willis said. "I've seen James Keyes place. He raised his house four feet, then six feet and still got buried in muck. Just the peak of his roof shows now, along with the tops of his dead orchards. Trees stickin' knee high out of the ground, lookin' like dry brush."

"Thousands of acres – fertile farmland, orchards, and pasture poisoned by slickens – hard compacted sand and gravel, no good to anyone," Ohleyer said in dismay. "Debris is killing the rivers and the land. Keyes is just one of many abandoned farms. George Briggs gave up fifty-eight thousand fruit trees when he threw in and moved south to escape the floods and not one mine gave him a dime for all the trouble they caused him. The same for Edwards Woodruff, our plaintiff in the Sawyer suit, his farm, seventeen hundred acres, ruined too." Ohleyer sat back in his chair, "And despite all of this, California is producing almost sixty million bushels of wheat this year. Think what we could achieve without these troubles?"

"The steam combine is making farmers even more productive. Hundreds of ships now sail the world selling California crops to far off markets. Shipping agents move wheat from San Francisco and brokers sell it an hour or so before it reaches port in Liverpool or Antwerp." Cadwalader let the fact sink in before dropping his ace card, "California now earns twice as much through agriculture than we do through mining, even *with* all these nuisances."

"It's a tidy sum, alright," Reed said. "You have my sympathies and support. I'm acquainted with Mr. Robinson and his chief engineer, Hamilton Smith. I don't know that you can call either of them bad. They're just doing what they know how to do. Don't make it right, but it's the world we live in until Judge Sawyer decides."

"Quite right, Mr. Reed," Cadwalader said. "May he rule wisely."

"And if he doesn't?" Willis asked.

Ohleyer sat grimly for a moment, "We've called upon our young men and formed the Anti-Debris Guard. Not just in Marysville but Sacramento too. We've provided uniforms with blue sashes, symbolizing that the water must run free and clear of sediment."

"Sacramento."

"Yes, like Marysville is captive to hydraulic mines on the Yuba, Bear, and Feather rivers, so too is Sacramento with the American and its namesake river. Sacramentans want an end to the incessant floods and turbid water plaguing them too. They've even built holding pools for drinking water, hoping the silt would settle to the bottom and clear. Days go by and the water never clears. They then tried building a so-called sanitary water pipe, but shut it down when people drinking from it were poisoned by lead in the pipe."

"I've spoken to the volunteers," Cadwalader said earnestly. "Our numbers grow each day the miners persist with their outrageous actions. We're prepared to take up arms to defend our natural and lawful rights to our own property."

Reed looked to Willis, who gave a nod of ascension. "Let me tell you about the North Bloomfield Mine, some things to look for. First, get there early. I don't mean going to the mine's front gate and introducing yourselves. You've got to go in using the back door through Humbug Creek. That's where all of the debris is being discharged from the mine. Better you get this look-see before you get led on an *official* tour of the diggins."

"We've heard of holding pools and a small lake and dam within the mine to capture debris," Cadwalader said.

"L.L. and Hamilton Smith will gladly show you these when they lead you on a tour. They'll explain how the lake and dam are holding back the larger, coarse debris, allowing for the sediment to settle, before it's pushed out of the mine, but you know for yourselves none of it is true," Reed said, looking to both men.

Reed continued, "The brush dams outside the mine don't work and neither does the one inside. There's far too much earth being moved for these remedies to provide relief. Your own numbers on the rise of the riverbed bear this out. All manner of debris is dropped from escape boxes in the flumes and sluices. Everything is moving out from their lake, over the spillway and into the tunnel. It all washes down a number of vertical shafts to the mile-and-a-half long tunnel located deep in the bedrock below. You do know of the drainage tunnel?"

"It has been mentioned in testimony to the state legislature and during court proceedings and has taken on a mythical status."

"Yeah, they're proud of it, a major engineering feat, I don't doubt. Point is, just get yourselves to the end of the tunnel, where it flows into Humbug Creek. There's a full head of unrestrained water there, discharging all matter of debris. It's the nuisance material that's clogging the riverbeds, overflowing brush dams, and ruining your fields and towns."

Willis added, "There's a trail where Humbug Creek flows into the South Fork of the Yuba. You boys need to get there early and walk up it. The trail follows Humbug Creek all the way up to the mine. You'll get an eyeful when you see the commotion at the end of the tunnel. You've never seen a bigger rush of muck in your entire life. Like Charlie says, get a gander and you'll see for yourself where all your troubles begin."

George Ohleyer looked to George Cadwalader. Ohleyer spoke, "Thank you Mr. Reed and Mr. Connelly. We're grateful for your advice and we certainly intend to heed it."

"Mr. Robinson is expecting to meet us at noon in two days," Cadwalader imparted. "I would wager a considerable amount that the tunnel is running at peak capacity before our arrival. An early surprise inspection, before we make our presence known, is very much called for."

"Good luck, gentlemen," Reed said, standing, offering his hand.

"And to you, Mr. Reed," Cadwalader said in return. "We are indebted to your help and appreciate your candor."

"Will everything be ready by tomorrow?" Reed asked John John as they observed men drilling with spears and swords. Mr. Chang led the men, who were separated into three groups based upon the weapon they held.

"Mr. Chang is doing his best and pledges the men will be ready."

"Who would have thought old Mr. Chang would be a…what did you call it?"

"*Jianke*, professional swordsman, master of martial arts."

Reed shook his head in wonder, "What else don't I know about him?"

J.J. raised an eyebrow, "He fought as a colonel for the Han during the Taiping Rebellion. Before that, he studied as a Zen Buddhist monk at the Shaolin Monastery."

"A monk and a warrior, some combination," Reed said. "Chan told me about the rebellion and its aftermath – famine, plague, lawlessness, the reason why so many Chinese fled to America. She said it lasted fifteen years and ended sometime during our own Civil War. We thought ours was bad but this was far worse, millions of people dead. Some say the worst war ever."

"It was a very difficult time. In some ways, we fight the rebellion again. Dai Lao is Manchu," J.J. spit, "part of the Qing Dynasty that ruled China, very corrupt, venal leaders. They used opium to enslave the Chinese masses to strengthen their rule. The Heavenly Kingdom army was briefly successful disposing of the Qing, but it too proved to be equally inept, losing support of the people and sowing division when it attacked Chinese customs, Buddhist and Confucian values. They too knew only the ways of brutal militarism and nothing about building a society through civil administration."

"So you traded one bad leader for another?"

"Yes and the country descended into chaos. Mr. Chang fought the flag gangs that rose up, bandits who plundered temples, towns and villages, as civilization crumbled. He grew weary of battle, fleeing China for America as our land grew more hopeless."

J.J. looked to Reed, "It is why I came to California too – *Gum San* – Gold Mountain. Even with the passage of time, opportunity in China is poor. I say this even though Chan and I were born to successful parents, who befriended the English, building ties and trade, moving from the Kowloon Peninsula to Hong Kong. My success in California has allowed me to send money back to my parents, who have used it to further grow our family businesses. They no longer sell and export just tea and silk. They have expanded into jewelry – jade, pearls, and fine porcelain."

"How come you never told me about your sister?"

"We are a reticent people, Charles. A wall divides our cultures, even though our partnership is successful, I do not wish to burden others with the problems of myself or clan. Needless to say, over the past months, I have enlisted the aid of others in the search for Chan. I learned of her abduction months after it occurred, when a message arrived from our parents. Through agents and friends, I learned a woman fitting Chan's description was auctioned in the flesh dens of San Francisco. I believed she was still there. The Chinese community is large in the city, secretive, many doors barred based upon family and allegiances. To learn she is captive just down the street, a prisoner of Pig Face, is one of life's surprises."

"And that your partner is in love with her," Reed added.

J.J. remained stone-faced, still considering the reality – its implications.

They stood silently for a moment. J.J. broke the silence, "If you say it is so, the truth from your heart, I believe you. Why else would you do so much to free a woman? I know, to you,

Chan is not merely a prostitute, an object, but something more – a person to treasure, someone to sacrifice for. Freeing her will not be easy. Many will be hurt, even killed, but I am grateful we do this together."

"It's a fight you're not going to keep me out of. Were you able to get the chests of opium?"

J.J. nodded, "Yes, arrived from Sacramento this morning. Thank you for the money and the idea. The balls of dope are being distributed quietly, individually to Dai Lao's men, who are greedily snatching them up."

"Good. It should soften them up before we all square off in the streets tomorrow."

Nearby, Reed and J.J. watched Mr. Chang decapitate a straw man, demonstrating the proper technique of wielding the *jian*, the long double-edged sword, King of Weapons. He expertly twirled it over his head, the steel flashing with blinding speed, striking its mark, an extension of the man, returning to his side in proper defensive posture, balanced repose, ready to lash out again.

J.J. said, "Mr. Chang may not be one of the legendary Ten Tigers of Canton, but he is well-versed in their teachings. He is happy to extract this revenge on Dai Lao and the hated Qing Dynasty, who attacked and burned the Shaolin Monastery to the ground." J.J. gestured to Mr. Chang, who sprinted the short distance to both he and Reed.

"Mr. Chang, J.J. has been telling me all about your story. I appreciate all you're doing to help us free Chan."

Mr. Chang's grasp of English was halting. J.J. translated Reed's words. Mr. Chang replied with a short bow and a rapid string of words, staccato bursts of Chinese.

J.J. interpreted, "He says, he is an old man, and learned much over a lifetime. He is pleased with the men's progress and relishes one more chance to do battle with the Qing."

"What's that on his arms and chest? Some kind of armor? Looks like fish scales."

J.J. spoke to Mr. Chang, who replied, explaining the intricacies of its design.

J.J. said, "paper armor, many layers, joined in an elaborate pattern with cloth, silk, and cotton. Supple, very light weight but deceptively strong. A modern bullet can penetrate, but it will offer excellent protection from blades, arrows, and other blows." J.J. added to Mr. Chang's explanation, "Taoism teaches that the soft overcomes the hard. Paper absorbs and disperses a blow through its many fibers better than any single hard metal plate."

Mr. Chang spoke again.

J.J. translated, "He says he will moisten the paper before we fight. The water will make the armor even stronger."

"How does the colonel feel about our strategy for getting into Dai Lao's place? Those are some heavy doors."

J.J. and Mr. Chang spoke. Chang's pace of words slower, deliberate, growing more hushed as they spoke. Reed could tell there was something he was not going to hear, a secret to the plan.

J.J. again, "The plan is a good one. As the groups engage, we should be evenly matched. There will be much taunting and posturing before the battle begins, insults made to test each other's courage. When the fighting begins, the men will match up. We will stay hidden and race directly to the door, through the fight."

Mr. Chang pointed to Hai Lon, who twirled two butterfly knives.

Reed caught Hai Lon's eyes as he finished his demonstration, smiling. "He's as good with those knives as he is with cards."

J.J. pointed to Charlie One and Charlie Two, two large laundrymen, who were also identical twin brothers, saying, "Each will carry a large shield and they will use them to battering ram through anyone in our way, cutting a path to the entrance. Mr. Chang insists we must follow along closely and rapidly in their steps, as a tight group. Once at the door, they will defend the sides and Hai Lon and I will defend our backs."

"That leaves me and Mr. Chang facing the doors. We can't chop our way in with axes. Pig Face will have slit Chan's throat long before we can ever break through," Reed said, puzzled, "so how do we get in?"

J.J. and Mr. Chang spoke again in more measured, hushed tones. J.J. stating simply, "Mr. Chang knows a way through."

J.J. said this as if it were magic, as if Mr. Chang could turn himself into smoke and seep in through a tiny crack in the doors. Reed knew Mr. Chang was a monk and no genie, "So we have someone on the inside we can trust," Reed asked, "who will be at the door and open it when we get there?"

J.J., after a time, nodded to the obvious. "The same person who is seeing to it that all our surplus opium is now filling the pipes of Dai Lao's men."

"Okay, so we're in. I go straight for Chan, probably up the stairs in her room, you and Mr. Chang for Pig Face, Hai Lon, and Charlie One and Two follow us in and take on anyone in our way."

"Speed and surprise are most important," J.J. advised. "They will not account for a small force striking boldly into their den as the battle rages outside in the street."

"I'm not traditionally armed like you," Reed said, drawing his revolver and spinning it to a stop from finger to palm. "I plan to shoot anyone in my way. Once my revolver goes off in that closed space, I figure the sound alone will take the fight out of a lot of them. Take a bullet or recline back down into the comfort of a pipe. It'll be an easy choice for some, but maybe not all."

Auburn, California 2013

"The place is crowded. You think we can get in?" Jen asked me as I returned from inside The Auburn Alehouse.

"Ten, fifteen minutes, they'll text me when a booth opens up. Any sign of Kendra, Helmut, and Gregor?"

"I saw their motorhome drive by, up the street. They'll have to park it farther away since there's not much parking around here and they need a bigger space."

"Busy, isn't it?" I said looking up and down the streets of historic Old Auburn, Gold Rush era brick buildings housing small stores, boutiques, and restaurants – a bistro here, a beer hall there.

"Look there's Carpe Vino. It's a wine bar, supposed to have really good food. A lot of Bay Area people stop there on their way up the mountains. Four stars, so says Yelp."

"There they are," I pointed as Kendra and our newfound

168

German friends came into view.

"Dad, we've got to get one of those. They're so awesome inside, really sleek and modern."

"Another Yelp review," I said to Jen. "All for it, except for the price – start buying lottery tickets now. It'll take a Gold Rush strike to buy one, even a used one."

"I'd happily sell it to you, Tom, but you know we are only renting," Gregor said.

"I appreciate the offer, but let me buy you guys beer and dinner. It's the least I can do after you helped me out of my splash down in the tunnel."

"Thank you, Tom, Jen, that is very kind of you," Helmut said. "Interesting old town. We passed a Joss House up the street. It was closed, but an historic site. The marker out front said it is used by the Chinese community and that its altar dates back to the Gold Rush."

My phone made a quick buzz. "That's our text."

We wound our way inside to the hostess, a young woman, who led us to our booth. I saw a crowded bar and in the back, large stainless steel tanks behind glass, where the craft beer was brewed.

"I hear Gold Digger is a very good double IPA, but they've got everything – pale ales, red ales, imperial ales, stouts."

"What is an imperial ale?" Helmut asked.

"Triple hops, high alcohol, can be very bitter, need to check the IBU's," Jen answered.

"IBU's?"

"International Bitterness Units. It's a scale from one to a hundred. Hops create bitterness. You feel it on the back of the tongue. A lager is light and has five to ten IBUs, a blonde ale fifteen to thirty, and an India Pale Ale forty and way, way up," Jen said, showing off her beer expertise.

"Craft beer is now coming to Germany. Many English and Americans are opening taprooms, so we are not just lagers anymore. I think I will try a brewer's flight tasting," Helmut decided.

"Ja, I agree. I have been adjusting my palate to the bitterness, with pale ales and going up, but a flight is a good way to sample," Gregor added.

"Good choice, guys. Jen, Gold Digger IPA?"

Jen nodded.

"Me too. Sorry Kendra, a few more years."

"It's okay, Dad. I don't even like beer."

A pleasant waitress introduced herself and took our orders. The old brick building was doing brisk business, its high walls retrofitted with steel support beams, earthquake proof, bringing the old-time confines up to code. Large banners on the walls displayed beer label art work – Old Prospector Barleywine, Fool's Gold Pale Ale, Shanghai Stout, among others.

Jen said, "Were you two as fascinated on that hike as we were? The entire canyon was man-made. It's hard to believe they washed an entire mountain down that drain tunnel of theirs."

"We only stumbled through the old Hiller Tunnel, the little one," I said, looking to our German guests. "Can you imagine walking through the mile-and-a-half one further below that collapsed years ago?"

"Ja, working deep underground everyday. Es ist interesting to see the ghosts of such activity, even the vertical shafts that remain, filled in or still oozing waste wasser," Gregor said.

Kendra provided dimensions to the discussion, referencing more of her downloaded files. "'The North Bloomfield Gravel & Mining Company extracted $3.5 million in gold, while excavating 41 million yards of gravel and soil.' All of it flowed down the creek we hiked beside, all the way to the river and beyond."

"I wonder what that is in current dollars?" Jen asked and I was already working on it with my phone, finding an inflation calculator.

"One 1883 dollar is now worth almost $24. Three point five million dollars is…wow, over $83 million today."

Kendra said, "In the Nevada City Courthouse, there's supposed to be a mold on display to a 512 pound gold ingot that came from the mine. A second mold is located somewhere in The Ferry Building in San Francisco."

"Next time we get there, you and your mom can hunt for it while I stand in line at Blue Bottle Coffee. It'll give you plenty of time to find it," I said.

"I wonder what's it costing now to clean up the mess?" Jen speculated. "Forty-one million yards, laced with mercury, is a lot to clean up."

"Oh, it's much more than that Mom. This is just one mine among many." Kendra cleared her throat before reading, sitting up straight. "'On the Yuba River watershed 684 million cubic yards of debris were washed downstream by hydraulic mines. In comparison, 262 million cubic yards were excavated in the combined French-American effort to build the Panama Canal.'"

"No wonder why Marysville and Sacramento were building

so many levees with all of that pouring down. Yuck," Jen said.

"I read somewhere that Marysville was supposed to be the New York City of California. Instead it became a walled in city, unable to grow because of the flooding and debris," Helmut added.

"That small Podunk town we drove through? New York City?"

"Ja, a financial and transport hub for the Sacramento Valley, using its waterways to San Francisco and on to international markets."

Kendra said, "When hydraulic mining was going on, over a foot of debris was filling San Francisco Bay every year. What is that over a hundred-fifty plus miles away? The scale of this is off the charts."

Our waitress returned with our food, plates balanced up and down her arm.

Helmut said, "We have been looking things up too. We read that during the Gold Rush, 26 million pounds of mercury was used to retrieve the gold, with ten to thirty percent of it lost downstream into the rivers. I don't know that I told you, but I am a chemist. All of this mercury forms into methyl-mercury. It concentrates into phytoplankton eaten by fish. Large fish eat smaller fish and creates much higher levels of toxicity. To this day, people must be very careful when catching and eating fish."

Our waitress, overhearing, said, "You're talking about mercury? Yeah, people still worry about that around here because of all the mining. We have a doctor who stops by. He's on the water board. He told me how they've partnered with The Sierra Fund to dredge Combie Lake. They're removing mercury before it reaches the downstream reservoirs that hold all our drinking water."

"So people are still working on the problem, long after the Gold Rush?" Jen asked.

"I don't know all the details," the waitress said, "but Bear River flows into Combie Lake and with each storm more legacy mercury is released. They've got a big machine that dredges all the sediment going into the lake, separating mercury and other heavy metals from the water and properly disposing of it. Some huge amount is being dredged. It'll expand the lake for more water storage, which we need with the drought, but he also said, as they separate the poisonous heavy metals, they're collecting gold. Once they finish up at Combie, they'll move on to other nearby lakes and rivers."

"Hopefully, the gold will defray some of the cost," I said. "So you've lived in the area long?"

"Local girl, born and raised. I've hiked about every trail between here and Lake Tahoe. I used to ski, but with so little snow the past few years, the season has been short to non-existent. It just doesn't seem to get as cold anymore. Snows only at the highest elevations. I was hiking Castle Peak, near Donner Summit in January and there were just patches of snow on the ground. That time of year, there should've been ten feet of snow all around. I'm almost," she covered her mouth with her hand, mumbling her age for no one to hear, then silently holding up five digits on one hand and a thumb index finger "0" with the other, "years old and I've never seen anything like it. Everyone is hoping for a big El Nino or even just an average rainfall year to help things out. Without the snow pack, we can't ski and the reservoirs and canals don't have the runoff to grow all the crops in the valley."

"What are the farmers doing about it?" Gregor asked.

"Let the ground go fallow or tear out fruit trees. Some are drilling deeper wells and pumping all the groundwater out, but what do you do when that runs out? Never mind the fact that all this pumping of groundwater is causing the Central Valley down south to sink a foot or more a year and who knows if the groundwater can ever return once the ground gets so compacted?"

"Pretty grim, but we appreciate hearing your local perspective. Anything you'd care to recommend as we pass through the area?"

"You're in the historic part of town now. This building goes way back. It used to be a restaurant called the The Shanghai, run by old Charlie Yue, who was a leader of the Chinese community, and later his sons. There's a picture of him in a piece of artwork behind the bar, across the street at Carpe Vino. Before that, this was a saloon, run by some gambler and his Chinese friend. Charlie worked here as a child."

She thought for a moment before saying, "If you want to see where it all started, just take Highway 49 toward Coloma. It's not too far. You'll come upon Sutter's Mill. It's where James Marshall discovered gold. The state parks have really improved it. It's worth a stop."

"TripAdvisor, four-and-a-half stars, 138 reviews," Kendra said, staring at her device.

"Thanks for the recommendation."

"You're very welcome. I hope you enjoy the rest of your trip. Can I top anyone off before I go?"

"Ja, this is wunderbar, the pilsner," Helmut said, pointing to one of his flight glasses. He reached into his pocket and tossed the Class B keys to Gregor. "Ja, a glass, bitte."

The evening moved on. We drank more beer and discussed a variety of topics, like places to see and things to do in Germany – how Berlin has shaken off its East German decay and where to find the best currywurst. We picked up on the earlier conversation with our waitress, the "what's the deal" exasperation with Americans to climate change and health-care? Agree, agree, the table signing on to a new global treaty and law in the span of two seconds. We tapped out with a debate on which sports organization is the most craven – soccer's FIFA or the International Olympic Committee? Jen proposed an American contender, the NCAA, billions of dollars in TV revenue, everyone getting rich but the players, who graduate without degrees and whose major study is staying *eligible*. Exhausted by each group's shortcomings, the debate ended in a draw.

The hour grew late, our energy waning, the conversation slowed to a standstill. Kendra broke the lull, "Helmut, Gregor, are you going to ask or do I have to?"

"Ask what?" I said.

Gregor spoke first, sheepishly, "We proposed this idea to Kendra on the drive over, but…" He stopped and looked to Helmut for an endorsement before proceeding.

Helmut replied with a "sure, why not ask" shrug of approval.

Gregor continued, "You see, we have a favor to ask."

Jen and I looked to each other. Jen said, "This is beginning to sound ominous."

"Oh, nein, not really. It's nothing illegal," Helmut said.

175

Gregor's face made a slight cringe in disagreement, "Well, technically, it sometimes is...depending where you do it."

Jen leaned forward, "Okay, I'm officially intrigued. What are you two talking about?"

Helmut sat up, and leaned forward over the table, his chin poised above scoured plates and empty glasses. He faced up squarely to Jen, melodramatically, their noses inches apart. He then side-eyed me with a look of faux seriousness fueled by multiple beers. He placed his hands lightly on the table, adding to the theatrics, "What do you know about BASE jumping?"

"Oh, my God, that is you," Jen gasped, as we gathered in the motorhome's plush interior. Gregor held his tablet up, playing the YouTube video for all to see. We watched transfixed, wind buffeting the audio with gusts sounding like blasts from a cannon.

Gregor was recording himself, speaking in German, a smile on his face, with his GoPro camera. The selfie ended when he pulled the camera back, flipping it around, placing it in his chest housing, so that we could share his visual point of view.

"What are you standing on?" Jen asked.

"A nacelle."

"A what?"

"Oh, you're on top of a windmill," Kendra said.

"A *wind turbine*," he smiled.

We watched him walk along the top of the nacelle, out to the hub, where the turbine blades met, the German country-side in the distance.

"Oh, my God, the blades are turning," Jen gasped again.

176

"The engineer turned the turbine off before we took der lift up the tower, but, ja, still moving," Gregor said.

We watched as Gregor made a right turn onto one of the huge propeller blades that was moving downward, approaching horizontal. I could only let out a brief chuckle at the brazenness.

"How high up are you?"

"Ninety-seven meters, just over 300 feet, not very high for a BASE jump."

The GoPro camera continued to provide Gregor's perspective as he moved step by step, walking out toward the tip of the blade as it slowly rotated. We watched as it went past horizontal and was now sloping down at an ever-increasing angle.

"Are you trying to make it out to the tip?"

He smiled a "we shall see" grin.

Our stomachs clutched as the blade's slant increased, steeper and steeper downward. Gregor's feet reached out in longer more rapid strides, his feet turning over quickly, darting in and out of view from the bottom of the screen, sprinting down a hill to nothingness. He managed one last desperate step near the tip, hurling himself in a dive away from the structure, before the blade's geometry made the decision for him. We watched the massive propeller blade fall away, the wind turbine's tower streaking by as Gregor's velocity increased, sunlight blinking on, off, and through its steel lattice. It was all happening so quickly, the camera filling with the lush greenness of a rapidly approaching Fatherland, details of the landscape sharpening – treetops, bushes, a man looking up and pointing, leaves rustling, blades of grass. For a few agonizing seconds, we watched before the pilot chute deployed, releasing the ram-air rectangular main chute, the camera jolting as the canopy snapped to attention, each of the nine air cells filling in resistance to the ground, a whoosh, a scream of delight, a massive rush of adrenaline for Gregor and for us. In just seconds he was on the ground, Helmut jogging toward him with a smile, a hearty slap on the back, end of video.

"What a gut-check," I said. "You two must be charter members of The Adrenaline Junkies Club."

Gregor and Helmut said simultaneously, "We hate that term."

I mumbled, "Sorry," renewing my tenderfoot patch for the next five years.

Jen, still wide-eyed, repeated "Oh, my God," over and over again, her fingertips to her mouth. "How do you do that? That's so dangerous."

"It happens so fast. There's no margin for error," I said, recovering from my faux pas.

"Ja, es ist difficult to jump from so low. I use a larger pilot chute so the ram-air chute opens faster."

"So no backup chute?"

"Es gibt keine Zeit."

Jen and Kendra looked to me for a translation, their faces turning in unison, as if they were tracking a tennis ball over a net from Gregor to me.

"Gregor says, 'There's no time.'"

"The biggest danger ist nicht der Boden," he said and then, pausing, finding the English words, "is not the ground." He continued, "Es ist the tower or whatever you are jumping from. If you have what ist called an off-heading opening, you can lose control and hit the tower so es ist very important to get clear and use your canopy skills to maintain a safe distance from the BASE object so you can make it safely to the ground."

"None of it looks 'safe' to me," Jen said. "Remind me what BASE stands for?"

"Buildings, antennas, spans like bridges, and earth, natural formations. We're diversifying with wind turbines," Gregor said, "but our next will be from a span, a bridge nearby."

"This must be where we come in?" Kendra asked.

"Ja, we need a ride," Helmut responded. "If you help out, we can both leap from the Auburn Bridge. Usually only one of us can jump because the other must be ready to drive, how do you say, getaway, since almost every BASE jump involves trespassing."

"I take it you didn't jump when you were in Yosemite National Park?" I asked.

"Two-thousand dollar fine and they will confiscate your equipment. So we just hiked up Half Dome instead. Though, it would be nice to be allowed to jump from El Capitan if only for a few days each year," Helmut lamented.

"I can see for a few days a year, especially if you're an expert," Jen agreed, "and it's a lot higher up than a windmill, I mean, wind turbine."

"El Cap ist 900 meters, about 3,000 feet, very high up," Gregor explained.

"The park service doesn't even allow a *leashed* dog to walk on *any* trail in *any* national park," I reminded Jen. "If man's best friend is shut out, BASE jumpers have no hope," I predicted.

"The Auburn Bridge ist nicht der national park," Gregor said. "Es ist the tallest bridge in California and the fourth highest in the states. Few people live in the area and traffic is very small on the bridge."

"You're right. There's a lot more tourists packed in Yosemite than around here. I grew up in the suburbs of Sacramento during the 1970s. Our school went on a field trip that drove over the bridge when it was new. My class toured what was going to be the site of the Auburn Dam, the dam that was never built. We heard all about the giant lake that would be formed by the dam and how the bridge would span the lake from Auburn to Foresthill. I remember our guide saying that the water level was supposed to be just a few feet below the bridge, but without the dam and lake, it's still a canyon gorge with the American River some 700 feet down below."

"Why did they not build the dam?" Helmut asked.

"They learned the dam site was on a major seismic fault line. My understanding is there's evidence that the massive weight of the water in a lake behind a dam can induce an earthquake." I stopped and recollected a dormant memory from years ago. "About 50 miles from here is the Oroville Dam. It's an earthen dam and the tallest in the U.S. I went there on another field trip. If I remember correctly, it was hit with a 5 or 6 magnitude earthquake and it spooked the geologists and engineers so much that construction was halted on the Auburn Dam. The experts thought the weight of Lake Oroville had caused its own fault line to slip. Arguments went back and forth and the funding dried up so no Auburn Dam, but the whitewater rafting is great."

"Interesting, Tom," Helmut said. "I must say, we are very

grateful to have met each of you on this holiday. You are good people and we are learning so much, making for a memorable holiday. Danke, to you, Jen and Kendra," he said with an appreciative nod to each of us.

"We've learned a lot from you guys, too," Jen said. "You've added a lot of spice to our outing."

"I am so ready for this," Kendra gushed, her eyes bright. "What do you want us to do?"

Helmut and Gregor explained their plan, which emphasized speed, get in and out quickly without a summons issued. Jen would drive the motorhome onto the bridge, the Teutonic Two along with Kendra would exit the back. Kendra, camera ready, would record the leap from the bridge, while Jen would drive on over the bridge, turn around and pick Kendra up on the return run. I would be stationed at the bottom, at river level, at the confluence of the North and Middle Forks of the American River, where Highway 49 and Old Foresthill Road meet. I would case the State Park Kiosk near the river for any rangers on duty and if all was clear, the jump would take place. I would record the event with my own camera, and then move the Honda from the State Park parking lot to a nearby spot across the river, where Old Foresthill Road intersected with the Confluence Trail. Helmut and Gregor would use their steering lines to glide their parachutes, landing on the Confluence Trail. They would then run a short distance down the trail to meet me. I would clear space in the back of the Honda as a hiding place. They could lie down and then be covered up with some of our camping gear. We would then speed away, rendez-vousing with Jen and Kendra, many thanks to Google Earth for all the street level views used in the planning of this operation.

"When is D-Day?" Jen asked, eager to go now, enthused to step away from our everyday conformity to bask in the excitement of a monkey wrenching moment, completely out of character.

I have to say, I, too, was thrilled at the prospect of this dash of chili powder spice enlivening our vacation feast.

"Tomorrow, around lunch time, when everyone, even rangers, like to eat," Gregor said with a wry smile.

Auburn, California 1883

J ohn John stood on the rooftop balcony of The Golden
Star of Shanghai, gazing out at the scene unfolding
below. He was flanked by Mr. Chang and Hai Lon,
with young Charlie Yue standing a step behind in deference to
the older men. J.J. looked on intently as his tong and that of
Pig Face faced off against one another in the street below. A
hum of many angry voices and the vibration of anxious
movements charged the air around them, tinder ready to ignite.
Sharp taunts rang out in challenge, a rapid-fire call of
Cantonese followed by a Mandarin response, escalating words
as both sides tried to intimidate the other – insults and
obscenities attacking one's tong, demeaning one's courage,
and crudely disparaging one's sexual prowess. The men were
packed tightly, some wearing tin helmets and shields, weapons
ready, thrusting *qiang* spears, *dao* sabers and *jian* swords
slicing the air. The overture for battle was in full fury,

beginning with a deadly ballet, chosen men alternating to and from the ranks, demonstrating each side's training and lethal skills. It was an elaborate prelude to the impending melee. Crimson rivers would soon surge into the street, spurting forth from severed veins and arteries. In the aftermath, the dusty street would soak up the gore. Bloody trails would dry and darken, laced together in an intricate web of pools and tributaries staining the ground. It would form a battle map – detailing each man's struggle and marking those whose fate would meet with mortal misfortune.

The tongs had drawn onlookers. A large contingent of town residents had gathered in ever-deepening rows at the outskirts of the plaza, spectators awaiting the clash as if it were a horse race.

John John spoke, "Charlie, bring Charles Reed here now, quickly."

A brief moment passed and Charlie was back with Reed, Willis, and J.C. Boggs, their eyes on the storm brewing below.

"I haven't seen so many people in Auburn since we had our last hangin'," J.C. recollected. "Seems fitting to be fighting in the same spot we strung Jim Freeland up for murder. That was way back in '56, when I fitted him up with a California collar." He looked up at the high sun, dabbing the back of his neck with a kerchief. "It was a hot day then, too."

"The townsfolk are placing wagers," Willis said. "They say Dai Lao has too many men. He can't be beaten."

"Well, we know that ain't true," Reed said in a determined voice.

Mr. Chang spoke. The men patiently waited for him to complete his thoughts, the white men attentive to the unknown words, hearing in its tone and cadence sagacity combined with an iron will.

J.J. translated, "Mr. Chang says 'a smaller, more dedicated force can overcome a larger army.' He says, 'See for yourself, Dai Lao's tong has smoked all of the opium we have spread through their ranks. They move sluggishly, many standing off in the back, leaning on posts and walls, in the shade. They are empty sacks of flesh with no backbone, merely drawing breath. They will flee, thinking only of themselves once the battle is joined.'"

The men saw what Mr. Chang meant. J.J.'s tong owned most of the street. They were the more aggressive group, passionate and active, despite being outnumbered 2 to 1.

Mr. Chang spoke again, J.J. looked to him, translating, "'Our fighting spirit is strong and our men and weapons move constantly with speed and daring.'"

J.C. took in the scene again, leaning out over the balcony rail for a better look. "Yeah, I agree. We got the tougher bunch." He looked up smiling, "That's why I put a $100 down on us to kick their ass."

"Helps to offer a bonus too, eh, Reed?" Willis smiled.

"We haven't won yet. We still need to get Chan out of there and deal with Pig Face, but we've used our time well, not much more we can do but get it over with."

"Asa's off taking a prisoner to Sacramento. He's going to miss out on the hubbub," J.C. noted. "The rest of the deputies aren't soft in the head. They're stayin' out of this fight. This is something for the Chinese to decide. Asa will just have to read about in *The Placer Herald.*"

"Look at that fat bastard over there, giggling, sucking on

his pipe," Willis said with disdain.

Pig Face and his lieutenants occupied their own rooftop, turning it into a theater box. The two rooftops watched each other carefully, warlords using the high ground in a bellicose staring contest, like those below, testing each other's resolve. Reed saw Pig Face sitting on a makeshift throne, a wooden chair with a high back, a small silk canopy affixed to blot out the sun. The covering wasn't nearly big enough to prevent the corpulent one's skin from flushing red in the sunlight.

"That big curly wolf is with him too," Willis said. "Reed, you best watch yourself around him. That big bruiser is trouble."

"They are not the ones I called you to see," J.J. said. "Is that not the Dutchman, under the wooden awning, beside the post office?"

A collective surprise was expressed by Willis, "Sure as shit, that's him."

"Rance Mueller too," J.C. Boggs observed, "that god-damned varmint's done and outlawed up again."

"McGirt's got to be nearby. Of all the times for them to reappear," Reed said, shaking his head at the turn of events, a complication no one needed. "We need to change the plan. Willis, J.C., get after them. We can't have them standing in our rear once we make our charge."

"Then who's going to cover you from above when you make your run to Pig Face's place?" Willis asked.

"No one," Reed said grimly. "We'll be on our own. Mr. Chang, I sure hope that friend inside is reliable. We've got to get through those doors."

A stoical look of calm resonated from both Mr. Chang and

J.J. Mr. Chang turned to Reed and said in halting English, "If you are facing in the right direction," he gestured with his hands, pointing, "all you need to do is keep walking."

Everyone mulled over the words of wisdom.

"Uh-huh," J.C. said, "Maybe so, but I say runnin' is better than walkin' right now. We've got to make up our minds fast. Reed, you sure about peelin' me and Willis off? I wouldn't make that run without someone lookin' out, ready to impose the law of the shotgun."

Willis said, "I've heard of *riding shotgun*, but what the hell is the *law of the shotgun?*"

"It's my own law, made it up myself. Once I pound a few barrels from this scattergun into the street, I promise *everyone* gets out of the way," J.C. said with a scowl. "Ain't seen no one yet who didn't comply."

"We'll make it without your people mover, J.C.," Reed said decisively, biting down on his lower lip. He shared a confident look with J.J. and Mr. Chang, all three nodding in agreement. "It'll take only a few seconds to get to the doors. We can't afford to catch a bullet in the back from McGirt or the Dutchman once we get out in the open. They've got to be dealt with."

"We best get movin' then," J.C. said. "The pot's ready to boil over and everyone's bound to see an elephant soon enough. Willis, we can light out back and loop around past the Orleans Hotel, catch them desperados from behind."

Reed grabbed Willis's arm as he turned to leave, saying, "McGirt, the Dutchman, they're lookin' to kill you on sight. It's a duel. You look to kill them first."

"You can count on me, boss," Willis said with grit in his

eyes. He followed J.C., running down the stairs.

"Charles," J.J. said, drawing his attention back to Pig Face's rooftop.

Reed watched as Chan appeared, pushed and shoved to Pig Face's side, her hands bound, fear etched across her face. Many conflicting thoughts and emotions raced through his head. She was beaten, certainly, but what else? He wanted to speak, to cry out to Chan that her ordeal would soon end, but such an expression now was beyond premature. Reed felt the weight of this deadly game, cards replaced by people of different ranks and values, the chips all-in for this penultimate pot. Never had the stakes been so high, time to play the game out, to see whose world survives, the victor breathing the air of a new morning.

Reed and J.J. watched mutely as Pig Face spoke to the Baotu. Chan began to move away, recoiling in opposition to Pig Face's words, tension mounting. The Baotu violently grabbed Chan, once again tearing her bodice and under-garments from her skin, stripping her bare and naked to the waist. The Baotu clutched her by the throat, lifting her off her feet. He presented her prostate form to Pig Face, who was out of his chair, dancing with sick, childlike glee. He moved in close to Chan. His face inches from her, smiling his small yellow teeth. He obscenely flicked and darted his reptile-like tongue in and out of his mouth, grunting the sounds of a fornicating animal. She fought against the Baotu's grip that bit into her neck, trying to turn away from the hideous creature. As their cheeks touched, the bitter scent of opium wafted up her nose, a pungent odor leaching from his pores. She spit into the fat face defiantly, screaming, "*Puk gai!*"

Pig Face's malevolent lust was undeterred and he was even more determined to humiliate this woman, to conquer her into submission. He slapped her hard across the face with the back of his hand. The stunning force of the blow allowed him to smash his thin lips into hers, opening his wet mouth, sucking up and down with a thrashing fish-like pucker. He pushed his tongue up against the fortress of her clenched teeth. The two stood locked together in an awkward, grappling dance, his mauling hands pinching and groping her flesh. Throughout, Pig Face's lieutenants looked on laughing, encouraging the assault. A low, guttural sound signaled a renewed attack. Chan opened her mouth for an instant and Pig Face recognized his error immediately, slithering his tongue swiftly from her lips, but it was not fast enough. Chan snapped quickly, cutting deep into the tongue's tip before it was withdrawn. She regretted her inability to shear it clean from his body, missing the opportunity to spit the pink flesh back into the owner's face.

Pig Face glared at Chan's biting visage, staring at her angry smile and tasting his own blood. He spit a mouthful in Chan's face, who cringed in revulsion, the spittle of red juice running from her face and staining her chest. Pig Face embraced Chan tightly, pinning her arms to her side. He spun Chan's backside to the men assembled on the roof of The Golden Star of Shanghai. Pig Face used a hand to tap on Chan's offending tattoo, screaming, *"Wo de jinu*, my whore!" and began to pump his hips into hers, over and over, in exaggerated thrusts.

Chan endured the degradation, wishing she had teeth below to cut his root to size.

Then it was over. Pig Face flung Chan to the ground, landing at the feet of the Baotu. He then faced Reed and J.J., hands on hips, his belly jutting out. He reached out a hand, palm down, his fingers wiggling rapidly, a mocking invitation to come on over, spitting a challenge into the street below. Satisfied, he turned and stomped away, only to stop abruptly, commanding a lackey to fetch his long bamboo pipe. The coterie plus pipe trailed in the fat man's steps. Chan was scooped up and tossed like a saddlebag over the Baotu's shoulder, her bare skin the last thing Reed saw.

Reed said nothing, moving to the stairs with speed and purpose, his own men falling in behind him.

Russell McGirt, Wim Van der Hoof, and Rance Mueller rode into Auburn from Mueller's cabin in Foresthill. Each man trailed a pack mule loaded with their goods. Rance's carried everything he owned of value, which wasn't much, the Farmer's Almanac his most prized possession. He abandoned everything else, though he wished he had brought along the Harper's magazines now that he and the Dutchman had made space by draining two bottles of whiskey crossing the canyon.

"Somethin's afoot," McGirt said, "look at all the commotion."

Rance and the Dutchman looked up from their stupor, no longer gripped by the monotonous sight of one hoof turning over another. Their soused eyeballs saw nothing but dark specks dancing about amongst the waves of heat brimming up from the horizon. The two swayed upright in their saddles, the whiskey that filled their bellies staking a claim on their heads.

"What of it?" the Dutchman slurred.

Rance said nothing, slack-jawed, taking McGirt's word for

it. He stood up in his stirrups, trying to raise his head, leaning over his pommel. It kept him, momentarily at least, from falling off the back of his horse. He looked down at the ground to steady himself, trying to find some point of reference to latch on to, but the ground kept moving even though his horse didn't. He caught himself by hooking a hand around the saddle horn, pitching forward, his head down alongside his horse's neck. He was lucky not to have lost his hat.

McGirt kicked his horse into a canter, riding up on groups of townsfolk marching from High Street in East Auburn. They were headed down the hill away from the Central Pacific Railroad depot to nearby Old Town Auburn. The town was a tale of two halves. Old Town Auburn rose with the Gold Rush. Later, East Auburn was established with the arrival of the Transcontinental Railroad. To the consternation of Old Town, the tracks were placed a mile east. The town was slowly unifying itself, filling in the gap between with shops and residences.

"You there. What're you all runnin' for?" McGirt demanded.

Albert Ford, a shopkeeper, stopped, while others kept to their pace. He flinched at McGirt's appearance, recognizing the hoodlum, regretting he had stopped to acknowledge the voice. He said meekly, "The Chinese is goin' to fight. We aim to see it."

"Chinese? What're they fightin' for?"

Ford, growing ever more frightened at having to speak to a wanted man, one with a $250 bounty on his head, stammered, "W-w-who knows, they's Chinese." He looked away from McGirt, seeing the stream of townspeople moving ahead of him, fearing he would lose out on a good viewing spot. "Lookie here, I n-n-eed to get along. It's Charles Reed and his Chinaman. They're takin' on the other fat celestial, the one with all 'em whores and miners." Ford gave up on the conversation, loping away, trying to catch up with his companions, hoping not to be shot in the back.

"Mueller, go get them horses you bought from the livery and meet us in Old Town, take our mules too," McGirt ordered. "Dutchman, let's go have a look-see."

The two rode toward Old Town, pulling their horses up as the crowd thickened. They hitched the animals to a post on Sacramento Street, following the throng to the plaza.

"You go that way, on that side of the street and I'll go the other way. You see Reed or that bullwhip partner of his, shoot 'em down," McGirt growled. "We get separated, we meet back up at the Anthony House on the old Virginia Turnpike near Deer Creek. We're gettin' after that payroll next."

The Dutchman moved off. McGirt yelled one last command, "And keep an eye out for Mueller."

The Dutchman pushed his way through the crowd, turning left into the first saloon. Everything could wait until he got more to drink.

McGirt could see a whole heap of Chinamen in the street, two groups raising spears and funny looking swords. He pushed his way along, shoving a man, then another to the ground, in search of a closer view, grumbling, "Get outta the way."

He could see the yellow men were as mad as a hornet's nest, hopping up and down at each other. His eyes moved upwards, to the rooftop of The Golden Star of Shanghai. There he was, Reed, the bastard, he thought, standing alongside three of his Chinamen. "I'll kill the son of a bitch," he muttered. It would be a long shot, but he'd take it. He just needed to find his way out of all of these people, into an opening to get a clear shot. He bumped and jostled one, two, three people when his knee caught 10-year-old Casey Winkles, knocking him painfully to the ground. The little boy winced, distress etched into his face, rubbing the spot where the knee smacked his ribs. Despite the pain, Casey was able to stand and grab an egg from a barrel out front of Nathan Cohen's Grocery & Dry Goods. Casey Winkles cried out, "Hey, Mr.! You dropped something!"

McGirt, hearing the voice, turned around and searched the wooden planks of the walkway. "What're you talkin' about? I don't see anything." And with those words, McGirt looked right up into an egg hurled by young Casey. It exploded in his face, leaving behind a goopy mess – streaks of yellow yolk, albumin encrusted with shell fragments.

Casey Winkles was elated, "Aaah, got you! How do you like it scrambled!" he crowed.

"You little runt, I'll...," McGirt barked, drawing the Colt from beneath his coat.

People gasped and screamed, "He's got a gun," "He's gonna shoot that little boy," and "That's McGirt, the murderer."

McGirt absorbed all of these voices, like bees buzzing his head, attracting more of a crowd than the Chinese in the street. "If you know what's for, you better stay back!" he threatened, waving his revolver side to side, keeping the crowd at bay. "Stay back, I say!"

Dorothy Winkles rushed in, wrapping her shawl and arms around Casey, whisking him out of danger, away from Murderous McGirt. Casey would become a local legend for the act, a little known footnote to the Great Tong War. He would tell the story to anyone who would listen up until the time of his death in 1948.

McGirt found himself encircled by men, all unarmed but tough, no-nonsense men.

A loud voice boomed out, "Everyone step aside." It was J.C. Boggs fighting his way through the crowd. "I see you McGirt," he yelled. "I'm going to collect the bounty myself. Going to buy me some fruit trees by seein' you hang."

McGirt saw the big lawman pushing his way toward him, a twin barrel shotgun in his hands. It was more than he wanted, his bottle was full and he needed to skedaddle. There would be better times than this to deal with Charles Reed. Get out of here, rob the payroll, hire someone to walk in and shoot Reed dead, while he played cards, just like how it was done to Wild Bill Hickok in the Dakota Territory.

McGirt cocked the hammer to his Colt, sighting straight down his arm, "Step aside! Anyone that tries to stop me is goin' to get a hole in the head." He began marching directly through the crowd, startled faces, giving ground, hands up in surrender. They melted away as he yelled "Gun! Gun!" over and over. He punched one man and pistol-whipped another for standing too close. He looked back once to see Boggs still struggling to make his way to him, finding the throng difficult to navigate without a gun shoved in people's faces. The townsfolk thinned, with more daylight to run through, then no one in his way. McGirt raced to his horse. He wiped yolk from his eyes, the yellow staining his glove with small pieces of white shell attached. He mounted, kicking his horse to a gallop, riding off behind Old Town and toward the Anthony House on the South Yuba.

"Where's McGirt?" Rance Mueller asked the Dutchman, who was slouched up against the bar, a half-empty bottle of whiskey and a dry shot glass anchored nearby. A few saloon patrons and the bartender himself were straining their necks staring out the windows, taking in the spectacle outside.

"Don't know," the Dutchman said, more sotted than before. "Here have some. No one is looking."

The Dutchman reached over and under the bar, coming back with a new bottle. Rance's eyes widened. "You are on your own for a glass," he slurred.

"Don't need one." Rance pulled the cork and upended the bottle, filling his mouth with liquor, a thin line of amber juice dripping from his chin.

"Hey!" shouted the barkeep. "You ain't paid for that," forgetting the scene outside and remembering his job. "You two pay up and get the hell out of here."

The Dutchman gathered himself from the bar, unhooking one foot from a rail, teetering a bit. He dug a coin out of his pocket and dropped it on the floor. "Come on," he said to Rance, walking a drunken strut of mismeasured steps out the door.

"McGirt's out here somewhere," the Dutchman muttered. "If not, then we meet him at the Anthony House." He stopped for a moment, wondering to himself, "Is that what he told me?" Convinced he had it right in his head, he nodded, saying to Rance, "Let's go that way."

The two pushed and shoved their way through the crowd, staying close to the buildings. When the horde became impassable, they turned ninety degrees and just shoved their way to the front. They stumbled into an open view of the street, the Chinese war dance still in progress.

"When're they going to fight," the Dutchman demanded.

A bystander said, "They been at it for an hour, jumpin' up and down, workin' themselves into a frenzy."

"An hour? I can't wait any longer. We want to see a fight," the Dutchman exclaimed.

Rance, even in his dilapidated state, knew the Dutchman well enough to retreat from the red-headed demon once the Devil got his grip on him. He slyly moved away, figuring the road to the Anthony House was the best place to be before all hell broke loose.

"Fight! Fight, you yellow devils!" the Dutchman growled. He pulled back his coat and withdrew his revolver, waving it in wild swinging arcs.

People scrambled for cover, with more cries of "gun" filling the air.

The Dutchman staggered forward a few steps, firing two quick shots in succession, the first high and through a window on the other side of the street, the bullet plugging to a stop inside a wooden beam. The second cartridge skimmed the heads of the assembled Chinese warriors, its speed snapping with a crackle as it pierced the air, crashing into a brick wall. A third shot followed, the Dutchman's legs steadying as a platform this time, his arm sighting lower into bodies of flesh.

Even he couldn't miss this time.

The shot went through the shoulder of Gam Soy, a laundryman for J.J., who dropped his *dao*, a bloom of blood expanding on his tunic, shock on his face. The bullet tumbled through Gam, redirected by his scapula, downward, out through his back. It lodged in the thigh of Jyu Hua, standing beside, who fell to a knee, clutching his leg in pain.

Few knew where the shots were coming from, the warriors thinking one side was firing into the other. Willis Connelly and J.C. Boggs knew otherwise and with McGirt already on his horse and out of town, they now renewed their attention on the Dutchman at the far side of the plaza.

The Dutchman jumped with delight, seeing two men fall. "Die, Die! you yellow heathen!"

With gunshots ringing out, the posturing challenges of the tong war ended. Both sides flung themselves into each other, launching a pitched battle of hand-to-hand fighting with sharpened points and steel blades.

J.C. emerged from the crowd, ten yards from the Dutchman. He raised his shotgun, but did not fire because of all of the people trying to flee the scene. The Dutchman had no qualms about bystanders and squeezed off a shot at the former lawman. It was an agonizing few seconds for J.C., who watched the Dutchman's barrel closely, leaning away from its deadly end, turning sideways, presenting less of a target. He dodged back in one direction and then the other, doing so quickly, as the Dutchman overcompensated, missing the mark. J.C.'s life saved by quick movement and the Dutchman's love of strong drink. A look of frustration crossed the Dutchman's face as he fled to an alleyway, attempting to dash down its length. J.C. had a clear shot for only a moment and fired a barrel from the scatter gun. The shell's 12 gauge cluster penetrated and ricocheted off a post that held up a storefront awning. The Dutchman flinched as splinters of wood struck his cheek and a single tiny lead ball nicked the tip of his left ear, the post the only thing that saved his life. The impact sobered the ruddy-faced redhead into a dead run down the alleyway. He reached the end, looked back and saw J.C. darting his head in and out from around the building's corner seeking his prey. The Dutchman fired his last two shots and hightailed it to his horse hitched close by.

J.C. thought about launching his own charge, but consider- ed the move rash, too risky. He could count and figured the Dutchman's Colt was empty, but he assumed it wasn't the only gun the outlaw carried. Besides, he knew Willis was working his way around to the other side, his role was that of a hound dog, flushing a bird into the open.

The Dutchman was dimly aware that McGirt's horse was gone as he mounted his own. He kicked the big black-maned bay to a gallop, giddy at his own escape. The celebration was short-lived, ending when Willis Connelly's whip snapped, its popper stinging the bay with a burning bite. The horse panicked and leapt in fear, its bucking movements irregular and spasmodic. The Dutchman had no hope of holding onto the wayward steed and was soon pitched high into the air, his fate in gravity's hands.

Willis watched the Dutchman tumble, landing with a heavy thump. The impact produced a cloud of dust that competed with the horse's vanishing trail, the bay running as if a mountain lion had set its teeth and claws into his backside.

Willis kicked the Dutchman in the chest, keeping him down on his back. He pulled the pair of H. Ahrend handcuffs that J.C. had provided from his pocket, shackling the dirty Dutch hands together.

"Well done," J.C. congratulated. "That horse kettled like none other. I sure could've used you as a full-time deputy during my term."

"You know I earn too much teamstering and workin' for Reed," Willis said with a wry grin. "What should we do with him? He's knock galley west and won't be wakin' up anytime soon."

"Asa said the Nevada County Sheriff wants McGirt for the ruckus at the North Bloomfield Mine. He didn't say nothin' about the Dutchman. We know he's guilty of whole lot and would do some time for the mayhem he caused back in town, but he wouldn't swing."

"That's not good," Willis said.

"Nope. And I wouldn't want a fellow like this walkin' behind me, lurkin' in every shadow, not knowing when or where for the rest of my life. It's why I got out of the law. Too many people find their sympathies is with the bad guys. Makes no sense to me. McGirt, the Dutchman," he said, kicking the downed man's boot, "they're just a bunch of takers, after your property, your life."

"I hear you," Willis fervently agreed.

"Tell you what, we take him out into the ravine. It ain't far. Hole him up in one of the abandoned mines in the hills. There's plenty of 'em. Tie and gag him up there, deep in the ground. When we catch up with Reed, we can see what he wants to do," J.C. suggested.

"Yeah, that's if Charlie Reed is still standing," Willis said, looking into J.C.'s eyes. "Who knows what's happened by now."

"Those are gunshots," Charles Reed said. He pulled back the door wide enough to see both sides launch into each other. "Fighting's started. We've got to go now."

Mr. Chang called Charlie One and Two to action. The thick men braced their heavy shields against a shoulder and formed up side by side. Mr. Chang stepped in directly behind the wide pair, followed by Reed, J.J. and Hai Lon. Reed held his Remington and J.J. and Mr. Chang the double-edged *jian*, while Hai Lon spun one of his two butterfly knives, nodding he was ready.

Reed shouted, "Let's go, all the way. We stop for nothing."

The doors to The Golden Star of Shanghai burst open, Mr. Chang yelling, "*Kuai, kuai!*" faster, faster. The wedge of men dashed into the street, leaping from the porch walkway and into the bright sun. Mr. Chang had planned well. Three men in the back ranks carrying 10 foot long *qiang* spears, charged into position ahead of the flying wedge, poised in front of Charlie One and Two's shields. They extended their spears forward, leading the way with a war cry, "*Diu na ma! Da tamen ying!*"

One *qiang* struck home in the abdomen of a Pig Face minion, who released a hideous scream, eyes bulging from his head, neck muscles contorted, mouth askew. The man fell aside, opening a gap in Pig Face's ranks. Others, defending the fat man's realm, considered the value of their own skins. Impaled at the end of sharpened lance or cut to pieces by a *jian* was becoming an all too real possibility, a toll few were willing to pay. Fear permeated the ranks of Pig Face's legion, guiding their actions. The idea of fighting made sense so long as someone else was doing the fighting. With each moment, more men came to this realization. Their will sapped, many fled in terror, or shrank away down alleyways, out of the sun and into the shadows, thinking of their own preservation, and a life filled with more drawn breaths from a bamboo pipe.

Charlie One and Two's shields widened the gap, knocking anyone nearby off their feet. Mr. Chang exhorted them forward, shouting, "*Jou!*"

Reed fired two shots into the air to keep Pig Face's herd in fast retreat. The wedge remained tight as the men stepped on and over the fallen. Those who had chosen to fight now clutched wounds small and large, some merely maimed, others gravely stricken, dying in the hot sun. For the mortally wounded, expressions of shock and disbelief filled their faces, the horrific realization that their lives were ending. For these pawns, the last moments were ones bearing witness to their own demise. They sensed the weakening hearts in their chests, the beats slowing with the loss of blood, helpless, beyond aid. As the end neared, each discovered a final thought, touched by a flash of memory. In the fading light of their lives, they relished it before darkness consumed them.

The wedge reached the black doors. Reed looked back to see just pockets of the fight still raging, the first skirmish about to end and the second about to begin. J.J. and Hai Lan assumed a defensive position in the rear as Charlie One and Two's shields bracketed the entrance. Mr. Chang moved forward banging three times on the black lacquer doors, shouting,

"*Zhima kaimen!*"

J.J., both hands gripping his *jian*, smiled at Mr. Chang's pass-phrase, *open sesame*, from Ali Baba.

The men heard the heavy bolt slide. The two doors swung open, the ancient woman stood impassively, slipping a daggar back into her sleeve, a second doorkeeper, prone on the floor, a wound in his back.

Mr. Chang stepped forward. Reed thought he was about to embrace or kiss her, but knew that such a display in a restrained, dignified culture was strictly forbidden. Mr. Chang merely made a quick bow, said something in Chinese, and moved inside, his blade ready. The ancient woman stepped past Reed, her eyes meeting his for an instant. She ran into the street, making her escape in the direction of The Golden Star of Shanghai.

Reed stepped in next, entering the lair, eyes adjusting from the bright sunlight to the dim interior. He saw Mr. Chang spinning and cartwheeling, arms, legs, and blade striking out in continuous, blinding motion, high then low, the sword's white tassels a distractive blur to the vision of his opponents. To Reed, he looked like a human sawmill blade ready to cut down a forest of men, kicking chairs and tables out of his way, driving Pig Face's hatchet men back against the wall. Reed looked to the staircase to the left which led to Chan. A Pig Face lackey was descending the stairs, moving in behind Mr. Chang. Reed shot the man as he raised his *dao*, dropping him to the floor.

Reed spoke to J.J. and Hai Lon, who had held the position at the doors as Charlie Yue and other loyal men appeared, consolidating their gains. "I'm going up. Help Mr. Chang get rid of Pig Face. I see him cornered in the back, trying to push his men forward. I'll see you when it's done."

"Good luck, my friend," J.J. said, sprinting forward to reinforce Mr. Chang with Hai Lon and Charlie One and Two.

Reed climbed the first three stairs, his Remington aimed out in front of him. He looked up ahead, moving from the wall to the railing, adjusting with every few steps to improve his view. When he made it to the top of the flight, he saw the door to Chan's room open, sunlight from her window backlighting her form, hands tied and strung upward to a hook mounted onto the wall above her head, blindfolded and gagged. Another silhouette loomed beside her, a Pig Face henchman ready to knife Chan in the back, ordered to kill her the minute anyone attempted rescue.

Reed held his gun on the man, stepping forward slowly. "Don't do it. I'll pay you gold, *jin, jin* to drop the knife. Let her live. Pig Face has lost. Everyone else is running away."

Reed said all this thinking the man doesn't understand a word of English. He tried again, seeing the sharpened blade ready to strike down. "*Nin jin, nin jin,*" you gold, you gold. Chan was screaming into the cloth material packed into her mouth, violently straining and twisting against the restraints.

As Reed moved forward the face of the henchman became more visible in the dim light. He was young and agitated, jumpy. His body quaked with a tremor as he entered the room. Reed stopped, put up a hand to calm the man, "Just take it easy. We can work something out." Reed had $200 in greenbacks in his coat pocket. "*Qian*, money," he said.

It didn't calm the man, who screamed, "*Xianzai!*"

The arm of the Baotu swept into view, knife in hand, the

blade plunging into Reed's chest. Reed fired a shot into Chan's executioner, who was dead before he hit the ground. Reed staggered backward, collapsing down in the hallway, stretched out upon his back. Chan's struggle intensified, panic driven, pulling and jerking against the restraints that bound her, fighting mightily to rip the cordage and hook from the wall. Each tug caused the rope to cut deeper into her, blood running from a wrist and down her arm.

Reed brought his chin up and was met with the unnerving sight of a blade and handle embedded in his chest. His eyes focused upward, beyond the knife, seeing the Baotu emerge from his hiding place. He had stood with his back against the wall just inside Chan's room. He revealed his entire self now, his large shape filling the doorway. Even in his shadowed form, Reed could see the sinister smile. Reed made a heave and a gurgling sound and the Baotu's smile grew broader – the white Devil's death near.

The Baotu understood his time with Pig Face was over, the battle a loss. But he would need his knife, travel back to San Francisco and join the Hip Yee Tong there. They could always use his services. He bent over Reed, reaching for the knife. He looked into Reed's eyes, expecting a frozen wide-eyed stare, a bright glassy-eyed dilation of death. As he leaned closer, taking a knee on the darkened hallway floor, Reed turned his head slightly, clear-eyed, staring directly into the big thug's eyes, who recoiled backward, uncomprehending. Reed put the Remington into the trough of the man's neck, the depression every man had trouble shaving, pulling the trigger and blowing a hole up through his head. The Baotu arched his back reflexively, as if he was trying to touch the ceiling with his nose. He found a balancing point, rigid and upright, holding the pose for just an instant, motionless, a cut tree ready to fall. The death throe provided Reed time to roll away, the behemoth's last act a lurch forward, body slamming dead upon the floor.

Reed released a deep breath, giving the Baotu a last look, glad to see his likes go. He entered Chan's room, placing a gentle hand on her shoulder, saying, "It's me."

Her writhing ended, the muffled screams replaced by a slowing sigh of relief, pulling air through her nose and into her lungs. He removed the gag and blindfold.

"Charles, I cannot believe it is you," she said, trying to catch her breath.

Reed untied her, turning her around, their eyes meeting. Her elation turning to alarm, seeing the knife fixed into his chest. "Oh, Charles, you are hurt!"

"It's nothing really," he said, pulling the blade out and holding the knife for her to see. He shrugged while she ran her hand's up over his chest.

"What is this?" she said, touching the hole the knife blade had made, unbuttoning the white shirt beneath his coat. "No blood?"

She opened the shirt.

"It's paper armor. Old Mr. Chang and John John, I mean, Wei Lu, your brother, insisted I wear it. Tough material. Just shows you how hard it is to shove a knife through a book," Reed said smiling.

"Good thing for you, but not for your suit coat," she said, sticking her index finger from the inside out through the hole and wiggling it.

"Just missed my trident," Reed observed.

She looked at the golden pitchfork on the lapel, scrutinizing it.

"Don't say anything. I've had enough opinions on it already."

She smiled through her tears and they kissed.

"I knew you would come for me, Charles," she said, her head against his chest.

"It's not over. It's just the beginning. We have to get you out of here. Your brother says taking down Pig Face will have consequences. We can talk about it later, once back at our place."

Mr. Chang's Shaolin breeze sword was winning the day. Eight of Pig Face's men cowered before its elegant move-ments, attacks hidden within – thrusts, cloud, and figure-circle swings. Mr. Chang nearly severed the arm of one who dared to cross steel, the man crumpling to the floor in agony, trying to squeeze the wound shut as blood ran between his fingers. One, two, three, then four men dropped their *dao* sabers in submission, humbled before the sword that moved like a light breeze through trees. The defeated wailed, "*Touxiang! Touxiang!*" surrender, surrender. The beaten men stepped forward hesitantly, bowing repeatedly, booted in the rear end by Charlie One and Two, who passed the toadies roughly along to comrades now occupying the illicit den.

The sight of surrender enraged Pig Face, who implored his men to "*Douzheng!*" fight. The remaining men balked, their skill level no match for this single old man, a wizard who fought like a dragon demon from myth. They had no chance against a *kung fu* master, futility compounded by the arrival of his fellow warriors.

Pig Face used his own *dao* to jab one of the men forward. The sycophant cried out in pain, reaching for the small puncture wound. He turned and spit at the feet of Pig Face, unwilling to submit any longer to his rule, exclaiming, "*Xiao bawang zhou tong*," wicked man.

Pig Face drew a gun tucked in his waistline, hidden below his changshan. He cocked the hammer and shot the man dead for his impertinence, thinning a member from his own herd, the sound of the gunshot reverberating in the enclosed space. John John, Mr. Chang and the others withdrew a step, Charlie One and Two moving into a defensive posture, protecting J.J. and Mr. Chang with their copper plated shields.

Pig Face spit on the man's body, "*Siren*," dead man. He looked at his remaining henchmen, spitting at them too, "*Nuofu*," cowards, he said with contempt.

John John reached out with his *jian*, tapping the nearest henchman on the shoulder with the flat of his blade, gesturing him and the others to "*chuqu*," get out – time to abandon their leader.

Pig Face watched the remnants of his tong run away, pathetic, he thought, shaking his head in disgust. He still held the gun, sweating profusely.

J.J. said, "You cannot escape. Drop the gun."

"You will kill me anyway. I should empty the gun into all of you," he threatened, raising the weapon at J.J.

"True, you could," J.J. said calmly, "But you need to consider how you wish to die."

Pig Face's brow furrowed, pulling the skull cap from his head. He exposed his Manchu queue haircut, shaven in front, forehead shiny with sweat, the long black braid dangling like a flaccid snake down his backbone.

J.J. made his offer, "*Lingchi*, hacked to death slowly, a thousand cuts, dismembered into pieces, unable to walk whole in the spirit world. Or accept our mercy – just one cut."

John John picked up a long bamboo pipe from the ransacked den. He waved it enticingly in front of the dope fiend, "We will even allow one last smoke."

Pig Face looked to the pipe, biting his lower lip with desire. He dropped the gun. Anything for one more pull on the pipe.

Charlie One and Two raced forward, grabbing Pig Face, twisting his arms behind his back.

"Place him in here," J.J. said, gesturing to a small side room, a tight windowless space. "Tie him down on a couch. We will not be heating up a small globule for you to smoke, Dai Lao. Your appetite is too great. You will need an entire crate of opium balls."

J.J. spoke rapidly to Hai Lon, who quickly located Pig Face's cache, box upon box of the potent poppy.

"I suggest drawing the smoke quickly into your lungs. It is the only mercy I will allow. We will have our retribution. You must be punished for what you have done to my sister." J.J. held the point of his *jian* under Pig Face's chin. "I promised one cut," he said. "It will be here," touching the fleshy jowls but not breaking the skin. "You will carry your head under an arm in the afterlife, explaining to other spirits how it got there."

Pig Face squealed in protest, struggling to break Charlie

208

One and Two's grip.

"Find me a keg, fill it with brine," J.J. ordered. He approached Pig Face, their faces inches apart. "Once your pig head is cleaved off, we will stuff your mouth, not with an apple, but with a ball of opium. I will send your pickled head to the Hip Yee Tong in San Francisco. They can feed it to their own hogs."

"*Meiyou!*" no, he cried, his body stiffening to the scheme.

J.J. motioned again to the small side room, "In here now."

Hai Lon followed, placing a large wooden box filled with balls of opium, some the size of oranges, inside the room.

"Gather all of the oil lamps and stand them in this room," J.J. ordered. "Clay pots on top with a ball of opium in each. Turn the flames on high so they can smoke and burn."

The men did as told and when complete, J.J. reentered the small room, filling fast with drowsy fumes. He told the remaining men to depart. He scooped up a globule of black paste from one of the clay pots, using a needle-like skewer to remove it. He then placed the molten paste in the ceramic bowl of Pig Face's pipe. J.J. studied the elaborate pattern etched into its silver saddle that held the detachable bowl, admiring the craftsmanship.

He held the pipe out in front of Pig Face's lips, saying, "We can hurry this along."

Pig Face seized the opportunity, drinking deep from the wooden cylinder. A soothing blankness washed over his face, followed by a slight smile, his body sinking deeper into the couch.

J.J. refilled the bowl as Pig Face greedily inhaled the vapor, over and over again until he slowed to a stop. J.J. tossed the pipe on the fat man's chest, leaving the room before he too became intoxicated by the addicting fumes.

John John shut the door behind him, no need to lock it. He pushed a small rug up tightly under the door, trapping more of the narcotic scent, filling the confined space with a sticky pungent smell of petals on fire. He would return shortly, blade in hand, to finish the deed.

Auburn State Recreation Area, 2013

"Nobody at the Park Ranger kiosk," I said aloud, using the Bluetooth to speak hands-free down Highway 49. I followed the winding road to the bottom of the Auburn Canyon. To my right, beyond the road's guardrail, the confluence of the Middle and North Forks of the American River. I noticed not much water running this time of year, what little Sierra snowpack there was had already melted and made the run months ago. Only slow moving fingers of water and stagnant pools remained, meager drops on a slow trickle to the parched valley lakes and reservoirs below.

"I'm driving past the kiosk, looking for a good place to park." I looked to my left, seeing the Auburn Bridge towering high above. I thought to myself, I can't believe they're going to jump from that. I then worried, what'll I do if something goes wrong? I looked up again at the dizzying height and cringed – no first aid class in the world is going to help if a chute doesn't open. New plan, in case of malfunction, burn rubber and get the hell out of here. "No, Mr. Ranger, I've never seen them before." What have we gotten ourselves into? We're all going to jail, probably some special enhancement for aiding and abetting foreign nationals in the commission of a crime.

"So nobody?" Kendra asked, calling from the back of Gregor and Helmut's motorhome.

"Just a few cars parked on the road, in the fee area. They look like hikers, people soaking their feet in the river," I confirmed, my D-Day jitters ending with a John Wayne spine transplant to get me back onboard. "Honestly, it looks good. No sign of any rangers or anyone that would issue a ticket. Like you said, they're probably all at lunch or, who knows? Budget cutbacks, for all we know, maybe no one is ever on duty. Where are you guys at?"

"We'll be on the bridge in less than a minute. We pulled off on the shoulder to let a couple of cars go by, but now there is no one behind us."

"Okay, I see the Confluence Trail next to the road. It follows the river, right under the bridge. There're a few spots here to park. I'm stopping and getting my camera ready." I put the car in park, stepped out, and closed the door. "I don't see any cars driving over the bridge. Everything looks pretty quiet."

"Great, Dad, we're on the bridge."

"I see you now," the metallic silver Class B motorhome floated into view, like riding a wave, the sun sparkling off of it. What a beauty, *gotta gotta* get one of those.

They drove about two-thirds of the way across, closer to the eastern bank of the river, where the Confluence Trail ran directly to me. I stood at the trailhead, my camera ready, video mode set. I looked one last time down the trail. Its contours reminded me of a railroad track moving off into the distance, converging lines meeting at a vanishing point somewhere off beneath the bridge. I began recording, bridge and trail, establishing shot. I zoomed the lens out and up to the motor-home. The back doors were both open, Gregor and Helmut out with their gear, followed by Kendra, recording with her phone. No traffic behind them, parked in the bike lane, Helmut closed the motorhome doors. They each stepped over a short concrete barricade and onto a pedestrian sidewalk. Jen put the motorhome in drive and drove off the bridge, parking in a vacant gravel area beyond the bridge. As I watched her drive off, I noticed a figure walking on the bridge. I zoomed in and saw it was just a young man taking in the view. Jen was out of the motorhome, finding a good vantage point to record the leaps with her own camera, moving down an embankment away from the bridge.

I kept recording, shooting forward, but looking all around for traffic, bystanders, any park rangers coming and going. Nothing, just a bobble in the viewfinder as I looked side to side. This is too easy.

Gregor and Helmut worked methodically, checking their gear one last time, serious and systematic, like two Wernher von Braun's working on their own moonshot.

Kendra was recording the final prep when the young man approached, long scraggly hair, concert T-shirt, cargo shorts, the whiff of the most recent bong hit touching everyone's noses.

"Dude, you're goin' to BASE jump," he krumped, "Outstanding."

"Bitte, please, stand back," Gregor said. "Helmut, bist du bereit?"

"I hear ya, man, don't let me get in the way," the young man bobbed and weaved a unique brand of body language, loose-limbed, rubbery. "Let me know if I can help. Whatever you need, brother, say the word. I'm here for you," he said, twirling his hands and ending with a theatrical "gotcha" index finger pointed at Gregor and Helmut. They shared a look with one another before returning to their equipment.

Kendra kept recording, figuring stoner kid added a bit of harmless color. "Do you live around here?" she asked.

"Yeah," he said enthusiastically, "down in the canyon. There're all sorts of places to camp out, listen to music, the birds…smoke some weed," he sniggered, his eyes lighting up. "I've got friends. We practically live down there, at least until the harvest. Then we hit the road and become trimmigrants." He made a snip, snip gesture with his hand, trimming an imaginary bud. "Pay's okay, all the weed you can smoke."

Gregor looked in both directions on the bridge and saw everything was clear and ready. He pommeled over the guardrail and did a half-turn facing out into the vast panorama of the canyon.

Helmut asked, "der Salto?"

"Ja, drei."

Helmut looked over the guardrail to the riverbed below, uncertain, "drei? Bist du sicher?"

Kendra thought "three, three something. Where's Dad when

I need a translator?"

Gregor yelled "abheben!" and leaped from the bridge, pulling his knees up to his chest, beginning the first of three inward somersaults.

Helmut, Kendra, and stoner kid white-knuckle gripped the guardrail, their heads leaning out over, mouths open, reflexively gasping for a breath to fill their startled lungs. Gregor slowly tumbled in his tight tuck, dramatically reducing in size as he accelerated toward the ground, gathering more and more speed, the 730 foot freefall all but consumed in a matter of seconds. Transfixed, the three above observed a strange contrast, an unnerving combination of slow motion somersaults with a high-speed plummet to river rock below. Anxiety spiked for the spectators as the gap between Gregor and Mother Earth decreased, each thinking, Gregor, you seriously need to pull out now. Suddenly, the chute deployed, popping open in a burst of captured air, the sound a fraction behind the sight of the canopy opening.

"Whoa, Mo-Fo!" the stoner gyrated, pumping a fist, spinning on the ball of a foot. "Go for it, baby, video that shit. That's so fuckin' gnarly, brother. Dude, he like held that til the very fuckin' end. That's seriously ballsy. Dude should be a stuntman in the movies or an astronaut or somethin'."

Kendra kept on recording Gregor's descent, keeping her hand steady despite the jolt of adrenaline pulsating through her veins.

"Ach, that triple took a while," Helmut said, relieved. "Gregor holds it far too long."

"Nailed it. Right on the trail," Kendra exclaimed as Gregor touched down.

"Nothing so dramatic for me," Helmut announced, bounding over the rail. He looked into Kendra's camera, "I'm the prudent one. See you soon," and dove straight out, no acrobatics, nothing fancy.

Kendra marveled at how fast the two had fallen away, beside her, then gone, really gone. She knew about terminal velocity but seeing people doing it up close and from so high up, made her spine tingle. She watched Helmut safely deploy his pilot chute well before Gregor's nerve-racking lateness. She recorded his glide, allowing him to fly further down the Confluence Trail, landing beside Gregor, who had already jogged almost a hundred yards down the getaway trail.

Kendra stopped her camera and turned around, sighing relief, "Wow, that was amazing."

Stoner kid agreed, nodding triumphantly. He rocked up and down on his feet, smiling satisfaction as if he had jumped himself, "*Boss*," he said in judgment, again, pulling on a gold ring earring. "I give them five gnarlys…So what're you doin' tonight?"

Kendra turned and stared into the canyon, shielding the sun from her eyes with a hand visor. She saw two dots jogging down the trail, meeting a third dot, Dad. The trail T-boned onto the road and she could see them load themselves up into the Honda. They were gone in seconds, climbing Old Foresthill Road, looping up, around, and out of the canyon free and clear. They would cross back over the bridge in a few minutes, this time traveling from the east.

"Uh, I'm really just into myself at this time," she fumbled. "Um, focusing on school," she lamely sputtered. "I have a boyfriend…any or all of the above."

"That's cool. I hear where you're coming from. I can respect that."

"Beep beep," the motorhome horn sounded as it braked to a stop, retracing the path back to Auburn. Kendra saw her Mom behind the wheel, big round black sunglasses, smiling, giving a thumb's up.

Traffic was clear and Kendra walked across a lane to the motorhome, turning to say, "What's your name?"

"Jason."

She walked backwards, rounding the front end of the vehicle, out of view. She poked her head back around, shouting, "Jason, remember to watch YouTube. We'll post the video soon. You're narration really captured the moment," she said before disappearing into the motorhome.

Jen hit the gas, waving goodbye.

Jason smiled and nodded, jutting one shoulder left and the other right, rocking his neck in rhythm, dancing to his own tune, "Sweet."

Auburn, California 1883

"Mr. Chang, good work with the spears. The...what do you call them, *qiangs*? I didn't know you were going to do that," Reed said. "It really put some Texas longhorn into our stampede."

Reed considered the sturdy man before him, saying, "I don't know that I owe a man more than I do you."

John John silently agreed. They were both indebted to this old man, monk and warrior, devout and disciplined, placid and serene as a Buddha statue. The man was truly a marvel, a worthy friend and ally.

"I've never seen a man move a sword the way you do and the fact is I'd be dead if I didn't heed your advice on the paper armor," Reed smiled appreciatively. "You'll always have my gratitude and thanks."

"*Our* gratitude," Chan added, taking Reed's hand into her

own.

Mr. Chang made a slight bow of acknowledgement.

"You understand more English than you let on," Willis said with a grin.

As Mr. Chang straightened from his bow, he arched an eyebrow and shared a knowing look with Willis that everyone noticed. "True," he said.

"One word, that's old Mr. Chang. You're the smartest person in the room, I bet," Willis replied.

"The lack of needless chatter quiets the mind," J.J. observed.

"Shoot, I've got one of the quietest minds around. It's just my mouth that don't shut up," Willis joked, causing everyone to laugh, even Mr. Chang.

When the laughter ended, J.C. offered, "John John, you're a young fella but I think there's a lot of Mr. Chang in you. I think you're somethin' of a disciple."

"Hell, we should all be disciples, after seein' this man in action," Reed said.

"I don't doubt it," J.C. remarked, "There's somethin' George Washington-like about you, Chang, old boy. Pick up a sword when you have to and then return to your plow once the fightin' ends. Slow to stir to anger, I can appreciate that."

Mr. Chang lowered his head, studying his steel blade, melancholy in his voice, "The sword is a cursed thing that the wise man uses only when he must." He raised his head, saying in a slow, measured manner, "We seek pathways to end suffering, *dukkha*. Spears and blades have provided an escape from evil," turning his gaze to Chan, "but do not dwell on this past pain. Through wisdom and compassion, we can attain happiness and a better understanding of ourselves and others. When we do this, the experience will feel true and real. We become the person we are meant to be, without pain, helping to guide others, especially those we love, along the same path to enlightenment."

"Such purty talk, I'm beginnin' to feel like I'm in Sunday school," J.C. said.

Chan smiled into Mr. Chang's eyes. She looked to Reed, her eyes filling with tears.

Reed returned the smile, squeezing her hand, saying, "I think we found a road to happiness, but the struggle isn't over yet. Right, John John?"

"The Hip Yee Tong will not let this stand. We must continue with the rest of our plan before more hatchet men arrive."

"What is that plan, brother?" Chan asked, looking to him and then back to Reed.

"Charles?"

"We're shutting down for a few days," he said, surveying the faces of those gathered in The Golden Star of Shanghai. "We'll keep a few things open, like the laundry and kitchen, but shut down the saloon and all the gambling."

"But why, Charles? I am free now."

"We're taking you to San Francisco. Like J.J. said, the Hip Yee Tong is going to want revenge, because nobody is supposed to stand up to them. We figure we have about a week before they send someone to survey the damage, might get rougher after that. It's a matter of principle for them, I guess, but this is the hard part," Reed said, hesitating, "you're going back to Hong Kong, to be with your parents. J.J. is going too.

You can be protected there by your clan."

"No, Charles, I will stay here with you."

"There will only be more bloodshed if you do. It's safer for you to go away for a spell, the anger of the moment will pass. We'll then do what Pig Face should've done, strike a bargain. We buy your freedom from Pig Face's boss and no one loses face."

"Except Dai Lao," J.J. said, gesturing to the keg holding his pickled head.

"We just need to get you on a ship and to safety."

"Sister, Charles is correct. The *kongsi* of Hong Kong will protect you until Pig Face's Dragon Master is appeased," J.J. said. "No more discussion now. Please, Mr. Chang, introduce us to your friend."

Mr. Chang escorted the ancient woman from Dai Lao's lair forward, the doorkeeper.

"Ming Ni, these are my friends."

The ancient woman with a steady gaze peered into the eyes of those around her, acknowledging each, saying nothing. Polite eye contact with everyone, though she consciously settled last on Chan. Their eyes met and held, unspoken history moving from one woman to the other, ending with a deep sincere bow in Chan's direction. Chan sensed Ming Ni's own burden – abduction and enslavement decades ago, abuse and debasement as a whore, ruined, untouchable, a doorkeeper crone and now, finally, an agent of her salvation.

Chan smiled and returned the bow, extending a hand in friendship that Ming Ni wrapped into her own, like receiving a gift. Chan studied the aged hands caressing hers, slowly, tenderly. With each stroke, Chan realized that Ming Ni was reliving her youth, seeing in her ivory skin the beauty she herself once possessed. For Chan, the weathered hands, each line and wrinkle, symbolized a lifetime of pain and suffering. Without Ming Ni's help, and those in this room, Chan was certain she would have shared a similar fate. The thought profoundly shook Chan's heart and when she looked up, she saw Ming blinking tears onto her cheeks. Chan wrapped her arms around the old woman who had stood silently in her own prison, opening doors, delivering food, doing what she was told, deferential to all, reduced to a ghost. They held on tightly to each other, knowing the ordeal was over. For Ming Ni, even this late, life could begin again.

J.C. broke the silence, "Looks like a whole lot of, whatcha call it? *Dukkha* up and rode out of town. Let's hope it keeps up."

Mr. Chang placed Ming Ni's hand into his own, a wise, venerable hand clasping a beaten but undefeated hand. They smiled at each other.

"Mr. Chang met Ming Ni at the Quong Hi Company store. She too purchased vegetables from Mar Ying Toy and his wife Leo Gim Moy," J.J. explained, looking to the elder couple. "Theirs is a friendship begun some time ago."

"Without her, we would never have gotten through those big doors and busted you out, dear," Reed said. "Mr. Chang and Ming Ni are going with you and J.J. to Hong Kong. They'll protect you on the journey."

"But aren't you coming, Charles?"

"In time, I'll join you, but I'm going to look after our investments, all of our goods. It's not likely the Hip Yee Tong will take me on or any white folk with so much anti-Chinese venom in the air. They don't want the law on their backs, not at this time."

Reed knew the answer was insufficient, entailing nothing but hardship for he and Chan, but it was the proper course. "We can talk more about it later. Time to rest, get everyone patched and cleaned up. Tomorrow we celebrate. Hold a banquet to reward everyone for a job well done, then we get on with some other chores."

By mid-morning, plans for the evening banquet were taking shape. Smells from the kitchen wafted throughout The Golden Star of Shanghai, raising everyone's expectation for a memorable feast. Mr. Chang retired his sword in favor of a chef's knife, expertly cutting mounds of vegetables with Charlie Yue and the rest of the kitchen help – duck, chicken, and pork all on the menu.

Reed had spent the morning seated at a card table studying his bank books. In reality, he was observing Chan, dressed in a new white lace dress, the skirt flowing as freely as she felt. Her joy was contagious, bringing a smile to everyone she encountered, Reed most of all.

Willis called out, "Hundley, the photographer, is here."

Reed stood and pointed to an area already set up with chairs near a window. Willis clapped Hundley on the back, directing him to the area where he could set up his new Pearsall Compact Camera.

"Come on," Reed hollered. "We're all going to get our pictures taken."

"What is this, Charles?" Chan asked.

"Here, have a seat, dear. Hundley, nice to meet you again," Reed said, shaking the man's hand. "We're going to get pictures of everybody."

Hundley opened a gap-toothed smile, the corners of his mouth bookended by a thin forest of red muttonchops. He removed his derby, exposing a white snowdrift forehead untouched by the sun, "That would be splendid, Mr. Reed."

"Charles?"

"Once you leave the country, you're going to need proof, documents to get back in. With the Chinese Exclusion Act, Chinese can no longer immigrate to America. Those already here need to certify themselves or you'll be barred from ever returning."

"Ready, Mr. Reed. Is the lady first?" Hundley queried.

"Yes she is," Reed said, commenting, "That's a mighty interesting camera."

"The Pearsall is the newest camera available and the most portable. See, it's self-casing." He proudly worked the hinge mechanism, opening and closing the camera within its wooden protective box. "Very efficient, with a rear-viewing bellows, no more need to duck under a dark cloth. Can go anywhere with it, even a baseball game. I'm making a tidy sum taking photographs of all the players and teams sprouting up."

"That's amazing," J.C. gawked, leaning in closer to examine the newfangled device. "People keep comin' up with new and better things."

"We'll make sure we get a picture of you leaning on your shotgun," Reed offered.

"I'd like that," J.C. said, smiling broadly. "Thank you kindly, Reed."

"There's a mirror over there," Willis interceded, steering the big man across the room. "Hook a thumb under your arm and start leaning on that shotgun. These two need to speak, so give 'em a moment, will ya? You just get to work practicin' your pose and that over-the-horizon gaze."

"Now little lady, just hold still," Hundley said as he adjusted the focus.

Reed stepped in behind Hundley, peering over his shoulder, looking directly at Chan. Their eyes met and she smiled.

"Wonderful," Hundley remarked.

"Wait. We need to take another with the two of us together," Reed said, sliding a second chair in beside Chan. He reached into his coat pocket and removed a gold band. "Slip this on, dear. Man and wife, even more proof."

A startled Chan smiled and extended her ring finger in a rush of emotions.

Reed slid the gold ring on, "It's engraved with both our names and the date we met."

Tears of joy rushed back again and she stood and they kissed, slow and tenderly.

"I am so happy, Charles," Chan said, wonderstruck. "My life is becoming a dream."

"You need to stop your crying or people are going to see this next picture and think I coerced you into this."

Chan laughed through her tears. "I'm not sad, only in love, darling."

Chan held herself tightly against him, using the moment to gather herself. She plucked the red kerchief from his chest pocket to wipe her tears away.

He whispered in her ear, "I'm sorry about Hong Kong. Not

long, I'll be there. We can have a ceremony there in front of your parents. J.J. says your father will insist on something elaborate."

"*Fuh mouh*, my parents, it has been so long since I have seen them. It seems so impossible that we will meet again."

"They'll be so glad to see you, but, Chan, remember," Reed said, his eyes on hers. "We need to show courage for each other. There's goin' to be a lot of distance between us, but we can both light a lamp for each other. Even if we don't see it, we'll know that it's burning, a flame to brighten the path that will bring us back together. It won't be long, I swear."

"There is no need for a lamp, the light burns so brightly from my heart. It will never fade, Charles," she said, kissing him again.

When their lips parted, each exhaled a mutual sigh of longing. Reed agreed, "We're not going to have a problem. I think we'll be able to see each other from the moon."

She laughed and gave him a playful tap on the chin, coyly releasing him from her grip.

Composed, they sat down side by side, a ringed hand conspicuously on top of the other.

"I think we're ready, Mr. Hundley," Reed said, feeling the squeeze of Chan's hand.

Hundley manipulated the shutter and the loving couple's image was instantly captured upon a light sensitive plate. It all seemed like magic.

* * *

"You ever eat so good?" Willis asked Chan, who was seated across the banquet table. They were beginning to clean up now, plates, bowls and utensils, all moving back into the kitchen for cleaning.

"Delicious. Dai Lao," she stopped to correct herself, "Pig Face provided nothing more than *zhou*, gruel, for everyone but himself and his lieutenants," she said. "Ming Ni can say whether it is true or not, but there was a rumor that Pig Face was one of your customers, sending faceless lackeys or paying a town drunk to walk over and fetch his *wancan*, his supper."

"If that's the case, we shoulda been sprinklin' poison on top," Willis said. "Woulda saved everyone a whole lot of hurt."

"It's done now," Reed said. "We can all start worrying about something else besides Pig Face. Say, where's Alice? She was right here a minute ago."

"Oh, she's back in the kitchen cussin' a blue streak at Mr. Chang."

"Why's she doing that?"

"He won't part with his recipe for that sauce that comes with the duck, hoisin sauce," Willis said.

"Yes, it was very good," Chan said, "the *char siu* pork was exceptional."

"Alice liked that one too. Hell, she likes 'em all. She can't get enough of Mr. Chang's cookin'. Now he's goin' back to China and he refuses to show her how to make it."

"You need to let her know young Charlie Yue is taking over the kitchen so she'll still be able to get her fill of grub," Reed reassured.

"Good thing you told me so, because Alice is used to

havin' it her own way with her young 'uns at school." Willis leaned across the table, speaking directly to Chan. "See, Alice is a schoolmarm, attended Smith College. Don't know what she sees in a teamster like me. Anyway, figured it would come down to Mr. Chang pullin' that sword of his just to get her out of the kitchen."

"Alice is your wife, Willis?" Chan asked.

"No, not yet, but I figure your own plans will put the whip to our own. We'll aim on somethin' smaller. I don't see us goin' as far as Hong Kong to be married. Maybe down yonder as far as Newcastle, out at J.C.'s new place with all them fruit trees. Make for a nice settin' with the sun goin' down."

"Speakin' of marriage," Willis discerned, casting a glance back over his shoulder. "You best get Hundley the photographer back. J.J. is goin' to need his own picture of Ah Cy," he gestured again, slyly arching his eyebrows. "The pretty filly, sister of Leo."

Reed stood from his chair and beckoned Chan to stand too, spying a look toward the back of the room, where John John, Ah Cy, Leo Gim Moy and her husband Mar Ying Toy were happily getting along.

"They're mighty impressed with J.J. ridding the town of Pig Face," Willis said. "No doubt, he's the boss Chinaman in these parts now."

"I wondered where he's been all night," Reed said with satisfaction. "Yep, we need Hundley."

"I think our wedding will be a double wedding," Chan said.

"Triple, if we can only convince Willis and Alice to come aboard," Reed offered.

Willis waved a hand and shook his head, no. "Just get back

in time so as to be a part of ours. I can ride and push around about any stock that walks this earth, but I don't do well ridin' on a boat. The Pacific is a big ocean and I'd spend the whole time ridin' the rail, pitchin' my insides out."

"Just as well. When we're away, you'll be in charge until all of us return," Reed said.

"Here she is now," Willis called out," eyeballing the broad voluptuous hips of Alice Sweeney, who sashayed in from the kitchen. Willis reached out from his chair with a wide swing of his arm, slapping her behind with a "whap." "Is it the bustles or your rump that's gettin' bigger?"

Alice bopped Willis on the head, "A little of both," she said with a flirtatious smile.

"Dang that Mr. Chang," Alice said looking up to all, "he's ornerier than some of them mules you drive."

"Alice, you've never been able to get far with Mr. Chang and those recipes."

"Well, to think he spoke English the entire time I was asking. Asking nicely, too," Alice complained. "All those 'I don't understand' looks, 'no speaky English.' What a heap of horseshit."

"Woman, you sound like you've been spendin' your summers workin' on a ranch," Willis teased. "Hope you're not like that in front of your pupils?"

"Hell, no," Alice said straight-faced. "I teach school, not Sunday School."

"It's not very ladylike," Willis replied.

"When did you ever complain? *He* with his own salty tongue."

Willis smiled, "Well, you've been missin' all the marriage

talk. And, I was thinking, maybe I should marry you, get you along with a few little critters so as to put an end to that blue streak of yours," Willis winked to Reed and Chan. "Can't have you swearin' profane oaths around the children."

"Willis Connelly, you trying to save me from myself with all your corral dust talk? You're worse than all them Temperance women bossing their husbands about," Alice fired back, cocking an arm, ready to bop him on the head again. "Besides, it's too late. I already spoke to J.C. like we planned. He said he and Louisa would be right proud to host the shindig to celebrate our nuptials."

Willis looked around the room for J.C. but saw he had already cut a path home. He shrugged, "Okay, then. We can get Charlie Yue to cook all the food. He's been learnin' from Mr. Chang and is goin' to take over."

"Young Charlie, he won't stand a chance with me. I'll have all them secrets from the kitchen," Alice boasted. "Hell, soon enough, I'll be cooking for this place."

"You're goin' to need a Chinese name before they let you stand over any wok," Willis said. He looked to Chan. "How do you say 'princess' in Chinese?"

"*Lihwa.*"

"There you go, sweetie. You're *Lihwa* and not that *Mm moh fan ah lei* name they been usin' on you. Say, Chan, what does that mean?"

Chan shook her head, "You do not want to know."

Willis and Reed chuckled, Reed, saying, "I'm sure they meant it affectionately."

"You two can laugh at my brash ways, but you best speak to young Charlie, because you might need a cook sooner than you think," Alice countered. "He's hatching a business with Mr. Chang that doesn't involve any cooking."

"What kind of plan?" Reed asked.

"Bones. They have some scheme to disinter the Chinese buried here, shipping them back to China so they can rest in their homeland with their families. Charlie will do the shipping from here and Mr. Chang will take care of the Chinese end. All done in accordance with tradition and respect."

"They told you all of this?"

"It's not like they were sharing Momma's secret recipes. They wanted my opinion and I said it sounded like a right fine idea reuniting everyone in the afterlife. If you come here to work, far away from home, sending money back to families, I can see how the last thing shipped home would be yourself. Plan for it now, before you step on that last rattler."

"It makes sense," Chan said.

"Don't you think?" Alice said, agreeing, "Seems almost like a public service."

"Speakin' of public service, you givin' any more thought to our Dutch problem out in that old mine?" Willis asked Reed.

"I have and we're waiting on the delivery of a gift."

"A gift? What kind of gift?"

Reed stopped Willis with a hushing motion, "Ladies, if you will excuse us, business you don't need to trouble yourself with."

"Come along, honey, the men folk want to talk all by themselves. Let's head to the kitchen and see if we can pry any recipes loose. Just don't mention anything about us working in cahoots," Alice said winking and smiling. She shook her hips playfully, petticoats rustling with the get along movement.

Chan leaned into Charles, whispering before she departed, "I like them. They like to tease each other."

"Even more than we do. They make a lively pair, and are good for each other."

Chan ran her hand down the lapel of his coat, looked into his eyes before turning to go. The two women walked side by side to the kitchen, the heavy folds of Alice's skirt buzzing through the air. Both men watched them go, overhearing a snicker and a giggle targeted at one or both of the men.

"Good to see them gettin' along. Reed, I think we done better than most in the women department. Don't you think?"

"We just need to live long enough to enjoy it. We need to tie up a few things, like the Dutchman holed up in the ravine."

"What have you got planned?" Willis said, flipping his chair around backwards and sitting back down, closer to Reed. He folded his arms over the top, leaning forward to nest his chin on his shirt sleeves.

"I sent a telegram to L.L. Robinson explaining our problem with an abandoned mine. He replied that he 'understood' and that 'they're very dangerous.' He offered to help and a package is 'on the way.'"

"Package? What kind of package? When's it supposed to get here?"

"L.L. sent it straightaway, said it'll be here tomorrow, so Charlie One and Two will need to stay on top of the Dutchman until I'm back from San Francisco, seeing Chan and everyone else off. But just take the package in," Reed instructed. "And make sure you place it somewhere safe, far away from people."

"What the hell could it be?" Willis said, puzzled. "I mean,

are we talkin' about an old mine or are we talkin' about the Dutchman?"

"Oh, I assure you L.L. understands completely what and who we're talkin' about. He said the gift originates from The Giant Powder Company and will solve all our problems."

"Giant Powder Company, we're talkin' dynamite," Willis whistled, shaking his head in comprehension. "Yeah, that'll seal a mine up plenty good."

Malakoff Diggins, North Bloomfield, California 1883

L.L. Robinson crumpled the telegram after reading it, tossing it into an ashtray. He lit a cigar and held the match to the paper, watching it burn. It wasn't the most incriminating telegram, but best to handle things promptly, leaving no evidence behind.

Hamilton Smith approached, studying the charred remains. "I suppose this has something to do with the problem down in Auburn?"

Nothing to hide from Smith, L.L. disclosed, "I just dispatched a fifty pound crate of dynamite to Charles Reed. It should help him deal with the Dutch mining problem that plagues us both."

"Reed say anything on the whereabouts of McGirt?"

L.L. shook his head, "No, nothing. Left the area after he was seen fleeing Auburn."

"Have you read *The Union* today? Some trouble in Auburn, rioting amongst the Chinese. Do you think McGirt was involved? The newspaper mentioned a few Chinese miners were killed in the melee."

L.L. thought about it, "Undoubtedly, he was, in some peripheral way, though Charles Reed seems to have played a bigger hand in the affair, along with his own Boss Chinaman. Rivalries, clan hatred, *business*…we cannot judge Charles too harshly since the episode seems to have brought about the apprehension of the loathsome Dutchman. Besides," L.L. said ironically, "why should we be concerned with a few less Chinese miners. All they do is pick over our tailings, scavenging after the ten percent we lose through our process. I'd just as soon see it washed all the way to San Francisco Bay and out to sea."

Miss Potter entered the banquet room, "Mr. Robinson, your noontime appointment, Misters Cadwalader and Ohleyer, from the Anti-Debris Association are here to see you."

L.L. derisively voiced, *"Anti-Debris Association."* He looked to Hamilton, "Just saying those words feels like stepping into a field of cow chips, steaming butt nuggets on a pair of new boots."

Hamilton laughed, "Now L.L., you're always a congenial host, even to these likes. The case has been heard. We can afford to be gracious while Judge Sawyer deliberates."

"I still do not know why I agreed to this *inspection.* Has everything been taken care of?"

Hamilton removed his pocket watch, studying the time. "It'll be a quiet afternoon."

L.L. pulled from his cigar, holding the smoke for an instant before puffing a blue-gray cloud from the corner of his mouth, smiling, satisfied. "Miss Potter, please send them in and let me know when the chicken and champagne arrive."

Miss Potter responded, "Yes, sir." She withdrew and returned with two men, both in dark suits, their hats in hand.

"Mr. Robinson, Mr. Smith, this is Mr. George Cadwalader and Mr. George Ohleyer from Marysville," she said, taking the men's hats, closing the banquet doors behind her, adjourning from the scene.

L.L. smiled and stepped forward, "Welcome gentlemen, please have a seat at the table. Lunch will be along shortly, but let's do take this opportunity to sit and meet. Mr. Smith and I are most interested in discussing the plight of the valley's farmers." L.L. placed a hand on both men's shoulders, leading them ahead of himself to the table. He could not resist glancing back over his shoulder to Smith, making a quick wink.

Hamilton Smith laughed silently to himself bringing up the rear. L.L. was incapable of turning off his charm, even when it was disingenuous. Time for diplomacy and lunch, a tour of the mine, smiles all around, and please don't come back.

Pleasantries, social chatter ensued, with almost every topic discussed except mining. The men gorged themselves on some "wonderful" chicken, eating like field hands.

"Miss Potter, please, more champagne for Mr. Cadwalader," L.L. said smiling. "I saw how much you enjoyed the chicken. The bubbles will aid in digestion."

"Most generous of you, Mr. Robinson," Cadwalader replied, "splendid fare." He raised his glass, "a toast to Mr. Robinson, our genial host."

"You are too kind. I owe all of my manners and refinement to my late friend Francois Pioche. He introduced me to fine French cuisine and gained for me entry into every San Francisco cultural association. He took a naïve, ambitious young man from western New York and molded me into what I am today."

"Which is?" Cadwalader, the lawyer, queried.

L.L. thought a moment, "At heart, an engineer, railroads and mining. But now, we are no longer considered builders. I believe the term is capitalist."

"Surely, you are more than that, Mr. Robinson," Cadwalader ventured. "We are all capitalists in one form or another. No, sir, you are something more exalted – a tycoon."

"You are mistaken, George. I am not a member of that most exclusive club – the Big Four. Francois, myself, we did not get rich on fat government land subsidies and cheap Chinese labor that built the Transcontinental Railroad."

"But you wish you had," Cadwalader challenged.

"Don't we all wish? No, we lost that battle long ago," L.L. said with dismay, remembering his early railroad days, the lost opportunity. He said in consolation, "but we did manage to compel Stanford, Huntington, Hopkins, and Crocker, now there is a detestable man, to acquire our Sacramento Valley Railroad, which allowed for our purchase of the Market Street Railroad in San Francisco, converting it from horsecars to steam engines."

Hamilton spoke, "Gentlemen, have you ever seen the Spite Fence?"

"Heard of it, never saw it." Ohleyer said, sucking on a chicken bone.

"Symbol of one man's power over another," Hamilton explained. "Crocker, not to be outdone by Stanford and Hopkins, built an enormous mansion on the top of Nob Hill, a complete city block, all except for one lot owned by a young man and his family. He refused to sell to Crocker." Hamilton threw up his hands theatrically, "Naturally, the great man could not be denied so he built a 40 foot fence, looming over three sides of the poor man's home. The views of the Bay, the Berkeley hills, even fresh air through the windows, all gone. People said it was like living in the bottom of a well."

"Walled in like Marysville with all its levees," Cadwalader said dryly, striking a match for affect, lighting a two-bit cigar.

L.L. grimaced, "Yes, that's a *great* story, Hamilton," admonishing the man with a mere look for his choice in tales.

Hamilton felt like Henry Perkins, embarrassed, stepping into his own self-made field of ass biscuits.

"I think it's time we tour the mine, gentlemen," L.L. said, breaking the tension. "You can observe for yourself how we capture the coarse debris in the mine. I'm sure once you see and understand our operation, it will ease your minds."

In short order the men had descended to the bottom of the great hole. Cadwalader and Ohleyer made a complete turn, surveying the vast amphitheater and its 600 foot walls. L.L. and Smith could see that the men were awed by the spectacle – everyone is.

"All of this done by man," Cadwalader said, wonderstruck by the accomplishment but discouraged at the result.

Red, muddy water flowed slowly along the bottom of the mine, westerly to the small dam and lake inside the mine. In the distance, three monitors were blasting away and less than twenty workmen could be seen.

"Not much happening, so little dirt flying," Ohleyer called out. "How come so few monitors? Where are all the workmen?"

"The real labor was building the mine – the ditches, tunnels, and piping," Smith explained. "We now operate the mine itself with little over one hundred men."

"So as you can see, gentlemen," L.L. said, "this operation is not nearly as big as you think. We could not possibly be the sole source of the calamities suffered by the valley."

"Few men, but one big hole," Cadwalader remarked, dissatisfied.

"Let's take a look down there," Ohleyer said, pointing to the low end, to the dam and lake. "That's what we come to see. What you're doing with all this muck."

L.L., annoyed, gestured onward, nothing to hide, "Please, lead the way."

Ohleyer and Cadwalader strode ahead confidently, marching side by side, speaking to one another in hushed tones. L.L. and Smith did likewise, both pairs assessing the meeting so far.

The men reached a large flume. L.L. suggested, "We can take the gangway so as to better see the dam and settling pool. The men climbed a short ladder to the gangway, walking the wooden planks beside the flume that conveyed debris-laden water. After a short walk, they reached a good vantage point, allowing for close up observation of a dam restraining a small lake.

Smith explained the function of the dam, "The dam was constructed so that the sluice boxes empty into the lake, where the coarse debris settles and the water is cleared. Heavy debris is captured behind the dam and does not escape over the spillway."

L.L. picked up the narrative, "This smaller material, far less

238

volume than you think, then travels to our *famous* tunnel, running through underground sluices for over a mile-and-a-half, where most of the gold is collected. What remains," L.L. said, dismissively, "is a watery remnant, similar to the silt your own farms create. It's then discharged into Humbug Creek and to the Yuba River below and certainly nothing to worry about."

Ohleyer, unconvinced, continued walking beside the flume and past the dam. Cadwalader followed a few steps behind.

L.L. looked to Smith, their eyes meeting. L.L. called out, "Nothing to be seen down there."

The men kept to their pace with L.L. and Smith reluctantly joining in behind.

Ohleyer finally stopped. "That, that there is what we come to see," pointing an accusatory finger. "It's the escape box for all your sluices. All the big debris goes right through that bottom you've got so cleverly hidden. We know all about it. You can't hornswoggle us."

L.L. regrouped, he hadn't expected this, "Gentlemen, admittedly, there are times when some large objects do slip past the dam," he said soothingly, "but these occurrences are rare…"

Cadwalader interrupted, "No, sir, they are not. We know for a fact that heavy debris is routinely discharged down the tunnel and that it is standard practice for your mine to do so."

L.L. considered stopping the man, but sensed more was to follow and he was correct.

"You see, Mr. Robinson, we did not arrive for this meeting directly from Marysville at high noon as you might suspect. No, Mr. Ohleyer and I spent the morning inspecting the mine by way of Humbug Creek. What we saw at the mouth of your drainage tunnel is nothing akin to the balderdash you show us now."

L.L. stared angrily straight into Cadwalader's eyes, who met the challenge by raising his voice, "We witnessed a torrent, a full head of water discharging heavy debris from the tunnel, a wicked muddy avalanche destined for the valley farms. It is nothing like this silt ridden stream, this mere trickle you attempt to deceive us with now," he waved a contemptuous hand at the meager flow crossing the spillway.

Ohleyer jumped on board, "I threw several rocks, big ones, weighing more than 30 pounds each, into your river of muck and it just tossed them away like pebbles. You were doing all your heavy work all morning, right up until we arrived, you dumb son of a bitch, but we saw it all anyway."

L.L. had heard enough, his own rage boiling up inside. He exploded, "Get the hell out of my mine, you arrogant flatland shit kickers!"

Cadwalader smiled grimly at the bluster, speaking a final rejoinder, "Thank you, sir, for confirming our long held suspicions and for the delicious luncheon." He tipped his hat in mock ceremony, manners prevailing. "We will find our way out posthaste."

Cadwalader turned and joined Ohleyer, both men smiling at their success. Cadwalader reached into his coat pocket, removing one of the fine two-bit cigars L.L. had dispensed. He bit off the tip, spit, and smiled, chewing on the end. Theirs would be an enjoyable journey back to Marysville.

L.L. looked to Smith, "Hamilton, get on the telephone and call the Bowman reservoir. I want the water flowing again.

Ready all of the monitors. I want everything back to full blast, do you hear me! And get the goddamn lights on. It will be dark soon. We're going to get every last fleck of gold out of this ridge!"

Auburn, California 1883

Willis borrowed the stage, the one he would drive later that morning, to take his friends to the train depot. It was only a short distance up the hill to High Street. The mile-and-a-half went by in quick order under a ferociously blue sky that spanned the canyon to Foresthill, reaching far away into the distance, crowning the peaks of the Sierra Nevada. Clouds would move in later that day, thunderstorms in the mountains, Willis thought, best grab my slicker. He glanced back at his passengers as they pulled into the depot, Chan's head peering out the window, trying to see everything. He was bound for Nevada City and above and they were going in the opposite direction, iron horse to the coast.

Baggage attendants removed John John's heavy Saratoga trunk from the stage's rear boot and he checked it with the railroad agent. The elegant trunk, with its round dome lid, assured it a preferential position high atop the baggage car. Chan, Mr. Chang, and Ming Ni toted their new carpet bags, remnants decorated with fine oriental prints capped with leather handles, stuffed with all their belongings. They walked a short distance to the raised wooden platform that bisected two sets of tracks. They stood idly by, only a few people about, waiting for Reed to return with their railroad passage to

Oakland, the western terminus for the Transcontinental Railroad, then a ship, a steamer bound for the Far East.

When Reed returned, he gestured toward the train hissing steam trackside, the engine looming large and black, smelling of oil and metal. "Everything's on time. We best get aboard."

Willis said his goodbyes moving down the line, shaking hands and clapping J.J. on the shoulder. "I seen you with Ah Cy, so I know you'll be back," the remark caused J.J. to smile broadly. Willis then made a tiny handshake with Chan, holding just the tips of her fingers. She smiled and he said, "It was nice to finally get to know you. I know you mean so much to Charlie, here, but we'll see you return soon enough once this blows over."

"Please thank Alice for me. We had so little time together. She was a most generous escort showing me the ladies shops, helping me to fill my bag," Chan said, lifting the bag an inch.

"Alice likes to spend money, especially if it's mine or Charlie's. She woulda been here to see you off, but she's teachin' young 'uns today. You just get back to us safely, so you can wear some of those fancy duds around here. It's goin' to be a rough time till we get the two of you back together again."

Chan forced a tight smile and looked away, suppressing a wave of emotion that welled up in her chest. The immensity of all this change, so sudden, freedom to flight, leaving the man she loved. Only a short time together remaining, followed by loneliness at sea, a personal island moving in a direction that felt backward, returning to her beloved parents, but her future was here, in this place, with Charles Reed.

Willis recognized the pained expression and discreetly

moved down the line, bowing to Ming Ni and bowing even deeper to Mr. Chang.

"Learned a lot from you, Mr. Chang. We're all goin' to miss you in the kitchen, well, you know, Alice, especially, but I'm really goin' to miss all them needles you stuck in my bad back. I know I was leery of the idea early on, but, dang, that Devil's Magic done the trick with my pain," Willis boasted.

"Much life energy in you, Willis," Mr. Chang said. "The needles redirect the spirit in your body."

"Shoot, don't talk to Alice, she'll have you redirecting it away from down here, where it counts," Willis said, peering over the top of his belt buckle, "to someplace else where I don't need it."

Mr. Chang laughed heartily, "spoken like a true emperor."

"Everyone go ahead and get on board," Reed said. "I'm going to have a word with Willis."

The two men watched the entourage move to a mostly empty passenger car and up the stairs, each holding the handrail up. John John led the way, with Chan stepping up last. She turned and looked back to Reed. He waved a hand of reassurance to her, nodding everything is okay. She smiled and turned, entering the car, finding a seat. Reed watched her silhouette pass down the aisle and descend onto a bench seat.

"Anxious," Reed said, "vulnerable, a whole lot happening at once. She's finally feeling safe and now we part, but…"

"I can tell you now, if gettin' on this train is hard, gettin' on that ship is goin' to be even harder. You, J.J., and me, we all know it's the best course to follow. It's just going to take a little while is all." Willis stopped and looked at his friend, knowing the power of his words were of dubious value. He changed tack. "How you holdin' up?"

Reed shook his head, displaying his own melancholy, "I've shoved it all down into my craw where it can stick. Nothing to do but to be strong about it, I guess."

"That's the best example you can set. It'll give her strength."

Reed changed the subject, "I spoke to the station agent inside. The dynamite is here, off on a side rail. Told the agent you'd be by to pick it up."

Willis nodded, "I'll take it back with me now and run it out to the ravine. See how the Charlies are doing. Forgot to tell you, the Dutchman tried to escape last night."

"Escape?"

"I wasn't goin' to bother you with this, but, yeah, the Dutchman had to shit so Charlie One unties him and sits him on a bucket," Willis recounted. "He lunged up snapping and biting like a viper, but Charlie Two was ready. He chopped him hard in neck, caught him right in the throat. It took the fight out of him. They cuffed him back up and cut a hole in the back of his pants, tying the bucket onto him. He ain't goin' anywhere."

Reed considered the ruckus and its result, nothing worthy of a reply. "Okay," he shrugged, "I'll see you back here in a couple of days."

"Remember, I'll be returnin' late that day," Willis reminded, "drivin' the stage up past Nevada City and on to Downieville. Don't worry about anything around here. J.C. is goin' to stop by and keep an eye on things."

Reed nodded "good" and said, "Hai Lon is ready to get the faro tables running again, Elsa back on the piano along with the dancing ladies, the saloon open, Charlie Yue holdin' down the kitchen, we're back in business sooner than I expected."

Willis said nothing. It all sounded so anticlimactic to both men.

Reed clapped Willis on the shoulder, "in a few days then," and walked to the train.

When he entered, he saw the back of the conductor standing over Chan, the twitch and jerks in his movements setting off an alarm in Reed who increased his speed down the aisle. He placed a hand on the back of the conductor's blue coat, giving him a slight shove, "Any trouble here?"

The conductor turned, startled, his gin blossomed nose and glass eye meeting Reed, mouth agape, as if caught in mid-sentence.

Like with his quick draw, Reed took the initiative, firing his words first. "What are you saying to my wife?" he said stern-ly, a cross look on his face.

Surprise followed by comprehension moved across the conductor's face. He said nothing as his single eye darted to a stop, bouncing like the marble in a game of roulette. He simply drew his frame up, at full attention, touching the bill of his conductor's cap in mock courtesy, saying, "My mistake, sir."

He shuffled down the aisle, his head turning to and fro from John John, Mr. Chang, and Ming Ni, scrutinizing each as he passed by. When he opened the rail car door, he looked back to see Charles Reed still standing, staring at him. He closed the door, moving quickly on to the next car.

Chan slid down the bench seat next to the window and Reed sat down. He placed his hand on hers and their fingers interlaced. Reed could see tears on her cheeks as she looked out into the day's sunlight.

More steam hissed, brakes released, and the train jolted to a start, every passenger pushed back into their seats, a bobble of inertia.

"He said I needed to be in the Chinese car."

"I know. It's informal. They don't label the cars, just figure all Chinese know they need to sit together, but don't let it get you down. I'm here now."

"But what will I do when you're not?"

"We just need to get you all on the steamer. Everything will be fine after that. No one will give you trouble," Reed reassured.

"I meant when we part. What do I do until then?"

"That's not so easy to answer," Reed admitted. "The country is going through its fits and starts with the Chinese. I guess, in some ways we are too, but this isn't the end of us. You just have to believe it isn't over."

She smiled, holding his hand tighter.

The train passed from Auburn, leaving the foothills and winding down into the Sacramento Valley. "Such open space, the mountains, the valley and soon the sea. It is so expansive, overwhelming. It is difficult to believe I am free, not imprisoned in a room, or lucky to venture out into the sunlight to labor in a field just a few feet from my confinement." Chan sat quietly for a moment, "My world was so small. Only you made it bearable, Charles."

He put his arm around her shoulder and she leaned into him.

"Charles, tell me of the other girls, newly freed from Dai Lao?"

"J.J. spoke to China Mollie."

"Chuey Fong?"

"Yeah, I guess that's her name. She's going into the madam business. Go Sam, in the kitchen, says he'll help her out so some are staying on. She says she's strictly a madam and won't be peddling balls of dope."

Chan spoke her name slowly, "China Mollie," unsurprised that she would be leading and organizing those remaining in the oldest profession.

"Some ladies ran off with their favorite miner once the street fight ended," Reed continued. "We did find a cache of Pig Face's money and handed it out. J.J. said the girls were stunned speechless by the display of kindness."

"In our world, such displays were foreign, though you always shielded and protected me during my dark time."

"I couldn't help everyone but now we can," Reed replied. "When we helped ourselves, we helped a lot of others too. I suppose some will want to get back to China and others will try to vanish now that Pig Face is dead along with their debt, though I suspect someone from the Hip Yee Tong will be along shortly. They'll try to enforce new terms. J.J. offered the best advice, just get on a train and head to Oregon or all the way up to Seattle. With so few Chinese women, and no more coming to these shores, he told them to find a good man to marry, be selective and choose wisely."

The train stopped for an extended time in Sacramento, taking on passengers and cargo, grain bound for foreign markets. The group dined at a nearby Cantonese restaurant that was more than a chop suey joint, paying the flat price for anything they could eat, which included delicious fare, like abalone, duck, oysters, and cuttle-fish, along with rice, bamboo shoots, and cabbage. They boarded the train fully sated, moving on uneventfully, through stops in Davisville, Fairfield, and Vallejo. Upon reaching the Carquinez Strait, between Benicia and Port Costa, the entire train was rolled on to the deck tracks of the world's largest railroad ferry, the *Solano*. This immense sidewheel paddleboat measured 424 feet long and 116 feet wide, much wider abeam than the upcoming steamer bound for Hong Kong. The group marveled at the ease with which the crossing was accomplished, smooth and efficient, employing skilled railroaders and boatmen, who worked closely as a team, their movement rote and practiced through many crossings.

Brief stops in Richmond and Berkeley followed. The last leg was a short run to the western terminus in Oakland, the train arriving in the early evening hour at the 7th Street station near Broadway. Reed settled the group into a neighboring boarding house, whose rooms faced out across the bay to San Francisco. The group supped on a greasy pot of stew and bread, nothing like the lunch in Sacramento. Reed excused himself, walking to the Port Authority of Oakland, where he located the agent in charge, who could stamp, sign, and date the Certificates of Identity, allowing for reentry into America.

The agent looked closely at the picture of Chan on the certificate. "She's your wife?"

"She is."

He paused, studying Reed, commenting, "Well, she's pretty for a sing-song girl." He stamped, signed and dated Chan's certificate, moving on to John John's. "What's his story? Why does he need to come back?"

"I'll vouch for him. Works for me, Chinese kitchen and laundry," Reed said, not betraying the true nature of their partnership that would only raise suspicions and pose more questions, like illegal Chinese ownership of land and property.

Convinced, the agent applied a quick pop of the stamp, ink pad to paper, followed by another signature and date. "What about these two?" the agent said, glancing up at the big clock on the wall. "Look mighty old, you sure they can even make it back?"

"If they do, they won't be working or taking anyone's job. They'll be living out their years with family and friends. Look, I'm just giving them a choice, if they ever want to return. I'd wager this is their last trip, going home to die. They want it to happen in the old country so their bones can rest there."

The agent stamped, signed, and dated, opining, "I don't think they're ever coming back."

He handed all of the Certificates of Identity back to Reed who said, "Obliged." He turned and walked his way out of the building, impressed he was able to hold his tongue, glad to have this chore complete.

Last night in an Oakland boarding house, four walls surrounding a bed and sparse furniture. Reed sits nude on the floor, a thin sheen of sweat cooling his body as he leans against the wall beneath an open window. He smokes a cigar, its tip glowing with each inhalation. He exhales a stream of blue-gray smoke softly into the moonlight, while a faint breeze causes the parted curtains to gently stir. Chan sits in a chair, looking out over the waters of the East Bay, toward the lights of San Francisco and its Barbary Coast, a pillow beneath her and another at her back as she reclines into its comfy confines. She draws a sheet up over the top of her bare breasts to protect against the cool marine air. They said little that entire night, all attention on this last act of love, a surging tug of war between two hearts, its energy and passion passing like a gift to and from each body, a storm of arousal punctuated by its own lightning, a climatic jolt, flashing out like a beacon, illuminating their time together. It was more than a memorable act between two lovers, both astonished by their desire, their lust and intimacy for one another. It was an inerasable joining of hearts that combined the vivid past with the promise of a joyful future together. No words are needed during this time of contemplation. They think and feel as one, bonded together, forging their relationship into something new and profound, something absence could never conquer. For both, in a lifetime of encounters, this moment would always stand out, thrilling, poignant, unshakeable, unifying their love forever.

Henness Pass Road near Freeman's Crossing, 1883

Willis Connelly was anxious to get back to Auburn. The first day driving the Telegraph Stagecoach rolled by uneventfully as the crew and passengers climbed beyond Nevada City to their destination in Downieville. Jim "Buckshot" Simmons sat perched beside him as shotgun messenger. He was a talkative sort, filling the air nonstop with stories, observations, and opinions. All you had to do was say, "How you doin', Jim?" and he would pretty much rattle on from there. It reduced the normally loquacious Connelly to mute silence, an occasional nod or grunt his only contribution, expertly timed between pauses in Buckshot's sentences or when he drew a breath. As the return journey progressed, the acknowledgments grew fewer, the speechifying wearing a rut into Willis the same way the stage's thin iron wheels cut a trough into the road. Willis could only be run over for so long, so he adjusted his listening from polite obligation to voluntary indifference. His mind was more on Auburn, joining back up with Reed, and ridding themselves of one of the two men menacing their lives.

Buckshot spoke, elbowing the brooding Willis from his thoughts. "I say, Willis, you ever see so much game skitter about on this stretch?"

Willis looked off to his side and watched a doe and her fawn leap quickly over a downed tree and off through the brush, darting a course deeper into the chaparral, finding gaps in the thorny twigs and branches. "Yeah, something about," he said, "maybe a bobcat or mountain lion…we'll be at Freeman's Crossing soon."

"Reminds me," Buckshot said, "before the Transcontinental Railroad, this road used to be filled with freight wagons, one after another, all the way to Virginia City. It was so crowded that the six stagecoach lines all ran at night."

Willis interrupted, "Take a look at the river. It's swellin' up. Somethin's wrong."

They continued the stage at a gallop, driving to the river bend, where they saw a tangle of debris – timber, brush, boulders, even the remains of a small cabin – forming a temporary dam a short distance from the covered bridge at

Freeman's Crossing.

"What the hell?" Buckshot exclaimed. "Look across the river, Willis. There's Tom Freeman helping his blind wife git to high ground."

"The English Dam must've collapsed. We best get over the bridge before that debris field breaks free. It's the only thing holdin' back the river. Yah! Yah! Get along," Willis shouted, snapping the three reins he laced through the fingers of each of his gloved hands, repeating the command over and over.

"We're going to make it easy, Willis. You don't need to drive the team so hard."

"I ain't takin' no chances. You see folks movin' to high ground, then we best get there too. Start throwin' them stones we got. We need all the speed we can get."

Buckshot disagreed but laid his shotgun aside and began hurling stones at the horses, stinging their backsides, joining Willis in a noisy chorus, encouraging the team forward.

They sped past the large obstructing pile, the shattered cabin teetering at a strange angle on top, its front door bobbing like the pendulum to a clock. Willis and Buckshot's eyes widened upon close examination, the inundating water rising quickly up the side of the mound of waste, working its way around and through the detritus, weakening it. The swirling current, more water by the second, could not be held back for long. It would soon crest over the top.

"I see your point, Willis," Buckshot hollered, tossing a handful of stones with greater force, "Get after it, you doggies! Giddap!"

They raced the remaining 100 yards, looking back to see more and more rivulets of water streaming over the top. Water filled the cabin and began pouring out a back window. In mere seconds, the shack gave way, forced from its perch atop, tumbling down the pile and breaking to pieces, yielding to the onrushing tide.

Willis slowed the stage, braking momentarily to make the tight turn up onto the abutment to the covered bridge. The stage's thoroughbraces strained, swinging the coach compartment wide, as the passengers inside, including Judge O.P. Stidger, released gasps of consternation. Willis leaned inside the turn, while Buckshot did the same, leaping from his seat, firmly grasping the side of the bench, as he braced his 200 pounds out over the front inside wheel, trying to keep it down on the ground and the stage from flipping over. They shared a brief second of worry before the stage swung back to center, the weight of the stagecoach returning to all four wheels. Buckshot clambered back to his seat, narrowly missing the beam to the bridge's southern end piece in doing so. He slipped just inside with inches to spare, seeing the beam's tight wood grain up close as it sped right past his nose, grazing the rim to his hat, turning it sideways on his head.

Willis renewed the charge forward, driving hard and fast through the bridge's darkened interior, the wooden plank deck clanking and clattering, producing a deafening commotion in the enclosed space. Their spines stiffened when they heard a sharp crack through the bridge siding. They knew what it meant. The debris field had given way, a flood of oncoming water and tons of wreckage was rushing toward them. The stage burst into the sunlight and onto the opposite bank, shooting forth from beneath the bridge's soon to be forgotten shake shingle rooftop. The horses lurched forward in unison, snorting and straining on their collars, traces snapping taunt. Willis beckoned for more speed, climbing up away from the river.

They raced pell-mell up the embankment, seeing Tom Freeman, his wife, servants, and workmen standing along the bluff, not looking at the stage but over its top, pointing back to the river as the huge pile swept down on the bridge, a giant raft of rubbish gathering speed. Willis reined the horses in beside the onlookers, setting the brake. He and Buckshot jumped to their feet, standing atop the stage as the passengers inside squeezed their faces into the windows facing the river. Judge Stidger unlatched the stage door and stumbled out, face first, falling in a heap upon the ground. He shot back up out of the dust, a tear in his fine trousers, the price paid for improving his view of the spectacle.

Some simply "oohed," others stood stoically, Tom Freeman, most of all, as the massive pile crashed through his toll bridge, taking his hotel, broom factory, blacksmith and carpentry shop along with it, doubling the pile of debris in size. They watched dumbfounded as the tremendous weight of the water, the whirling rapids, shoved the large mass before it, filling the canyon like a giant land schooner steaming from port. They remained speechless, all but bidding it bon voyage as it sailed from sight, surging downstream to the towns below, North San Juan, Graniteville, Smartsville, out of the foothills and into the valley, on to Marysville.

Buckshot Jim broke the silence. "Whoo-eee! Tarnation, Willis Connelly! The late great Hank Monk himself would be damn proud of how you handled that stagecoach. He couldn't have done a better job himself, may he rest in peace."

"What are you talkin' about?" Willis said. "Hank ain't dead."

Buckshot removed the hat that still sat sideways off his head and held it to his chest, lowering his voice to just above a whisper. "Afraid so, just a few days back in Carson City. Pneumonia done got him."

Willis shook his head, remembering the last time he saw his friend at Miss Ellie's in North Bloomfield, with his bad cough. Hank shoulda stayed in bed, let Ellie tend him, get some power back into his lungs. "You done all that talkin' for two days and *now* you say Hank's dead. Buckshot, you need to learn to put the important matters at the top of your speakin' list, in front of all that other hogwash you pack my ears with."

"I'm sorry, Willis. I thought you knew. It was in all the newspapers."

Willis spit and kicked a stone in frustration, launching it from the edge of the bluff and almost to the river, disheartened to discover an old friend and mentor had taken up residence in tomb town. Willis brought his boot back down, "Not your fault, Buckshot. Sorry day is all, a friend dead and this calamity ain't helpin' matters." Willis raised his voice, "I hope folks below know this pile of muck is headed their way."

"N.C. Miller, the ditch superintendent," Tom Freeman said solemnly, "he used that long distance telephone of his to start warning people up and down the line, sending riders out in both directions, upstream and downstream when the dam gave way early this morning."

Tom peered out at the scene below, assessing what was left of his property. Later, when he added up all that was lost, including the 200 pound anvil that was nowhere to be found, he would place the total at $12,000 in damages, a life's work. He whispered something into the ear of his blind wife, who began to cry. He gave her his kerchief, placing an arm over her shoulders. She quickly grabbed his hand, stroking it repeatedly as her chest heaved. "We got our lives," he said, his voice choking with emotion. "We should be grateful."

The assemblage watched as five Chinese miners, soaking wet, climbed from the riverbed, exhausted. One spoke English, explaining how a companion ignored their warning and returned to his cabin to get his clothes and drowned. The five had searched for his body, but it was hopeless.

Nobody said anything after that, continuing their vigil, bearing witness, shaking their heads at the enormity of the disaster. With the blockage displaced, the current rushed by more potently than ever, churning left to right, mesmerizing in its monotony. They all shared a version of the same thought – we coulda been down there under all of that, dead like that Chinaman. But they weren't. They had survived.

Above, higher in the mountains, the English Dam, what remained of it, sat in ruins, its dry stone encased in 3 inch planking yielding to the maelstrom, tossed aside, bits and pieces of wreckage strewn below, as if hurled from a high window. The lake, one of the largest reservoirs in the state, was out from behind its barrier, spilling down the watershed. George Davis, watchman at the dam, in the employ of the Milton Water Company, owners of the dam and the vast volume of water, was now taking stock. He had seen it all, beginning at 5 a.m. Water had penetrated the dam, he had no doubt, causing the wooden middle portion to collapse. He was no engineer, but he knew enough about water to know that it could find its way through anything. He had witnessed the power of the water monitors and understood how water pressure on the back of this dam, even a slow leak could grow and spread like some infestation, weakening the structure, causing its destruction. Once the upper portion was removed, he witnessed the rest of the dam's demise, the 130 foot height crumbling down gradually, stones and all. It would take an hour-and-a-half for the reservoir to empty. He stared out at the mammoth sink left dry. He thought of the Milton Mine and other smaller mines around French Corral who counted on this water for their operations. No hydraulic mining for them this year. The water was gone, unused, free of slickens, washing out to the valley and beyond, all the way to San Francisco Bay. Those miners are all going to be out of work, Davis thought. He mulled it over some more before deciding he would need to seek new employment, too. He took one last look and turned and walked away.

All through the morning and into the afternoon, people scrambled to escape the deluge. The use of the Ridge Telephone line, notifying call stations to the approximate time high water would reach designated points saved many lives. The Black brothers, up earlier than usual, saw the flood and eluded it by climbing a tree, saving their skins but losing their house and barn. Tom Fainweather, a ditch tender with a new bride, survived the flood by mere inches, finding sanctuary on high ground, escaping with their prized new furniture. But not everyone was so lucky. Near Graniteville the water rose over 100 feet above normal, the massive wave destroying a half mile of flume and the small Eureka Lake Company dam that directed water to the San Juan Ditch. It was near here that the older Reese brother drowned, aged and decrepit, though still mining, perishing despite a heroic effort made by his younger, more vigorous brother.

Scenes of destruction kept repeating from the mountains to the valley – 4 Chinese and 1 Italian drowned, the 80 foot trestle at Bloody Run Canyon demolished, the American Mine flume smashed. At 11 a.m., the wall of water arrived in Smartsville, pushing the immense floating bridge before it, thick with logs, driftwood, and other debris. Those who saw it thought the mass solid enough for a man to walk across if he dared. None did, preferring to watch the tangled mass parade out of town, killing 40 head of cattle on its persistent march.

Word quickly spread that the flood would reach Marysville by 2 p.m. Citizens gathered near the D Street Bridge, placing bets on the probable height of the water, treating the whole matter as a thing of jest, giddy with anticipation. The show proved a disappointment. People watched as the thick syrupy water choked with mining debris ran beneath the bridge, flowing down the Yuba River to its confluence with the Feather River and on to the Sacramento River. The seething, all powerful wave that everyone expected, never waylaid the town. The crowd soon dispersed, going home, complaining of the pitiful display. It would be a day or two before *The Marysville Appeal* would report on the levee failure in the Linda district seven miles east of town, relieving the pressure of the flood, sparing Marysville. B.P. Hugg, deputy assessor, described the event. He was the first to notice the damage to the levee while standing on top, watching it grow from 1 foot deep and a yard wide to 40 feet wide in 15 minutes. He warned the men harvesting crops in the fields below to flee, which "they did with great urgency, but sizable damage was done to the crops," Mr. Hugg stated.

Questions abounded, with both sides speaking out in the aftermath. George Cadwalader of the Anti-Debris Association, lashed out at the hydraulickers, using the English Dam collapse to, yet again, disparage the miner's proposal for a debris dam to be built in the Yuba narrows. Cadwalader declared the plan "foolhardy" and a "wasted expenditure," reaffirming the argument that "only Judge Sawyer can end the scourge of hydraulic mining and that no miner's dam can be relied upon to keep the cities and towns of the valley safe." Robert Lincoln, son of a revered President and the current Secretary of War, agreed. He held the purse strings to $250,000 in federal money allotted to the waterway, stating it "not wise to build the dams with the continued operation of the mines."

Henry Perkins, engineer for the North Bloomfield Mine, speaking for the Hydraulic Miners Association, asserted the English Dam's destruction was deliberate and not accidental. He claimed the dam was blown up by powder, all but suggesting the culpability of valley grangers in the matter, conniving at the behest of Anti-Debris Association agent's intent upon sowing discord. Further, Mr. Perkins declared that he himself had recently inspected the dam's 450 foot length, proclaiming the structure "perfectly sound in all its parts." Perkins concluded his statement by offering a "$5,000 reward for any information that will lead to an arrest and conviction of those responsible for the deadly deed."

Of course, no evidence of an explosion was ever found and no one was ever convicted, but plenty of evidence for a poor design and an unmaintained dam was later uncovered. It all came as no surprise to the former dam watchman George Davis, who was now working in dry goods.

Auburn, California 1883

A Republican and a Democrat sat on the porch to The Golden Star of Shanghai, a table between them, playing dominoes, watching the town mosey on by. J.C. Boggs took a swig of steam beer, not sure if he liked it. "I only beat you in the election of '79 because that Sonie son of bitch from the Workingmen's Party ran for sheriff too," he said.

Asa Huntley nodded in agreement, "Yes, he peeled off a wagon full of Democratic votes I was counting on," he said with no regret, seeing as he now had the job.

"It wasn't *that* many," J.C. countered with a chuckle. "I was a mighty popular constable, favored by the Auburn citizenry."

"Good thing folks discovered their horse sense when it comes to all the rabble-rousers in the Workingmen's Party of California, Denis Kearney most of all," Asa said, wondering, "Kearney still in jail?"

J.C. thought a moment, examining his bones before placing one at the end of the line. "I think so. Still inside for inciting a mob, but which mob? There were so many. Did you know McGirt and the Dutchman served as sergeants at arms to their convention?"

Asa shook his head, thinking of the race riots and the chant, "The Chinese must go" and "No more cheap labor." He said, "You know the Workingmen's Party biggest mistake was singling out the Chinese and not staying after the Railroad Barons and all the other tycoons who filled their pockets by way of the Chinese. Those rich bastards could pay working people more, but they'd rather build fancy mansions, collect European art, forgetting the little folks of every color who made them king of the hill."

"Speakin' of Chinese, you know these two?"

"Never seen them before, but they sure look like Hip Yee Tong to me," Asa said, watching two hatchet men approach, anger in their eyes, surveying the loss of Dai Lao's lair.

J.C. grabbed the shotgun propped against the wall. He traced their movement with the twin barrels, aiming it at their middles. He stood and yelled, "Fill your pipes somewhere else. Closed down, nobody home!"

The two tong enforcers turned and saw the shotgun pointed at them. They shared a look, thinking what to do?

"Get your asses back to San Francisco, you hear me!" J.C. called out.

Asa stood, too, his badge prominently pinned to his vest, his hand moving and resting on the handle to his holstered revolver. "John, they don't understand a word you're saying."

"Yeah, but they know what this shotgun means."

The stare down continued for a few more tense moments. The taller Chinese broke eye contact and looked to his shorter companion, whispering something. The short one answered with his own whisper. The tall one then returned his attention to J.C. and Sheriff Huntley. He made a small bowing gesture, hands together in front. He then straightened and strode away briskly, the shorter one following behind.

"That's right, get the hell out of town," J.C. said, lowering his shotgun. "Asa, I ever tell you about the law of the shotgun? How it's a people mover?"

"Only a few hundred times," Asa said with a smirk.

J.C. returned the shotgun, propping it back into place. He reached for a paper bag. "These peaches are somethin' special. I'm thinkin' of growin' some. You tell me if you ever tasted anything so delicious? Here, go on, take one to your wife, but you watch it. They bruise just by lookin' at 'em."

Asa bit into one, succulent juice filling his mouth, "Sweet."

Oakland, California 1883

The small fishing boat first appeared as a distant lantern, a tiny golden dot, off in the darkness. It was the only light moving this time of day, well past evening but not yet morning. Reed, Chan, and the others studied the light, growing larger as it steered a zig-zag course across the bay, through the foggy mist, from San Francisco to the Oakland Pier where they stood. John John blinked his signal lantern twice and the group waited. The amber light, bobbing in the bay, blinked once in reply. Good, Reed thought, saying, "There's our ride." J.J. began to wave his lantern in a slow arc, guiding the boat into dock. The boat was no longer just a lantern. It was now a darker, more shadowy shape set against the backdrop of the bay. As it drew closer, a mast and sail became visible, then an entire vessel, not more than 20 feet long, the outline of a man at the tiller. The silhouette raised his arm in friendship, a single wave, arriving silently on the wind. He glided the boat skillfully into dock, dropping the last portion of the triangular sail along its angled, raking mast at just the right moment. The group watched as the green painted hull of the *Libby May*, exhausted its speed, drifting the short remaining distance to a stop, just inches from the pier. The skipper tossed a rope to Reed while Mr. Chang took hold of the bow. Together they moored the boat securely to cleats on the dock.

"Ahoy," Jacob Langtry shouted, stepping over the rail, planting his feet firmly on the wooden planks. "You must be Charles Reed?" he said, extending his hand.

"And you Jacob Langtry. Asa Huntley speaks kindly of you," Reed said in return, shaking his hand.

"How's that old merchantman doing, now that he's swallowed the anchor, given up the sea for the foothills?"

"No regrets, that I can tell," Reed responded. "He's spoken often of his travels seeing the world, the times you spent together, Central and South America, the Orient. Said it was rewarding but difficult work, the kind only young men can and should do."

"Asa and me, we got our fill, glad to have survived it. We both came to the conclusion that the life of a seafaring mariner, without roots, no port to call home, was for men starting out. We'd seen the world and it was time to step away so others can have a look."

"But you are still on the water," J.J. said, as he and Mr. Chang moved the large Saratoga trunk onboard.

"Aye, that's true. I'm a fisherman now. I have a home and a wife, Libby May," he said, gesturing proudly to the red lettered moniker on the side of the boat. "I bought her from an Italian man, who built it himself. It's called a felucca, the most common boat in the bay, the kind used in the old fishing villages of the Mediterranean, sturdy, sails well tacking against the wind."

"The way you maneuver it, right up to the dock, we can see you enjoy your time on the water," Reed said.

"I can't sing Verdi like some of the other fellas and wish I could because good voices stand out in the fog so you don't get run over by the bigger ships. Anyway, I'm in and out of the same bed each and every day and not a better place to fish, something to catch every month of the year, though it's getting crowded, must be 3 or 4 thousand of us fishing these waters. It's getting so big that the state is going to open a Fisherman's Wharf sometime next year."

"What kind of fish do you catch?" Chan asked.

"All sorts. After I deliver you up, I'll venture to the shrimp fields. Good shrimp to be found in the central part of the bay. The Chinese can't catch enough for their kitchens and a large amount is dried and shipped to China. I'd venture to say a few tons of it is in the hold of the ship you have passage on."

Mr. Chang smiled, "Yes, very good shrimp. We cooked and ate our share at The Golden Star of Shanghai, also salmon and sturgeon."

"The waters nearby, Oakland and Berkeley," Jacob said, pointing, "good salmon and sturgeon, plus flounder and herring can be had. Beyond that, there's always crab and smelt. The smelt teem in schools by the millions January through June. Curious little fish, thrives in both fresh and salt water. Tastes good too, batter 'em up and fry 'em in butter."

He completed his tour of the fisheries of the bay by saying, "Sail further south, toward Richmond and San Pablo Bay and you'll come across clam beds and oysters, pockets of them are all about."

John John asked, "Other than the shrimp, what else can you tell us about our ship, the *City of Tokio?*"

"She's a fine vessel, used by President Grant on his world tour a few years ago when he left office. The captain's a drunk, who spends most of his time asleep in his cabin. The first officer, a fine fellow, Mr. Oliver, impressive and most capable, he runs the ship. You have no worries. Spoke to him last night and everything is arranged. He'll have a gangplank ready for our arrival so we can avoid the entanglements Asa mentioned in his message."

"Yes," Reed said, "We figure too many Hip Yee Tong spies ply the Barbary Coast and will see us if we board directly through San Francisco."

"It's a wise decision," Jacob seconded. "The tong's reach is long and they have many eyes in port. With fewer passengers, and less ships on the route, it's easy to observe any *irregularities,* coming and going from that part of the world. You best watch yourself once on board. I'd wager Hip Yee Tong members will be sharing passage with you, unaware of your presence. Stay in your cabins as much as you can."

"We will exercise caution," J.J. said, looking to Mr. Chang and Ming Ni, who silently agreed.

"They're a nasty lot, so be mindful," Jacob added.

"We've had some experience with them recently," Reed shared, "out our way in the hills."

"They can't import women like in the past, now with the

Chinese Act. Bribing port officials no longer works, but the Hip Yee are devious, resourceful. They've discovered ways around the law. Smuggling is most active these days, lucrative." He looked to each member of the group, "You don't need me to tell you that the most valuable cargo in the hold of any ship isn't tea, shrimp, or even opium. It's people, young ladies especially."

Jacob returned his gaze to Chan, who met his with her own. Asa hadn't disclosed all the details, but it was plain to Jacob, one young lady was finding her way home.

"We best get going," Jacob advised. "Better to do this in the darkness, before the morning sun rises."

Mr. Chang and Ming Ni lifted their carpet bags and stepped aboard, the small boat rocking with the added weight. John John approached Reed, Chan standing at his side. "I have everything," he said, nodding to the trunk. "Our clan will act as intermediary and begin talks with the Hip Yee Tong. We will stress Dai Lao's conduct was bad for everyone's business." He looked to his sister and then made a formal bow to Reed.

"When peacemaking, remember to not call him Pig Face, might cause umbrage, slow down negotiations," Reed said wryly.

J.J. smiled and Reed reached out, saying, "You're family now," and embraced John John, who stiffened like all Chinese to so public a display of affection. "Speak to your parents. I figure we can expand their merchandise beyond tea and silk to many other goods." He looked to Chan, "I think we can profit by re-exporting European goods by way of Hong Kong to America."

John John nodded affirmatively, "We will pursue any opportunities." He stepped away, ready to take his leave, then hesitated. He returned to Reed, his back to Chan, offering final words. Reed heard the steel in his voice, though it was just a whisper, "Kill the Dutchman," John John implored. "The same for McGirt, track him down, end his miserable existence. Do it before they kill you and Willis. My sister must have you to return to."

Reed agreed, nodding, he nibbled his bottom lip out of habit, saying, "It's on my mind. Goodbye, my friend."

J.J. returned the nod, satisfied. He turned and studied Chan. He could see she was prepared for this moment, "Sister, better to do this now, rather than on a rocking boat, squeezed in together with the others."

Chan's eyes said everything. John John moved off, gesturing to Jacob Langtry and the two of them stepped over the short rail and onto the boat. Jacob took his seat at the tiller, while John John found a place in the bow with Mr. Chang and Ming Ni, ready to release the mooring line.

Reed held Chan's hand and they walked a few short steps along the wooden planks, finding privacy in the moonlit darkness. Intuitively, they were both thinking of their time earlier at the boarding house and its affirmation. This was only a respite, a pause in their life together.

Reed smiled, as they gazed into each other's eyes, his hands on her waist. "Only an intermission, dear," he said reassuringly.

She smiled and wanted to pull the brim of his hat down in a playful display, but resisted – Charles always confident, a man with a plan and always a twinkle in his eyes. "It still hurts," she said.

"A sacrifice tendered so we can make matters right, be together in the end."

"A sacrifice on the altar of love," Chan agreed. "May we enjoy good health and prosper until the moment we are rejoined."

"We'll get our time back and I know we'll use it well. We settle things with the Hip Yee Tong and you can come back or I'll come to you. Never been to the Orient before, would look forward to it."

"Please tell me, Charles, it will not be long."

"It won't be. Neither of us would allow it. And when we reunite, we'll live our life together the best we can for as long as we can. I never speak of this, but I had a baby brother. He died of fever, never got a chance in this world. He would have grown into a fine man. Then my mother and father, just a few years later," Reed shook his head at the unfairness, his voice halting on the emotion. He managed, "Life can be awfully harsh," pausing some more, gathering himself, "There's a fellow named Jasper Fanch. He'd say all the woes in the world are caused by sin, and we live with the retribution as part of some grand, unseen plan, but none of it's true. It's just a simple way to scare everyone, casting blame and punishment on the living, a piddling explanation for all the hardship and senseless death around us. People are hardy because they have to endure so much. Some lives just burn for an instant and are then extinguished. Some go on longer and it doesn't matter if you're good or bad, just lucky. We've seen people die over nothing, but I know *we're* lucky."

Chan stared into his eyes, transfixed, softly murmuring,

"Yes, we are."

"We can beat what the world throws at us, make the most of our time before we join everyone else buried in the ground or piled up on a pyre. Chan, the world doesn't care about our love. Everyone's got their own troubles. Only we care, care enough to make it back to each other's side, but somehow if we don't, remember that we carry on for each other. Our love never fades if one of us is still standing, drawing breath."

They embraced and held each other tightly. Chan proposed, "We have an engagement to meet again, Charles Reed."

"If it's San Francisco, we'll stay at The Palace Hotel and dine at The Poodle Dog. It's French and L.L. Robinson highly recommends it."

"If it is Hong Kong, my mother and I will cook." Chan pulled his face closer, her arms weighing on the back of his neck, "And if fate takes us, may we walk together in an eternity of our own making. For if our love perishes, we, the two of us, will know that it existed and that it was true and beautiful. Our last thought will be for each other, oblivion, our ashes cast together on the wind."

"We'll make our own paradise. I'm confident of it."

Chan placed her head against his chest, arms around each other for one moment longer. They glanced back at the small boat and saw their privacy remained intact. They kissed, holding each other, remembering the sensation, locking it away in their memories as sustenance for the lonely times ahead, until this exile, this separation, ends.

They walked arm in arm slowly back to the boat. He held her hand as she stepped aboard, steadying her as she found her balance and faced him. The bow and then the stern, moved quietly away from the dock, their hands still held, arms extending as the distance increased. Who would let go first? They timed their release perfectly, by mutual accord. They smiled at each other, fingers now parted into a low wave of goodbye. Jacob Langtry raised more sail, adjusting the yard and the boat gently slid into the bay, gathering speed. Reed watched for a short time, but this time there was no lantern glow, only two hearts dimmed by considerable distress. Chan vanished into the enveloping darkness and mist, and he could already feel the gulf between them, soon to expand to the width of an ocean.

Auburn, California 2013

It's going to be hard to top this road trip," I said hoisting my pint glass at Knee Deep Brewing. We were all seated at a picnic table inside the taproom's warehouse space, concrete floor, surrounded by a towering array of stainless steel fermenting tanks. For a craft brewery, the production floor, with bottling equipment, was large, business obviously good.

"Ja, very successful jumps," Gregor said, smiling, lifting his own beer in salute, "because we lived to drink another beer."

"Here ist to holidays and those who take them," Helmut added, clinking his pale ale with our own glasses. "We are very lucky to have met you Tom, Jen, and of course, our cinematographer, Kendra."

"We've had a great time together. I'm sure it's taking the sting out of the expense of the motorhome rental," Jen teased.

"Ach, don't remind Helmut. He will only worry more," Gregor said.

"Nein, nein, I am not worrying. We have received our money's worth," Helmut conceded.

"Here, look everyone," Kendra said, flipping her phone for us to see. She launched the video of Gregor leaping from the bridge.

We watched with rapt attention, quiet until the parachute opened, then the celebratory audio kicked in, screams of relief along with stoner kid commentary. "Man, that's so unbeliev-able," I said. "I totally thought you were going into the river."

"*I know*. Why'd you do that to us Gregor?" Jen complain-ed, nudging him in the shoulder with her own, spilling a smidgin of her double IPA. "I thought I was going to have to call 911."

"Should've called it anyway, to restart my heart," I said.

"Ja, I did not, drehen, spin at a safe rate," Gregor explained, "too slow and I fell too far before deploying the canopy. Next time zwei instead of drei der Salto," he smiled, taking a mouthful of beer and offering a nonchalant shrug toward the Grim Reaper.

I thought to myself, the frivolous way people risk their lives, seemingly invulnerable. The entire subculture of daredevils online struck me as some strange arms race, action-packed selfies vying to one-up each other. And for what? an adrenaline rush that lasts about as long as the temporary celebrity status it conveys. It seemed absurd, risking one's life creating a death-defying clip to compete with cat videos. All the things that can be done with the Internet and, for many, it's just a stage to live life as a lark, striving for attention in a cluttered world where only the outliers standout. At some point, one grows out of this, I suppose. We get serious, though I worry Gregor sees this as a way to push barriers, the video a trophy to justify more thrill seeking, more extreme risks. I hoped, in the future, whenever we next heard from our new friends, it would not be terrible news.

Gregor pulled me from my thoughts, proclaiming loudly, "But I am here now and will do better next time." He finished his beer, a high alcohol triple IPA working on his innards. He spanked the empty glass on the table top. "I think I will have another one of those."

I looked to Helmut as Gregor stepped away, saying in a low voice, "That was scary. This might be the jump to retire on."

Jen added her own take, "Three flips, *inwardly*, I'd be happy and call it a career, undefeated."

Helmut nodded, "Ja, we are meticulous checking each other's equipment, packing our chutes, but I worry Gregor is becoming too reckless. Even proper equipment cannot save one from poor judgment, a minor mishap, trying too many acrobatics. The, how do you say…margins, are very slim. The difference between exhilaration and death is just a heartbeat." He swallowed the last of his beer, disclosing, "Gregor did not receive a promotion with his firm. Ever since…the wind turbine jump, too low, tollkuhn, foolhardy. Now this jump, much, *much* too close to the river." He looked into each of our eyes, "We do not need to record our own deaths. This ist my last BASE jump. I will try to direct our energies elsewhere, perhaps, more cycling and skiing."

"That might work," I said, "something with speed. I don't

think either of you are ready for bocce ball yet."

Jen asked, "Say, who was that kid with you on the bridge? He was funny. When you post, you've got to leave his remarks in."

"That was Jason," Kendra said. "His narration has to stay, but once the chutes open, I would launch into an Electro House beat and then into a Euro Dance riff once you touch down and begin running the trail to Dad, plenty of synthesizer."

"What do you think of the music choice, Jen?" Helmut inquired, playfully nudging her with his shoulder, maintaining the levity.

Jen motioned to Kendra, "Talk to my daughter, she knows modern music better than me. Did The Smiths ever get back together?"

"No," Kendra answered, "and neither did the Beatles."

"These are good ideas," Helmut said. "We will work with you on the finished video once we return to Germany. I hesitate to post now, since there is a chance someone will see it and recognize us. We could be cited for trespass. Better to be back home in Germany."

"Yeah, make 'em extradite you," Jen said before worrying, "Oh, Kendra, make sure none of us appear. We don't need the police knocking on our door."

"Mom, I think the police have bigger things to worry about," Kendra eye-rolled in exasperation. "It's not like they're going to send a posse after us."

Helmut and I could only chuckle.

I put my head down in shame, mumbling over the rim of my glass, "What a pathetic *Monkey Wrench Gang* we turned out to be."

Jen playfully kicked me under the table and my "Ow!" exuded more laughter.

Gregor returned to his place bookending Jen on the bench with Helmut. He placed a tray of beers on the table, the celebration continuing, though it was tinged with melancholy since we all knew this would be our last day together.

"When she was filling the glasses," Gregor said, "I asked the barkeep what is Auburn known for. She said great beer, growing pot, and the Western States 100 mile endurance race."

"Yeah, I've heard of that race," I said, "running over the tops of the Sierra Nevada's, Squaw Valley to Auburn. You get a nice belt buckle if you can do it in one day. I can't even imagine running 100 miles."

"Train, I bet you can do it," Gregor said matter of factly.

"I'm too far over the hill to be running over *those* kind of hills," reality in my voice.

Kendra, on cue, reading from her phone, "'Runners ascend 18,000 feet and descend 23,000 feet over the 100 mile course. Men's record, Tim Olson, 14 hours 46 minutes and 44 seconds, women's record, Ellie Greenwood, 16 hours 47 minutes and 19 seconds. Runners completing in 30 hours receive a commemorative bronze belt buckle, under 24 hours a silver belt buckle.'" Kendra held up her phone, "Here's what the belt buckle looks like."

We all leaned forward, admiring the shiny metal award, Jen saying what we all thought, "Oooh, that's cool. Like the mountain lion on it, '100 miles' in '1 day.' Better than just a video clip leaping from a bridge." She nodded and winked at Gregor.

"That seems like something we can do," Helmut proposed.

"We should look into endurance racing when we return to Germany. There must be a club."

Gregor nodded affirmative to the possibility, the challenge it presented. You could already see his jaw setting.

I looked to Jen and Kendra and the three of us shared a sly look with Helmut, who managed a slight smile.

We finished our beers with a bite of tacos from the food truck parked outside. More conversation, Kendra describing her college plans, which, fortunately, involved in-state schools. We talked about where to from here? They were getting on the road to Oregon, stopping for the night at Grants Pass before reaching Bend, where they would day hike the Green Lakes Basin Trail. After that, Portland, the Olympic Coast, with a final stop in Seattle, where they would turn in the motorhome, tallying up all the miles, then Lufthansa back to Deutschland.

We shared our plans, walking to our vehicles, more local hiking in the Gold Country, a combination of camping, small hotels along with Airbnb rentals, then home, more souvenir magnets to place on the fridge, our belt buckle for another successful road trip.

A passerby obligingly took a group photo of us and we hugged goodbye, exchanging contact information, promising to stay in touch. Helmut and Gregor offered to host a reunion, hiking the Bavarian Alps that elicited yelps of agreement. I'd like to think this will happen, but who's to say? Lives are complex, things happen, we go our own way. Maybe this encounter was just a one-off kind of thing, happy moments that can never be rekindled, existing only in the time you live them, glad that they happened at all. At that moment, though, I sincerely hoped that we would stay in touch, sending Kendra for a year abroad in Germany, a family emissary reestablishing ties from a memorable summer.

As they entered the motorhome, Jen said, "I'm so sad to see them go."

"Me, too," Kendra said, her eyes watering. "They were so nice."

"It was fun alright," I said, grateful for the experience. We began waving as the Class B rolled up beside us. Helmut stopped and opened his window.

"You will need this when you begin searching for your own Wohnmobil," he said, and handed Jen a thick, glossy Class B motorhome brochure that detailed interior features and specs. Jen flipped it open and we all gushed at the photos, shimmering vehicles parked in front of iconic national park backdrops – Half Dome, Yellowstone.

Helmut tapped the horn, smiling, seeing our eyes light up. Then he and Gregor drove away and we stood there waving, not knowing if this was a departure or a final farewell.

Auburn Ravine, California 1883

"Get that bucket off him. We've got something new for him to sit on," Reed said, "and hitch up his britches."

Charlie One and Two lifted the Dutchman to his feet, waking him from his slumber, keeping the blindfold in place. They untied the bucket covering his backside, seating him down on the wooden box that Reed and Willis had carried in with them.

"Yellow bastards, take your hands off me," the Dutchman protested, then stopped, sensing others. His hands were already tied behind his back as the four men lassoed his ankles, looping the rope a few times around the box and then around his waist. When they were done with all the lifting and twisting, tightening knots, Reed removed the blindfold, pulling it down under the Dutchman's chin. The mottled face looked up toward Reed, his eyes slowly focusing in the mine's dimness, illuminated by two lanterns. "You and the shitkicking teamster who smells of manure. Stand closer to the slant-eyed laundrymen who stink of lye and you won't be so offensive to my nose," he said with disgust.

"I'll stand where I like and you best keep your sass to yourself," Willis warned. "I shoulda blown you in two that day you and McGirt walked into The Golden Star of Shanghai. Birds of a feather, you two. Flock with crows, you die with crows."

"I piss on all of you."

Reed stepped forward and looked down on the dusty mop of red hair. "Isn't it true a group of crows is called a murder?" Reed answered his own question, "they get together and decide the fate of another crow." He paused and said, "Let's talk about what you've done, Dutchman, starting with the most recent. You put a bullet through Gam Soy. He's on the mend, but Jyu Hua lost his leg. Hurt like hell when the surgeon probed for the bullet."

The Dutchman laughed, "Am I supposed to feel *sorry*? Yes, sorry that my aim was not true and that I did not shoot more of the little yellow men. If they are going to fight, then fight. I can't stand around waiting all day."

"Took your mind off killin' us," Willis remarked, "just couldn't help yourself, seein' all those Chinese in one place."

"Yes," the Dutchman said evenly, as if there was no other explanation, "Why send them back to China where they can breed. Shoot them now, send the heathens to hell," he spit. "I'll shoot you yellow loving white men too and if it isn't me, then Russell McGirt will finish the job."

"You got it backwards," Reed asserted, walking to a 3-legged table that could only support its weight by leaning against the cave wall. Reed loosened the draw string on the sack that sat in the middle, removing a bottle of whiskey. "How many Chinese, hell, how many people of any color you and McGirt kill?"

The Dutchman studied the bottle more than the question. His eyes lighting on it, the days in this hole without a drink, he shook, an involuntary convulsion of longing, then nodded his chin in quick reflexive jabs at the glass container and its all-important liquid.

"This?" Reed said, raising the bottle. He walked to the Dutchman, removing the cork stopper. The Dutchman made a grunt and opened his mouth, beckoning Reed to pour it down his throat. Reed obliged, pouring a mouthful that the Dutchman swallowed. He hungrily grunted for more and more he got, swallowing mouthful after mouthful. Reed stepped back and examined the bottle, a little more than half remaining.

"So how many people you and McGirt kill?"

The Dutchman sat back, relaxed by the whiskey, a grin on his face, eyelids drooping. "I won't count you two yet, but it is many," he nodded. "Russell and I met during the San Francisco riots, in a crowd in front of City Hall. The Workingmen's Party was just starting and we demanded anti-coolie action. Those speakers, so-called *leaders*, cowards who hesitated," he said with dismay, "held their tongues. So it was up to us to lead the throng, and they followed, chanting, 'On to Chinatown.'" He looked up to Reed and Willis, disappointed, "We only lynched four Chinese during those two days, but we did destroy many Chinese businesses and pelted their temple with rocks, smashing windows," he said, satisfied. "After the second night, the state militia arrived, so Russell and I retreated to the valley, then the foothills."

"And you've stayed ever since," Willis retorted.

"We cleaned the Chinese out of a few towns, Roseville, Rocklin and then started in on those working remote claims on the Yuba, Bear, American, Feather rivers, below the large hydraulic mines, enforcing our own Chinese Miner's Tax," he cackled, exposing the gaps between his teeth. The wheezing effort forced him into a coughing fit. He stopped and rested, gathering breath, searching for more memories in an alcohol addled mind. It was like rifling through a chest of drawers, all empty but for one. He opened and closed each, like a thief, until he found something of value, something that could spur the narrative forward. He muttered back to life, saying in a low voice, "The yellow man picking through the tailings of the white man's mines, like vultures," he raged, clenching his face in repugnance. "Soon they would run whenever they saw us, but we were successful, taking the white man's gold back from them."

Reed and Willis could see that the Dutchman viewed these actions as duty-bound, upholding a racist manifesto, rather than as brutal crimes. He giggled, recollecting, "Russell grew angry when I shot too many. He'd say 'how are we goin' to get more gold if you keep shootin' every yellow hide you see. Nobody left to steal from.'"

The Dutchman said this last part voicing an imitation of McGirt, remembering all the killing as if they were good old lively times. He came out of his revelry, demanding, "More whiskey."

Reed poured more down his gullet, keeping the tongue

lubricated. "But you didn't stop there, did you?"

"Black men, Indians, greasers, they were next. Then some white men, true, but the strong have to survive," he said oblivious to the carnage. "It ended," he corrected himself, "*slowed down* once that punk Robinson at his big mine hired us to oversee the diggins, which provided new opportunities."

"Quite a tale, Wim. Pretty much jibes with your reputation, what we know about you," Reed said tersely.

Willis looked at the Dutchman with contempt, "You're a right tall hog at the trough. I'm tired of hearin' you airin' out your lungs."

"I left a lot out," he slurred, malevolently. "Did you know, the Chinese, you can never tell them apart, the big round straw hats, the baggy clothes." He looked to Reed, "Sometimes you find women under all of that." An evil smile crossed his face, eyes narrowing into a menacing glare, "better than gold, looking into those dark slant eyes, the last man they will ever know," his blood burning with a carnal rage.

Reed's anger almost bested him, but he checked himself, looking to Willis, who stared back at Reed with his own steely determination, ready to put the mad dog down. Charlie One and Two took a step forward. They too were seething with rage at the white devils, Wim Van der Hoof and Russell McGirt, who shot Chinese down in cold blood and bragged about it. It was only through their loyalty to John John that they had not killed the red-haired animal already. They did not understand the Dutchman's words, but they recognized the tension they produced, the angry reaction of Reed and Willis, provoked by insulting, remorseless words. The laundrymen followed suit, suppressing their anger, too. They knew why they were here, and wholeheartedly agreed with the verdict.

In the silence, Reed's ire abated, settling to just below a boil. "All that wrongdoing, the villainy and cruelty, you're an abomination, Wim, and you're going to pay for what you've done. You should've been hung long ago, but never a witness, nobody to testify, though plenty of people, even white people, seen your deeds."

If his hands weren't tied, the Dutchman would've waved one of them disparagingly, "A white man testifying for the yellow man against another white man…it sickens my stomach. Never happened to me or Russell, though we once shot two men through the foot in Nevada City to help them better remember what they saw."

"It's all coming to an end. You're sitting on a gift of fifty pounds of dynamite. It was sent to us by your former employer, Mr. L.L. Robinson," Reed said, adding, offhandedly, "Did you know L.L. used to be the president of The Giant Powder Company? Before he took over the North Bloomfield Mine? You worked there, out in the pit. You know they use explosives, blowing up debris that clogs the tunnels. Yeah, they've got plenty of dynamite to spare."

The Dutchman grew quiet as the meaning grew clear, a worried expression came over his face as he examined the wooden box and its proximity to his being.

"The thieving, murdering, intimidation is over," Reed declared. "We mean to kill you, Wim, and Charlie One and Two are here to witness it. And the funny thing is, like those men you shot in the foot, I don't believe they're going to see anything either, but I know they're goin' to be happy with the result."

"We're goin' to walk away from this the way you and McGirt have walked away from everything," Willis added.

The Dutchman stared at each man, stopping on Charlie One, who raised his hands to cover his eyes. Charlie Two slit a finger across his throat and the two brothers smiled.

"You dirty devils, I'll dance on all your graves," the Dutchman ranted, as he began yanking and tugging against the restraints, the muscles in his neck as taunt as his bindings.

"You never did figure it out, did you, Dutchman?" Reed explained. "Not every bird is a crow, some are eagles, hawks, pigeons...and it's the same with people. We're all a little different but we fly the same skies, drink the same water, and we've decided your fate."

"You have no right," he complained bitterly.

"We've been deputized plenty times before," Willis shrugged, "just another public service."

"You see, Wim, some people don't deserve to live in society, not even a prison society," Reed stated. "For the good of everyone, it's time we cull you from the flock."

Reed returned to the sack on the table, removing a bundle of dynamite he had earlier taken from the box, seven sticks wrapped together. "Here, let me show you, Dutchman. It's much safer now, with these blasting caps and fuses, not like the early days with black powder and nitroglycerin, one shake and ka-boom." He inserted a blasting cap into one of the sticks, attaching the fuse. "What do you think, Willis? Six feet of fuse? Gives us three minutes to lope on out of here."

"Sounds about right."

Reed stretched the fuse line out, measuring a couple of arm lengths, plus a little more, cutting it, connecting it to the blasting cap. He placed the bundle on the ground, between the Dutchman's feet, up against the box containing the remaining dynamite. He extended the fuse outward on the ground, as the Dutchman's feet wiggled away, trying to create enough slack to kick the explosive away.

"That ain't goin' to work," Willis objected. "I tie a lot of knots, moving all that freight. I'm somethin' of an expert. You're done for Dutchman, no tombstone for you." Willis stopped and eyed the cold dark surroundings, "not goin' to find many mourners passin' through here once that roof comes down."

"Wait, I did none of the things I said," the Dutchman protested in desperation. "McGirt made me do them. You let me go, I tell you where he is."

"You'd just lie," Willis said with disdain. "Your time's up, nothin' is changin' that."

Reed looked to the whiskey bottle, an inch remaining. He made an offer, "You tell me where McGirt is and you can have the last inch."

The Dutchman hesitated, his mind racing, unsure what to do. The silent indecision caused everyone to resume their preparations for departure. Reed bit the tip from a cigar, lighting its end. He rolled the end in the flame, pulling on it until it glowed. He gestured to Charlie One and Two to withdraw. The two men nodded and approached the Dutchman, scorn in their eyes. Charlie One said, "*Puk gai*," die in the street, and spit on the Dutchman's boots. Charlie Two followed, issuing his own oath, "*Ham gaa chaan*," death to your entire family. The two then made their retreat to the surface, trotting down the tunnel with one of the two lanterns, their footsteps dwindling to silence as they marched away.

"Wait! Wait!" the Dutchman pleaded.

Reed approached with the bottle, shaking the remaining liquid in front of his eyes, "You talk first, then you can have a last swallow."

The Dutchman's tongue licked his upper lip, swaying back and forth in an alcohol induced storm. "Russell is with Rance Mueller. They are ambushing the stage carrying payroll for the North Bloomfield Mine. They will make that lecherous punk Robinson pay for his depravity."

Reed still held the whiskey at bay, shrugging, "So?"

"We know its route and schedule, even guarded it," he laughed softly, "during *better* times." He elaborated, "The mine makes a gold run to the San Francisco Mint every two weeks. The mine's managers, accountants in San Francisco are always there directing the exchange, make the deposit…our weight matches their weight, receive sacks of gold coin in return. It all goes in bank accounts there. It is all so tedious, really," he said as an aside to Reed. "But always there is payroll to return with, first by train and then by stage from Marysville to North Bloomfield. Russell will stop it on the steep grade above the Anthony House."

"When is this going to happen?" Reed asked.

"It already has," the Dutchman blurted, "while you kept me down in this dark hole."

"Your talk ain't worth a damn," Willis scoffed. "They're long gone, then, out among the willows."

"Mueller," the Dutchman disclosed. "He knows the hide-outs from the early days. Places nearby, speak to Sheriff Boggs, he will know."

Reed grimaced, looked to the Dutchman, who assumed his open mouth position. He dumped the remaining whiskey in, tossing the empty to the side, where it thudded to a stop in the shadows.

"Last gut warmer for you," Willis taunted. "Time for you to pull your horns in, no more troublemaking from you." He looked to Reed and both men nodded "ready."

"You will burn in hell for what you do to me," the Dutchman raged. "I will hunt you down in the afterlife and take my revenge."

"I don't think so," Reed replied. "We're bound for different places." He lit the frayed end of the fuse with his cigar and the double strand of yarn wrapping a core of black powder hissed to life, burning one foot every thirty seconds. Reed dropped the fuse on the ground, and took one last look at its destination, the deadly red bundle nestled in between the Dutchman's feet. He grabbed the remaining lantern.

"You can try spittin' on it, I suppose," Willis joked, "but fuses are varnished now, waterproof, and, well, it is your only light."

"Damn you! Damn you!" the Dutchman screamed as Reed and Willis showed him their backs, striding away down the twisting underground passageway.

They moved quickly, no dawdling. When they emerged from the hillside, the sun's brightness slowed their pace, eyes adjusting to the world above. They could see Charlie One and Two a little ways below. They moved toward them, just a few steps away from the abandoned mine's entrance, when the ground rumbled. They felt the heavy vibration from the blast through their boots and up their spines. Both turned back to the entrance. In a matter of seconds, a cloud of dust appeared, exhausted by the mines collapse, the falling rock and soil displacing the underground air, venting it out from far below.

Willis broke the silence as the dust wafted on the breeze, "I thought he'd spit that last swallow of whiskey back in your face."

Reed shook his head, "No, he needed it too bad."

"If it were me, I woulda just poured the whiskey into the ground."

Reed said nothing, but inside his heart, he regretted it too. Wim Van der Hoof deserved no pity. His victims received no quarter and neither should he. Killing this man was a chore that needed to be done, for both he and Willis's peace of mind. McGirt was now the only prey remaining. He would still be hard to track down, but they had hunted men before and were confident in their abilities. Reed looked to his friend, "Half our problem is gone. Let's get after the other half."

Newcastle, California 1883

"Nobody is sayin' it's McGirt, but I don't think anyone would be surprised," J.C. Boggs said from his front porch. The sun was setting in the west, haloing row upon row of plum and persimmon trees in golden light. From the porch, the Sacramento Valley stretched out below, clear and majestic, the Sutter Buttes stood in the foreground, above Marysville and Yuba City, Mount Diablo further to the southwest, then a strip of purple on the horizon, the Coastal Range. J.C. thought, looking out at all the beauty, "done good, hell of a place to retire to."

Reed and Willis sat nearby, sipping a libation. "Oh, it's him alright," Reed said. "Have it on good authority."

J.C. leveled his considerable stare on the two, having heard the rumble from out in the ravine, "Uh-huh," he said, leaving the topic there, details of which the former lawman need not know. He sipped his own drink and then provided details of the robbery. "Asa said the bandits were masked. Used sticks propped up in among the rocks to make it look like the stage was surrounded by gunmen. Ain't seen that trick since Black Bart rode these hills. Old is new again, I reckon." He chuckled, thinking the phrase applied more to himself than to a robbery, the fruit farm venture invigorating, more enjoyable than he anticipated.

Alice and Louisa Boggs joined the men on the porch. "It's so beautiful, J.C.," Alice gushed.

"Right there, below, beside the garden, we'll make an arch and you and Willis can stand there with the justice of the peace," Louisa suggested.

"Oh, it's perfect, Louisa, thank you so much. Willis, what do you think?"

"Perfect," Willis said in a flat, neutral tone.

"No butterflies in this man's belly," Reed said, jostling Willis in a friendly way with a knock to the shoulder. "You need to be helping Alice plan your nuptials."

"She don't need no help. Alice can have whatever she wants," Willis said, recovering his old self, smiling at his bride to be.

J.C. laughed, "More afraid of the altar than McGirt."

"Damn right, there," Willis conceded, "I feel like a mustang colt gettin' his first saddle throw'd on his back."

J.C. laughed, "You're greenbroke already but don't know it. Louisa and me, we've been married 26 years, goin' strong. You two will do the same."

Alice returned the smile, "Thank you, J.C." She then shot a stern but frisky look to her future husband. Willis cringed, putting up his hands in playful surrender. "I need to find Charlie Yue. I've got a food list a mile long for him to prepare."

Louisa said to all, "We'll be eating soon ourselves so get your appetites ready." She and Alice returned inside the home, sitting in the parlor, reviewing Alice's meticulous plans organized in a journal.

"Alice's got a book on how to hold a weddin'," Willis said with some resignation. "Every time she writes a new page, I see more money comin' out of my pocket."

"Aaah, quit your complainin', you only do this once," J.C. joshed. "We can all use a good shindig once this business with McGirt is over."

The men grew silent, as if the viper's presence was sharing the porch. Reed spoke, "What else did Asa say?"

"Two masked men, identities unknown, though we now know it's McGirt and Rance Mueller. Rance can show his face in town, but McGirt can't. They're still after him for what he done when he left the North Bloomfield Mine. I'd suspect they're still hid out in the hills. Wells Fargo agents are after them and the local jurisdictions are all notified."

"The Dutchman said Rance was along because he knows all the hideouts from the early days," Reed commented.

"*Early days*," J.C. thought. He went inside the house and returned with a map, spreading it over the porch rail as a makeshift table, Reed and Willis stood and joined him. "Robbery took place somewhere near the Anthony House."

"On the steep grade," Reed confirmed.

J.C. took a long stare at the map, contemplating the road, the hills and terrain, thinking back over thirty years hunting men in the area. He could see the robbery in his mind, "Here, on these hairpins going up, probably the last one. It then flattens out there for a stretch. That's where I'd do it. Make my escape this way," he pointed, tracing a path with his finger. "Ground's thick but not impassable, a few ups and downs, keep moving west of Nevada City. Not much in this area, few people, just the Excelsior Ditch and the Newtown Ditch. I can see this," he said nodding his head, "then to Deer Creek and on to Boston Ravine outside Grass Valley." J.C. faced Reed and Willis, "Rance Mueller would know this. He's been there before. I'm sure of it."

"J.C., what makes you so sure?" Reed asked.

"I ever tell you about Ned Whitney and his wicked bunch? Like McGirt and the Dutchman, they took it out on the Chinese. Rance ran with them ruffians long ago – Spanish John, Curley Bill, Wabash Dan, Buckskin Bill Riley. They'd all drink till blind at Harrison Morgan's bit house saloon in Foresthill. Morgan ran with them too when he wasn't sellin' his cheap Indian whiskey, tasted like coffin varnish. Anyway, once them cutthroats shoot themselves into some money, they'd retreat out to Boston Ravine, where they had a cabin to divvy up the loot."

"So that's where they've gone?" Willis said, unconvinced.

"Nothin' is 100%, but it'd be the first place I'd look, especially since there ain't much out there now, very remote.

Can't figure McGirt would show his face anywhere near town people. He'd need Rance to lead him to some old ace in the hole, settle down awhile till everyone grows tired of the chase, then make a getaway."

Reed nodded agreement. "Willis, we're headed there in the morning. We leave early. It'll only take a few hours."

"Stay for supper first," J.C. reminded. "Louisa's got plenty of food prepared and, like I said, they ain't goin' anywhere. Besides, better to have a good meal and sleep before we strap on a pistol and load up a shotgun."

"No, you ain't goin' this time, J.C.," Reed protested. "You've got a fruit farm to run. You've done enough for me and Willis already. We can't have you risking your life for us anymore. McGirt's our problem and we mean to get him."

"McGirt's everyone's problem," J.C. countered. "He and the Dutchman tried to bring the bad old days back. Ruin my life's work. These bullies, you'd think we'd be done with them by now." He paused, thinking in retrospect, "The day of the gunslinger is over. The farmer and merchant, they're buildin' this state into somethin' new, prosperous, a better place."

"Well, you're part of the new change, growing fruit and you're staying here," Reed said firmly. "Willis and me, we need our own challenges, our own stories to tell from our own porch."

J.C. nodded, understanding, "I'll draw you a map of the ravine, where the cabin's located and a path in up through the hills along the tree line, where you won't be seen."

"Whatever happened to Ned Whitney's gang?" Willis asked. "I'd like to hear."

J.C. hesitated, then spoke, "Oh, they left the area. Ended up killin' constable John Leary down south in Columbia, a fine man. Morgan was caught and lynched by the good citizens of Columbia. They hung his body from a flume." J.C. picked up his glass and gulped some bourbon. "What was left of the gang came back here and robbed a mining camp. Tracked them down to where they were holed up in French Ravine, near where you're headed, below Grass Valley. We had a shoot-out," he said solemnly, "Undersheriff Van Hagen, Deputy Ed Burrell, and two citizens we deputized, fellows named Lockwood and Dennin, good men like you two, willin' to help out." J.C. stopped his storytelling, "We ain't goin' to eat at this rate."

"No, go on, my appetite can wait," Willis encouraged.

"Yeah, but mine can't," J.C. said, reluctant to continue, his humility stopping him because there was enough tall tales and braggadocio in the world and not enough men with the good sense to hold their tongues in the company of others. But these two men knew the work and the risks. J.C. wrapped the story up quickly. "It was late, dark out, when we confronted them. I put two bullets into Ned, gunfire everywhere. Lockwood was hit in the arm, bleedin' bad. We had to make a retreat. Took Lockwood to a doctor in Grass Valley, who saved the arm. We came back the next morning with reinforcements, but they weren't needed. We found Buckskin Bill asleep on the porch, shot through the thigh, busted femur. He was lyin' there in his own pool of blood, usin' Ned's corpse as a pillow."

J.C. added a postscript, "Once them renegades were dead, things really began to quiet down." He looked to Reed and Willis, "you get rid of McGirt, it'll get even quieter."

"Quiet is good," Reed said, "we all need peace and quiet."

* * *

The next morning Reed and Willis took the earliest stagecoach from Auburn to Grass Valley. They both studied J.C.'s hand drawn map, familiar with the whereabouts, but soaking in J.C.'s dotted line approach to the cabin hideout, climbing a ridge and moving down the upper reaches of the ravine, obscured by timber. While Reed filled canvas bags with water and stuffed feed bags for themselves and their stock, Willis spoke to the hostlers at the Telegraph Stagecoach corral, men he worked with often. He saddled a reliable dun-colored mare for Reed, a dark stripe running along her back from mane to tail. For himself, he found a handsome copper-tanned sorrel named Rusty, small, rugged, and tough. He tapped him gently, saying in a low tone, "hello there, Rusty," continuing to pet the side of his neck as he fed him the bit. Rusty nickered happily, nostrils flaring to life at the prospect of getting out of this fenced enclosure. The white blaze on the horse's face bobbed up and down in delight. Willis smiled at the enthusiasm and walked the two horses from the corral, hitching them briefly to a post. He then entered another corral and cut his favorite mule, Mr. Pebbles, from the herd. He wasn't goin' anywhere without the mule, whose reputation for endurance and tenacity was only matched by his uncanny instincts – part animal, part human. It was a strange quality nobody could quite put their finger on, but as the stories grew, the legend increased, especially in detecting danger, be it rattlesnakes or inclement weather.

Willis approached Reed with the horses and mule. They loaded their supplies, the horses bearing rifle, pistol, and extra cartridges for Reed, the same for Willis except the rifle was replaced by a shotgun and shells. Mr. Pebbles would be burdened with all else.

"This the mule you and everyone speak so highly about?" Reed asked.

"Yeah, this is Mr. Pebbles. He's got mystic abilities. Just look at that gaze."

Reed studied the mule and had to admit the stare was unusual, along with the rest of his countenance – the way the mule carried himself, looking you in the eye, measuring you and everything up, very attentive. "Most peculiar," was all Reed could say.

"Oh, he's been touched," Willis vouched. "He's Mr. Pebbles for a reason, 'cause he can hear a pebble fallin' three canyons away. Just watch for his signs – a twitch of his ears, turn of the head, nose to the air, the sway of his tail – he'll let you know what's comin'. Bet he can smell a ghost cat ten miles away."

Reed didn't doubt it. From all the stories, he half expected the mule to pick up a newspaper and read it.

"He ain't a bloodhound, but you could probably train him to be," Willis asserted, cinching a leather strap and patting him on his flank. "Isn't that right, Mr. Pebbles?"

"We don't have far to go," Reed said, "just slow going, once we get off trail. We'll follow J.C.'s advice, move east of the ravine down below the southern end and then climb up into the cover of the trees. We should be able to locate and spy the cabin from above."

Willis nodded, agreeing to the plan of approach. They mounted up and Willis led the way, trailing Mr. Pebbles. The men and animals backtracked two miles along the stagecoach road between Auburn and Grass Valley, locating Little Wolf Creek.

Reed removed J.C.'s map from his inner coat pocket and studied it, "This looks about right," he said, eyeing the forest covered ridgeline. They dismounted, abandoning the road, going off trail, leading their mounts and mule on a zigzagging course up the hillside, climbing through stands of sugar and ponderosa pines. It was exhausting work carving a trail among rocks, boulders, downed trees and thickets of brush, the horses moving slower than the sure-footed mule. They stopped often to catch their breath and as they neared the crest, Willis took the lead with Mr. Pebbles, who moved forward at a comfortable pace but slowed down noticeably once they crossed over, Boston Ravine below to the west.

"That mule tired?" Reed asked.

"Oh, no, somethin's afoot. Probably picked up a scent blowin' out from the ravine. See look, he's standin' up, stretchin' his neck, flaring his ears and nose to better catch the smell."

They stood and watched the mule do his work. When sufficient time passed, Willis chirped a chittering sound that signaled the beast forward. Willis provided plenty of slack on the rope attached to the bridle, stretching it out behind the mule who led the way, dropping low, then climbing high, then back down low again. This went on for about a quarter of a mile, before the mule stopped and turned his head back toward Willis, twitching muscles around his eye as if raising an eyebrow.

Willis froze and looked down the length of Mr. Pebble's

nose, following the mule's line of vision down into the ravine. Below Willis saw the rooftop to a dilapidated shack, Ned Whitney's old hideout. "We're here," he said in a hushed voice to Reed, who had used the pause to take off his hat and wipe the sweat from his forehead with the back of his arm.

"I know we had a map, but that's still pretty good trackin' by a mule," Reed complimented.

"Let's go back aways, and tie up the horses and Mr. Pebbles to some trees," Willis suggested. "We can feed and water them and then come back and work our way into position to see the front of the cabin."

Reed agreed and they soon returned, locating a shadowed gap deep in a thicket, about fifty yards from the cabin. It provided a hillside view to the cabin and its approaches along the bottom of Boston Ravine. Reed and Willis swallowed some of their own water and had a bite of jerky, sitting down on the ground, trying to find comfort on their watch. They said nothing for a short time, studying the silent scene. Reed craned his neck, looking all around at the emptiness.

"Ain't nobody down there," Willis said in a whisper.

"Not now, but someone was, not long ago, either."

"How can you tell? We're too far out to see tracks."

"Take a look at that hitching post, that mound of turd below. It's standing tall and fresh, not beaten down, pale, flat, and dry."

Willis saw the unmistakable dark, moist pile, chagrined, he said, "What else I miss?"

"The privy over yonder, looks like someone's hung pages of paper on the hook. You can see them flapping in the breeze. If nobody'd been here, those pages would have blown off long ago. Also, the woodpile, on the chopping stump, someone's stood a log up on end ready to be split. Can't imagine that could stand long by itself without falling over." Reed stopped and examined the scene some more, "That little stack of wood, next to the larger stack, it was chopped recently, ready to be hauled into the cabin."

Willis leaned forward, shading his eyes, moving from Rance Mueller's almanac swinging from the outhouse to the wood pile. "Dang, Reed, no wonder you beat everyone at cards. You see all the tells," Willis said in amazement. "Good thing you're honest and don't mark cards, but I guess you don't need to when you can tell so much by just lookin' at a man."

Reed shrugged, "Pays to look hard at things," he said. "Now we wait. Someone will be along."

The time passed slowly. In some ways, this was the hardest part, trying to stay alert amongst the tedium. Willis regretted not bringing a blanket to sit on and the two alternately stretched their arms and legs as blood pooled in their limbs with pocket watch regularity. Reed bade Willis to nap, saying he'd take the first watch. Willis removed his hat and laid the shotgun aside, resting his head on a rotting log, absorbed halfway into the ground by bugs and moisture.

Reed kept vigil, eyes moving like a pendulum, rocking back and forth from the cabin and down the ravine. As the sun crossed over, the shadows deepened, darkening the western slope to Boston Ravine. Reed watched the silhouettes cast by the crowned points of trees reach out in a slow progression to the canyon floor, descending like an immense wave of ants from the hillside, providing a crooked pattern of dark and light.

Two birds fluttered out from his right, flying down the gorge in a rapid rush, soaring up and over the cabin and into the trees above. Reed concentrated his attention on the right, as far as he could see before his vision was obstructed by a wall of pine. Reed elbowed Willis from his slumber. He rolled up just in time to see Russell McGirt ride out from behind the stand of trees, trailing a mule toward the cabin.

"He alone?" Willis whispered.

"Appears so," Reed replied. "No, wait. Here comes Rance Mueller dilly-dallying behind."

"Look how far apart they are, not talkin'," Willis observed.

The two watched as the outlaws arrived at the cabin separately, with Mueller hitching his own horse and mule well after McGirt had done so. McGirt entered the cabin, but Mueller remained outside, walking to the privy and removing a few pages from the hook. He then walked back to the wood chopping stump and knocked the still standing log to be split aside, taking a seat, one that allowed him to view the front door of the cabin.

Reed noticed this and said to Willis, "Something's gone wrong between them. Look how wary he is. Doesn't want to be anywhere near McGirt."

"Who would?" Willis answered.

"I guarantee you he's looking over the tops of those pages to see if McGirt steps through the doorway and when he does, I'll bet you his hand moves to his gun," Reed predicted.

Barely a moment passed before McGirt stepped from the darkness of the cabin and into the frame of the doorway. Mueller's head twitched up almost in reflex at the sight, his right hand touching the pistol grip before landing in a neutral position across his thigh.

"Goddamn, Reed, you're turnin' into Mr. Pebbles," Willis exclaimed, suppressing the volume to his voice. "What's he yellin'?"

"Wants something to eat. Guess Rance is supposed to make it."

They watched Mueller rise reluctantly, slow walking into the cabin, saying nothing to McGirt as he passed by. Soon smoke could be seen emerging from the cabin chimney, fire from the stove. McGirt walked outside and took in the view of the ravine, scanning the hillside. Reed and Willis froze, even though they were well hidden in the thicket. They knew movement, any kind of movement, draws the eye. Satisfied that nothing was about, McGirt stepped around the corner of the cabin and pissed a stream near the wood pile. When empty, he secured himself, looking both ways in the process. He then gathered up some cut wood from the smaller stack, carrying it back inside. Not long after, Rance Mueller returned outside, with what looked like a plate of beans. He sat back down on the stump, shoveling spoonfuls into his mouth, his jaw muscles chomping up and down vigorously until he had cleaned the plate. He stared at the emptiness and then began licking the surface, lapping up the last morsel of bean juice. When done, his posture inclined upright, spine straightening, and he released a belch from deep inside, like a geyser of gas spouting upward. His body then settled back down into a relaxed, hunched recline. He pulled the folded pages from his pocket and got back to his reading.

Reed said, "Notice how no whiskey bottle is at hand. Biggest drunk in California and even he's resisting, trying to stay alert."

"Yeah, he must be plenty spooked by McGirt to give up the bottle."

"He'll drain a cask of Old Red Eye in one gulp if he gets out of this alive," Reed said. "He's realizing he ain't getting his share of the payroll heist."

A half hour passed before Mueller stood and walked to the outhouse.

"He gettin' more reading material?" Willis guessed.

They watched Mueller remove a few more pages to his precious almanac, unhitch his britches and take a seat, closing the ramshackle door. No sooner than it had closed, McGirt strode from the cabin in a determined march, left turning directly to the outhouse. Halfway to his destination he drew his Colt hand cannon, cocking the hammer. McGirt grabbed the door handle with his left hand and tried to rip it open. Mueller had hooked a small latch into its ring screwed into the wood frame and it resisted. Mueller reached for his gun down around his ankles, fumbling for the grip. He got his hand on it, lifting it upward before it snagged part ways up on his lowered trousers. A wave of panic spread through him and he accidentally fired a shot down through his foot. He yelped in misery at the sharp hot spot burning through his boot, searing pain that compounded his consternation. Frantically, he jerked and pulled on the gun that refused to rise. Desperately, he altered course, bending over, head between his knees, he worked to untie the gun from the folds and cuffs in the denim material. With more of the gun exposed, he placed both hands on the grip, gritted his few remaining teeth and yanked on it as if it were the world's most stubborn weed. All the while

THE GOLDEN STAR OF SHANGHAI

McGirt was yelling, "Mueller, you son of a bitch!" as he tried to kick the door in. But Mueller heard none of this, including the ripping sound when the gun finally tore free, his hearing blown out by the deafening sound of his first premature shot going off in the enclosed space.

Mueller scrunched back down in his seat and pointed his gun upward at where he thought McGirt's head was located, firing a shot in the seam between two planks in the door. The bullet ricocheted out but not into McGirt, who jumped backwards and unloaded two shots of his own through the door, the first whizzing through Mueller's hat and the second into his shoulder. Mueller winced in more pain. He managed a low shot through the door, missing, trying anything to put up resistance. McGirt fired again, lower, the bullet splintering more of the door, striking home in Mueller's left knee and the old outlaw dropped his gun onto the shithouse floor, sobbing at his predicament.

McGirt stepped back, breathing heavily, staring at the punched in door and the little latch that would not give. He studied the pattern of bullet holes in the wood, muttering, "Goddamn door." He turned and ran to the wood pile, fetching an axe. He hit the cross beams at the top and the bottom with two swings from the blade, splitting the door in half. He tossed the axe aside, drew the Colt again, and pried the door open, flinging half of it onto the ground.

Mueller, caved in and crumpled, raised his blood-soaked hands defensively, pages of the almanac sticking to the flannel sleeves of his shirt. He barely uttered a weak "don't" before McGirt put two bullets into his chest, one of which traveling first through his right hand, blowing three fingers off. Mueller didn't move or say anything after that. His eternal silence upstaged by the reverberating echoes of the gunshots that killed him, receding down the ravine and into the same nothingness.

Reed and Willis had watched the slaughter with revulsion. Reed regretted that he did not have the rifle, his revolver and Willis's shotgun ineffective from this distance. They watched as McGirt toppled Mueller from his throne, tying up his britches and taking an ankle in each hand. He lifted them up to his waist and dragged the body awkwardly from the outhouse and out behind the cabin. McGirt reappeared and reached for a short shovel loaded onto one of the hitched mules, who shuddered and kicked at his approach. He wrestled the shovel free from the outside of a pack and hit one mule across the nose with the flat of the shovel and sliced a cut into the flank of the other trying a second kick. The animals writhed in pain, crying out. He spit on one and retraced his steps back behind the cabin.

"Now's our chance," Reed said. "He'll be out back digging a grave for some time. I'm going down into the cabin. I'll wait for him there. You get down closer, behind the wood pile. Once he comes inside, you follow him in from behind with the shotgun."

"We can both go to the wood pile. I can cover you from there, until you get inside, just in case he comes back unexpectedly," Willis advised.

Reed nodded "good" and together they crawled from the thicket, staying low in a sprint from the brush, all the way to the wood pile. Reed looked back one last time at Willis who lifted the shotgun, providing cover as Reed moved quickly over open ground and into the dark confines of the cabin.

Out back, McGirt's enthusiasm for digging was waning. He rolled Rance Mueller's stiffening corpse into the shallow slit that could scarcely be called a hole. He tossed a few of the almanac pages that had detached themselves haphazardly back upon the blood-soaked chest, chuckling, "Now you got plenty of time to read about the weather." He used the shovel to quickly cover the body with a thin layer of dirt, twigs, and leaves. It was a mockery of a burial, obscenely performed by a murderer. He took one last indifferent look at the face of Rance Mueller as he cast the last earthen debris into his wide, unflinching, dead eyes. He dropped the shovel, satisfied he had done enough to cover the crime, worms could do the rest.

The mules brayed a warning as McGirt returned from his grave digging chore. The animals moved as far away as their ropes and leads would allow, straining against the hitching post. McGirt ignored them and marched through the still open cabin door, oblivious to their fear. He filled his mouth with the last morsel of beans sticking to the pot atop the stove. He froze upright at the sound of Reed's Remington, the hammer cocking back into position. He dropped the spoon, lips tightening. He swallowed the half-chewed, undercooked beans. They felt like gravel going down. He turned his head slowly, seeing Reed seated nearby.

"Keep your hands where I can see them," Reed said calmly.

"How'd you find me?"

"The Dutchman," Willis said, entering the cabin, his shotgun aimed at McGirt's middle. "Told us all about the payroll robbery. Sheriff Boggs helped with the rest."

"That lousy traitor. Where is he?" McGirt demanded.

"He's holding up a mine, not doing too good of job of it," Reed answered.

"What are you talkin' about?"

"Doesn't matter, he's dead. You've run out of partners. Why'd you kill Mueller?"

"He had the mule with the loot after the getaway. We got separated and he buried it before we met back up here, at his old hideout."

"And he made the mistake of showing you where he buried it," Reed deduced.

McGirt smiled, "That's right, knew his mistake right away, lollygagged all the way back here. He shoulda just made a run for it, but I woulda caught 'im and killed 'im. Don't need 'im leadin' the law back here outta spite at not gettin' his share."

"Some partner, so where's it buried?" Willis asked.

"You ain't gettin' your hands on it. It's mine now. Robinson and his big mining outfit can do without, down payment on what he owes me."

"Willis, take a short walk. See what Mr. Pebbles is up to."

Willis turned to Reed, giving him an "are you sure?" look.

Reed nodded and stood.

Willis slowly backed out the door, uncertain, moving off just a short distance, staying at the ready.

"L.L. Robinson owes you? For what?"

"He's a punk pecker tootin' pansy. I'm goin' to let everyone know it. Wrote letters, I done. It'll wreck his reputation. He ain't messin' with me no more. I'm messin' with him."

"And what are you going to do to me? Still think you're going to kill me, like the last time we saw you in Auburn?"

"I figure I'll still get around to it," McGirt answered flatly.

Reed just shook his head at the insolence. "Nothing worse than a man who thinks he has a place in this world when the world's done with him. I'm done with you McGirt. The world's done with you."

"I ain't tellin' you where them gold coins is buried, you or the law. I'll hang first."

Reed stared into McGirt's eyes, pointing his gun directly at his center, the pressure from his trigger finger increasing ever so slightly. McGirt's nerve broke, seeing Reed's steady gaze that betrayed no fear, only resoluteness.

"We didn't come here as some posse, looking for you to stand trial. Trial's over. You're sharing the same fate as your friend. I'm here to carry out the sentence. Sometime, later tomorrow, Willis and me, we're going to ride into North Bloomfield with your dead body over that mule you were hitting. All them miners you beat and abused, they'll celebrate all night long, dancing a jig at your demise."

McGirt was grimly silent, then spoke, "Okay, I'll tell you where the gold is. I'll lead you to it." He said this as if it were some grand concession, rather than a feeble attempt to bargain for more time, trying somehow to turn the table, to gain the advantage over Reed.

It didn't take long for McGirt to realize his mistake. There was no more time. It had run out and would never come again. McGirt reached for his Colt, playing the last card in the weakest of hands, drawing on a faster man who already had his gun out and aimed. Reed pulled the trigger to the Remington and the barrel jerked, firing a shot into McGirt's stomach. He bent at the waist and then tried to stand back up, mouth open, gasping. He had a stunned look on his face, the look of surprise everyone has at being shot.

Reed stepped in close, his mouth near McGirt's ear, "Keep your secret. Don't care about any gold coins. Just want you dead."

McGirt's body slumped down like a tree slain by one mighty chop. Reed lifted the large Colt that never cleared leather, disarming the brute as he fell, his backside thudding down upon the floor.

"All those shots you fired at Rance Mueller, you only have one bullet left," Reed said, looking down at McGirt, "better I have it." He opened the cylinder and pointed the gun upward, the lone bullet slid from the chamber, bouncing to a stop on the wooden floor.

Reed watched as McGirt rolled into a sitting position, back against the wall, his hand pressing against the wound, filling with blood as he tried to stem the flow. The stunned look was replaced with one of bewilderment. He examined the bloom of blood staining his front, growing ever larger, wet and sticky, leaking from his shirt down into his britches.

"For everyone a day comes that's our last," Reed ruminated. "We try to live a life that's good and worthwhile, enjoying our time, finding love, losing it, and trying to get it back. Anyway, most people I know want to leave the world in a better place than they found it." He paused, "Me killing you does just that."

McGirt grimaced, found lucidity amongst the enveloping cold that drew his limbs inward. He jutted his jaw forward, stretching his neck and face menacingly toward Reed, who looked on unmoved. McGirt's mouth opened and two lines of blood ran from the corners, dripping intermittently from both sides of his chin. A tense rage boiled until his lid blew, defiantly uttering, "I still ain't tellin' you where the gold is, you China lovin', no good, son of a…"

The Remington jerked again, Reed shooting a hole through McGirt's forehead, just above the ugly pink scar left by their earlier encounter at the mine foundry, the one that never quite seemed to heal. Reed watched as the head snapped back, body recoiling off the wall and falling over face first into the pool of crimson that was once the life sustaining river that ran inside him.

"I told you. I don't give a damn about the gold."

Willis's shotgun barrel appeared, peeking through the doorway. He looked in, then out quickly.

Reed said in a steady clear voice, "Come on in, Willis. It's over."

Willis stepped inside, slowly at first and then relaxing once he set his eyes upon McGirt's dead form, lowering the shotgun barrel. "Shee-it," he said, "you had me worried, ole buddy, sending me out like that. I want this man dead as much as you do." Willis walked over and looked down at McGirt, offering his own assessment, "No, sir, I don't believe he's goin' to be able to rub that one away."

"What stopped you from rushing in?"

"Oh, I'm familiar with the sound that gun of yours makes. Knew you were doin' all the talkin'."

Reed walked to a table and began to study McGirt's belongings. He opened a leather satchel and dumped a number of letters out. He picked them up and flipped through the stack, examining who they were addressed to – L.S. Calkins editor *Nevada City Transcript*, C.D. Dawson editor *Marysville*

and "It's the Devil himself, good riddance," rose up from the crowd. Others, mostly miners, just made hard stares, some spit tobacco juice on the blackening face, doing in death what they would never dare in life. Mr. Hawkins from the *Nevada City Transcript* stepped in with his camera, beckoning the crowd back in order to take a picture. He took two of the outlaw's faces and then someone located a board and slipped it under McGirt's back, tying him to it and propping him up. The deputies and others stepped in beside the upright corpse for their own pictures, smiling for the camera. It made for a macabre, gruesome spectacle, lasting until the undertaker arrived to remove the bodies.

Reed and Willis did not see this, writing and signing their statement that Sheriff Carter read through the small rectangular glasses perched upon his nose.

It all took some time, and when Sheriff Carter finished reading, he asked, "Any sign of the Dutchman, Wim Van der Hoof? He still ain't been found."

"Nope, never saw him," Reed answered.

Willis just shook his head "no."

"Not surprised," Carter said, "figured he must've split up from McGirt when they fled the mine after killing Wendell Akins, not wanting to be an accessory to murder. No sign of the payroll?"

"Backtracked their route aways from the hideout," Willis explained, "tried to follow their sign, but the terrain's too tough. Could be buried anywhere."

Carter looked to Reed, who said, "If Willis can't find it, ain't no way I can."

Carter leaned back onto the back two legs of his chair, the

same way J.C. Boggs does. Reed thought, it must be something all sheriffs do.

"Boys, you done something good here," Carter beamed. "The county has a $250 reward for McGirt and the North Bloomfield Mine has a $1,000 reward for the murder and another $500 reward for the payroll robbery. Pretty good work for you two. I'll see to it that you get the county reward, the other you need to take up with the mine."

"I'm acquainted with Mr. Robinson," Reed said.

"My then, you run with some big company, Mr. Reed, but, then again, you two don't look like typical bounty hunters." He stopped and studied both men, taking their measure. "J.C. said you do it because it's needed and we all need to take an interest in the towns we make." He nodded his head affirmatively, "kind of support I like to see." He rocked his chair back down on all four of its legs and stood, "I won't hold you any longer and no need to check your guns," he said reaching into a desk drawer. "Allow me the honor of pinning these deputy stars on you and to offer my personal thanks." Carter walked around the desk and pinned a star on Willis's vest and the other on Reed's lapel, below his trident. "Say, what is that, a pitchfork?"

Willis almost giggled and Reed said, "It's just a pin."

Carter raised his eyebrows and adjusted his glasses, taking better measure, "Nice, looks made of gold," he said in appreciation. He removed his glasses and shook both their hands again. "There's a grateful community out there that wants to buy the two of you a drink, several, in fact, so watch yourselves," he said smiling. "Good luck. I hope we meet again, and much obliged for your help, a dead McGirt ends a dirty time for this town."

"Yes, he made his miserable mark in plenty of places, not a man to shed tears for," Reed said, tipping his hat as they departed.

Reed and Willis walked a short distance. It was dark now, early evening, the street illuminated by a smattering of artificial light.

"I'll meet you at Miss Ellie's," Reed said. "Going out to the mine, let L.L. Robinson know what happened."

Willis looked at Reed, hitting him in the shoulder, "We done it, Charlie, got rid of McGirt and the Dutchman. I'll do nothin' sweeter again for the rest of my life."

"We've got a long time to live," Reed said, sharing the same smile of satisfaction. "We're both good and lucky, plenty more lively times ahead."

Willis agreed and then asked, "You still thinkin' of Chan, I bet?"

Reed paused, "Every second of the day."

There was only one guard on duty as Reed approached the North Bloomfield Gravel & Mining Company gate. The guard only looked at him once, nodded, and then moved along, having remembered Reed from his earlier visit. Reed opened and closed the gate behind him, making his way toward the office. To his left, the glow from the great pit extended skyward. Reed studied the power of this dome of light, marveling at electricity's ability to penetrate to such lofty heights before the weight and immensity of the night sky suffocated it. The surrounding stars, twinkling in the darkness above, reminded Reed of the gold flakes living in the soil below – the reason for all this activity, lights on, jets of water flowing, boring deeper into the earth, the 24 hour cycle operating as strong as ever.

Reed entered the office and caught Miss Potter on her way out, her ledgers put away, the pince-nez glasses in her drawer and a shawl over her shoulders. She smiled widely and wrapped her arms around Reed's neck, saying enthusiastically, "Mr. Reed, it is you."

She kissed both of his cheeks in elation, gushing, "You did it. You killed McGirt. I'm so happy, so happy that I could just cry." And she did.

Reed retrieved the shawl that had fallen to the ground and placed it back upon her shoulders, "Everyone seems to know?" he said.

"My yes, word spreads quickly in this town." She dabbed her moist cheek with a kerchief from her sleeve. "Please go inside, Mr. Robinson is expecting you."

She opened the door to the well-appointed banquet room with all its books, where the earlier games of faro and poker were played. Reed stepped inside as Miss Potter closed the door. L.L. stood from a large chair positioned near a window, facing outward to better see the mine, its glow, his empire.

"Charles, good to see you," L.L. said, smiling jovially, walking the length of the banquet room to shake his hand. "Come, please join me."

L.L. pulled up another chair near the window, pouring a glass of wine for Reed and refilling his own. He raised his glass in salute, "To the death of McGirt, a renegade and scoundrel who earned more than damnation in his lifetime."

They both took a sip. Reed's swallow was not even complete before L.L. added, "And to you, Charles Reed, for sending the monster back to the hell that spawned him."

"Thank you, L.L., and for the dynamite. It got rid of the first problem."

They drank more wine, with Reed describing the death of the Dutchman, the payroll robbery, Rance Mueller, and the final moments of McGirt.

Reed then stopped and looked about, observing, "Quiet around here. Where's Hamilton Smith and Henry Perkins?"

"Gone, I'm afraid. Hamilton is off to Venezuela, working for the Marquis de Carledo. He's bringing the unique mining process invented in California to the rest of the world." L.L. stood and retrieved a box of cigars, "Henry, dutifully, is in Sacramento, still working on the hydraulickers behalf." L.L. opened the lid, offering Reed to partake, which he did, striking his own match, while L.L. lit his with an ornamental lighter, carved leaded glass, as grand as the crystal bar set sitting nearby.

L.L. puffed the cylinder of rolled leaves to life, saying, "All the best engineers have left. California isn't the only place with alluvial gravels." He said offhandedly, "I just heard the other day that Gardner Williams of the Spring Valley Mine is off to Africa. He's leaving to build diamond fields for the British, for some fellow by the name of Cecil Rhodes."

L.L. sat back down, "Ironic isn't it, all the large orders for equipment are coming from around the world and not from California." L.L. tapped a finger on the table for emphasis, "Richard Hoskins, now there's a valley man who will rue the day we close, his Marysville factory building monitors for everyone but us."

"What's changed? You don't sound as confident in Judge Sawyer as before," Reed asked.

L.L. provided a thin smile, looking a bit older. He tapped an inch of ash onto a silver tray. "Public face I have to put on as the leader of hydraulic mining. I'm not blind to the machinations around me, politicians, Judge Sawyer, though I was with McGirt, too involved in the legal fight to see the bully in my midst." He shook his head and reflected, "Our time mining this ridge, eighteen years, will soon end and, you know, I only have myself to blame."

Reed puzzled, "How so?"

"It's my fault because I set the precedent years ago, when I won my own lawsuit against a coal mining company." L.L. turned to better face Reed, "They were dumping their tailings in streams that ran down on to my farm along the San Joaquin River. It ruined the farm, made the land worthless."

Reed was astounded at the revelation. "*You* set the precedent?"

L.L. explained further, "The Black Diamond Coal Company appealed the decision. It went to the State Supreme Court, was upheld, and I received damages."

"So the principle is already established in law, mining companies can't dump their debris into streams and rivers?"

"Not without regard to all those farmers, *like me*, who hold riparian rights." L.L. pulled and exhaled a large cloud of smoke. "How's that for a hypocrite," he said, laughing at still more irony.

Reed could only laugh along with him.

"Now I don't feel so bad," Reed confessed, "telling George

Cadwalader and Ohleyer what to look for when they made their call on the mine."

L.L., surprised but unperturbed said, "So that's how they knew."

"Not much of a disclosure," Reed admitted, "*everyone* knows debris gets out of here somehow."

"Fortunately, we pulled enough out of the mine, barely, to cover our investment costs, but out there, in the darkness," L.L. stood and tapped on the glass pane, "there's a ridge...$70 million buried deep down in those gravels and no one is ever going to get it," he said in annoyance.

Reed then realized the chair was not positioned to oversee a mining empire. It was there to slowly bid it goodbye.

"I'm sure Governor Perkins and old Governor Stanford will be happy to be rid of the mining mess. Did you know Leland Stanford appointed Judge Sawyer to the San Francisco district bench before he was placed on the federal circuit court? He and the Big Four always hated me, my partners, for trying to get our share of the Transcontinental Railroad. They received all the government money, the generous land subsidies that amounted to thievery." L.L. sat back down, "Now look at the railroads, they're more despised than ever." He stroked his mustache flat, with a thumb and index finger, staring out at the glow, "Nothing better for Stanford and Sawyer than to take my great mine away from me."

They sat quietly for a while, each playing the recent times back in their heads.

Reed broke the silence, "What's next for you?"

L.L. shrugged, "Plenty of ways for a man to make money. I have a home in San Francisco that I have no use for. I'll probably return instead to my estate on Suisun Bay, see how much of the bay we filled in with our debris. I can plan my future there, then more mining, maybe in Mexico, insurance, oil drilling, that's the next big business. What about you, Charles?"

"Return to Auburn, I've got a saloon, kitchen, and laundry to run." Reed paused, "but before I go, there's something you should know. I found some letters, nasty ones, written by McGirt. Before I killed him, he told me he was going to send them to newspapers, your enemies, try to ruin your reputation."

"I see," L.L. said with a note of alarm followed by resignation.

Reed continued, "Like all things McGirt, it wasn't well thought out. No one plans blackmail staring down the barrel of a gun held by an adversary." Reed shrugged, "So no worries. The letters are gone. I tossed them into the fire. Nobody is ever going to read them."

"Thank you, Charles. I am indeed in your debt," L.L. said sincerely, "please excuse me, I'll be right back."

L.L. withdrew from the banquet room and into his office, returning with a thick envelope. He untied the string clasp and began counting $100 banknotes issued by The First National Gold Bank of San Francisco. He licked his thumb and stacked five stacks of ten banknotes each, piling the currency in front of Reed and then stood back, "Your reward, please accept this in gratitude from me, the mine, and from a grateful citizenry."

"That's more, much more, than the reward offered," Reed said, stunned at the generosity. "If the mine's closing, you might be needing that for yourself."

L.L. just waved a hand dismissively, "I'm a rich man, Charles, not as rich as Crocker or Stanford, but I'll do fine. Like I said, opportunities abound and you've earned every cent of this."

Reed thought for a moment and nodded, "Thank you, then, L.L. It's much appreciated. It will help me settle some personal affairs I need to tend to."

L.L. rocked back on his heels and studied Reed's face, hitching a thumb under his arm, waiting to hear more.

"You see, I have a wife," Reed solemnly confided. "Well, we're not married yet, officially, but will be. She's Chinese and on a boat back to Hong Kong. Her name is Chan and I love her dearly. She had to leave. It wasn't safe here. I hope to get her back soon and when I do, I'll introduce you to her. I know that some people are bothered by the color of her skin, the shape of her eyes. A white man marrying a Chinese woman will never sit too well with them, but you wouldn't be put out by it."

If Reed's admission of a Chinese wife and lover were meant to shock, L.L. betrayed no impact. He merely appreciated the candor, offered when none was expected. He placed a hand on Reed's shoulder, "She must be very special to you and I would be highly honored to meet her. I understand how important it is to have someone to share a lifetime with," the thought of Francois welling up, choking his voice, "Even if it's just for a short time, their presence fills your heart with joy, makes life worth living. But, remember, Charles, life is all so fragile and short, people come and go rapidly and we need to cherish those close to us while we can for as long as we can."

Reed agreed, "Loneliness is humbling." He paused, "*Alone,*

I can't think of a sadder word in any language."

"It's a difficult burden to bear."

"But we don't have to bear it forever," Reed said, managing a grin of optimism.

L.L. patted Reed's shoulder, breaking into his own smile, "Good, then you have a plan to reunite, excellent. I wish you luck and good fortune. You *both* must come visit me as my guest when you and your bride return from the Far East."

"We shall," Reed said, bidding goodbye and taking his leave. He walked back to Miss Ellie's in the dead of night, wondering what Chan was doing right now.

Reed stepped through the doorway and was immediately greeted by a big kiss from Miss Ellie, planted right on his lips. "That's for getting' rid of that no good outlaw," she said, tapping the deputy badge on his lapel. "You and Willis done good, mighty good."

"Where is Willis?" Reed asked, smiling.

"Comin' out of the kitchen. I needed to put some food in his belly, with all the whiskey people been buyin' him."

With that, on cue, Willis staggered down the narrow hall from the kitchen, "How you doin', buddy," he said, trailed by nubile Betty, who looked at Willis longingly, her hero. She pouted her moist lips and rubbed up next to Willis, touching an earring dangling from her earlobe, then lacing a pinky finger with his own.

"None of that, Betty!" Miss Ellie shrieked, "You scat. This man's gettin' married to his sweetie, Miss Alice, so stop your foolin' around, run along now, you hear."

Betty made a stamp of a heel and walked away toward the boisterous noise emanating from further inside the boarding house. Willis watched her go, eyes fixed on her shapely figure, jaw ajar. Reed elbowed him out of his desires. "Best you keep your mind on Alice and all the reward money we come into. You've got a wedding to pay for."

Miss Ellie said, "The girl's heart's in the right place. She spent time upstairs with McGirt, broke her nose, and, well, best I don't say anything more other than he and that filthy Dutchman were never allowed back in here again."

"Understandable, then," Reed said. "I hope you have room for us, Ellie. Just me and Willis boarding ourselves for the night, anywhere that's convenient."

"You two are heroes. We got room for the both of you, but the way this celebration is going, I doubt anyone is gettin' any sleep."

"Reed, everyone says Judge Sawyer is goin' to rule any day now. The whole town's got so much liquor in stock that they need to drink some of it now," Willis announced. "A dead McGirt's got the whole shebang a goin'."

"I just wish Hank was here to see this," Ellie said, wiping a tear from her cheek. "Hank done loved a good shindig, miss that old knight of the stage somethin' fierce, added a lot of color to my life."

"We were all sorry to hear about it," Reed consoled.

"That's right," Willis said a little too loudly, his voice still enlivened by the bottled spirits. "Hank was a mentor to me, taught me everything."

"Well, life goes on, I suppose," Ellie said. "I still got the two of you to keep me entertained."

She put herself between them, hooked an arm in each of theirs and led them both through the batwing doors. A thunderous cheer greeted their entry, the raucous "whoops" going deep into the night, a celebration that blew the roof off the town.

Marysville, California 1884

The invitation was waiting for Reed and Willis when they returned to Auburn from North Bloomfield. With the Sawyer Decision imminent, George Cadwalader had invited both to Marysville, as his guests, to be on hand when the momentous decision was announced. Reed and Willis thought about it and then sent their "thanks" and "regrets," preferring to settle back into their lives, which felt empty with those dear so far away. Weeks passed without a decision, the New Year coming and going. On January 6, a second invitation was delivered, this time by telegram, requesting their attendance. Enough time had passed, and both Reed and Willis shrugged, "Why not? Let's see it to the end." They were in Marysville the next day, put up in the United States Hotel, where President Grant had once stayed.

Late that afternoon, they had a convivial lunch with George Cadwalader and George Ohleyer, the twin stalwarts of the Anti-Debris Association, both of whom exuded confidence, summarizing the legal case up till then, the injunctions, winning the first phase of arguments, and so on.

Reed asked, "How long before a decision?"

"Tomorrow, two days at most," Cadwalader answered,

"We have a rouser of a bonfire planned to draw the attention of everyone within 50 miles. Also, if that isn't enough, we'll shoot rockets and light Roman Candles on top of the Sutter Buttes as a signal for the townsfolk to gather in Cortez Square. Every town in the valley is doing the same."

"Well, we'll look to see you then," Reed said. "We know both of you are following the court's actions in San Francisco and we won't keep you. Both Willis and me want to thank you for your hospitality."

They downed the remainder of their coffee and shook hands. Excitement was in the air, flags and bunting going up, people buzzing about, giddy, preparing for the event or just burning off nervous energy. With everyone a little off their kilter, Reed played cards at The Silver Dollar Saloon, winning a tidy sum from the grangers and other visitors who came and went from the table. These folks were undoubtedly distracted and impatient for news of a decision, anxiety that affected their play. Willis smartly avoided the table, knowing Reed would clean up under these circumstances, walking instead to the Kelly Brothers Stables to look over the horses for sale.

Evening approached and the chairs went empty, everyone avoiding Reed's play, moving to the bar – better to drink their money than to lose it. Reed reclined back in his chair and studied the contrasts, the deserted gaming table and the long line of backsides, squeezing in at the bar, the hum of loud conversations reverberating off the walls and ceiling with his own silence. He watched the comings and goings from the second floor brothel and recognized one of the patrons mounting the stairs as a player from earlier in the day. Reed thought, at least the man was wise enough to keep some money in reserve, enough to buy a ride in the saddle. Only gamble with what you can afford to lose was a motto few heeded.

Reed stood and retrieved his hat, adjusted it on his head and sought out supper. He returned to a good place he and John John had once dined at, just a few blocks away, in Marysville's Chinatown – *Sam Fow* – the third city in California for Chinese immigrants, behind San Francisco and Sacramento. The area was quiet, desolate, Reed the only customer at a table.

The old man server asked, in fractured English, "Where your friend?"

"John John, Wei Lu, he's in Hong Kong, with his sister Chan."

"Oooh, he leave too?"

"No, he, *they*, will be back. I plan to go fetch them."

Another, "Oooh," which sounded like an echo of the first. "Everyone go, so few Chinese remaining." He looked all around his establishment, taking in the city. "Once second largest Chinatown in America." He scrunched his lower lip upward in irritation, almost touching his nose, "No more, all gone, only a few, like me, remain."

"Yeah, sorry, it looks that way," Reed said in commiseration, "miss my friends too."

"How you like food?"

"It was delicious. I'll finish my tea and get out of your way. Let you close up."

"No worry, take time. Maybe you follow me to temple. I show you."

Reed swallowed his tea, considered the offer and said, "I'd

like that," handing over a gold coin in payment for the meal. The old man bowed in gratitude, making his way to the kitchen and returning with a heavier coat.

The old man led Reed from the abandoned Chinatown and its smattering of burned out storefronts, to the still busy streets of central Marysville. Reed witnessed the sneers and glares the old man incurred and wondered if he would receive the same treatment once he set foot in Hong Kong?

For a spell, Reed thought the old man was taking him back to The Silver Dollar Saloon. They passed right in front. Reed watched the old man locate a dark passageway next to the building. He vanished into the inky blackness and then reappeared, saying to Reed, "Follow me, watch step."

They shuffled slowly beside the saloon's brick wall, taking care with each step so as not to stumble in the darkness. Once past the saloon, the old man stopped abruptly. He said, "wait," and Reed waited. The old man's shadowy form crawled down amidst some bushes, returning with a lantern hidden in the shrubbery. He lit it, illuminating his and Reed's faces, "Now we go."

It was mere feet to the Bok Kai Temple, sitting directly behind the saloon, a levee and the Yuba River just beyond. The old man unlocked the gate with a large key, opening both doors, each elaborately carved with Chinese symbols that Reed could not decipher. They stepped inside, the old man in front, carrying the lantern to an ornate altar, Reed trailing just a step behind.

"First temple burned down. This new one, not three years old."

The old man sat the lantern on a table and pointed to the

altar, explaining, "This is temple of many saints, but one, *Bok Eye*, god of water, is most important. He controls rain, floods, irrigation. See, in the middle."

Reed leaned in and had a look at the porcelain figure, a warrior holding a sword, sitting on a throne, one foot on a snake and the other on a turtle. "With all the anti-Chinese agitators, let's hope *Bok Eye* keeps some water handy so this place doesn't burn down again," Reed said. "I mean that with no disrespect."

The old man took no offense and dropped to his knees before the altar, his forehead nearly on the ground. He whispered a prayer in a language Reed wished he better understood. When he finished, he stood back up and faced Reed.

"I pray for you, for a blessing," he said, pointing to another deity set upon the altar. "*Sing Moo*, goddess who protects travelers, those who cross oceans. You go safely, return safely."

"That's most kind of you," Reed said.

"There are three jewels to Tao – *kindness*, *simplicity*, and *modesty*," the old man said, holding up three fingers. He turned again to face the altar, reaching in his pocket for an offering of fruit for the gods. He placed a plum on a plate before the altar and bowed deeply, the last movement in this ceremony before departure. He lifted the lantern and, extending an arm outward, beckoned Reed to lead the way back out.

They walked silently, Reed thinking how hard it must be for this man to follow his faith as his friends and family are driven away. The old man closed the two doors with care, noiselessly. He locked them, pulling on the handle to insure they were secured.

"Thank you for showing me this. Perhaps, it's time we get everyone together to create a fourth jewel," Reed suggested, "*understanding*."

The old man smiled and nodded, "Yes." He then said, "Me, no know your name."

"Charles Townsend Reed," he said slowly, enunciating each syllable.

The old man tried to repeat it, mangling, "arlz own-sen eed."

Reed winced, "close."

"Me, Li Qiang."

"Li, is easy for me to say," Reed said. "You can just call me Charlie."

"No, Charlie," Li said, speaking slowly, "you *peng yao*."

Reed smiled, recognizing the word, "Yes, *friend*."

The next morning the sun was bright, but cold in Marysville due to a north wind. Judge Lorenzo Sawyer had entered his San Francisco courtroom, 125 miles to the west. The courtroom was packed with attorneys, newspapermen, and other interested parties, as the judge began reading his 225 page decision. It was a long and arduous process, the judge, in painstaking detail, repeating what was already well-known – the destructive impact of mining debris on the valley and its crops, the ineffectiveness of two debris dams to contain the nuisances at a cost to taxpayers of over $500,000. On and on the judge droned, until he finally made it to the crux of the matter – the climax of two years of litigation – 2,000 witnesses, 20,000 pages of testimony. Chairs began to creak as backsides were repositioned, the movement waking many from a slumber. Notepads were placed at the ready, everyone now alert in their seats. Judge Sawyer took no notice and stated once and for all that the North Bloomfield Gravel & Mining Company and other defendant companies were "perpetually enjoined and restrained from discharging or dumping into the Yuba River and its tributaries any tailings, boulders, cobble stones, gravel, sand, clay, debris or refuse matter."

A gasp went up from the courtroom, followed by a number of voices all saying a version of the same thing, "The miners lost." Many newspapermen leaped up and rushed from the courtroom, brushing past bailiffs and anyone else in their way. They furiously scribbled messages cobbled from their notes to a batch of telegraphers, steady fast hands, who began tapping out the news to the rest of the state, to the towns in the hills and cities and communities all along the valley floor.

Judge Sawyer glanced briefly over his glasses to witness the commotion, raising an eyebrow before continuing his oration from the bench. He kept the wordy speech going for three-and-a-half hours, stopping periodically to sip water. In that time, the judge closed all the miner's loopholes, further ruling that the large companies were forbidden from allowing anyone the use of their vast water supplies for hydraulic mining purposes. It was a total victory for the valley farmers. Judge Sawyer had slain the hydraulickers and this most destructive form of mining. The debris would end, the water run clear again, teeming with returning fish, and its only practicable use would be for agriculture.

In Marysville, like elsewhere, people gathered near the telegraph office. The first message from the courtroom arrived at 1 p.m. and the celebration began. The steam whistle at the Swain & Hudson Mill released a prolonged shriek, which drove everyone into the streets. Reed and Willis heard the signal and stood from their half-eaten lunch, dropping their napkins to join the crowds assembling outside. They were greeted by church bells and a marching brass band. Everyone seemed to be shaking hands and offering congratulations. Reed looked to Willis and both men smiled, a procession of strangers came and went, thrusting out a hand and backslapping with the other. The first fireworks were lit and their percussive pop would sizzle and crackle deep into the night, until the town's supply was exhausted. Copious amounts of liquor flowed, irresistible to even the most staid and stuffy, the stiff and priggish, all of whom found reason to engage in foolishness on this one special day – sobriety and respectability be damned, a big time for everyone.

Further telegrams arrived, each a variation on the same theme, "success on every point." The steady stream of good news and congratulatory messages soon became dull and humdrum. The telegraph office was quickly abandoned once news spread that the Empire Foundry was preparing a flying anvil salute. Reed and Willis joined the crowd, walking not running, to witness the spectacle. They arrived in time to see a large, heavy anvil stacked upside down on another. The concave space formed in between the anvils was packed with black powder. A foundryman lit a match and hightailed it once the fuse sparked to life. The crowd held their breath in anticipation, standing safely back as a thunderous boom launched the top anvil skyward, all eyes watching it soar over 100 feet into the air, trailing white smoke against the exceptionally blue sky. It thudded back to earth, impacting six inches deep into the packed roadbed, fortunately missing the two drunkards who had raced out from the throng, competing to see how close they could come to the flying iron object without getting hit. The crowd watched the two drunks argue about who was the closest and to "pay up" the shot of whiskey wager. A few men stepped forward to arbitrate, drunk too, amusing the crowd even more. The unruly jury reached a decision, saying the first anvil was a tie and that another needed to be launched to break the deadlock.

Reed and Willis could only shake their heads at the stupidity, Reed saying, "They send another anvil up, bet you one of them ends up wearing it as a hat."

"Ain't touching that bet," Willis said, "best you don't get drunk around mules that kick and anvils that fly." They didn't stick around for the rematch, which was declared a draw after the anvil misfired, pin-wheeling up and over the crowd. It came to rest crashing through the roof of a tool shed.

By 5 p.m., more people from the outlying area had reached town, swelling the streets. The bonfire in Cortez Square was struck, its flames roaring into the early evening darkness now casting a blanket over the town. The evening festivities began with a 40 gun salute fired by Captain Colford's battery atop the levee at Third and G Streets, followed by more skyrockets and steam whistles. George Cadwalader, flanked by leaders of the Anti-Debris Association and other dignitaries, spoke, the bonfire lighting his presence at the dais. A good portion of those gathered heard the words, but many were too sloshed to understand them. They would read about the speech the next day in *The Marysville Appeal*.

Reed and Willis listened carefully to the hour long speech, having moved closer to the stage, knowing that George Cadwalader's leadership and advocacy would be critical in the aftermath of the Sawyer Decision. His strong voice addressed the significance of this day – the first day of victory – not in a gloating, but an even-handed way. He explained that the "bitter struggle was far from over and that the valley could not rest on the great tidings of one day. Enforcement would be a challenge but crucial in order for the valley to survive and thrive." He mentioned "the hard-fought existing injunctions and using these to vigorously prosecute any outlaw mines with fines and imprisonment." He further reminded his fellow citizens that "even without any new debris, the nuisances still existed, choking streams and rivers with a slow moving avalanche that still threatened the valley and the delta, all the way to San Francisco Bay."

George Cadwalader then paused and, if possible, stood even taller, gazing out at the gathering, measuring it to see if *these* people were up to the task. "*We* can do it," he said reassuringly. "The federal court of Judge Sawyer has saved California from its own legal paralysis and legislative obstructionism, fostered by the *once* all-powerful mines. Their reign has ended," he declared and then boldly launched into an appeal "for more help and assistance from Washington so that California can reclaim its vast river system, the lifeblood that sustains the people and commerce of this great state." He predicted that by doing so, "California would become an agrarian colossus, capable of feeding the nation and the world." He stopped and pointed a finger at everyone, warning that "this will not be an easy task, but it is all-important work that must be done, and will be done, even if it takes years to complete. Perhaps not even in our lifetimes, but we must rise to the occasion." The crowd roared its approval, following the tone and tempo of the speech, if not all the words, knowing a climax when they heard one.

Reed thought the speech visionary, charting a course of sound investment, enabling generations of progress without the miner's mess. George Cadwalader closed his speech by acknowledging the crowd, extending both arms, imploring it to settle down. He smiled at everyone, "Thank you to Marysville and the citizens of the valley. The time to rejoice is now. Our long suffering is over. We have prevailed in this most righteous fight against the unrestrained privileged few, greedy miners who would turn our beautiful state into a poisonous pit. Now is the time to build for the future, prosperity for all Californians. Together we can achieve greatness."

Another roar went up, George Cadwalader stepped from the dais, shaking hands with those sharing the stage. Other speakers came and went that night, echoing George Cadwalader's refrain, but none with the passion and energy. When it was all over, Reed and Willis found George Cadwalader, visibly tired, offering their congratulations.

"Good speech, George," Reed said with a smile, "words like that will get you elected governor."

"I'd vote for you," Willis said. "It was inspiring."

George waved a nonchalant hand, "It was no Gettysburg Address," he said humbly, tamping down his own ambitions for the office he secretly coveted, one that he would ultimately be denied, tragically thwarted by a weak heart and premature death just 4 months from now.

"Well, it sure got the crowd goin'," Willis said, enthusiastically. "Marysville's hotter than a whorehouse on nickel night."

George laughed heartily, "Mr. Connelly, your words constantly amuse me. If I could bring half as much observation and homespun wisdom to a courtroom, then I would be a happy man, indeed."

"Are you headed back to Sacramento?" Reed asked.

"Yes, to my law practice and to follow events there. Then back to San Francisco, where I have a home. Yourselves?"

"Back to Auburn," Reed said, "things will slow down, but the railroad still comes through. I suspect the mood is a fair bit more somber in places in the hills, like North Bloomfield, Nevada City, Timbuctoo, Rough and Ready – all those towns are going to die."

"I am not immune to their plight, Mr. Reed," George said. "It will be a slow death, but this sacrifice is necessary in order for the state to live, bloom, and become the Eden the first Californians envisioned before gold was discovered. Mr. Reed, Mr. Connelly, look around you. This is a vast inland empire with waterways reaching to far off markets, unlike any in the nation. It's a place dedicated to the farmer, who nurtures the soil. All this water used for mining can now grow crops. Grain has surpassed gold even now. You can grow anything in this soil, and people will. Agriculture, the farmer, has supplanted the miner. That's our future."

George Cadwalader looked in each man's eyes, assessing the impact of his words. "Come now, you must be convinced,

Mr. Reed, with that farmer's pitchfork pinned so prominently on your lapel."

Willis laughed and Reed too.

"You already had me convinced before," Reed said with a sheepish grin. He burnished the golden object with back of his coat sleeve, "You're right. Today, I am a farmer."

"**D**id you ever find an answer to your 'Why are covered bridges covered?' question?"

"It's like we thought," Jen said, hiking the narrow trail single file behind me, "protects the beams and support structure from the weather so it lasts much longer."

"That was a nice serendipitous stop, the longest covered bridge in North America, over 200 feet long."

"I was just thinking about the one way toll, 5 cents for a hog or sheep," Jen said, "$1 for a one-horse buggy. Tom, you calculated inflation earlier. What was it, the equivalent to $25 today? That's a steep toll."

"They collected over $20,000 the first year the bridge opened in 1862. That's over half a million bucks today. It really paid to be in the bridge business back then, well, at least until the Transcontinental Railroad came along and ended the good times."

"Nice to see the state stabilize the bridge so it can be restored and people can walk on it again. It really is a part of all this Gold Country history. Hate to see it lost because no one stepped in to save it."

"I was talking to that docent in the South Yuba Museum, the old fellow. He said all the other covered bridges in the mountains are long gone, wiped out by flooding over the years. I looked it up. Bridgeport survived a 1996 flood only because the bridge was raised in 1971. The river rose 26 feet above its low water mark. The flood waters just barely made it under the deck, clearing it by inches."

"Tom, you're getting as good as Kendra at finding out things with your phone."

"Where is Kendra, by the way? She shouldn't get out too far ahead on the trail. There's bobcats, mountain lions all through these hills. I should be carrying bear spray."

"Let's just keep moving. She's probably just around the next turn."

"I wonder," Jen asked, "how much of that big North Bloomfield Mine is still out there in the rivers? That big canyon they made, they washed the whole mountain down through here."

I shook my head not knowing the answer, taking my sun hat off and wiping the sweat from my brow with a scarf. "And it was just one of many mines."

"Suppose anything like that can ever happen again?"

It didn't take me long to think of an example, "Oil fracking in Oklahoma, all the wastewater injected underground, lubricating the fault lines, causing earthquakes. I read somewhere that there were only two magnitude 3 earthquakes a year in

Oklahoma. Now, with fracking, there's hundreds every year. It's the most seismically active place in the country."

I sat on a rock and retied my hiking shoes, "Maybe it's not tons of debris washing down on towns and causing floods, but who's going to repair every home every time an earthquake strikes – broken windows and pipes, cracked foundations, walls, driveways? You make repairs then another earthquake hits the next day and the damage is right back again. It's like the farmers who kept raising their houses with each flood, building levees higher and higher each year and nothing helped until hydraulic mining ended."

"Earthquakes are the 21st century debris," Jen agreed, sipping some water from a bottle.

"I'm sure it's all tied up in the courts, waiting for a new Sawyer Decision. Frackers saying prove to me my well caused the earthquake that damaged your house. It's just like the hydraulic miners who said prove to me that debris came from *my* mine and ruined your crops, buried your town."

I stood and drank some of my own water, "I can't see the Oklahoma state legislature doing anything since they're politicians elected with energy company money. Their clout, an army of lobbyists clogging the halls at the capital, will keep it all going with the usual arguments, 'we don't know enough yet,' 'more study is needed,' and 'this is an energy state.'" I just shrugged at the inevitability of history repeating itself, "It'll be up to the feds to rein it in – tell the frackers you can't profit by destroying everyone's homes and property but, in the meantime, filibuster in court – get what you can, while you can, before they start shutting wells down."

"You're right," Jen said with dismay. "It's the history of

hydraulic mining all over again."

"Hey, there's Kendra, way out there. I told her not to go off trail. This place is full of abandoned mines. What did she tell us last night? over 47,000 in California alone."

"I'm more worried about ticks," Jen warned, "none of us need to come down with Lyme disease."

I yelled, "Kendra, get back over here!"

She heard my voice, making a big wave with her arm for us to "come here."

We bushwhacked to Kendra, avoiding the star thistle, but not the other dry grasses and weeds, picking up numerous stickers in our socks, their points jabbing annoyingly into our skin.

"I hope this is worth it, Kendra," I said, walking up behind her. She was busy studying something up in an old oak tree, one that cast a welcome canopy of shade. Jen and I were preoccupied looking down at our feet, plucking stickers from our socks.

"It just caught my eye as looking strange," Kendra said. "It's an old bottle hanging by a string."

Jen beat me looking up, "Why would someone hang a bottle by a string and then sit it on another branch below?"

I got into the act, with all three of us scrutinizing the bottle, craning our necks for a better view. I looked at the tree trunk, charting a path upward, locating hand and footholds. I removed my backpack and began climbing up toward the bottle.

"Tom, don't get killed. You fall, we can't carry you out of here," Jen said with scolding alarm.

"Always with the encouragement, hon. It's barely ten feet

up," I said between grunts of exertion. "I was the best tree climber in the neighborhood as a kid."

They silently watched as I reached the branch and began inching my way out to the bottle, crawling like a snail on my hands and knees. I slowly made it beside the bottle, wrapping my legs tightly around the branch, examining the bottle, a cork stopper on top, the weathered string snapping with a gentle pull. "It's been here a long time," I said with astonishment.

"What makes you say that?" Jen asked.

"The branch below has grown up and around it. It's stuck in the bark." I grabbed the neck of the bottle and tried to twist it out and it didn't budge.

Jen yelled, "Don't pull so hard, you'll topple out of the tree."

I just shook my head, saying to myself, "yes, dear, the thought had occurred to me." I slowly dug my Swiss Army Knife from my pocket, maintaining my precarious balance. I began to whittle away on the bark, opening a small gap around half of the bottle. It was slow going, cutting and prying up chunks of bark and the only encouragement from below were impatient peels of "Are you done yet?" and "Oh, forget it. Just come down before you get hurt."

I grabbed the top of the neck and pulled toward me, into the empty space created by my whittled trench. The bottle snapped loose with the suddenness of a picked apple. "Hey, hey, got it! Here, Kendra, catch." I tossed the bottle ten feet down to her sure hands.

I carefully retreated from the tree, knowing the trek down is often times more difficult than the one going up. I stumbled out of the tree, my presence forgotten by Jen and Kendra, surviving with a couple of light skin abrasions on my knees and a small tear to my cargo shorts. I walked up on Jen and Kendra who had the bottle open and were trying to shake something out of it. "Thanks for the help getting down."

"Oh, pipe down, Tom," Jen said, mesmerized by the mystery of the bottle. "There's a rolled up piece of paper inside that we can't get out."

"You could break it, Mom, but that would be a mess."

"It's definitely old," I said, "I wouldn't break it. It'd make a good souvenir to stand in the garage." I pulled the tweezers from the Swiss Army Knife. "Let me see if I can grab it." I used the tweezers to reach down the neck, inserting a small twig alongside to pinch the tweezers together, then pulled both out. The message came three-quarters of the way up the neck before the tweezers slipped off.

"Almost, Dad."

On the second attempt, I was able to latch onto the paper with just the tweezers, pulling it free, "Got it."

I held it up and Kendra plucked it from the tweezers, unrolling it. "It's a title page to the Old Farmer's Almanac, 1882."

"There's something written on the back," Jen noticed.

Kendra flipped the page over, reading, "Look to North Star."

"That's it?" I said.

Kendra held the page up to Jen and me, Jen saying, "Now what?"

Kendra had her phone out, using a compass app to establish north. She extended her arm outward, "There, on that line."

All three of us sighted down the line, studying the

landscape for a half minute. I asked, "Anything stand out?"

"Just those two big rocks," Kendra noted, "halfway up the hill."

I pulled the binoculars from my backpack and adjusted the focus, Jen eagerly repeating, "Whaddaya see? Whaddaya see?"

"Two big rocks," I said, deadpanning the obvious. I studied the scene some more, adding "with another smaller rock on top."

"Let me see," Kendra asked and I handed her the binoculars, still staring out at the distant rocks.

"It doesn't look right," I said, "like this bottle in the tree. How'd that rock get on top of those two big ones, sitting right smack in the middle."

"It's funny shaped, too, Dad. It looks almost square."

"We have to go check this out," Jen said excitedly.

"Okay, but let's each find a big stick so we can weed-whack a path out there."

We found suitable sticks beneath the old oak and slowly marched in and around the thorns and thistle, stopping briefly to let a snake slither by. It wasn't enough to deter us, reaching the two big rocks in shorter time than I expected. We gazed up at the square rock poised above us, Jen wondering, "Who would put that there, right on the edge, centered perfectly on a crack?"

"It's a different kind of rock, color's not the same."

Jen and Kendra looked at me.

"What?"

"You like to climb, get up there."

I laughed, "The thrill of the hunt."

"We all want to know, Dad."

Of course, I agreed, seduced by the mystery. I surveyed the base of the two large rocks, looking for the best route up. The seam in between offered the most promise and I quickly scrambled up the backside, covering the 12 vertical feet in a fraction of the time needed to climb the tree. I walked to the edge, looking at each side of the strange square rock.

Jen and Kendra both looked up, shading their eyes, "Well?"

"Strange how nature can make a cube-shaped rock like this. It's like it was made in a mold." I bent down near the edge and a chorus of "Be careful," rang out, just like it does when I remove leaves from the rain gutters back home.

I grabbed two of its corners and wrestled it away from the edge, spinning it toward me for a better look. It must've weighed fifty pounds. I worked my fingers underneath and flipped it over, exposing the unseen bottom. As it toppled over, I glimpsed the same dark handwriting as before, "Son of a bitch…"

"What? What's going on up there?" Jen yelled.

"Get back, get back, I'm going to push it off," I shouted. I looked down and saw Jen and Kendra had moved a safe distance away. I spun the square stone back to the edge and sat down behind it, using my legs and feet to push it off. I didn't see it land, but heard the dense, heavy thud when it cratered back to earth.

Jen and Kendra rushed to the stone. I hollered, "read what it says."

I retraced my way down from the two large rocks. I walked around to the front, just in time to see Jen and Kendra jointly bending to tilt the rock up, balancing it on its tipping point. Jen warned, "Watch your fingers," and they let it topple over, both standing from their crouch, their faces flush from the effort. I walked up and the three of us formed a circle around the stone and its exposed message, "50 paces west."

"*Oh my god, oh my god*," is all Jen could say.

"North's that way, sun's moving west, 50 paces that way," I said, staring out at another field of thorns and thistle. "Going to be hard to measure 50 paces out into that field."

"Hand me my big stick and follow me," Jen ordered, damning the torpedoes.

We watched Jen move off eagerly. Kendra and I located our own sticks, joining in the effort to create a path through the brush, making and finding gaps in the prickly tangle. We dead reckoned west, Kendra using her phone to zero in more precisely on a heading. We looked back at the two large rocks periodically, trying to gauge the distance, removing burs and stickers each time we stopped. When we reached our best approximation of 50 paces, we fanned out side-by-side, stepping gingerly amidst the thistle, looking down for anything unusual. We were at this for close to an hour, our hopes of finding anything receding, when Kendra, shouted, "Got something!"

Jen and I moved quickly beside her to have a look.

"It's a cairn of rocks," Kendra exclaimed.

"Here, let me knock some of this thistle down so we can get a better look." I swung for the fences whacking down a wide swath of the invasive plant that thrived in California's Mediterranean climate, the hated fibrous green stalks with their punk rocker spiked yellow heads and masochist's collar of thorns.

"Don't hit the cairn," Jen warned.

I battered a clearing around the cairn, doing so like a human Weedeater, inflicting revenge for all the pricks and stabs.

We could now see the base of the cairn and a triangular series of stones laid out, like an arrowhead, pointing back at the two large rocks. The cairn was only stacked four rocks high. We lifted each up, examining them for any message.

"Nothing. Now what?" Jen asked.

"We dig," Kendra said, using her stick to begin pawing at the ground.

We removed all the rocks and took turns digging straight down. I used my knife to make something of a point on each stick so that they could better penetrate the soil. Even so, it was hard going, our enthusiasm waning with each tortured turn in the expanding hole.

"This is ruining my nails," Jen complained but kept digging with the determination of a backhoe.

We were over a foot deep when a different sound emerged from the bottom of the hole. Jen dropped to her knees and used her fingers to probe the bottom.

"Hello, found something," she said. "It's metal, like the rim to a can."

Kendra and I bent down for a better look at the half-exposed metal top, the lid looking dilapidated and beaten, nearly rusted through. I said, "Look out, I'm going to dig around it." I broke my stick to the length of a hand trowel and leaned into the hole, digging out the dirt from around the side of the can. When I had excavated enough, I leaned back out of the hole, rolling onto my back, exhausted. "About the size of a coffee can," was all I could say.

Once I caught my breath, we all stood looking down at the

can in the hole, Jen's hands clasped under her chin, Kendra wearing the look of anticipation one sees when the river card is turned.

"If this turns out to be some kid's idea of a joke, some can of marbles with a "Ha, ha, ha" note, I'm going to pitch a fit," Jen firmly stated.

I looked at our filthy selves, the skinned knees, the nicks and cuts on our arms and legs, each of us probably with a case of poison oak, proposing in a slow drawl, "then we hunt the little runt down and make him pay."

"End the suspense, Tom."

I got back down on my knees and reached into the hole. I lifted the can just a few inches before I was forced to slip my other hand underneath. "Heavy," I said, heaving it up and out, just making it to the rim before I lost my grip. The can bounced to a landing, staying upright, but the lid popped open, just an inch or two. We moved in close and simultaneously discovered the faces and grooved edges to a trove of coins.

"*Wow, Wow, Wow!*" Jen screamed.

Kendra started jumping up and down with joy, saying over and over, "*You've got to be kidding! You've got to be kidding!*"

"*No way,*" I said in delight, knocking the brittle can over, spilling out the contents. I excitedly grabbed a handful of coins and began sorting through them, "Lady Liberty, this is a $20 gold piece. See the dates, 1866, 1877, 1883..."

Jen grabbed her own handful, holding one up, "Shiny, they look brand new," she said in amazement. "Are these really gold?"

"There's an "S" on them," I said. "They must be from the old San Francisco Mint that opened during the Gold Rush."

Kendra was reading something on her phone, shaking her head in astonishment, "These are really rare. They're worth a lot, a lot more than their face value. Just one of these is probably worth thousands of dollars."

We spent the next ten minutes going through each coin, handing them back and forth. When we were done, Jen wondered, "Where did they come from?"

"Who knows," I guessed, "someone who doesn't like banks, a stagecoach robbery?" my speculation trailing off to silence.

Jen made a brief glance at the sun's position, "We've got a few more hours," starting to say what we each thought – that there still might be more cans of treasure to unearth. I resumed digging while Jen and Kendra gathered up the coins, loading them into my backpack. The two then hiked all the way back to the car, hiding the coins in the spare wheel well. In time, they reappeared, traversing from the two large rocks back to my position, only their heads and shoulders visible above the scrub brush. They carried all three of our backpacks, plus a snack and more water, but it was the hand shovel from our camping gear Kendra waved high over her head that caused my eyes to light up.

"How's it going?" Jen said as they stepped back into the clearing.

"See for yourself," I said, smiling, tapping a second can of coins with my stick. "That shovel is really going to help."

Jen handed me the hose to her hydration bladder and I took a long pull. She then passed me a sandwich to eat. "We have the head lamps too, so if it gets dark we should still be able to manage our way back down the trail to the car."

I nodded "good," chewing on a mouthful of ham and cheese. I gobbled down the sandwich and jumped back into the hole with renewed energy, the sharp edge of the shovel doing the work of ten sticks, plus two. In short time, a third can emerged, followed by a fourth. We were more and more dumbstruck by each discovery, wondering how many more can there be? It turned out to be one more, five total, when the big dig came to a halt.

"It would be nice to have a metal detector right now," Jen said.

I shrugged, "That's why I dug three feet beyond the cluster of cans, just to make sure."

"What if this is just the top layer, and there's more cans deeper below?" Jen hypothesized.

I thrust out the shovel, "Have at it."

Jen peered again into the hole, "I think you went deep enough, dear."

Kendra then bounded up with her phone. "I've got the GPS position, plus pictures of everything here, the two large rocks, the whole area, and I'll take more as we leave so we have this place well documented."

We loaded the treasure up, two cans for me and one each for Jen and Kendra. It made for a heavy load, the straps cutting into our shoulders, but the pain was soon forgotten once we reminded ourselves of the contents. We stopped often, happily bearing this pleasant burden, lugging it all the way back to the trailhead parking lot, the few cars seen earlier now long gone, only our Honda remained.

It was dark out now, the backpacks placed carelessly on top of the other camping gear. We climbed inside and buckled our seatbelts. I placed my head on the steering wheel. We each sat exhausted, saying nothing, consumed by our own thoughts.

"What is it, Tom?" Jen asked.

I leaned back upright, "Our lives are totally different now."

"Yeah," Jen said warily. "How's this going to change us?" she wondered. "This is going to take a while to sink in."

"It's like winning the lottery," Kendra added dreamily.

"Exactly. And we need to take this slow and easy, say nothing to anyone. We need to do our own research, find a reputable expert, get the coins evaluated, find out what they're really worth," Jen said, the seeds of a plan beginning to germinate.

"A lot," I murmured softly, then finding my voice, "We take care of the necessities first, pay off the house, Kendra picks out a good school..."

"Don't forget the Class B," Jen chided, with a smile, touching my arm. "I'm going to start researching motorhomes the minute we get home."

I started the Honda and we drove off, stunned at our good fortune. At first, I thought our destination would be a camp-ground with showers, but the ladies demanded a bigger, more luxurious splurge – a motel or nice roadside inn. Within minutes, Kendra had located a three star hotel and I pointed the car in that direction, once we made it back to the main road. After a few miles of silence, Kendra's voice was heard from the backseat, "Yeah, you can call this the best road trip ever."

* * *

Worldwide Press
Friday, March 21, 2014

A California family is living their dreams with the auction of a trove of rare coins discovered during a hike last year. Pre-auction estimates placed the Sierra Foothills Hoard, nearly 900 coins with a face value of $18,000, at just under $7 million. Today's auction, conducted at the Old San Francisco Mint, exceeded these expectations, totaling over $9 million in sales by the time the last gavel was struck.

The auction was highlighted by the sale of numerous $20 Double Eagle gold pieces, an extremely rare coin sought by collectors throughout the world. A single 1866-S no motto coin, the finest of its type known to exist, alone sold for just under $1 million.

The coins date from 1849 to 1883 and many theories have been advanced as to the hoard's origin, with speculation ranging from a secret order of knights to any one of a number of stagecoach robberies that occurred in the region during the Gold Rush.

The family who discovered the hoard remains anonymous. They plan to pay off bills and travel, keeping a few coins as souvenirs to a great adventure.

Made in the USA
San Bernardino, CA
17 January 2018